When the Rainbow turns Black

by Peter Venison

Clink Street

Published by Clink Street Publishing 2022

Copyright © 2022

First edition.

ISBN:

978-1-915229-23-6 - paperback
978-1-915229-24-3 - ebook

Also by Peter Venison

Managing Hotels
Heinemann Profesional Publishing (London)
1983, 1984, 1986, 1988

100 Tips for Hoteliers
I Universe, 2005

In the Shadow of the Sun
iUniverse, 2005

100 Ways to Annoy your Guests
Clink Street Publishing, 2020

Out of the Shadow of the Sun
Clink Street Publishing, 2020

The Lottery
Clink Street Publishing, 2020

The Extraordinary Life of Niv Bloom
Clink Street Publishing, 2021

PART
ONE

Chapter One

It is January, 1970. Two little boys are starting school for the first time. They both live in Randburg, a suburb of Johannesburg, South Africa. They are both white. One of them, Gerhadus, is quite nervous; the other, Lance, can't wait. Randburg is a large suburb, covering several square miles and the two boys live in different areas, each with their own primary school. Gerhadus is attending the General Christian De Wet primary in Triomph and Lance, the Laeskool Jim Fourie in Crosby. They will both be taught primarily in the Afrikaans language, since their districts are heavily populated with Afrikaners, but, because English is the other official language in the country, they will also have lessons in English. They will be taught to neither speak nor write any of the other eleven languages in common use in the land of their birth; these are the languages of the native Africans, who make up 80% of the population.

Randburg is a mixed-race suburb. The "mix" is between Afrikaans and English speakers. Black children are not allowed to attend school in Randburg and black citizens are not allowed to live there, unless they are domestic servants with a special permit to do so. Blacks must live in specially designated areas, outside and often far from the white areas and, if they work in white areas, in anything other than domestic positions, they must commute daily to and from their work in overcrowded buses and decrepit and dented taxis. Kaffir taxis! If they do not have the fare, they must walk since bicycles are not commonplace. If a black is caught in a white area at night, without good reason, he will be jailed and most likely beaten up in the police van en route. There is a marked difference between the standard of homes in white and black districts. White homes, generally, are made of bricks, black ones with tin and straw. This is South Africa in 1970.

Not far from Triomph and Crosby, in the neighbouring suburb of Sandton, which is primarily an English-speaking area, a little blonde girl, Angela, is also attending primary school for the first time. She is very pretty. Everybody tells her that, so she knows it. Her mother, Sally, is an English immigrant who is married to a handsome Afrikaner. They have chosen to live in an English-speaking suburb because it was easier for Sally, but Dirk, her husband, has requested that their daughter attend an Afrikaans speaking primary school, lest his language be forgotten in their household. They have no other children. All suburbs are, by law, required to provide education in both official languages, irrespective of the preponderance of any one language in the area. Sally understands Dirk's position but is not thrilled about the idea, since she feels it will be difficult for her to relate to the other mothers. Sally knows that, for young mothers, their best chance of making friends in a foreign land is by meeting other young mums at the school. Dirk is sympathetic to her plight but has asked her to, at least, try to make it work for the sake of his parents and other Afrikaans relatives.

Both Gerhadus and Lance are strapping lads for their age. They have been brought up in the sunshine of the Witwatersrand, at the centre of the plateau on which

Johannesburg has emerged further to the discovery of gold. Their families are middle class Afrikaans folk. The bulk of the poor Afrikaners live in the southern suburbs of the city, so these two boys are privileged. Strom Van de Merwe, Gerhadus' father, owns and operates a small trucking company; that is to say he owns two large trucks, which he keeps in a siding next to their home in Triomph, much to the chagrin of his neighbours. Strom, unlike his son, is a stick of a man, tall, wiry and thin. He has piercing grey eyes and a neat little moustache. Strom's wife, Edna, is a housewife and mother. Unlike her husband, she is a large lady with strong solid legs and a spreading bosom. Gerhadus has one little brother, Frikkie, who is three years his junior. Frikkie is also a well-built boy; he absolutely idealises his big brother.

Lance's folk are less well off than the Van der Merwes, but both his mother and father work. His dad, Rudy Hermanus, works for the post office. Rudy is a large, well-muscled man with a ruddy face and a cheeky smile. A good joke is never far from his lips. Lance's mother, Becky, is a receptionist at the local doctor's office. Becky is very popular and gregarious. Everyone who visits the doctor loves her and she casts aside their anxiety. Rudy and Becky also have a daughter, Bibi, who is one year older than Lance. Bibi is a pretty child with jet black hair and an olive skin. Some of the neighbours wondered if the handsome black garden boy, employed by the Hermanuses, had anything to do with her genes.

Both the Van der Merwes and the Hermanuses are staunch Nationalists, who believe that South Africa is God's given country, that is, "given" to the Whites. Rudy and Becky attend church regularly; Strom and Edna do not, although Edna would really like to. Both families live in well-built single storey homes with generous back yards which are kept green through rain in the summer and the garden "boy" in the winter. Both families vote for the ruling Nationalist party. Black citizens of South Africa are not allowed to vote. The AFA (Africa for Africans) political party favoured by the Blacks has been banned.

Gerhadus and Lance, in their separate ways, get on very well at school. If anything, Gerhadus is the more diligent of the two, but Lance is the brighter. Gerhadus is quickly named "Gerrie" by his classmates, although it takes a couple of years before the teachers drop the formality of Gerhadus. Gerrie keeps himself to himself, but is not disliked or ignored by the other children. Lance is everyone's friend and is, by far, the most sociable kid in the class. Gerrie pays more attention to the lessons than Lance, but Lance does just enough to get by. Sports are very important to the Afrikaners. Through sport one can demonstrate the strength of the race, by determination, fitness, skill and the teamwork that is required. Through sport you can be measured. That is good for Gerrie and Lance, because both boys love the sports which they are allowed to take part in at school. Although, at primary school age, these are limited to sports with no physical contact, both boys, being big for their age, still excel at all of the running, jumping, and swimming events that they are permitted to participate in. Rugby, the national pastime in the winter, is not allowed on the basis that it is too physical and whilst elementary gymnastics are taught, boxing and wrestling are not allowed. Nevertheless, both Gerrie and Lance can run faster and jump higher than most of their classmates and both are in demand for their respective teams. Gerrie, the outsider, is brought into the fold through sport. Lance needs no invitation.

Meanwhile, in neighbouring Sandton, Angela takes to school with great enthusiasm. As an only child, she has been the Princess of the household. This could have made her unpopular in the classroom, but her natural charm and outstanding prettiness somehow propel her into leadership. Yes, she has been spoilt; yes, she can be haughty, but her enthusiasm for life and her attractiveness appeal to both her classmates and teachers. Some of the teachers think she can be bossy, but most applaud her confidence and quickness at learning. Yes, she can be manipulative, but she manages to get the other children to follow and admire her. Everybody wants to be on Angela's team. It is not long before Angela's name has been shortened to "Angel".

Gerrie, Lance, and Angel's birthplaces have all been in the beating heart of South Africa, in the province of Transvaal, a large state which, as its name implies, traverses the Vaal River. The Transvaal stretches across a huge plateau that varies between 6,000 and 8,000 feet in altitude. To the casual viewer the land is predominately dry and dusty, but, on closer inspection, it is rich in minerals. With the arrival of the short sharp summer rains, the parched land turns almost instantly green. When gold was discovered in the late 1800s, the sparsely occupied region in the centre of the plateau quickly became heavily populated with settlers and the seeds of the now mega city of Johannesburg were planted. First there were miners' cottages, small brick single storey simple homes with tin roofs, in staggering contrast to the mine owners' occasional colonial-style mansions. The land became scarred with digging and great mountains of excavated soil grew like golden pyramids around the town. The one storey cottages of the white Afrikaans workers were dotted around the mine shafts, whilst the bosses moved a little further north into nice family homes with cultivated gardens and paved streets, where, in spring, the blue flowering jacaranda trees bathed the area in soft colour.

Black workers are housed in two or three storey dormitories which serve as temporary accommodation, where they are forced to live in appalling conditions, four or even eight to a room, with unpleasant communal washrooms at the end of the corridor which offer no privacy. Unlike the white areas there are no hard top roads in these townships. In winter they are cold dusty places, despite the daily nonstop sunshine. In summer, after the torrential afternoon storms, the streets are canals of mud, which sweep into the tin shacks that surround the official dormitories. These temporary barracks have gradually become permanent and grown into massive black townships with no tarred roads and little sanitation. They are rough areas to live in, but the blacks are given no alternatives and they need the jobs in the mines to support their families back in the bush.

The success of the mines has attracted other commerce and soon, just north of the minefields, a whole new city has grown, with bankers, and builders, and factories, and shops, and a myriad of other commercial enterprises. A whole new downtown area has developed to house the workers in the non-mining sector, and the supervisors and managers have started to build houses in the north: pretty houses with red pitched roofs, or decorative thatched cottages. They have planted trees to line the streets, made parks and ponds and public gardens, built rows of shops, and eventually malls, opened restaurants, clubs and bioscopes. In short, Johannesburg has become a vibrant city, divided by the wealthy whites in the north and the poorer in the south, with the blacks out of sight in the townships and shanty towns. Gerrie, Lance, Angel and Bibi are all lucky to have been born and living in the north.

The predominant political party, the Nationalists, hold a commanding and impenetrable position in the government. Its policy is crystal clear. South Africa is a democracy, but only white South Africans over the age of 21 are allowed to vote. Not only are Blacks denied the right to vote, they are also denied the right to choose where they can live, where they can shop, where they can work, where they can eat, even where they can swim. Blacks and whites are not allowed to intermarry or cohabitate. They are also forbidden to form trade unions or to gather in public places outside of their own tribal lands. Every black citizen is obliged to carry the dreaded Pass Book, stating their name, tribe, and tribal address, with a photo. There is an inexhaustible pool of labour, so wages are kept low.

Most whites, including Gerrie and Lance's parents, regard this situation as being completely normal and wish to reinforce it by supporting the National Party. Angela's father, although Afrikaans, is not so sure that this situation is viable. Through his job, Dirk has travelled extensively. He has seen how others live and has felt the stinging criticism of his beloved homeland from colleagues and friends overseas. He has even married an English girl and brought her home to live. Like many immigrants Sally is, in principle, against this policy of Apartheid, but, then again, she has not found it too difficult to slip into, and enjoy, the benefits. Like most housewives living in Sandton, she has a black maid, Supreme, to help with the housework. Supreme has legal papers that allow her to live in a servant's room in the back yard, with nothing more than a cold water shower and a seatless water closet. Supreme sleeps on a bed raised by tin cans to keep away the togalosh. Sally does not treat Supreme badly and Supreme absolutely adores little Angela, but, after a while, it did not really bother Sally that her maid was denied the vote or had to put up with cold showers, even in the freezing Highveld winters.

Politics is the last thing on the minds of Gerrie, Lance and Angela as they progress through the formative years of primary school. For them, it is perfectly normal that all of the pupils are white skinned, as well as all of the teachers. It does not seem odd to them that the cleaners, maintenance men and gardeners, are all black, or that when they line up in the afternoons to be collected by the mothers, all of the people walking in the streets are black, whilst all of those riding in cars are white. These things, apparently, do not trouble primary school age children, and why would they, if they don't trouble their parents? Despite living in the less affluent of the northern suburbs, both of the boys' houses boast a swimming pool, the sun shines almost every day and when the much-needed rain does arrive, it is short and heavy, delivering just enough to magically refresh their lawns and fill their water tanks. Nowhere else in the world could a child of ten have such an idyllic existence, unless, or course, said child was black.

To the children in our story, the privileged life that they lead in sunny South Africa is perfectly normal. The fact that there are no black students in their school despite blacks making up 80% of the population of the country does not seem strange. The fact that Supreme has to use a cold water shower, even in the freezing winter, whereas, not twenty feet away, inside the house, there are two fully equipped bathrooms with all hot and cold facilities, does not trouble little Angel. That all the dogs in the neighbourhood (every household has a dog) bark at and chase after passing black pedestrians, explained by their parents as because blacks smell different from whites, is just accepted by the children. It does not occur to them that the passing black man probably has no access to a shower at all in the hot summers. Of course, he smells different. Neither does it occur to Angela or Gerhadus et al that you almost never see a white pedestrian in Randburg actually walking down the street; they all have motorcars, almost all of which are new and shiny and are kept clean on a daily basis by the garden boy.

Sometimes at night, when Angel is tucked up in her comfortable bed, she will hear a vehicle in the street outside screeching to a halt. This will be followed by some shouting in Afrikaans and the sound of a tussle and a few dull thumps. The pleading voice of an African man can be heard as he is shoved into the back of a police van and then there is a sound of doors slamming and the vehicle is driven off. Some poor fellow, caught out after curfew in a white residential area, has just been nabbed. He will almost certainly be worked over by the white cops and then shipped off to oblivion in his "homeland", thereby probably losing his job and his ability to provide for his family. Angel will have heard the kerfuffle, turned over, and gone back to sleep, happy that she is safely tucked up in bed, out of harm's way.

It does not really bother our group of youngsters that, unlike almost every other country in the civilised world, there is no television service available. This is not due to technical incompetence. It is deliberate censorship. The things that people might see on television could open Pandora's box. Keeping the box closed is a priority for the Afrikaans government. The people, at least the white people, have it so good; why promote change? For the blacks, however, things are dire. Supreme is one of the lucky ones – at least she has a job, even if she has no hot water. But even Supreme is isolated from her family. On her one day off a week (almost never at a weekend) she cannot travel over a hundred miles to her village and back. Even if it were physically possible for her to do so, on her pittance of a wage, she is not able to afford to. Her only social life is on the streets of the suburb in which she works, where she sits on the grassy kerbside and chats with her fellow domestic workers. None of these things bother Angel or Gerhadus or Lance or any of their friends or siblings. They are living in an artificially created bubble; sooner or later all bubbles burst.

Fast forward to 1976. Our three children are done with primary school. They are moving on to the big boys' (and girls') school. There are only two high schools in Randburg, one where the lessons are primarily taught in Afrikaans and the other in English. Both Gerhadus and Lance have graduated to the Hoeskool Randburg, where they meet for the first time. The school is a rather ugly two storey, red brick building, with crumbling white stucco, and metal window frames. They are placed in different classrooms.

It is through sport, rather than lessons, that they come together for the first time and it is at their first rugby practice that they meet. Up until now, in their school life, they have each been the biggest in the class. That is still the case, but, here, on the rugby field, they meet their equal. Gerrie and Lance are almost identical in weight. Gerrie is slightly taller than Lance, but Lance is somewhat stockier. Both eye each other with suspicion, but the practice session goes off without any physical contact between the two. The coach, however, has noticed the two newcomers; big lads like this could be a welcome addition to the school "under thirteen" team.

As with most school coaches, however, Coach Brennan is responsible for all boy's sport in the Hoeskool, and it is for another sport that he eyes up the two boys with interest: boxing. Coach Brennan runs a boxing club at the school. He believes strongly that boxing is character building for young men. In no other sport, in his opinion, bar tennis, are two opponents entirely left to their own devices, for at least three minutes at a time. In tennis, however, your opponent is not trying to hit you; in boxing, he is. For Coach Brennan, boxing is the ultimate sport; one that will make men out of boys.

When the boys appear for the next rugby training session on the concrete hard dusty grass field, Brennan makes his pitch to the team about the boxing club. He explains that you don't have to be big to join. Boxing, he tells them, is divided into different weight divisions, so only like-sized boys will fight each other. That is, of course, in all weight catogories, except the heaviest one, where there is no upper limit in regard to weight. Several boys at the rugby practice enrol. They include Lance, but Gerrie keeps his hand down. Coach Brennan is puzzled. Gerrie is as strong a young man as he has seen in the first year of High School. Why would he not be interested in learning to box? Brennan collects up the names of the boys who have opted to join and invites them to attend their first training session in a couple of days, telling them that they must show up at the school gym with shorts, a t shirt and trainers.

As the boys drift away, some of them throw fake punches at each other in jest. Brennan collars Gerrie and asks him to remain behind for a moment. When all of the other boys have left, the coach invites Gerrie to sit down with him on the changing room bench. "Sorry to hold you back, Gerrie," he begins, "but I am interested to know why you do not want to join the boxing club? I know boxing is not for everyone, but I have to tell you that most of the boys that come along, really enjoy it."

Gerrie, always the reticent one, is silent for a moment. Brennan waits patiently, his eyes glued to the well-built young man. "Well, coach," Gerrie finally says, "I suppose I'd never really thought about it. I'm not frightened of getting hit, or anything like that. I'm just not sure that I want to hit other people."

"Are you afraid, because you are a big boy, that you might hurt someone?" asks the coach.

"Maybe. I've never really thought about it."

"Well, Gerrie, I can assure you that you are not going to hurt anyone. Your fists will be gloved and bandaged to protect your opponent. And each bout will be closely supervised. If it gets a bit rough, the referee will step in before any damage is done."

Gerrie is dubious about that logic. "Surely," he thinks, "they will only step in after the damage has been done?"

Despite being a big lad for his age, Gerrie is, in fact, extremely shy. Volunteering for any sort of social activity is anathema to him. Putting himself "on show" in a boxing ring is just not his thing. Team sports, like rugby, are different.

Coach Brennan can see that Gerrie is reluctant, so does not push the matter. "It's a pity," he thinks, "because the lad really does have the build of a boxer, solid and strong."

"Well, that's okay," he says as he stands up, "If you change your mind, you know where to find me."

Whilst Gerrie was eating his supper that evening, he related the conversation he had had with coach Brennan to his mum, Edna. She thought about it for a moment. She knew that her Gerrie was a shy boy. True, he was big for his age, but this seemed only to make him feel more self-conscious. He was not naturally gregarious. "Like his Dad," thought Edna. "That's why he likes to cocoon himself in the truck. Perhaps joining a boxing club, in fact, any club, would be good for Gerrie, force him to mix with others."

"Well," she announced, after a little while, "I think you should have a go. You would be good at it. Why don't you think about it, my boy?"

Gerrie did just that. When he went to his bed he just could not get to sleep. His mind was mulling over what his mum had said. "Maybe she was right. Maybe he should join in a bit more? After all, he did love team games. So, why not give the boxing club a shot? Eventually he fell asleep, having first determined that he would seek out Coach Brennan the next day.

The new recruits for the boxing club were welcomed and weighed. They were then divided into groups, according to their respective weights. There were no other recruits as heavy as Gerrie and Lance so they were assigned to a group of older boys who were already members of the club and had undergone at least a year of coaching. Although most of the boys in their weight category were one year older than the two recruits, some were even two and three years their senior. This meant that none of them were novices like Gerrie and Lance. Nevertheless, instead of allowing Gerrie and Lance to spar with each other, Brennan split them up and partnered them with older, more experienced, boys.

The newcomers were duly allocated bright red boxing gloves and asked to copy various jabs and hooks, as demonstrated by Brennan, using one of the older boys as a punching bag. The gloves at first seemed strange to the new recruits. They felt clumsy in them, but were surprised how light they actually were, considering their bulk. The boys were then asked to pummel a heavy hanging leather bag for a few minutes. They were all astonished how tiring this was.

Coach Brennan then announced that the recruits would now be allowed in the ring to spar with existing members of the boxing club for three minutes each. The experienced boys would be "available" as targets, but would, of course, defend themselves. In total there were six new recruits, including Gerrie and Lance. Coach Brennan started with the lightweight boys who he matched up with some of the smaller, but more experienced, members of the club. He then fitted them all with the mandatory protective leather headgear. Some of the new recruits, having seen fights on films, had a natural instinct about throwing punches and defending themselves. Some were completely uncoordinated. Finally, it was Gerrie's turn to step into the ring. Brennan had saved him and Lance till last. It felt strange inside the ring. Everyone else in the gym was looking up at you. For about a minute, Gerrie danced around without doing much, just as he had seen real boxers do on the newsreels. In the second minute, he got a bit bolder and his opponent started to goad him. In the third minute, the older boy wished he hadn't, because Gerrie let fly with a right hook that knocked his opponent off his feet.

"Stop boxing," yelled Brennan, who, in a flash, leapt into the ring to attend to the fallen boy. He hadn't been knocked out, but he sure been knocked over. He was hurting, but so was his pride. He had gone from "instructor" to "loser" in a flash. Gerrie was as surprised as everybody else. He had floored the other boy with the first real punch that he had thrown. With the cushioning provided by the red leather glove, Gerrie had not realised just how hard he had hit the other boy. The gabble of all the boys in the gym suddenly stopped, replaced by an eerie anxious silence.

Everybody there had seen what happened, including, of course, Lance, who had yet to have a turn. He quietly determined that if that other large lad, Gerrie, could knock over a more experienced older boy, so could he.

Once the surprised Gerrie and his opponent had climbed out of the ring, it was Lance's turn. Coach Brennan had had his eyes on Lance during the practice sessions. To Brennan, Lance had seemed somewhat cocky. "Needs to have some of that cocksureness knocked out of him; otherwise, he might walk into trouble one day," thought Brennan. So, to spar against Lance, he selected one of his better club members, someone with a couple of years of experience.

When the two got started, Lance's opponent peppered him with short sharp jabs, almost all of them landing on Lance's face. Not that they really hurt Lance, but, after a minute and a half of feeling defenceless and even embarrassed, Lance let fly with a barrage of uncoordinated punches. The experienced boy rather dismissively evaded almost all of them, making Lance even madder. To Lance, three minutes was beginning to seem like an eternity. Finally, and somewhat luckily, just as the three minute alarm was about to sound, Lance let fly with an almighty and ungainly left hook. It caught his opponent flush on the chin and he went down like a felled tree. Once again, Brennan leapt into the ring and rushed to Lance's opponent, who was out cold on the canvas. This had been the only punch in three minutes that Lance had actually landed. The stricken boy had let down his guard for a split second as he eyed Coach Brennan moving towards the bell. That was all it took for him to be felled. Lance was jubilant and started jumping around the ring as if he had just won the World Championship. Gerrie looked on with amazement.

Brennan's main concern, of course, was the state of the boy crumpled on the deck, but whirring in his mind was the realisation that he had two new recruits to his club who could really pack a punch. The boy on the floor recovered and, although his pride was hurt, even cracked a joke. He knew that, for a split second, he had lost concentration. He had paid for it dearly.

Brennan, happy that his warrior had recovered, now turned his attention to his two new sluggers. He realised that they both had potential, but he did not want them to get cocky. Cockiness could lead to calamity. He pulled the six new recruits together for a pep talk, allowing the older boys to head for the shower.

"Now, boys, tell me how you felt in the ring," he started. Nobody spoke. "Come on, lads, I don't bite. Tell me what it was like."

"Three minutes seemed like half an hour," piped up one of the smaller boys.

"Yes, you're right," said the coach, who went on, "some boxers will tell you that every three minutes can seem like ten. But, when you think about it, even three minutes is a long time. In a 15 round fight (which is what heavyweights did in 1980) you are having to jog about, keeping your hands up high, for 45 minutes. That's the same as playing one half of a soccer match, but you've got the ball all of the time, with the other side's 11 men trying to get it away from you. No soccer player ever has to do that. Yes, my friend, three minutes can seem like a long time, and the one minute rest can seem very short indeed. What else did anyone feel about their first three minutes in the ring?"

"I felt alone," piped up another lad.

"Dead right, young fella. You are alone. There is nowhere to run. There is no one to help. It's just you, so get used to it."

It was then Gerrie's turn to speak. "I sort of felt helpless. The guy kept picking me off and I was too slow to stop him."

"Yeah, I felt a bit the same," chimed in Lance, "I wanted to kill him but I couldn't get near."

"And what does that tell us?" asked Brennan.

"That we've got a lot to learn," said Gerrie.

"Dead right," said Brennan, "but you've all learned a lot today. So off you go now. Get changed and I'll see you same time next week."

As the boys drifted off to the changing room, Brennan called back the two biggest boys from the new recruits. "You two got lucky today. Don't expect it to always be so easy to land a knockout blow. And remember, what you did today to another boy, someone can do to you tomorrow. You've clearly got the build and the strength to do well. I hope you'll both come back next week, because I'd like to help you learn to defend yourselves as well as attack. Well done, lads. See you next week."

Chapter Two

Over the next six months both Gerrie and Lance regularly attended the weekly training sessions and, on the advice of Coach Brennan, both were encouraged to visit the gym several times a week for body building exercises. By now the two boys were getting to know each other, but their personalities were poles apart. So, apart from light hearted chat in the gym, they seemed never destined to become good friends. This was odd, because of their shared interest in boxing and that they played together on the same junior rugby team. Beyond that, they had very little in common. They remained in separate classes and their lives, out of school, were lived apart. Gerrie in Triomph and Lance in Crosby. Gerrie found the school work quite challenging, but he was a good student, who worked diligently to score reasonable grades. Lance, of course, was the opposite, one of those annoying boys who appeared to do little work, was quite cocky, but still, somehow, managed to pass the various tests that came his way.

Their personalities were reflected in their performances in the training ring. Gerrie was a good student. He listened intently to the advice and instruction handed out by Brennan. He learned how to jab, how to keep his arms up, how to feint, and how to throw a devastating hook. Although right-handed in the schoolroom, for some reason, he could throw a fiendish left hook and found himself just as comfortable leading with the right or the left. He also had exceptionally solid legs. In this regard he luckily took after his mother rather than Strom, his sticklike dad.

"The strength of your legs is just as important as the strength of your upper body," Coach Brennan would often say. "It's your legs that hold you up if you're in trouble."

Lance could not have been more different than Gerrie in terms of his approach to life. There was nothing introverted about Lance. He was big, strong, and good looking. The cheeky, almost cocky, grin never left his face. He was sharp-witted and quick of thought. He possessed an amazing self-confidence; he was always the leader of the gang. The boys in his class admired him and the girls thought he was a hunk. He did not like hard work, but this did not seem to matter much, as things came easily to him. He had found that he could often get what he wanted without too much effort. Boxing was, therefore, good for him, because things did not always come so easy in the ring. Instead of cajoling everyone onto your side through charm, there was always someone against you, and that someone was intent on beating you up. There was no short cut to success in the boxing ring. You had to learn the craft, and particularly the craft of defence. Coach Brennan could see that Lance was possibly the strongest of all of his boys, but he was also the most reckless.

For a long time, Brennan kept the two boys apart in the ring. There were plenty of older boys for them to spar with, so this was not a problem. Sooner or later, though, he knew that they would have to fight each other, especially when it came to the school championships and other tournaments in the wider world. Brennan concentrated on teaching them the art of defence. That, in his view, was more important than attack; good defence was the basis of success, particularly with two young men with such a powerful punch. Then, slowly, as they mastered the art of defending themselves, mostly against older and bigger boys in the club, he started to teach them how and when to unleash their power.

After nine months of training, they were ready to enter their first tournament, which was to be against the Bryanston High School, the English-speaking counterpart of their Afrikaans High School. Like all local "derbys", this annual event carried a lot of prestige, and attracted quite a crowd of students, teachers and parents. The rules for the contest allowed each team to enter two fighters for each of the four weight categories. Although they were first year students, both Gerrie and Lance were eligible for the second highest weight tier. In other words, they were already two tiers above their age group. As a result, they each found themselves matched against boys two years older than them and, by definition, with two years more experience. Coach Brennan was taking a chance, because he could have selected two older boys instead of Gerrie and Lance. That, of course, would have denied them the experience of a proper tournament, so Brennan decided to let his two young "heavyweights" have a go.

When the boys from Bryanston High saw the age of their opponents on the schedule, they laughed. When they actually saw their opponents, the laughter stopped. The fights were scheduled for three, three minute, rounds. Lance had never fought for a full nine minutes; in training he had always stopped his opponent before the end of the second round. At the beginning of the bout Lance danced around in a fairly cocky manner, his hands almost by his side. After a minute or so he lunged forward with a powerful right hook, which, had it reached his opponent, would have ended the contest. However, as he was looping in the shot, he was hit full flush in the face with a straight right, followed immediately by a hard left as he staggered back. He did not go down, but one could say that he had the smile wiped off his face. For the rest of the round, he pedalled backwards and was grateful to find his seat in the corner.

As he sat on the stool, he did not hear a word of the advice Coach Brennan was giving him. He was mad as hell. He was determined that the other boy would not survive another round. When the bell went, a fully recovered Lance leapt off his stool and raced straight towards his opponent with the intent of knocking his head off. His first punch, a left to the stomach, winded the Bryanston boy, causing him to lean slightly forward. That was a mistake. With his opponent's chin slightly unguarded, Lance put all his weight into a straight right that made him stand up straight. With the following left hook, he knocked the boy out. Knockouts were rare at this junior level of boxing, partly because of the protective headgear, although, in this instance, it had had little effect. The crowd from the Hoeskool roared with enthusiasm. Lance took an unnecessarily jubilant and cocky lap of honour around the canvas. The Afrikaans kids in the hall all cheered.

Now it was the turn of Gerrie, who had heard the commotion from the changing rooms. Gerrie felt under huge pressure to match his team mate's performance, and he needed to, because the score between the two schools was level. Gerrie had to win for his team to capture the trophy. As he made his way through the crowd of spectators towards the ring, his heart was pounding. It was very noisy in the gym when Gerrie climbed in to the ring. Nervous as he was, he loved the atmosphere and the springy feel of the canvas underfoot as he went forward to be introduced. His opponent, like Lance's, was also two years older than him and had fought many times before. He was as tall as Gerrie, but more wiry. Gerrie noticed how thin his legs were. This was Gerrie's first real tournament. But, as he eased into the fight, moving gracefully out of reach each time the Bryanston boy jabbed him, his confidence grew.

"This boy," he thought to himself, "might be experienced, but he can't hurt me."

As the round wore on, Gerrie began to dance around his opponent, peppering him with solid blows. Gerrie's confidence was growing. The bell sounded.

"You're doing well," shouted Brennan into his ear above the din of the audience, "put three punches together, just like we've done in training. You can have him."

The bell sounded for the second round to begin. So far, Gerrie had not been hit hard enough for it to hurt. He continued to score with two and three jab flurries, but suddenly, he was caught with a right hook that really hurt and, as he stood in surprise, a left uppercut that, luckily, grazed off his chin.

Gerrie decided that he must hit harder. It was all very well throwing good punches and scoring points, but he had not broken this opponent's spirit. With seconds to go in the round, Gerrie tried to let rip. In so doing, he ignored his defence. It was a mistake. Another thundering uppercut from the Bryanston boy sent him hurtling backwards into the ropes.

The bell announcing the end of the round rang. Brennan leapt into the ring and helped his man back to the stool. "Do you want to carry on?" he shouted in Gerrie's ear.

"Yes," was all Gerrie could muster. There was an excited buzz in the hall. The crowd was wondering if Gerrie would fold.

The minute on the stool was long enough for Gerrie to regain his composure.

"You were winning when you boxed him," whispered Brennan. "Teach him a boxing lesson."

The bell went and Gerrie waited for his opponent to make the first move. "I'll make him think I'm all in," thought Gerrie. "When he goes for me, I'll nail him." Gerrie threw out a few tentative jabs. His opponent grew in stature and then, suddenly attacked. Gerrie was ready for him and picked him off, as he advanced with a flurry of hard and well-aimed shots. They all landed and they all hurt. Gerrie knew that he had his man. The attacks from his opponent had stopped; he now seemed intent on damage control. Gerrie moved in for the kill. A series of left jabs, undefended, pushed the English-speaking boy backwards. Instead of pressing forward relentlessly, Gerrie seemed to stand back, as if to examine his handiwork. That was a mistake. The apparently spent opponent suddenly attacked with a series of flurries to the head and the body. This seemed to re-engage Gerrie's brain and he retaliated with a barrage of hard punches that sent the boy to the canvas. The referee, as was often the way in amateur fights, moved in between Gerrie and the slumped figure and stopped the fight.

Both Gerrie and Lance had both won by knockouts and the tournament trophy was now secure. For the first time in four years the Afrikaans school had beaten its English-speaking rivals. The Hoeskool kids in the audience yelled and cheered and hugged each other, no one less than the prettiest girl in the hall, Angela de Kock.

Gerrie soaked in the special feeling of winning, especially in front of his schoolmates. He was quietly very pleased with himself.

The boxing team's victory was the talk of the corridors at the Hoeskool the next day. The Principal had proudly announced the victory at the morning assembly, which had elicited a huge cheer from the packed room. Those that had been present excitedly related the story of the two knockout fights. Morale was high. When the team members, including Gerrie and Lance, reached their respective class rooms, the other students cheered and clapped. It took a few moments for normal order to be restored. Lance was very pleased to be the centre of attraction. He had noticed that the prettiest girl in his class had come to the fight. This would need to be investigated. Gerrie, on the other hand, shyly accepted the compliments from his classmates, and then tried to turn his attention to schoolwork.

Several more inter- school matches followed over the next few months and the results were always the same. Neither Gerrie nor Lance lost a bout. They did not always win by knockout, but their impressive streak was always against older and more experienced opponents. Brennan continued to teach them the tricks of the trade and they were both good learners. He did not, however, put them into the ring together, except for specific training exercises. His instincts told him that this would be a mistake. The mystery of not knowing which of his two stars was the best was something that intrigued many. Brennan, however, was smart. He knew, from years of experience in the game, that this sort of mystery was good for the business of boxing.

However, the inevitable clash of the Titans was destined to take place soon. The Hoeskool boxing championships were looming. Lance and Gerrie were the same weight. They had the same number of bouts under their belts. Neither of them had lost. There was no way to avoid them meeting in the Hoeskool championship, and everyone knew it. They could be on the same team, but not, unfortunately, in their own school championship.

They were also in the same team on the rugby field. Rugby teams were selected by age group, not weight or maturity. This had given the Hoeskool a huge advantage with their forwards, since the inclusion of both Gerrie and Lance in the team was almost the equivalent of having an extra man in the scrum. As a result, the Hoeskool team was one of the strongest in the inter-school league. Not too many kids were up to the challenge of tackling either Lance or Gerrie when they were carrying the ball moving forward. It normally took two of more of the lads on the other team to stop either one of them.

It was in a fairly innocent looking maul that the accident, if it was an accident, happened. Whilst Gerrie was being pinned to the ground by a pile of opposing shirts, one of them stamped hard on his ankle. The ground was like concrete; there was nowhere for his ankle to go. There was an ominous "crack" and a yelp of pain from Gerrie. There was no question that a bone in his ankle had been broken. Any thought of dancing around a boxing ring for the next few weeks would be out of the question. The "big" match between the two boys would have to wait for a future time. As expected, without Gerrie on the card, Lance made short work of his lesser opponent. The fight was stopped in the second round and Lance was proclaimed the "Champion". Angel and her friends were there to watch.

Gerrie did not attend. The history books and the engraved honours boards in the gymnasium would not be mentioning his name. He was sure that he would have been able to outbox that show off, Lance, but history would not be on his side. Lance, of course, privately conceded, at least to himself, that he had not proven anything in winning the school title. The real opposition had not shown up. He would just have to wait for another occasion to prove that he was the best.

When boxing training began again the next term, both Gerrie and Lance reported to Coach Brennan for duty. The coach had decided that it was time for the two lads to be registered with the boxing board of control as amateur fighters, and should start to enter the board's official amateur tournaments. Since tournaments were held across South Africa with reasonable frequency, Brennan was able to schedule the participation of his two men on a staggered basis. This achieved two things; first, it was easier for the coach to concentrate his attentions on one or other of the fighters at an event, and secondly, it allowed him to stick to his schedule of keeping them apart. He knew the day would come when his two men would have to fight each other, but the more that date was postponed, the more interest it would create when it happened.

For the whole second year of their fighting careers, Brennan managed to keep them apart, at least in the ring. For the whole of the year, they were both undefeated and word, in the boxing community, was spreading across the country that there were two young heavyweights in the making that might be of national interest. His charges, however, were now both 13 years of age and things, other than boxing, started to attract their attention, including that beautiful girl at their school.

Chapter Three

Angela de Kock was also 13 and she was beginning to blossom. Further to her father's wishes she had eschewed the chance to attend her local high school in Sandton and enrolled in the Afrikaans Hoeskool in neighbouring Randburg. This was, strictly speaking, against the rules, but Angel's father, Dirk, had been determined that his daughter should not lose her Afrikaans' heritage by attending the local English-speaking High School. This decision had caused a huge rift in the relationship between Dirk and Sally, Angela's English mother. Not only did she have to fetch and carry her daughter in "Mom's taxi" far further than she would have done had the young lady attended the local school, but it also denied her of the opportunity of mixing with other English-speaking mothers.

At first, Angel, herself, was not happy at her father's dictatorial decision, but it did turn out to have some advantages, not least of which was the teenage crush that she had on the outgoing Lance. Angel felt sorry for her mum. "I will not let any man treat me that way," she thought, but she too, was a little scared of her dad. Just how Dirk had managed to persuade the school authorities that his daughter could attend a government school out of her catchment area, Angel did not know. Sally, however, was beginning to learn that the Afrikaner Broederbond was a very influential organisation. That's how, she realised, they had got a telephone line in their house before their English-speaking neighbours. In any case, Sally convinced herself, after a while, that Angel seemed to be perfectly happy at the Afrikaans school, so why rock the boat? If Dirk wanted to be dominant, that was okay. Dominance did have its place, even in the bedroom.

There was no question where Angel got her good looks from. It is true that her dad was handsome, but her mother, Sally, was an outstanding beauty. Her long blond hair and striking figure were reminiscent of Marilyn Monroe, the fated Hollywood actress. Dirk, her husband, was much envied by his pals. Luckily, Sally had passed on her genes to her daughter, who, at the age of 13, was beginning to develop in all of the right places. There was, however, one other young lady at the Afrikaans high school, that equalled Angel in beauty. That girl, Bibi, Lance's sister, was over a year older than Angel. Bibi was physically opposite to Angel in so many ways. Angel was blonde; Bibi's hair was jet black. Angel had a skin so fair that it looked as if it could break; Bibi was as tanned as if she had been born in Sicily.

Although they were in different classes at school, it did not take long for them to become good friends, and, soon, best friends, who went everywhere together and did everything together, as good friends do at that age. They would spend hours at each other's houses, only to be on the phone with each other for yet more hours once they had parted company.

It was through Bibi that Angel started to go to the boxing tournaments and, pretty soon, Angel had a huge crush on Bibi's brother, Lance. Naturally, it did not take long for Bibi to notice Angel's infatuation for her brother. It made her nervous. She knew how her brother spoke about the girls in his class when they were hanging out at home. At the age of 14, Lance had the confidence of a 19 year old and he almost had the body to match. Bibi feared for her friend, should she get involved with her brother. She, of course, knew her brother better than anyone. She believed that, despite all of the bluster and bravado, Lance had not actually followed up with action in regards to other girls. There had been plenty of opportunity, especially with girls of her age and older, who ogled him in the ring. As far as Bibi could tell, he had yet to utilise his manhood. This was partly because, at the boxing matches, Lance was surrounded by the adults in his life. Both Rudy and Becky, his dad and mum, attended almost all of his matches, as did Coach Brennan, so the opportunity to duck out with one of his fan club was not on the cards. Bibi was convinced that, unlike herself, Lance was still a "virgin". That, however, was not the case. At the tender age of 14, Lance had found several ways to impress a series of young ladies, all of them at least two to three years older than himself. Naturally, he did not boast about these escapades to his older sister. Angel's good looks, however, had not escaped him; she seemed to become more beautiful every time he saw her, and, although she was younger than his conquests so far, she was certainly prettier than anyone else he had met. She also seemed rather taken with him, but then, in his eyes, who wasn't?

Lance had plenty of opportunity to hang out with Angel, but only, it seemed when his older sister was there too. Bibi started to notice that Lance seemed to be spending more time than usual at home, especially when Angel visited. She had also overheard some of the older girls at school swapping stories about liaisons with their boyfriends. Lance seemed to feature heavily. "Having"

Lance seemed to be a badge of honour. This came as a bit of a shock to Bibi. She did not immediately discuss what she had overheard with her brother, nor with her best friend, Angel, but she determined that she would protect her friend, even at the risk of annoying her brother. She decided that, given the first opportunity, she would confront Lance, and warn him to keep his hands off her friend. Lance listened to his sister and assured her that he had no interest in Angel and that he only liked older girls. He was lying. For a while, Bibi, was content that she had nipped any danger in the bud, but, as much as she could influence Lance's behaviour, she could not control her best friend's hormones, anymore than she seemed to be able to control her own.

In the end, the mutual attraction between Angel and Lance inevitably won out. The deflowering of Angel took place in the woods between the high school and the Hermanus' home. Bibi, of course, was not sent an invitation. Lance had got what he wanted and so had Angel. To Lance, it was as if a challenge had been met; now on to the next peak to climb. To Angel, it was an indication of Lance's love for her. So, when Lance carried on with his social life as before, with scant attention to Angel, for a while, she felt completely deflated, although ever hopeful that her prince would return. Slowly, she began to realise that she had been used and determined to make her abuser pay.

Over the next two to three years, Angel physically developed into the most beautiful young woman in the school. All the boys were chasing her, all, that is, except Lance. Lance knew that none of them could claim the prize that he had already taken. But, in any event, Angel treated him as if he were carrying a deadly virus; she would make him be sorry for his earlier cruelty. By now, she knew that she could have any boy that she desired. Who needed that show off, Lance?

The friendship between Bibi and Angel, however, did not flag. They did everything together. They protected each other from unwanted advances and helped each other in wanted ones. They shared their amorous adventures and achievements. Angel had the Barbie doll good looks, but Bibi was just hot; she had a sultry demeanour that just captivated and entrapped boys, but also men. Bibi had such a calculating, almost emotion free, approach, that it sometimes worried and puzzled her friend. To Angel, love, even though it may be fleeting, meant love, not just sex.

Gerhadus and Lance's amateur boxing careers during these teenage years continued to astound followers of the sport. A year after Gerrie had been unable to compete against Lance in the Hoeskool Championship because of his broken ankle, the two finally met in the same tournament the following year, when they had both just turned 14. Up until this point, neither of them had ever suffered a loss in the ring, so, unless this match turned out to be a draw, one or other of them was going to lose that cherished record. They had both now fought in several bouts for the school team and, independently had won several fights as part of the Transvaal Junior team. Neither had yet competed at the national junior amateur level. Coach Brennan was working up to that.

The big day arrived at the Randburg Hoeskool. The gym was packed with spectators. Brennan had organised erector set seats to be constructed on all four sides of the ring. So many students wanted to attend that they were ultimately selected through a lottery, though there seemed to be plenty of gate crashers hanging from the wooden bars on the wall. When the two strapping lads stepped into the ring there was a carnival atmosphere in the room, with much whooping and shouting. Underneath there was huge tension. This crowd had waited over two years for this event. Coach Brennan was going to personally referee the contest; he was not taking any chances with his two prize students.

The Deputy Head Master, who also took drama lessons, had opted to be the ring announcer. He climbed awkwardly into the ring, catching his right foot on the rope and toppling over on his backside on the canvas. The spectator students hooted and whistled with glee as the embarrassed teacher picked himself up from the floor with the help of Coach Brennan. Then, his composure recovered, and with a booming voice, in imitation of the ring announcers he had seen on the newsreels, he called out the names of the two boxers and announced the fight. Lance waved at the crowd and danced around the ring, his gloved fist held high above his head, as if he were already victorious. Gerrie stayed in his corner and acknowledged his name with a slight nod of the head.

The bell sounded and the fight began. For a moment or two, as the two lads circled the ring, eyeing each other warily, there was quiet in the gym. Then, as Lance suddenly leaped forward with a flurry of wild flying punches the crowd erupted with noise. The young girls in the audience were screaming, almost all of them for Lance, who was continuing to press the attack with punches coming at Gerrie from all angles. Gerrie kept his cool. He dodged almost all of the blows and systematically landed short sharp jabs on Lance's undefended face. If the fight was to be won on aggression then Lance would be a clear winner, but, if the fight were to be won by punches landed, it would be Gerrie's. The bell rang for the end of the first round. For the first time in their careers, neither had Coach Brennan in their corner, since he was now the referee. To both, this felt strange.

When the bell rang for the start of the second round, Lance rushed across the ring and, almost before Gerrie had stood up, landed his first punch. It was delivered with such venom that it knocked Gerrie sideways. Lance sensed victory and followed up with another blow to the head. Gerrie went down on his knees and although he got up immediately, Brennan clearly scored it as a knockdown and waved the hovering Lance away whilst he started a count. Before he reached ten, seeing that Gerrie was on his feet, he waved the fighters to carry on. This short breather gave Gerrie time to think.

"Keep boxing him," he said to himself, "he's leaving himself wide open."

Lance, still sensing blood, resumed his furious wild attack, but Gerrie had recovered and easily dodged the blows, continuously countering with strong jabs to good effect. He could see Lance's nose getting redder and redder. Lance did his best to keep his guard up but, as soon as he did, Gerrie went for his body with a cluster of well-aimed jabs. Once again, by the end of the round, although Lance had scored heavily with a knockdown, Gerrie had more than made up with the number of punches landed.

The third and final round started. The crowd had become noisier and noisier as their excitement built. Now both fighters gave it all they had. Lance took a more measured approach which seemed to work as he got through Gerrie's guard through sheer force on several occasions. Once or twice he really rocked back Gerrie's head, but then Gerrie continued to box and frequently scored good points with alternate blows to Lance's head and body. Both boys were exhausted. They had given their all, and, as the bell went for the third and final time, they fell into each other's arms.

As referee, Coach Brennan was also the scorer; he knew exactly what to do. The bout had gone just as he hoped. As the boys' de facto manager, it was not in his interests for either boy to show a loss on their records. A draw was the perfect result and so, without any hesitation, he stepped forward and raised both boys' arms into the air, indicating that the fight was a tie. The crowd whooped and clapped in appreciation. Nobody could argue with that.

Chapter Four

The fight seemed to be a turning point in the relationship between Gerrie and Lance, at least for the time being. Their respect for each other had grown considerably and they now began to hang out together, other than at the gym. There was another reason for this: Gerrie had been a late starter in the romance department compared with Lance. Now, he had developed a crush on Lance's sister, Bibi. Not that he was in a position to do anything about it because Bibi was clearly out of his league. She was older than him and, being the stunner that she was, seemed to have plenty of suitors, especially guys that were much older than either of them. Nevertheless, hanging out with Lance and visiting with him at home, gave Gerrie the chance to spend time with his sister. Although he did his best to conceal his feelings for Bibi, her very presence caused his heart to race. He frequently saw her as she prepared herself for a date. Sometimes she would ask Lance and Gerrie what they thought of her outfit as she readied herself. Gerrie was always polite, but his heart pounded as she swirled in front of him; it was almost as if she was flirting.

A few days after the big fight, Coach Brennan called the two lads in for a meeting. He had a video tape of their fight. He wanted to show them because they both could learn from it. He also wanted to talk about their future. "It is time," he began, "to plan ahead." He mapped out the route forward. This would entail entering the State Championships, and thereafter, if successful, the National Championships.

"You both have the potential to win," said Brennan, "if you don't kill each other on the way. Whichever of you wants this the most can have it. It will mean more training and hard work than you can imagine. It will mean laying off all of the things that young men, like you, do. I'm not talking about girls here, I'm talking about booze and drugs and partying. If you want me to help you, then you must promise me that, for the next couple of years, you'll forgo the things that your mates will try to get you to do. There is no gain without pain. There is no luck either. As our great South African golfer, Gary Player, said, 'the more you practice, the luckier you get'."

Both lads promised Brennan that they would follow his rules. He then called for a meeting with their respective parents. Although Strom and Edna Van der Merwe and Rudy and Becky Hermanus were used to acknowledging each other at tournaments, they had never really spoken. All four, sat and listened as Coach Brennan spelled out what it would mean in their lives if their boys were going to challenge for national honours in their sport. They would all need to sacrifice a lot of their time and lives to keeping the lads on the right path.

"I am convinced," said Brennan, "that your boys have the makings of boxing champions, maybe beyond South African ones. If we're to give them that chance, we'll all need to make sacrifices – and so will they."

Both sets of parents bought into the prospect. They could all interpret Brennan's words into Rand, or maybe, even, dollars.

Over the next couple of years things went well for Brennan and his two proteges. Where possible, Brennan entered his gladiators in different events, but when it came to the State and National Championships, he could not keep them apart. When they were 16 and 17, they both reached the finals of the National Championship in their weight group. Brennan didn't exactly fix the result but it was interesting that Lance won one year and then Gerrie, the next, in fights where neither fighter seemed to break much sweat.

For a couple of years, Gerrie carried a flame for Lance's beautiful sister, Bibi. When he was 17, he finally had the guts to ask her out on a date. At the time she was dating a man of 25 who was a real estate salesman. To go behind his back with a 17 year old seemed a bit crazy to Bibi, but she had grown to really like her brother's friend and, sometimes, adversary. He was somehow so much older than his years. He was quiet, studious, and, it seemed, intelligent. He did, she had discovered, have a dry sense of humour, but, above all, he had a fabulous body – as hard as a rock. Bibi had to admit to herself that she did actually fancy him. So, she accepted to go out with him, just once. Their choices were limited. In South Africa, you had to be 18 to buy a drink, so the cinema seemed the best bet. The cinema was also dark. Gerrie had steered Bibi into the back row, which was almost empty. She did not mind. It did not take long before Gerrie's hands were exploring Bibi's body. She did not mind that either. In fact, the more he fondled her, the more she wanted to whisk him out of the bioscope, rip off all of his clothes, and have him make passionate love to her. That, of course, was not going to happen and, in his innocence, Gerrie probably had no idea of the effect his wandering hands were having on Bibi. In his eyes, a bit of fondling was about as far as one could go in the cinema. When they got home, after a stop at a fast-food place, for two pins Bibi would have whisked Gerrie up to her bedroom, but it was not possible. Instead, he had to listen to her dad, Rudy, cracking jokes and her brother teasing them about being a "couple". That night, in the privacy of her room, Bibi thought about Gerrie. Back in the Van der Merwe's home, Gerrie thought about her.

Training for the fights continued. Both young men attempted to follow the strict regime set by Brennan, but, as the next two years went by, Lance found it more difficult than his friend, Gerrie. Lance's outward going gregarious nature made it almost impossible for him to live his life like a monk. He was popular. He was good company. His schoolmates were always inviting him to join them at parties and other gatherings. He could not refuse. Both drink and drugs were available, as were young ladies. Lance just could not resist but join in. He rationalised that if he wanted to be the leader of the gang, which status he enjoyed, he would need to participate fully. "After all," he reasoned, "it didn't seem to be doing any harm. The odd hangover never killed anyone."

He still put himself through Brennan's vigorous training routines, but, in the ring itself, he was beginning to struggle. At the South African junior national championships, which Gerrie won, Lance had been beaten in the semi finals. Worse, he had been beaten by a black boy, who had reached that position without any of the advantages that had benefitted his opponent. Lance was 17; the black boy, one year younger. The following year, which was both Gerrie and Lance's last year as juniors, the title was again won by Gerrie, who outpointed and outboxed the same black lad that had beaten Lance the year before. Lance lost in the quarter finals. He had trained hard, but was too reliant on a big punch. He had failed to master the boxing techniques that Gerrie had learned, but worse, his overall lack of conditioning had betrayed him.

Brennan was not surprised. He was bitterly disappointed, because, of his two proteges he secretly felt that Lance, with his big hitting, would ultimately be the most flamboyant and successful of the two fighters. He had the greatest respect for Gerrie's craftsmanship and diligence, but Brennan had secretly considered Lance to have the most commercial potential, the sort of fighter that crowds love. But it was not to be. His boys had reached the end of the junior road. It was now time for them to make decisions. Would boxing be part of their lives going forward? And, if so, how?

It was quite normal for Junior National Champions to turn pro. Several champs before Gerrie had done so with varying degrees of success. Brennan encouraged Gerrie to do the same and offered to be his manager. Strom, his dad, had other ideas.

"Coach Brennan is not a business man, son," he told his lad. "He is a school teacher. A manager requires a business brain, like mine," he went on. "We should offer Brennan a cut for being your coach. I will arrange the business side of things and he can carry on with the training and preparation. We will make a good team."

Gerrie was not so sure. Yes, he loved his boxing, and he was proud to have been proclaimed the best amateur in the country, but he had also been a good student, with the possibility of going on to university. So, this was a big decision. Strom didn't think so. Strom could see the dollar signs.

So could Edna. "You can always go to university later. If things don't work out with the boxing, uni will still be there," she suggested. This seemed to make sense to the young man and so, within a few weeks of winning his second national title, he had signed the necessary forms to become a pro. Coach Brennan was offered 10% of any purses and Strom told his son that he would be taking 25% of his lad's earnings, to look after the business side of things. Secretly, Gerrie thought this was quite a lot, but how could he argue with his dad?

Lance, by now, further to his recent defeats, had decided that the life of a boxing pro would be too much like hard work. Instead, he signed on to be a policeman. This would require a period of training, but nowhere near to the rigorous routine he would have to endure as a professional fighter. The uniform of a law enforcer would also give him a certain prestige. He had no doubt that it would not be long before he was a senior officer, or even, one day, the Chief. Underneath his bravado, he was, however, quite jealous of his friend Gerrie. But he knew full well that Gerrie had earned his success by putting in the hard work that he had not. Lance was happy with the knowledge that, should he so desire, he could beat Gerrie any day; all he would need to do would be to take the matter seriously.

The South African boxing business was dominated by one firm; Shultz and Rosenburg. Steven Shultz was a lawyer and Trevor Rosenburg a sports journalist. Their firm, S and R Promotions, practically controlled the professional sport in the country. They also had far reaching contacts in the USA, UK and South America with other boxing promoters, from whom they could source foreign opponents for the local lads. To even get into the professional ring in South Africa, you needed to be under contract to S and R. Not that that was all bad. S and R had proved adept at advancing the careers of several South African boxers over the years, in various weight categories, and had several world ranked local boxers on their books. Almost all of these were in the lower weight divisions, and all of them were black. When Gerrie became available as a professional, he was a promoter's dream. First of all, he was white, second, he was Afrikaans, and, most importantly, he was a cruiserweight, and might soon be a heavyweight. Fight fans always wanted to see the big lads.

Strom didn't need to approach S and R. No sooner than Gerrie had won the amateur championships for the second time and turned 18, Trevor Rosenburg was quicker than lightning in reaching out to Gerrie's dad. Strom, of course, had no experience in contract law, so rather quickly fell under the spell of Trevor's smooth talk. He also had a great admiration for Trevor, who, before becoming a journalist, had been a star centre in the Springbok national rugby team. Soon, Strom had signed up his son for a two-year promotional agreement, in which S and R would feature Gerrie in four professional bouts per year, for a mere 33% of his earnings.

"But, Dad," exclaimed Gerrie, upon hearing the news, "that means for every time I fight, I get less than one third of the pay."

"Yes," said his dad, "you have to regard it as a sort of apprenticeship; everyone learning a trade has to go through one. After two years, when you are successful, you can call all the shots."

As far as Gerrie was concerned, he had already done an apprenticeship. He had been boxing now for over eight years and nobody had yet beaten him. He was far from happy about the arrangement that his dad had made.

It turned out that Steven Shultz was the brains behind the firm; Trevor was more of the PR man. Shultz was shrewd. He was delighted that the firm had signed Gerrie. He had watched Gerrie box. He knew that he was pure gold.

For the first three fights under the contract, Steven selected fighters who were past their prime. For the first time Gerrie would be boxing without the protective head gear. The professional fights would be longer than the amateur ones, starting for Gerrie with a four rounder and moving up, by the third fight, to six rounds. None of these, however, lasted more than three, with Gerrie easily disposing of his opponents. For his fourth fight, Steven pitched his novice against the number four ranked heavyweight in the country, over eight rounds. Coach Brennan made sure that his man was in tip top shape and it paid off, as Gerrie outpointed his opponent easily.

In the second year of Gerrie's contract he fought and knocked out the number two ranked South African. The press, through Trevor's manipulation, were now hailing Gerrie as a future world beater. But first he had to beat the reigning local champ, Tiny Robertson.

Tiny was far from tiny. Whereas, Gerrie was still, in truth, a cruiser weight, which is under 200 lbs, Tiny was a massive 250 lbs. He was also black, which somehow made him even more imposing. Coach Brennan struggled to find suitable sparring partners. He could source plenty of big black men, but none with the physique of Tiny. He would have to rely a lot on the heavy bag in training to simulate the upcoming opponent.

The bout of the relative newcomer and lighter weight Gerrie against the incumbent colossus, Tiny, had now attracted the attention of more than just sports fans. This was a rare David and Goliath pairing and the fact that Gerrie had never been beaten in the ring added huge lustre to the event. This did not go unnoticed by Gerrie, who not only felt that he was being grossly underpaid, but that his cut of the pay was extremely unfair. After all, he had to endure all the weeks of training and the constant punishment to his body, not his dad nor Steven Shultz. The seed of his discontent had been sown by his girlfriend, Bibi, who had been pointing out for a long time that Gerrie was being screwed, not only by S and R but also by his own father. At first, Gerrie had been resistant to Bibi's entreaties, but slowly he came to realise that she was right. He decided enough was enough. He was now almost 20 years old. Old enough to make his own decisions. First, he tackled his dad, not as a "dad," but as a "manager". That took guts. He pointed out that the fee he had negotiated with S and R was far too high, as was the fee he was taking as "manager".

Strom tried to give him the routine of "how can you be so greedy? After all I and your mother have done for you: supporting you through all these years!"

Gerrie wasn't buying it. "I thought that's what parents did," he countered. "I'll tell you what we're going to do, Dad," he went on, "You're going to reduce your management fee from 25% to 15% and I'm going to refuse to fight for Shultz and Rosenburg unless they give me twice the money you've agreed with them. That way, you'll still get more money and I'll get what I'm worth."

"But you have a contract with them. You can't just change it," said his Dad, rather meekly.

"Contracts don't fight, Dad," replied Gerrie with the firmness of one of his right jabs. "They can have something, or nothing."

It didn't take Steven two seconds to adjust the split. He knew when he was onto a good thing. "Of course, we can change the purse. I had been thinking of suggesting this anyway."

With that it was settled. From now on, Gerrie would negotiate his own terms. The two year deal with S and R was coming to an end. If he could become the South African heavyweight champion, he could call his own shots. All that mattered now was to win the fight.

S and R might have been greedy, but they sure knew how to put on a tournament. Trevor's handling of the press was masterful. In the two weeks before the fight, some story or other related to it appeared daily on the back pages of all the South African newspapers and, sometimes, even on the front. The hype surrounding the upcoming event was huge and so were the ticket sales. Everybody in the country, it seemed, wanted to be there. Gerrie was quite determined that for his next fight he would want a percentage of the gate, as well as a fee for fighting. Tiny Robertson had never attracted such a crowd, so Gerrie rightly assumed that he was the attraction, not the big black man.

At the same time, however, another news story crept into the pages of the national papers, possibly because it vaguely related to boxing. PC Lance Hermanus, the ex-amateur boxer, featured. Apparently, during an altercation between the police and a gang of black youths, one of the boys had been shot and killed. Unfortunately, he had been shot in the back whilst attempting to climb a wall to escape. Lance Hermanus had fired the shot. He, of course, had claimed that it was supposed to be a warning shot and that he was only attempting to do his difficult job, but there were many who thought that he was wrong and some were baying for his blood. The situation wasn't helped by Lance's apparently cocky and nonchalant remark to a pressman, that "it didn't really matter. It was only a kaffir that died."

The whole sorry mess was turning into a flashpoint of conflicting opinions amongst the public. Those in the outright racist right wing of the Nationalist party, were screaming for Lance to be given a medal, whilst the lefties proposed that he should be sent to jail. The right wingers would have probably won, but, somehow, the matter got some press coverage in Europe, and the ruling Nats found themselves on the defence internationally. To cool things down, it was decided that Lance should be suitably reprimanded, and the upshot was that a judge sentenced him, not to death, but to a year in jail.

Gerrie was sorry about his old mate and adversary's predicament. He had not seen Lance for over a year, even though his romance with Bibi had blossomed.

He wanted to reach out to Lance, but Bibi had little sympathy for her brother.

"Maybe a year in the slammer will bring him down a peg or two," she told her lover. "The real problem is that he'll be barred from being a policeman again."

Notwithstanding Bibi's view, Gerrie thought the decent thing to do was send a message of support to Lance. He vowed that, as soon as the fight for the Championship was over, he would go to see Lance in jail.

The day of the fight for the right to wear the South African heavyweight belt arrived. The atmosphere in the arena was exciting. Most of the money was on Tiny to crush his smaller opponent, but most of the hearts in the crowd were rooting for the underdog, not only because he was so much smaller, but also because he was white. Very few blacks had been able to afford tickets, so Tiny Robertson was definitely under supported. Basically, the crowd wanted the young white man to win, but would not be devastated if he didn't, because they would have at least got their ticket money back from their bets on the other man.

To the millions of black citizens of South Africa, Tiny Robertson was a hero. Very few black men had been able to reach the top of any sport in the country, not because of their innate lack of ability, but purely because of their lack of opportunity. Participation in team sports for blacks in the country was close to impossible. The very nature of team sports requires organisation and facilities; these, in turn, require funding. There were simply no funds available from government to provide training facilities or land for playing fields for black citizens. The hostels in which male blacks lived in the slum townships on the edge of all South African cities and towns, in most cases, did not even have the most basic facilities for personal hygiene. There was no way that any money would be made available for playing fields or courts. Boxing was one of the few sports that required limited facilities. Small gyms could be set up in the most rudimentary locations and you did not need a team of participants. Boxing was, therefore, one of the few areas where the black man could compete against the white man on more or less an even playing field, simply because there was no field required. As a result, there were quite a few black men scattered across the South African rankings, but, until Tiny Robertson came along, none of them had won the heavyweight crown. Tiny, however, had done just that. He had beaten every white man that had challenged him, proving to his black world, that the white man can be challenged and overcome. Tiny Robertson was a symbol of defiance. He needed to be crushed.

Chapter Five

For the first time in his boxing career Gerrie was nervous as he climbed into the ring. The fact that he was fighting for national honours suddenly hit him. As the South African national anthem blasted out from speakers around the arena, with thousands of voices singing along, he was somehow filled with emotion. This was it. If he were to be successful, he would go down in the sporting annals of his country: *his* country! His heart was pounding: not from fear of the huge black man snarling at him from the other corner of the ring, but from the weight of responsibility that he felt on his shoulders. Suddenly, his thought train was broken. He was being called into the centre of the ring by the referee, a South African Greek, Markus Roufus, for the introductions and the ritual recitation of the rules. When Gerrie's name boomed out across the arena with its eerie echo, the mainly white crowd roared their approval. And, to be fair, when Tiny's name followed, there was a healthy level of polite applause; after all, this was a sport.

It was really only then, once Gerrie found himself side by side with Tiny, that he realised just how large the man was. As he returned to his corner to await the bell, Coach Brennan must have read his thoughts. "Remember what they say," whispered Brennan to his man, "the bigger they are, the harder they fall." Ding…and they were off.

Tiny looked like a thug, but he was nobody's fool. He knew how to box as well as how to hit. He started rather cautiously. Gerrie danced. Clearly "dancing" was not what Tiny did, but he didn't need to dance to look menacing. Gerrie knew that, at any second, Tiny could unleash a sledgehammer blow. Gerrie kept moving and Tiny plodded after him, throwing a few jabs from time to time, trying to find his range. Nothing landed. On the other hand, in between the dancing steps, Gerrie found that he could pepper Tiny's face with little jabs. He knew they had landed because he could feel the thud through his gloves. Round One to Gerrie. The second and third round carried on in much the same manner, with Gerrie jabbing and Tiny swinging and missing. Up until now, Gerrie was giving the champ a boxing lesson.

At the beginning of the fourth round, it all changed. Gerrie was hardly off his stool when he got hit with a thundering right hook from the champ. Gerrie had never been hit so hard. Luckily, he went straight down to the canvas, because, if he had stayed on his feet, he would have been the recipient of several other hammer blows that probably would have ended the fight. At the count of six, Gerrie realised what was happening. His head was clearing. He stood up and raised his gloves in front of his face. "Box on," said Roufus, his sharp eyes looking for signs of Gerrie's condition. Tiny rushed forward to try to end things, throwing a series of vicious blows. They all missed. Gerrie's instincts to duck and move had saved him. Gerrie's head was now clear, so for the rest of the round he managed to keep out of further trouble, even landing a few scoring points himself. At the end of the round, however, no one could argue that Gerrie had won this round.

As Gerrie sat down with some relief, Brennan was quick to be in his ear. "You're scoring well, Gerrie…but you're not hurting him. Imagine that you actually want to kill him. When you see the chance, hit hard. Hit him as hard as you've ever hit anyone in your life."

Gerrie nodded. The first half of the next round proceeded fairly quietly. Gerrie continued to box and score points; Tiny continued to slug away without much success. Gerrie had now worked it out. He would let Tiny think that he was confused by the champ's lunges, almost encourage him to throw more. Then, at the right moment, when Tiny was unbalanced as he threw a big punch, Gerrie would hit him with the hardest punch he had ever thrown. It was as if Gerrie was winding himself up, preparing to throw a punch, not only with all his muscles but with all his mind.

With 15 seconds of the fifth round remaining Gerrie's chance came. As Tiny let go with a fairly vicious looking right swing, for a split second he was indeed unbalanced. Gerrie uncoiled the hardest blow he had ever unleashed. He hit Tiny flush on the jaw, not just with his fist but with his whole being. Everything he had was behind the punch, his arms, his legs, but mostly his mind. Tiny went down like a ten pin being hit with a bowling ball. He had not moved whilst Roufus counted to ten. Gerrie could not believe what he saw in front of him. The great hulk of a black man was out for the count at his feet. Gerrie was so stunned, he hardly noticed the deafening roar of the crowd. He hardly noticed Strom and Edna and his little brother, Frikkie, leaping for joy or Bibi with tears streaming down her beautiful face, her make up smudged beyond repair. It was as if he were dreaming. Suddenly, it was over. Referee Roufus was holding his arm aloft and Coach Brennan was hugging him in tears. This was Brennan's own dream come true too. He had no idea where Gerrie had found such a punch. It was as if, for one day, he had managed to combine the best of Lance and Gerrie into one vehicle. Anyway, whatever had happened, it felt good.

Tiny had been helped back to his stool. Gradually his brain resumed normal service. As Gerrie approached him to see how he was, Tiny was gracious in defeat. "I didn't see that one coming. Man, I ain't never been hit that hard before. What you got in them gloves? Lead?" He managed a laugh at his own joke. Gerrie felt good. At least the man didn't seem to be damaged. For the first time, too, Gerrie felt pride. All of the work in the gym, all of the gruelling road work, the sweat, the heat, the pain; it all now seemed worthwhile. He was the Champion of South Africa. It was a good feeling.

The ring was now crammed with boxing officials, clearly identifiable in their blazers, journalists, radio and television commentators, general well-wishers and posers. Gerrie was manoeuvred in front of a battery of cameras. Somebody handed him the championship belt. It weighed a ton.

"Put it on," someone yelled.

"Hold it up," someone else shouted.

Cameras flashed and whirred. Out of the corner of his eye he caught sight of Strom, his dad, squashed in a crowd on the far side of the ring. "Let my dad through," yelled Gerrie. A little corridor opened up in the crowd and Strom squeezed his way towards the centre with Frikkie in tow. As he approached, Gerrie gave him a big loving hug. The photographers caught it. It was an important and moving picture. Edna was not in the ring. She was no less proud than her husband, but there was no way, given her bulk, she could undertake to climb up to and through the ropes. Bibi, however, was not far behind Strom and Frikkie, and some of the best pictures that appeared the next day were of Bibi and Gerrie in a long embrace. When Bibi and Gerrie finally reached home that night, Bibi was still aglow with excitement. She was hot; hot, that is, for her man to make passionate love with her. But, Gerrie was exhausted; what he needed was an ice bath and sleep. Bibi was disappointed and, of course, frustrated, but that didn't matter; she was proud of her man as she watched him sleep.

When Gerrie looked at the papers the following morning, in the fresh light of day, he was interested to see who was featured in the pictures. There was a small picture in most papers of him with Strom, there were many pictures of him and Bibi, and, he was pleased to see, quite a few of Coach Brennan. However, if you had to tot up who appeared most it was, rather surprisingly, Steven Shultz and Trevor Rosenburg.

Messrs Shultz and Rosenburg were not slow out of the starting blocks. Tiny Robertson had not only been ranked number one in South Africa, but was ranked number seven in the world rankings, both by the WBC and the WBA, the two international organisations that somehow controlled world boxing. Given the fact that these rankings would now be revisited by their ranking panels, it would seem that S and R would shortly have two world-ranked boxers on their books, and, fortuitously, one of them would be white. For many years the heavyweight champions of the world had been black and, although it would be fair to say that some of them had been very popular with both black and white fans, having a white heavyweight champion again, could be massive in terms of potential earnings. The fact that their contender was also South African could only add to his value, because controversy paid well in the boxing business.

Both Shultz and Rosenburg had longstanding connections with the boxing establishment in the USA. There the business was effectively controlled by two men, Bob Levin and Louis Brown. Levin's company, Square Ring, had a weekly boxing television show. Levin lived in Las Vegas, where he was "tight" with the major casino owners, and frequently organised major boxing events in their showrooms. Bob had a host of fighters of all weights signed to him, but his speciality was Latinos. He had many contacts in South America and Square Ring was a route into the lucrative North American market for many aspiring fighters from the slums of Rio, Sao Paulo, and Buenos Aires. Bob was an unlikely fight promoter. He was a middle-aged, bespectacled, white lawyer, from a comfortable family background in suburban New York, who had slipped into the field of boxing when his firm represented an ex-heavyweight champion versus the Inland Revenue Service. Bob had been amazed at the lack of depth and ability in the management of the boxing business. He gradually took on more cases from the sector for his firm, until one day, he broke away to form his own company, representing fighters. It was not long before this enterprise had morphed into a fight promotions company as well as fighter management.

Bob's biggest competitor, Louis Brown, was a huge African American, with grey wiry hair like an upturned hairbrush. He had a booming voice and a smile as wide as the Grand Canyon. In his youth, as a gang member in Detroit, he had served time for abetting a manslaughter. Whilst incarcerated, out of boredom, he took some courses in maths and, ultimately, business management. He also made a friend of another inmate, Jimmy the Hammer, who had been a professional boxer. Jimmy told Louis how the boxing business was structured. How it was essentially controlled by white shady businessmen and, sometimes, the Mafia. He told him how fights were fixed. He told him that managers and promoters made off like bandits and how the poor guys getting pummelled in the ring were getting pummelled in the pocket. He explained how the Mafia knew who was going to win, how judges were bought and referees paid off.

Brown decided that maybe there would be room for a black manager, or black enforcer, in the boxing business, and, by the time he was released, not only had he made some good connections with the Mob, but he had compiled a list of the names and last known addresses of a host of black fighters. Armed with this knowledge and now in contact with the right people, one by one Brown ensnared his targets and soon he had many of the most promising black boxers under contract. It was not long before they found that they could not get a fight unless Brown was, in some way, involved, either as a promoter or manager in a sham company operated by his son. It was also not too long before Louis' huge grin was featured in all of the sporting magazines as the man who controlled boxing.

Steven Shultz knew both men quite well. He had supplied them with the odd South African boxer for these American shows, as well as taken some of their stable of fighters for matches in Africa. Shultz did his best to balance his relationship between the two men in the US, but, it did not take a genius to realise that he felt more comfortable dealing with Levin than with Brown. He often wondered what Louis thought about the pro white politics of South Africa, but, clearly, Louis didn't give a damn, just as long as he could make a buck.

In Gerrie Van der Merwe, Steven knew that he had a hot commodity. The fact that Gerrie was now being tagged as "Gerrie the Giant Slayer" also helped. He decided that the best thing to do would be to fly to the USA to see if he could carve out a lucrative path for his new local champion. He knew that the current world heavyweight champion, James Dubois, was one of Louis' men, and that Louis would probably do everything in his power to keep it that way for a while. He was not sure that he could trust Louis Brown with Gerrie's future. On the other hand, Bob had been starved out of participation in the heavyweight division. It might be very appealing to Bob to be representing a white challenger.

The first thing for Shultz and Rosenburg to do, however, was to secure rights to the new local champ. The two-year deal that Gerrie had agreed to was now over. Before Steven went anywhere, he needed to sign a new contract with their fighter and he knew now that this was not going to be as easy as before. He sent his partner, Trevor, to speak with Strom. Ostensibly, Strom was still Gerrie's manager and Steven knew that Strom had the greatest respect for Trevor, so this was probably the best starting point. Strom agreed that it would be in his son's best interests to sign a new promotional deal with S and R and promised to talk to him.

Gerrie, however, was taking a break. The championship fight had been a good payday and all sorts of offers were pouring in by way of sponsorship. Strom, in truth, didn't really know what was going on in Gerrie's head or with the sponsorship offers. Gerrie had a new manager, – not, officially, of course, but in practice. Her name was Bibi.

Chapter Six

One face that had been missing at ringside for the championship fight was Angel's. She had been in London, with her pretty mother, Sally. In fact, she had been in London now for well over a year, having been taken there, some 15 months earlier to be a contestant in the Miss World Pageant. She had not won, but had been named as first runner up. Sally, who had been estranged from Dirk, whom she had accused of mental abuse, had moved to London to be with her daughter.

To become a contestant in Miss World, Angel had needed to win the Miss South Africa title, which she had done two years before. A couple of years before that, a South African impresario, Jules Donovan, had spotted the lovely Angel, ringside, at one of Lance's bouts. He knew instantly that she was beauty queen material, and he should know, because he was the owner of the South African franchise for the Miss World Organisation, operating from London. To be more precise, Jules was the franchisee for the "white" Miss South Africa competition. There was also a "Miss Africa South" competition, which had been set up by Miss World in London (under pressure from black activists in the UK) for black ladies only. Miss Africa South was owned by a black entrepreneur, Daniel Buthelezi, or to be more precise, by his exotic girlfriend, Gloria. Interestingly, Daniel was, in fact, more interested

in white girls than black ones, but Miss Africa South did
at least open some doors to him internationally. Donovan
had no interest in the black version of the pageant; in his
view there was no money to be made there.

Having discovered Angel, he had taken her under
his wing, and this had led him to meet Dirk and Sally de
Kock, from whom he needed approval for their daughter
to compete in his beauty pageant, such were the strict rules
imposed by Miss World. Dirk de Kock had taken an instant
dislike to Donovan and did not endorse the idea of his only
daughter being paraded, like meat, in front of an ogling
crowd, even though he would have been quite happy to ogle
other people's daughters. As a result, there had been a huge
disagreement between Sally and Dirk as to what was right for
their daughter, which just added yet another thing for them
to argue about. Dirk's temper seemed to be getting worse by
the day and Sally often bore the brunt of it. Notwithstanding
Dirk's view, and under pressure from her daughter, she had
signed the paperwork that Donovan required.

Dirk was furious and physically beat Sally that night
before forcing himself on her. Sally decided it was time to
move on. The next day she consulted a lawyer and, within
a week, she and her daughter had left the family home.
Luckily, Sally had some independent financial sources,
both her parents in the UK having recently passed on and
left her their estate. Sally and Angel set up home together.
Angel left school and enrolled in a secretarial college and
Sally was offered a job as office manager by Jules Donovan,
whose main business was theatrical and entertainment
management. Donovan, although considering Angel as
the prettiest young thing he had seen in years, was actually
quite taken with her mother and went out of his way to
find a spot for her in his company.

Jules was quite sure that if he entered Angel directly into the Miss South Africa pageant, she would be a certain winner. Under the rules set down by the Miss World organisation in London, Jules was not supposed to influence the judges, but, in the case of Angel, he doubted whether this would be necessary. There was no question in Donovan's mind that Angel's beauty and allure would far surpass any of her competitors. Nevertheless, Jules felt that it would be politic for Angel to first enter the Miss Transvaal contest, both to gain some exposure to the cattle market atmosphere of beauty contests, but also to gain some credibility with the press and the other contestants, in particular, the other contestants' parents.

Jules explained to Sally the ropes of a beauty pageant and Sally set about fitting out her lovely daughter with an evening ball gown and a skimpy one-piece swimsuit. When Sally staged a dress rehearsal for Donovan, he knew, right then, that he was onto a winner. Angel looked fabulous. The blue swimsuit, high cut on the legs and plunging at the top, showed off Angel's figure to perfection. There was no way this costume could actually be worn in the water.

Jules, with permission from Sally, showed Angel how to move: how to put one leg in front of the other, how to stick out her chest, and how to sensuously slide her hands over her body. It felt odd to Angel, parading in a swimsuit with high-heeled shoes, but the bit of practice gave her confidence. Angel was a quick learner. Sally was surprised how jealous she felt at the sight of Jules, almost caressing her daughter with his demonstration. Then, when Angel reappeared a few minutes later, having changed from the swimsuit into the white ball gown that Sally had selected, both Sally and Jules clapped in unison. Angel really looked like a Miss World. Once again Jules gently showed

Angel how to stand and how to move gracefully in the long dress, and once again, Sally couldn't help but wish that Jules was touching her. It had been a long time since she had felt the tender hands of a handsome man.

The Miss Transvaal beauty pageant was held in a hotel ballroom in Troyville, a rather seedy part of Johannesburg. The room was packed with about three hundred people, mainly working-class white men and women. Most of them, it would appear, came from the extended families of the contestants, including mothers, fathers, brothers, sisters, aunts, uncles, cousins and even elderly grandparents. Most of them were Afrikaans. The elegant Sally felt completely out of place, but Jules Donovan just laughed and reminded her that these were their customers. Sally was also pleased that Angel's best friend, Bibi, had wanted to be there. Bibi had proved herself to be a very good friend.

The judges had been picked by Jules. They included a popular Afrikaans singer, the Mayor of Troyville and his Lady Mayoress, a previous Miss Transvaal, and the captain of the Springbok rugby team. A stage had been erected at one end of the ballroom and was draped with a backdrop of false red velvet. The judges were seated on multi-coloured plastic chairs at a long trestle table that had been set up facing the stage. The room was thick with smoke, made worse by the low stained ceiling. Popular music blared through the hotel's thin sound system. The room was filled with expectancy. There was a buzz of excited anticipation from the crowd. Most of the chatter was in Afrikaans. The hotel had set up a bar in the anteroom to the ballroom. Business was brisk. The Castle lagers were flowing.

Meanwhile the contestants, all twenty of them, had been crammed into an adjacent meeting room, which had been partitioned off with sheets to give some privacy. The room had seen better days. The walls were scuffed and the ceiling was a patchwork of stains from the dripping air conditioning system.

The first round of the competition required the young ladies to wear their swimsuits. Then, after a brief interval, they would have to change into their ball gowns, which were now hanging on the metal racks of the hotel's wobbly luggage trolleys. This makeshift changing room was bedlam with the high pitched squeals of the young girls. No men were allowed in the room, but each contestant could have the assistance of another woman to help them change into their evening wear. As Angel looked around the room at her fellow contestants, any anxiety she had had about her ability to compete disappeared. Her fellow competitors were a motley collection. True, there were some pretty girls, but, in Angel's opinion, none of them seemed to have what her mother called, "class". Most of them seemed to know each other. They had clearly competed before. They viewed Angel with suspicion. Perhaps they knew then, that they could not win.

In the main ballroom, Jules stood on the little stage and welcomed the crowd. He explained the procedure: first the swimsuits, then the ball gowns, then the judging. Then he introduced a local comedian as a Master of Ceremonies. The MC told a few well worn jokes about beauty pageants and then, accompanied by a great fanfare of trumpets from the tinny sound system, announced the arrival of the contestants.

One by one the girls filed onto the stage, each one trying to walk elegantly in high heels and swimsuit. Clearly, it is more likely that the contestants would have been used to wearing flip flops with their swimsuits, because they obviously were not at ease in their stilettos, especially on the uneven planks of the makeshift stage. Jules had taken the trouble, in rehearsing Angel, to make sure that she could walk elegantly in her costume and had made her practice on the rickety boards before the other contestants arrived. As the girls appeared, one by one, various sectors of the crowd let out whoops and cheers. When Angel appeared, there was almost a universal gasp. No whooping, no cheering, from attendant families, just a sort of combined, "Wow". They knew, right there and then, that no matter how much they hollered for their sister, cousin, daughter or whatever, there was no point. Angel was clearly the most beautiful girl in the room.

Back in the makeshift changing room, the girls knew it too. There was not much chatter as they climbed into their ball gowns. Most of them had nobody to help, so Sally kindly went around to aid those that needed a zip or a button fixed. Some of the evening dresses were obviously homemade and most with cheap and gaudy material. Angel stood out. In comparison with the other girls, Angel seemed really sophisticated. The girls in the dressing room knew it was all over. As they traipsed back onto the creaking stage to parade in front of the judges, the crowd politely applauded each contestant as they appeared, with the usual shouts of encouragement to their own, but they too knew that the newcomer had stolen the show.

The judging was a formality and it was not long before Jules was placing the sash of "Miss Transvaal" across Angel's delightful bosom. Sally looked on with pride. Bibi whooped and cheered. The local press took their pictures and Angel's pretty face duly appeared on the front page of the Johannesburg papers the next morning. Dirk, when he saw the pictures, was not pleased, but reluctantly accepted the congratulations showered on him at his work.

The girls at the secretarial college were thrilled for Angel. Just as at school, Angel was popular with her fellow students. Although none of them had attended the pageant, and, in fact, most of them had not known that their fellow student was a contestant, the word soon went around the college, as did copies of the newspapers. Back in the office, Jules Donovan explained to Sally the next step, which would be the Miss South Africa pageant to be held in Bloemfontein in three months' time. They would need to think about a new dress and a new swimsuit.

Jules was pleased that he had hired Sally. He looked forward to seeing her light up his office every morning. Jules had not been short of girlfriends. After all, as an entertainment promotor, he had lots of opportunities to date very pretty girls. Now in his forties, Jules had a history of affairs. He had once been married, some 20 years earlier, but this had not been successful and had, luckily, he thought, produced no offspring. His wife had been a dancer. They had married young, but had grown apart. When Jules found out that his wife was having an affair with a two-bit actor, he divorced her. Since then, he had had numerous liaisons, but none of them had developed into permanence, mainly because Jules had become quite a heavy drinker and had dabbled with dope. By the time Jules was 40, he had done it all, but, luckily, had pulled himself together and now concentrated on growing his entertainment business alone. He had not lost his eye for a pretty woman and, upon the arrival of Sally in his life, realised once again just how attractive the right woman could be. "This time," he thought to himself, "I am not going to screw it up."

Sally was also attracted to Jules. However, she was still married to Dirk, who had not yet agreed to a divorce. In fact, Sally had not pushed the matter; there seemed to be no urgent need. The more she thought about her new employer, the more she thought about getting a divorce. Not that she would need to if she wanted to seduce Jules, but there was no future in being married to that bully, Dirk, and now, with new interests in her life, she could well do without him.

Dirk did not oppose the divorce, nor was he particularly generous with a settlement. As far as he was concerned Sally had left him and he had got used to the idea. The split had been a long time in the making. It had really festered after the row about the Afrikaans schooling. As it turned out, Dirk should have married an Afrikaans girl, one who would do as he asked. As far as Angel was concerned, he had lost her a long time ago. She was too much her mother's daughter. No, he would be better off without them. And, since they had both left him, he was not about to split his wealth, not that there was really a great deal to split.

Sally didn't care. She just wanted out. Her growing infatuation for her new boss was really what was on her mind. She was also enjoying her job. Interacting with the cream of South Africa's show business was fun. Although, primarily, she dealt with the contracts, Sally always wanted to find out who was behind the paperwork and the signatures. She took an interest in the work that their clients were undertaking and they appreciated it. Jules noticed this. He also noticed an upturn in business for which he was grateful. He did not want to spoil this happy state of affairs by following his urge to bed Sally. Sally, however, had different ideas.

Her immediate focus though, was on preparing her lovely daughter for the Miss South Africa contest. To a large degree, this would follow the same format as the previous contest in the Transvaal, but the contestants would also be asked to answer a few ridiculous questions from the Master of Ceremonies, who was going to be South Africa's heartthrob and only real international movie star, Johnny Last. Johnny had featured in several Hollywood romcoms. He was seriously good looking with a rich tan, thick wavy golden hair, deep blue eyes and a gravelly voice. Sally had not met him yet, but had been thrilled to sign his contract on behalf of the agency. Secretly, Sally dreamed that Johnny Last would fall for her daughter.

The contest was also slated to be televised, which would be a new experience for Angel. So, this time around, as well as rehearsing walking in the costume and dress, Jules made sure that Angel practised answering questions, as if she were on the television.

"Putting on a TV face, is very important," explained Jules, as he filmed his role-play of Angel answering his questions and then playing it back to her. "Make your voice sexy," he told her. "Just like your mother," he thought to himself. "Imagine you are in a film with Johnny." It did not take Angel long to get it right. Jules was confident that she would steal the show.

Once again, the pageant was being held in a hotel but this time the venue was Bloemfontein's only five-star hotel. The ballroom was a grand room, with a decorative ceiling and beautifully panelled walls, a far cry from Troyville. The television company and the sponsors had done an excellent job of decorating the room, including the stage, and, instead of a tinny sound system, there was an orchestra, seated on a raised dais at the back of the stage. The contestants were all asked to be in attendance one day in advance of the show, which was to be beamed out live across the country. This annual event was one of the few live entertainment shows that South Africa's fledgling national television company managed to put on and, as such, it was eagerly awaited every year. For this reason, the contestants were all required to attend a full day of rehearsal, during which a stooge stood in for the famous Johhny Last.

Unlike Troyville, the contestants' dressing rooms in Bloemfontein had been properly planned and constructed in a series of meeting rooms, adjacent to the main ballroom. Each segment had a long dressing table with lighted mirrors and little canvas privacy cubicles for the girls to change in. The ballroom toilets had been sealed off for the exclusive use of the contestants; visitors would have to use the conveniences in the hotel lobby. Johnny Last was, of course, given special star treatment. He was to use the hotel's presidential suite and provided with a personal security man to escort him to the stage at the right time. Jules' attention to detail in organising the event, together with the television company, had left nothing to chance.

Sally studied the other contestants at the rehearsal carefully. There were one or two that exhibited some charm and, in one case, even sex appeal. But, in the main, they were giggly young girls. Most were quite pretty, but few exhibited sophistication. She was convinced that Angel would win. Sally had also been involved in selecting the judges, at Jule's behest. She had deliberately tried to find people with class; she thought that would work out best for her daughter. And it did. Angel carried it off beautifully. She moved better than any of the other girls and she was dressed better. There was no getting away from it, she actually was the prettiest young lady in the line.

But, if anything nailed it, it was her "interview" with Johnny Last. She almost seduced him on the stage, not physically, but with words. He absolutely loved it and played it up with great enthusiasm. There was no question who Johhny favoured, but so too, did the judges. By the end of the evening, Angel de Kock had been crowned Miss South Africa, and booked her ticket to the Miss World pageant in London. Sally was overjoyed. She hugged Jules in her happiness. He did not object; this was the first time that he could feel her attractive body close to his.

Chapter Seven

The Miss World pageant in London was a tightly organised event. The owners of the Miss World Company, Jane and Dick Michaels, had been running it for many years. They knew where the pitfalls were and planned everything meticulously. With over 80 pretty young ladies under their wing they could not afford to have any scandals. Jane employed a gaggle of trusted chaperones, each of whom were assigned ten girls as their charges. The entire party was lodged at the Hilton hotel on Park Lane, with each group of young ladies, together with their chaperone, on separate floors. At Jules Donovan's request, Jane had hired Sally to be a chaperone, but not for the group that included her daughter.

The competition was to be held at London's famous Albert Hall. The competitors would be required to parade three times, first in swimsuits, then in national costume, and finally in ball gowns. The actual show, however, was considerably padded out with a compere, and some musical dance numbers to which the contestants were required to provide a decorative backdrop. The whole performance was enhanced with short videos reflecting the different countries of the participants. This particular year's compere was the famous American comedian, Bobbie Smart, who in later years was convicted of sexual assault by a Florida court. Because the show was scheduled to go out live to a worldwide audience of many millions, several days of rehearsals were required. Chalk marks were placed on the stage to show each girl where she should be standing at any particular time. Progress was slow due to the difficulties of communicating instructions in so many languages.

Angel grasped what was required of her quickly. Some of the girls were a little slow to catch on. Possibly it was a language problem, but Jane and Dick had provided several translators. Angel soon concluded that some of the young ladies were just thick. On the other hand, there was a surprising sprinkling of professional girls, training to be lawyers, doctors, architects and so on. Sally and Angel were impressed how stunning many of the contestants were, particularly those entered from South American countries. Angel was particularly taken with Miss Israel, who reminded her of her friend Bibi, with her olive skin. Angel was sorry that Bibi was not with her; lately Bibi had moved in with Gerrie Van der Merwe and had been less available to hang out with her friend.

Once all the girls had arrived in England, Jane and Dick held a grand fundraising dinner at the Grosvenor House Hotel, which housed the largest ballroom in London. The girls were all asked to attend in their evening wear and were spread around the room at 40 tables of potential donors. Jane's charity, "Beauty for Good", had, over the years, raised and distributed millions of pounds to deserving causes around the world.

This was the first chance that Sally or any of the other chaperones and the press had to see all the girls together. When Sally got back to the hotel, she called a bookmaker to see what odds she could get on her daughter to win. She was amazed that the best she could get was four to one, which seemed pretty crazy since there were over 80 contestants. Somebody else, it seemed, agreed with her that Angel had a very good chance of winning.

A few days after the contestants had gathered in London, Jules Donovan arrived from Johannesburg. He too booked a room at the Hilton. Sally was really pleased to see him. She had not acted on her impulse to seduce him back in South Africa, because, since she worked for him and enjoyed the job, she did not want to jeopardise her position. Now that she had left the agency to return to London, she felt no such inhibition. The trouble was that, as chaperone, she was not supposed to leave the floor of the hotel where her brood were lodged, and Jules was certainly forbidden to visit her there. She would just have to wait until after the show. Whatever happened, she and Angel had decided not to return to South Africa. Angel had finished her secretarial course and would look for a job in England. She had also been approached by a modelling agency whose offices were in the Kings Road, not too far from the Hilton. The agency had scheduled a photo shoot. Angel had high hopes that this might lead to some extra work.

The Albert Hall was an impressive venue. Angel had never seen anything like it. There certainly wasn't anything like it in South Africa. The girls rehearsed their moves against a vast backdrop of empty red velvet seats. The sound of their excited voices echoed around the great hall, which had been a venue for many of the world's top entertainers. Angel felt proud to be there. This hall was part of the history of Great Britain; Angel could feel it. The big day finally arrived and the girls and the chaperones climbed onto a trio of buses to take them on the short journey through Hyde Park to the Albert Hall.

Angel had made a point of making sure that Miss Africa South made her way safely onto the bus. Since they had arrived in London, Angel and Sally had taken their black compatriot under their wing.

When the buses arrived at the Albert Hall, their passengers were shocked to see a huge crowd of protesters, whom the police were trying to push back behind metal barriers. The three buses waited. There was too much mayhem going on to let the girls safely off to run for the performers' entrance. As far as Angel and Sally could tell, there were two protests going on. One part of the crowd was screaming "Down with Beauty Pageants!" and the other, "Boycott South Africa; Stop Apartheid". The sheer numbers of protesters had obviously taken the police by surprise. The delay was a serious concern for Jane and Dick. The show they had been rehearsing was going to go out live. They could not afford to start late.

The police showed no signs of being able to quell the crowd. When the protesters saw the three buses full of girls the coaches were suddenly surrounded with an angry mob, banging their fists on the metal panels of the vehicles. Some of the girls were screaming with fear; some were crying, which was ruining their carefully applied make up. Sally and Angel remained calm. Suddenly, Angel rummaged in her little suitcase. Although she had been issued with a Miss South Africa sash for the Miss World pageant, which was now inside the hall with her costume, she had carried, for luck, her original Miss South Africa sash from Bloemfontein. Without consulting her mother or her chaperone, Angel moved to the front of the bus and and pressed the "open door" button, much to the consternation of the driver. As she did so she draped the sash around her neck and across her bosom.

The mob close to the bus was completely taken aback. Here, right in front of them and two steps above, stood a beautiful young lady, her head held high, with the words "South Africa" emblazoned across her chest. She started to speak. Loudly, but not shouting.

"We have heard you," she said. "You have made your point. I will carry your message back to South Africa. There will be change. Now, please let these young ladies through. They are not from South Africa. It is not their fault. Please do the decent thing and stand back."

The crowd by the door, mainly young boys and girls, was amazed at this fearless and beautiful girl defiantly standing two steps up in the open door of the bus. Several of them had been shouting through megaphones. Somebody in the crowd said, "give her the megaphone", and a bright blue metal object was handed through the crowd.

Angel, now feeling that she had their attention, took it and repeated her message, "Please let the girls through. They are not from South Africa. If you want, I will stay behind as your hostage, but please be fair."

Somehow the words got through. The shout went up, "Let the buses through."

The crowd moved back and slowly the three buses edged up to the doors of the hall. By now, police reinforcements had arrived. The crowd was dispersed. The passengers disembarked and the frightened contestants rushed for the stage entrance of the hall.

Several of the rioters had managed to find their way into the hall, having bought tickets or by other means. It was their intention to harass the participants every time Miss South Africa appeared on the stage. In the first round of the events, there was a barrage of boos from a certain section of the crowd, which was met with hissing from the rest of the spectators. But, by the time Angel appeared for the national costume section, word had gone around about her heroic stand in the doorway of the bus. Angel was no longer the villain of the piece; she had earned their grudging admiration; she was also very pretty. The rest of the show went off without a hitch, but when it came to the section where the compere, Bobbie Smart, posed his questions to the contestants, Angel made full use of the platform.

"There are things wrong in my country; there are in all countries. However, I have heard the protests, and, if elected, Miss World, I promise that I shall do all in my power, to work for change in my country. Apartheid must end!"

There was a roar of approval in the famous hall. Sally was now convinced that Angel would now be crowned Miss World. She was definitely one of the prettiest contestants, and had now become the most popular.

When Dick Michaels stood up in his black tuxedo to announce the judges' verdict, there were five girls left in the hunt. As was his custom, Dick, with his slight London East end accent, began by announcing the fifth placed contestant.

"And the fourth runner up is –" Long pause. "Miss Colombia."

Miss Colombia smiled a disappointed smile and took her place on a chalk circle marked five.

"And the third runner up is –" Another long pause. "Miss Thailand."

Miss Thailand burst into tears. Jane handed her a tissue and whispered "Pull yourself together" in her ear.

"And the second runner up is –" An even longer pause. "Miss United Kingdom."

Huge roars of support from the audience. Then there were two young ladies left standing, Miss South Africa and Miss Israel. They just stood there for what seemed an eternity. Dick, shuffled his paperwork, then, finally held up the mike again.

"And the runner up for the Miss World Pageant is…"

This time the silence was broken by a long roll on the drums. Dick raised the mike again. "Miss South Africa!"

Angel smiled a gracious smile of disappointment. There were boos from the audience. Sally didn't know if they were anti-South African boos or boos because those booing thought that Angel should have won. Whatever they were, they were quickly followed by Dick's final announcement.

"And Miss World for 1981 is Miss Israel."

And with that, it was all over. The rest of the girls gathered round to congratulate the Israeli. Sally somehow knew that her daughter had been robbed. There was no way, it seemed, that Jane and Dick would ever have countenanced a South African girl as Miss World. Their life on tour with the beauty queen would be impossible. Sally was disappointed that Jules had not warned her; he must have known.

Later that evening at the wrap party back at the Hilton, everybody let their hair down. This was the first time in two weeks in London that the girls had been allowed alcohol. They were also now finally free from their chaperones and, of course, the chaperones were free from them. The whole evening had been one of high tension for Sally. First, there was the incident in the bus and then the tension of the announcements at the end. Sally was bitterly disappointed that her daughter had not won and she hit the bar with gusto. Jules, being a Miss World licensee from South Africa, was also invited to the party.

Sally had been cross with him for not warning her that the judging was rigged, but one sight of this handsome man, whom she had desired for so long, dissipated any antipathy she had. She could not wait to dance with him and hold him tight. As he held her close, she could feel his enthusiasm. They kissed, and kissed again.

"Let's go upstairs," he whispered.

She nodded in agreement. They did not stop to say good bye or thank their hosts. They could not get into the elevator and into Jules' room fast enough.

Within seconds they had disrobed. All the tensions of the evening's competition drained from them. The wait for each other had been worth it.

When Jules opened the bedroom door the next morning the newspapers had been delivered. Sure enough, all of the front pages showed a picture of the sultry Miss Israel, complete with crown and sash. However, the headline in the *Sun* read "The Angel from the South", with a large picture of Angel, standing in the door of the bus, complete with blue megaphone and, clearly visible, a South African sash. Pages two and three of the *Sun* and the *Daily Mail* were both full of other, earlier, pictures of Angel, taken in South Africa. She was described as the saviour of the event. Both Jane and Dick had joined the act with lengthy interviews in which they praised the bravery and good common sense of Angel. Miss Israel had been absolutely gazumped in terms of press coverage. Sally called a few friends back in Johannesburg. Yes, it was the same thing there. Her daughter, Angel, had gone from Miss South Africa, to the heroine of the nation, despite having publicly denounced her own government's policy.

"This," thought Jules, "should be really good for business."

Sally was so happy that she had finally consummated her longstanding relationship with Jules. She had not been disappointed with what had transpired the night before. It had been a fitting culmination to an exciting week in London. Nevertheless, she was troubled. For some time now Sally had felt nervous about the future of South Africa. She had enjoyed being in London again with her daughter and was hopeful that Angel would now prefer to settle in the UK rather than build a life in the country of her birth. Falling in love with Jules, whose business was in South Africa, could be problematic.

Sally was curious that she, alone, in her circle of friends and acquaintances seemed to fret about the future of South Africa. Surely, she thought, the writing was on the wall, spelling out that things had to change there for the country to survive. It seemed just downright wrong that four and a half million white people could keep over 40 million blacks in continued subjugation. Not only did Sally feel that it was morally wrong to do so, but she also worried about its practicality. Clearly, the rest of the world, was opposed to the regime in South Africa and that had been brought home to her by the protesters at the Albert Hall. The rest of Africa had gone black. Why, in the end, should South Africa be any different? True, this rejection of European colonialism in Africa had not always been a success in economic and social terms, but the alternative of continued white domination was clearly not right in Sally's mind. She did not know what the answer was, but she feared that it would involve violence, and she did not want herself or her beautiful daughter to be caught up in it.

Recently, the neighbouring country of Mozambique had fallen into the hands of a black terrorist movement that had swept out the Portuguese rulers. This momentous event had received little attention in the South African press and, to Sally's amazement, had caused little concern within her circle of friends nor, it would appear, to the ruling National party. Surely, thought Sally, the anti-colonialist movement that had swept through Africa would not stop at the borders of South Africa.

Sally was not a political creature, but the obvious tide of black control troubled her. She could only see severe difficulties ahead, and would rather that she and her daughter were not caught up in the mayhem that could ensue. Only last year there had been riots in the black townships surrounding Johannesburg. The trigger, apparently, had been a revolt in the schools about the continued insistence by the government that Afrikaans should be the "go to" language in the schools and that all study books should be written in that language. First, the students had marched in protest, soon to be joined by black workers in support. A lighted match had been thrown into the tinder box. Although the ensuing riots and violent put down from the police and army, which resulted in numerous fatalities, were not widely reported in the South African press, they were extensively covered by international journalists and news of the event slowly seeped into South Africa. Even then, almost all of Sally's friends could not accept that their privileged way of life was under threat.

Sally had frequently discussed the situation with her trusty maid, Supreme, who reluctantly related some of the bad news from the township. Supreme, like many domestic workers, was clearly nervous to discuss these matters with her employer for fear of creating conflict which might end her much needed employment. But she had said enough to have made Sally deeply aware, and ashamed, of what was actually going on.

The whites in South Africa, although, in the main, hard workers and loyal family-oriented citizens, were living a privileged existence as compared to the rest of the world and certainly as compared to their fellow black citizens. There were really no opportunities for poor blacks to lift themselves out of poverty. What South Africa needed, in Sally's view, was the creation of a black middle class, that could boost the economy and give poor blacks a target to aim for. Some of Sally's friends agreed with her, but most just believed that blacks were incapable of any work, other than menial.

By far the majority of white South Africans had never been into a black township. Since all cities and towns in the land prohibited blacks from living in designated white districts, they were forced to live in informal townships that were just "over the hill" and out of sight from the white areas. Out of sight is out of mind, so, although whites would drive past these informal settlements on their way into or out of town, they would never dream of actually entering them. Had they done so, they would have seen how horrendous the living conditions were. There were no tarred roads or paved sidewalks, no proper drainage or sewage systems, often no electricity. Row upon row of little tin roofed houses normally stretched as far as the eye could see. There were no back gardens, nor driveways, nor fences between the homes, which normally consisted of one communal room for cooking, living and eating, and one bedroom, no matter how many children there were in the household. Often the most productive thing for unemployed men to do was to ensure that the children kept coming.

In the summer, the tin roofs acted like heat conductors and, in the winter, the reverse. When it rained, water gushed down the muddy unpaved streets and often into the little houses. In the hot dry season, the dust from the same roads almost choked the inhabitants. Such awful living conditions were so much in contrast to the average white homesteads, that the colossal difference must have been an ongoing slap in the face to the army of black domestic workers in white homes. Furthermore, even the poorest white families seemed to have domestic help in the form of maids or nannies, so the contrast from home to workplace for these workers was strikingly evident on a daily basis. It was unheard of for a black family to have any domestic help. White mothers, when asked by their children why their pet dogs always barked at black passers-by, opined that blacks had a different smell to whites. The mothers did not explain that there were no hot showers in the black townships. Indeed, there was mostly no plumbing of any sort in the little tin houses. Water had to be gathered from a communal pump, which could be located hundreds of yards away from ones home.

Despite this, there was often a buoyant community spirit in the townships which kept the spirits of the downtrodden inhabitants up. The older residents seemed to be more accepting of the abysmal conditions but more and more youngsters were joining the AFA, in the hope that they could change their lives for the better.

Through the Miss World pageant, Sally had been able to reconnect to her own homeland, England, just at a time when things were going well for her native land. Once removed from the constant tension of South Africa, much as she loved the place, it was as if a heavy weight had been lifted from her shoulders. She hoped that Angel would feel the same. Now, this new emotional entanglement with Jules had been sent to test her. Did she love Jules, or was she just sexually attracted to him? Would a relationship with Jules be more important to her than her concerns about the future of herself and particularly her daughter about the fate of Jules' homeland? These were questions that would need to be answered.

Chapter Eight

Back in South Africa the plight of the black community was the last thing on Gerrie Van De Merwe's mind. His thoughts were all about maximising his current good fortune. Gerrie's rise to riches had coincided nicely with the overall rise in riches of the average white South African. Gerrie now knew that, as the South African heavyweight champion, to a large degree, he could call the shots regarding the future shape of the pot. He would still need his faithful mentor and coach, Sean Brennan, and, until he had his foot more firmly on the international rankings, he would still need Shultz and Rosenburg. He knew that they had the contacts overseas. He did not, however, really need his dad anymore and Bibi was the first to remind him – constantly. Bibi had moved in with Gerrie, who had acquired a large house, surrounded by a high wall, in Atholl, a suburb next to the emerging sector of Sandton City. The house had four bedrooms, spacious entertaining quarters and a sparkling pool. A row of cypress trees on either side of the back yard protected Gerrie and Bibi from snoopers, which was especially useful since Bibi was in the habit of sunbathing topless by the pool.

Although Gerrie now realised that his dad was out of his depth in the international business of sports promotion, he had much respect for his common sense. He also knew that his dad loved him and was proud of him. As a result, he did not want to cut him out of his share of the spoils, even though he knew that Bibi disagreed with him. There was something else where they did not see eye to eye. Gerrie was determined to visit his old adversary/ friend in prison. Bibi had been ashamed of her brother for shooting a man in the back. She didn't care whether the victim was black, white or brown. She just thought that it was a callous thing to do and that her brother deserved to be taught a lesson by cooling off in jail for a year. By association, she thought, Lance's actions had tarnished the reputation of her family and herself.

Gerrie disagreed. "These things happen in the heat of battle," he reasoned. "It's difficult being a cop."

Although Bibi called most of the shots in their partnership, she also knew when to give in if something was really bothering her lover, so, finally she agreed that they would pay Lance a visit.

It was a big deal at the Kyalami jail near Pretoria. Almost all of the staff at the prison were white Afrikaners, Gerrie's breed; so, they were excited that their heavyweight champion was paying them a visit. They had not expected the bonus of his attractive partner. Their captive, Lance, was being well treated. Apartheid was at work in the prison. The black inmates were cooped up together in cells with two bunks and four occupants. The white prisoners were in larger cells with one set of bunks, a desk, closet and little dining/work table.

To many of the wardens, Lance was not a criminal, he was a hero. He had shot a kaffir who was trying to evade custody. What was wrong with that? He shouldn't even be in jail; he should be given a medal. Such was the depth of opinion amongst the warders that Lance had initially been allocated single occupancy of a double cell.

However, after a week of effective solitary confinement, he had asked to be put into a double cell and had found himself locked up with a white lawyer, Bruce Heidelburg.

Bibi and Gerrie were allowed to meet Lance in the prison library, which had been temporarily closed off to other prisoners.

"Not a bad place you've got here," quipped Gerrie as the two men gave each other a hug.

"You wait till you've seen my bedroom!" Lance quipped back. Lance sensed that his sister was a little cool. "What's up, Sis?" he started. "Can't he get it up, or something?"

"You always were a cynical bastard," she replied, but, nevertheless, moved forward and gave her little brother a long and affectionate hug.

"The boredom here is what kills you," Lance told them, "that, and the food."

The three of them continued to have a good natter. Lance wanted to know about the fight with Tiny. Gerrie and Bibi wanted to know what plans Lance had when the time came for him to leave jail. Obviously, he would not be allowed back in the police force.

"Why don't you box again?" asked Gerrie, out of the blue. "You could use this lockup year to train and get fit. I am sure that there are a few big black blokes in here who would like to knock your head off. You could run boxing lessons for the inmates. Maybe, as champ, I could pull some strings, get the equipment, that sort of thing. Then, when you come out, I could get my guys to get you some pro fights. What do you think, mate?"

"I'm not so sure I'm up to it," replied Lance, completely out of character.

"Of course, you are, bokkie; you were always better than me. Just had too many girls and parties. That won't

93

happen to you in here. It's the perfect place to train. And think what a story it would make; you could earn some big money."

By the time Lance was escorted back to his cell the idea of starting training again seemed to motivate him. Before reaching the cellblock, he had asked his guard if he could possibly set up a meeting for him with the Chief Warder as soon as possible. He explained that his visitor, the SA champ, would like to donate some equipment to the jail. The guard agreed, and, two days later, Lance found himself, unhandcuffed, in the relative luxury of Superintendent Geldenhy's office, sitting in the most comfortable chair he had seen in over a month. He explained his plan. To set up a boxing club, for inmates, at which he would be the trainer. He explained that he had been a successful amateur and that his best mate was the SA champion, who happened to live with his sister. "Gerrie Van de Merwe will supply the ring, the gloves and all the other equipment needed, if you can find us a suitable training room. I will give the lessons and, hopefully, from time to time the champ will come here to train or to coach. The boxing club will be open to all, black and white."

Geldenhys listened with interest. This seemed to him to be an uncommonly good idea. Maybe, even some of his guards could benefit from some gym time. What he was not keen on were the implied multi-racial aspects of the proposal. Somehow he would have to find a way to organise the training in compliance with the prevailing rules.

"Well, Prisoner Hermanus, this seems like a good idea. I will give some thought as to where we might locate your gym. I will need to meet your sister's boyfriend, the champ, to verify all of this, and I will need to get authority from my boss, the Minister for Prisons. But, overall, I do think your scheme may have some merit. Do I have your permission to contact Mr. Van der Merwe?"

"Of course," said Lance, "this is where you will find him." He reached out and wrote done Gerrie's phone number on the pad on Geldenhys' desk.

"That will be all," barked the Super, his voice returning to that of an officer of the law. "Guard, you may escort prisoner Hermanus back to his cell."

A month later the Kyalami Prison sparring gym was up and running. Gerrie had responded immediately to the request for equipment, all of which was donated by the suppliers, the Minister for Prisons had been delighted to get, at last, some good news out of a prison, and Geldenhys had converted an old storeroom into a gym. The word had gone out to both black and white prisoners that boxing lessons would be available and at least a third of the population put their names on the list, if, for no other reason, than to get out of their cells for a while. It looked as if Lance's new cell would be the gym. First, though, Lance had to get fit himself. Then he had to remember all of the things that Sean Brennan had taught him. Maybe, if he could reach out to Sean, he would make himself available to help out at the gym from time to time. He would ask Gerrie on his next visit.

Gerrie was really pleased with Lance's positive reaction to his suggestion and he made up his mind that he would do anything he could to help. Bibi too seemed pleased; after all, Lance was her brother. However, where Bibi had changed her position re: Lance, she had not changed her mind about the involvement of Gerrie's dad in his future, or to be more precise, his specific involvement in the negotiations for Gerrie's future fights, nor in the lucrative sponsorship deals that were beginning to emerge.

"You can give your dad all your purse, for all I care," pouted Bibi, as she addressed Gerrie, "but don't let him negotiate deals for you. It's not his bag." Gerrie knew that his lover was right. Negotiating with big numbers was not Strom's strength. He was too much in awe of the other side and Gerrie knew it.

Gerrie went to see Strom. He wanted to see him alone, but Edna was so happy to see her son that she did not read the signals. She was pleased that he was visiting them without Bibi in tow.

"Dad," started Gerrie eventually, "I need to talk to you about the future. Now is the time we can all make some money, and, if we play it right, some really big money. We also need to reboot our agreement with Shultz and Rosenburg. We still need them, because of their contacts in America, but not on the same basis as before. Also, I'm getting approached by all sorts of companies, offering me money to endorse their stuff. So, I've decided to appoint a business manager. I'm not going to take away your 15% of the purse going forward in recognition of all you've done for me, but I won't need you to be involved in the negotiations any more. I will come to you for strategic advice because you're a wily old fox, but I won't be needing you for the day to day business decisions. Do you understand what I'm saying?"

"Of course, I do, my boy. You want me out. I've got the picture." Edna grimaced. This wasn't like her boy.

"No, Dad, I'll never want you out. You're my Dad, and I love you. It's just that I want to appoint a professional."

"And who might that be? Who is this professional?" said Rudy.

"Well, I think it should be Bibi."

"Aha," Rudy exclaimed, as if he now understood everything, "that girl's got you by the balls, my son. You'll live to regret it. And, while you're at it, you can keep my 15%."

With that, he stomped off, out of the room and busied himself cleaning the pool.

"Now you've upset your dad," said Edna, unhelpfully. "You must go and apologise."

"No, Mother," said Gerrie. "It is what it is. He will have to get over it."

Gerrie let himself out of the house. He was sorry that he had upset his dad, but he did feel that his father was reacting rather emotionally. "Hopefully," he mused, "he will get over it, especially when he gets the 15%. It will be more than he has ever earned in a year."

Gerrie was now ready to return to work. Bibi phoned Steven at S and R to ask for a meeting with herself and Gerrie.

"What about Strom?" enquired Steven, "is he out of the picture now?"

"Not entirely," said Bibi, "but Gerrie wants to make his own decisions."

When Steven told his partner Trevor about the call, they both agreed it was a pity, since they knew how to run rings around Strom, or, at least, Trevor could.

"Gerrie's making his own decisions now," said Steven, mimicking Bibi's Afrikaans accent. "Like fuck he is," he continued. "It looks like Bibi's in charge now. Watch out!"

The meeting took place a few days later in the S and R offices in downtown Johannesburg. Steven announced that the latest WBA and WBC world rankings had just been issued. Gerrie had gone straight into the top ten at number six, replacing Tiny Robertson who had now fallen to ninth. Steven also announced that, should Gerrie appoint S and R, he would go immediately to the USA for exploratory meetings with both Bob Levin and Louis Brown, to ascertain where Gerrie might fit into their plans. Before that, however, the two promoters needed to have an exclusive agreement to represent Gerrie.

"What we propose, is that, as your representative and promoter, we take 40% of all proceeds accruing to our side. That is to say, 40% of your purse and 40% of any other revenue, including gate, television and film rights, and proceeds from promotional material. Such an agreement will last for your next five fights. And naturally, the basis of the 40% is after all expenses, yours and ours, have been deducted."

Bibi and Gerrie sat and listened. When Steven had finished, Bibi got up out of her chair. "Come on, Gerrie, there is no point in carrying on with this meeting. These guys are out of their minds." Gerrie stood up too.

"Now wait a minute, you two," interjected Trevor. "Can't we discuss this for a moment? Which part of the proposal don't you like?"

"Fucking all of it," yelled Bibi. "Do you think we're mad?"

"Well, if you sit down for a minute, maybe we can fine tune the thing a bit," said Trevor. "After all, we all have a long history together. Why don't you tell us where you're coming from?"

Gerrie made a move back towards his chair. Bibi did not look happy, but, after a moment, she too moved back to the table and sat down.

After an hour of haggling the four finally worked out a deal. Since the potential earnings from now on were going to be in dollars, they decided to set their agreement in that currency. S and R would get 25% of all revenues, less relevant expenses, from the next five bouts involving Gerrie, up to a maximum of $125,000 per bout. The revenue would include Gerrie's purse, and any cut from the profits of all ancillary income, less all expenses involved, including travel, training camps, transport costs, payroll costs and so on. All costs incurred by each party, prior to any revenues being available from an event would need to be funded by each party and reimbursed later. So, for example, Steven's proposed trip to the USA would be for his cost until it could be reimbursed out to the takings. In other words, if he failed to nail a fight, then he would not get recompensed for trying.

Bibi did almost all of the talking for Gerrie and she was good at it. Gerrie, however, had one important thing to say; "I shall have a veto as to who I fight. Unless I approve of the opponent, no matter how rich the deal is, there will be no fight. Do you all understand? You'd better write that into the deal."

When Bibi and Gerrie finally left the S and R offices some three hours after they had entered, they both had a smile on their faces. The deal was far better than they had set out for, especially the cap on S and R earnings. Gerrie was very proud of his new "manager". In one way, though, she had really stabbed herself in the back. Now, Gerrie would never marry her, because, if he did, she would potentially be getting 50% of everything that he earned. Gerrie may have kept quiet in the meeting, but his head had been screwed right on; he knew exactly where he was coming from. Now, he had everything he wanted, at least for the moment; he was champion of South Africa and was living with one of the most glamourous women in the land. No matter if she thought she was in control; that, he didn't mind, as long as it was only in the bedroom.

Chapter Nine

With the contract signed, Steven Shultz set off for the States. He had agreed that it would be best for Trevor to stay behind to babysit their protégé, who had started light training in order to keep in shape. Often, Trevor, no mean athlete himself, would jog with Gerrie; he thought it was a useful way to bond.

At the time, due to boycotts, there were no American carriers flying into or from Johannesburg, so Steven had to fly on South African Airways which only routed to Atlanta. From there, he thought it was sensible to fly directly on to Vegas, where he could meet with his old friend, Bob Levin. Bob, over the years, had supplied S and R with quite a few lower-ranked fighters to feature on their regular shows in South Africa, so the two had a long history of doing deals, albeit small ones. This time Steven had a larger fish to fry and someone he knew would be of interest to Bob. Steven was well aware that it had been a long time since Bob had been able to participate in the heavyweight division, since six of the top ten ranked fighters were signed to Louis Brown and two of the remainder were being managed by Louis' son, Buddy. Steven knew that Bob would give his right arm to promote a heavyweight and maybe both arms for a white one.

Bob's office was one block removed from the famous Las Vegas Strip. Square Ring Promotions occupied a small suite in an unpretentious mid-rise building. The décor was far from plush. Clearly Bob was not a big spender, no matter how many millions he had in the bank. The walls, however, were plastered with posters of famous encounters in the ring. All the big names in the sport were there, and all of the big venues. For Steven, a lifelong student of the sport, a visit to Bob's place brought the history to life.

Bob greeted his visitor with genuine warmth. Bob's business with Steven, although never huge, had been a welcome trickle of revenue for Square Ring over many years. Steven's promotions in South Africa had also been a useful training ground for some of Bob's stable.

"Now, here's the thing," drawled Bob, after their preliminary greetings were over, "your man Gerrie might be a good boxer, but nobody's ever heard of him in America, so we won't get big money. His exposure on the television has been zero. We've got to get him on the box here. On the other hand, he is famous in Africa, so it's there we can make good money at the venue."

Steven waited for Bob to continue, but Bob sat in his chair and said nothing. He was thinking. Through the window behind him, Steven could see the flashing neon signs of Las Vegas even though it was broad daylight. This was a magic city like none other, a perpetual adult fairground.

"What a strange place to live," thought Steven through the room full of silence.

Finally, Bob seemed to awake from his slumber. "This is the plan," he suddenly announced, his voice now spirited with enthusiasm. "We put on three fights; the first two, you will promote in Johannesburg; the third one, maybe in the USA, maybe not. We need to get Gerrie up the rankings to number two; that way Louis Brown's champ will not be able to ignore him; the money will be too big."

Bob was now in full flow. Steven just sat and listened.

"Gerrie is now ranked number six. I've one fighter in the top ten, who's at number eight. I could sacrifice him. You put on the fight down there; I'll make sure it gets prime time viewing here on the undercard for my world middleweight card coming up in two months. That won't move him up the ladder but it will get TV exposure. My man is black. Your man will knock him out. Then, we should put him in the ring again with Tiny Robertson. We'll say that the winner will get a crack at the world title. This will draw a big crowd for you but will be great for our TV because it will be a repeat David and Goliath. The public here love that."

At this point, Steven interrupted the flow. "Don't you think that's an unnecessary risk? Tiny is a big powerful bloke."

"Nah," said Bob. "The public will love it. Just make sure the payday is enough for Tiny to retire. Now," he just carried on, "there is a fighter in the UK who's the only one in the top six not controlled by Louis. He's managed by my British associate, Mickey Luff. His fighter's a black English lad. Louis and Mickey don't speak to each other. I'm sure your man will have the beatings of Jim London, that's his name; this is one I can't completely control, but your man is the better boxer. When Gerrie's won all of those fights, he'll be big news here and a fight against whoever is top at the time will be a promoter's dream in Vegas. I know I could get that financed. A white South African against a black American; that's a promoter's dream."

Finally, Bob stopped talking. For a minute the room was filled with silence, only punctuated by the whine of police vehicles in the street outside. Suddenly Bob seemed to awaken once more. "This is the deal," he announced, "First two fights, you keep the gate, I keep the TV money.

You can pay Gerrie whatever you want. Second fight, against Tiny: same thing. You keep all the local revenue, but you pay the retirement gift to Tiny, and I'll keep the US TV money; you can have the pittance from SATV, but you've got to provide me with the feed and the fight must be in your evening, so that I can get it in the afternoon for my show. The fight against the black Brit; we'll have to work this one out later because there is the British promoter to cut in. When we get to the Championship of the World, we split whatever we get, but, one way or another, we will guarantee Gerrie a minimum of 2 million dollars." Finally, he stopped. Again, there was a long silence. Steven wondered if Bob was going to say more, but he didn't. He just sat there, rocking in his chair, and peering, it would seem, at nothing out of the window. Finally, he swivelled, looked straight at Steven and actually smiled, with a slight upward turn of the lips in one corner of his mouth. "Let's go and have lunch."

As they walked across the road to a diner, Steven took stock of what he had heard. Bob wanted to be part of team Van de Merwe, but he wanted a big part. Four fights from now, Gerrie could be World heavyweight champion. His next fight he would win, because Bob would ensure the opponent would lose. The second fight Gerrie would win because Steven would be required to make sure that Tiny would not put up much of a fight, the third fight was less certain, but Bob's friend in London would be on our side, and the championship fight would happen because Bob knew how to manipulate the rankings committee in Mexico. That was the long and the short of it. Steven would now have to put pencil to paper to work out what that would all mean.

Meanwhile, he would enjoy a hot pastrami sandwich and a Coors. Oh to be in America! But Steven was now tired. He had been on an uncomfortable plane for 17 hours to Atlanta and then another few to Vegas. He decided to take a nap before agreeing to anything. He thanked Bob for the lunch, announced his plan to sleep and agreed to meet Bob again at ten the next morning. Bob offered to draw up some form of draft agreement for them to look at the next day and they parted. En route to his bedroom in the hotel, Steven dropped some loose coins into a few machines as he went past. To his amazement, one of them came to life like a fire station. He had won $10,000.

Steven woke at 4am the next morning. He really was doing a bad job at jet lag management. However, he was now wide awake. He chuckled to himself as he suddenly remembered the ten grand. His bedroom was large, but it was ghastly. He must have been really tired the evening before because he had not really focused on his surroundings, although he had needed to look for a safe to hide his 10,000. Now he noticed that one wall of the room was covered with shiny silver palm tree wallpaper. The ceiling was typical American plaster board panels but the area above the bed was mirrored, with a fancy frame of plastic fruit and cherubs. The carpet was grey shag. There was a red velvet couch and a shaggy pouf. Steven's taste was minimalist. Nothing in the room appealed to him. Nevertheless, it was too early to go anywhere, so he ordered some breakfast on room service and picked up the little pencil and pad beside the phone.

His assumption was that all three proposed fights would take place within a year. Since the first two fights were entirely within his control, predicting the numbers would be easy. He estimated that fight one, against Bob's supplied American, could draw a crowd of at least 20,000 people in South Africa, plus prime time television coverage. He predicted that this fight, after expenses, could net around $400,000 of which $100,000 would be due to S and R and the balance of $300,000 to Gerrie to share with his coach and dad. Fight number two, also under his control, would be much bigger, since it could be marketed as a revenge fight for Tiny. Steven thought that the live fight could attract at least 40,000 fans and the SATV take would be large, even though there would only be South Africans fighting. For this fight, after expenses, he reckoned that there could be a profit of over one million dollars. S and R would get their agreed max of $125,000, leaving Gerrie with well over $800,000. Obviously, S and R would have to cough up around $50,000 as a retirement present for Tiny, but he figured they would more than make that up with some well placed bets on the outcome of the fight, since they already knew it.

Fight number three would be more difficult to forecast, since there would be a third party involved: Bob Levin's British promoter and his fighter. Because of the risks involved here, and all of the unknowns, Steven was nervous that Gerrie would not agree to this without some guarantees, and he would be right. He therefore decided that some sort of minimum purse should be negotiated in this regard, before he signed the contract. Steven would suggest a modest minimum of $500,000. When all was said and done, should things work out as planned, in three fights leading up to a world title crack, Gerrie would be able to bank well over one and a half million dollars and he and Trevor would net close to $300,000, without counting anything they could make on sure fire bets.

"Well worth the trip," thought Steven as he munched on his cold leathery toast and wondered why they never have any marmalade in American hotels.

When Steven reached Bob's office, Bob was ready and waiting. He had prepared an agreement which covered as many of the points they had discussed that could be incorporated into a document. Bob agreed to enter a minimum payment to Gerrie for fight number three, but pared it down to $350,000 from the half a million suggested. "After all," he observed, "he's not the champion yet. That's when he can command the big bucks." It took an hour or so for the document to be tidied up and made ready to sign. Bob allowed Steven the use of an office where he pondered his next move. There was little point, it seemed, of going to New York to see Louis Brown. On the other hand, since he was in the country, a courtesy visit might be sensible. He would not, of course, let Bob know.

When Steven arrived in New York, he headed straight for the Plaza on Central Park South. Steven loved this old hotel. It stood on the premier site in Manhattan: probably the most expensive piece of real estate in the world. The rooms overlooking the park were obviously the highest in price, but Steven was happy with his Fifth Avenue view. From his window he could see the comings and goings of the clientele as they climbed out of their yellow cabs, Cadillacs or Rolls Royces. The Garden Court at the Plaza was definitely the place to be seen, and to see.

He called Louis Brown's office to let him know that he was in town. A few minutes later the phone rang and the huge voice of Brown bellowed down the phone. "Hey, Bro, no one done told me you were in town. How long you here for? How's it going down there in Apartheid land? Do you want me to send you some nigger fighters? They won't get arrested, will they?"

Big guffaws followed at his own joke.

"I'm just here for two days, Louis. Just some legal business for a client in SA. If you've got time for a drink, that would be nice. You know I represent Gerrie Van de Merwe now. Maybe we can arrange something one day.?"

"Yeah, Bro. That would be great. How about the bar at your hotel? Say, 6pm, okay?"

Steven got to the bar earlier than 6pm. He sought out a corner table and ordered a beer. He happily watched the suited clientele, probably from the offices on Madison, a couple of blocks away. "Why are all Americans so loud?" he asked himself.

At 6.30 there was a kerfuffle at the door. Quite a lot of loud talk and laughter. Louis Brown had arrived. As he was escorted to Steven's corner table, heads in the bar turned. You couldn't miss Brown: a huge black man, with a large head and even larger smile, showing perfect gleaming teeth. His greying hair pointed upwards like a brush defying gravity. Steven stood to greet him. He felt like a midget. Louis squeezed his big frame into the chair and ordered a Jim Beam.

"I suppose you'd like to arrange a fight for your Gerrie boy," he launched straight in. "I saw the tape of him fight Tiny. He's impressive. But, the trouble is, that nobody here knows who the fuck he is. See if you can get him to fight Tiny again. This time I'll get it on the TV here and we can start to build up his name. I reckon that he needs another four or five fights before he can really be a challenger. You should bring him to America to train. It would be easier that way."

Would you be able to promote these fights, Louis?" asked the South African.

"Well, of course I could," said the big man. "If you hadn't already gone and done a deal with Uncle Bob."

Steven had to fight hard to stop his jaw dropping. How the fuck did Brown know about the deal with Levin? The ink was barely dry on the paper.

"I see you're a bit surprised, my friend. You should know that nothing happens in boxing, without Big Louis knowing about it. Now, I doubt whether your Gerrie will like the deal you've done and I'm sure he ain't signed it yet, so if you get to change your mind, come back to me. Four fights for $50,000 a pop within the next year and then a title crack for minimum £1 million. If he wins, which he won't, I get the rights for the return or first two defences. You'd better talk to your man. I gotta go." With that, the Jim Beam was tossed back and Louis was gone.

Steven was stunned. How did Brown know what had transpired in Bob's office the day before? Should he question Levin about it? Had Brown spoken directly to Gerrie? Too many unknowns. Getting out of the deal with Bob would now be tricky and certainly subject to a legal dispute. Going over to Brown did not look too profitable. Better get on a plane and let the dust settle a bit. There was a flight to South Africa, leaving Atlanta at midnight. Steven would just have time to make the connection. On the plane, he found himself sitting next to the Chairman of South African Airways, Piet Homer. They got talking about their impressions of America. "The trouble with America," said Piet, "is that it is 80% full of white kaffirs!" Steven nodded in agreement.

Chapter Ten

After a night of passion in Jules' room at the Hilton, Jules and Sally checked out. Jules had a tiny flat in Onslow Court, Chelsea, which he had owned as a London bolthole for many years. It had been useful for his business, since he often had to book acts in London and Europe for shows in Africa. Over the years it had served as a love nest for many a one night stand. Jules was now hoping that Sally would not turn out to be at the end of a long list; she had been in his employment for a couple of years before opting to live in London. He had longed to make love to her but, whilst she was an employee, had resisted for fear of spoiling a good thing. She too, had resisted, for much the same reason. But now, things were different. In one night at the Hilton the power of their combined withholding had burst asunder. Both now wondered why they had waited so long.

Next morning Sally called Angel, who had also had a good time partying with the other contestants, and was still with her roommate in her hotel room, nursing a throbbing head. She gave Angel the address of Jules' flat but they agreed to meet back at the Hilton coffee shop for lunch and to make plans.

Under Angel's contract with the Miss World Organisation, as the official runner up, she was obliged to be on hand for Miss World appearances, should some mishap occur to Miss Israel. This didn't seem likely and it didn't mean that Angel could not go home to South Africa. Angel, however, had other ideas. She was due, the following day, to keep her appointment for the photo shoot at the studio in the Kings Road; there was no way that she was going to miss that. Sally and Angel met for lunch. A lot of heads in the coffee shop turned to see two radiant women, looking so alike and lovely. Angel announced to her mother that she had no plans to return to South Africa; London seemed so much more vibrant. Sally agreed. She knew that Jules would want her to go back with him, but Jules apart, she too would rather have stayed. They agreed to look for an apartment for Angel to rent, since there was not room for a third person at Jules' place. Mother and daughter has been renting rooms in the rather seedy district of Balham. Now, as the trajectory of their lives seemed upward, they had decided, even before the pageant, to find more permanent quarters. Sally would set this in motion after lunch and agreed to collect Angel from her photo shoot the next day to look at what was available. Sally went back to Onslow Court, via an estate agent on the corner of Kings Road and Beaufort Street, to initiate the flat hunt for her daughter. Then, on to her own love nest round the corner. Jules had been to get supplies; there was no need for the two of them to leave for the rest of the day.

The guys at the Mood Agency in Chelsea were all over Angel, when she arrived for the shoot; they just knew that she was such a "find". They had watched the Miss World pageant on television. They were shocked that Angel had not won, but they were also happy. If she had, there would be no way they would have been able to prise her away from Jane Michaels. They had asked Angel to bring the swimsuit she had worn in the pageant, as well as her ball gown.

The photographer was a handsome young man, Tony, who looked permanently windswept. Surprisingly, Angel thought, he was not gay, far from it. In fact, Angel thought he was rather sexy. He asked her to change into the swimsuit, which she did in a little canvas cubicle. He then dabbled around a little with her make up. She felt his strong body almost touching hers. He then asked her to pose, using a few props that he had on hand, but he was clearly not happy.

"You look too much like a beauty queen in that swimsuit," he proclaimed. "I want you to look wilder."

There was a pause as he thought. Then, "Come with me," he said, grabbing her by the hand. "Let's go next door and buy some clothes."

With that he tossed her his raincoat. "Here, wrap this around yourself. We are only going next door."

He grabbed her hand and she tottered after him in her high heels, swimsuit, and oversized Burberry mac, down the stairs, out of the front door, five yards along the busy pavement, and into the lingerie shop. Here, Angel was in heaven. She took her time, caressing the beautiful materials, and then proceeded to the changing booth with her selection. Meanwhile, Tony made his own selection; that is to say, his selection for her. As he thrust it through the opening of the cubicle instructing her to "try these", he caught a glimpse of her uncovered breasts.

"Spectacular," he thought, "I must get them on camera."

By the time Sally arrived, Tony had plenty of pictures in the can. Many of them were pure fashion plate stuff: Angel in the gown, Angel in the one-piece swimsuit, close ups of Angel's pouting face, close ups of Angel's happy smiling face, shots from the front, shots from the back, and shots from the side. But, also in his portfolio was a series of stunning shots of Angel in lingerie, and, after a little, but not much, cajoling, Angel spilling out of it too. Tony was deliriously happy with his work, which he had shown to his model. Angel, too, was pleased. However, when Sally arrived to collect her daughter, Tony's delirium went to new heights.

"Jesus, Ange," he exclaimed, "is this your mother? Jesus Christ, she could be your sister! I have to get pictures of the two of you together. They will be sensational. Come next door, Mother. We must find something for you to wear!"

Magazine covers are planned several months in advance, so it would be some time before the pictures Tony took of mother and daughter would appear. In the meantime, the Mood Agency had acted quickly, signing both Angel and her mum for lucrative modelling contracts. The little flat that Sally was planning to show Angel after that first photo shoot was no longer necessary. Angel would be able to afford something much more glamourous, so the realtor was called and re-instructed. Within a week, Angel had signed a lease on a beautiful apartment on Cadogan Square, a stone's throw from Sloane Square in one direction and Harvey Nicks in the other. Angel was ready for the next heady phase of her life.

Three weeks after the pageant, Angel got a call from Jane at Miss World.

"I've got some good news for you, my dear," started Jane. "We have had to ask Miss World to resign, so, as runner up, you will now be crowned Miss World and will take over her duties. You will, of course, also take over her salary for the year. Could you please come to our offices to sort this out?"

Angel was flabbergasted. "Why has she had to resign?" she blurted out, "What on earth has she done?"

"Well, my dear, it's a long story, but, in a nutshell, we have found out that she is married and has a baby daughter. As you know that is against our rules. A newspaper in Israel is about to break the story."

"Can't you bend the rules; you make them?" asked Angel.

"Fraid not," said Jane. "But you will make a fine replacement."

Angel, now with a lucrative modelling contract in her pocket, was not so sure that this was good news, but agreed to make her way to Golden Square in Soho, to meet up with the redoubtable matriarch of the Miss World organisation. On her way there she thought about it. To perform her duties as Miss World, Jane would probably expect her to travel all over the globe, promoting their competition and anything else that they had signed for Miss World to endorse. This could well be a complication in regard to the modelling that she aspired to. On the other hand, it might make her even more in demand. She decided to tread carefully. Also, she worried that the contract she had signed with Mood might contravene something she had earlier signed with Miss World. Hopefully, this could all be worked out.

"But," she thought, as the taxi inched its way towards the West End, "these are high grade problems for a young girl who has just finished secretarial school in South Africa."

Angel had been right to worry. It transpired that, in signing up to Miss World, she had agreed, if she won, to fulfil a huge number of engagements in at least 25 different countries over the year of her "reign". The fact that she had not actually won didn't seem to matter, because, deep in the small print, she had agreed to all of this, should she be lucky enough to be "runner up" or second "runner up". The Michaels had been here before. They had covered all eventualities. All, it would seem, except the one that was Angel De Kock. Angel took great heart from something she had heard Gerrie Van der Merwe say one day, when presented with agreements that he had signed but no longer liked – "contracts don't fight." Well, the contract she had with Miss World did not require her to exactly fight, but it did require her to do all sorts of things that she no longer wanted to.

It soon became clear to Jane and Dick Michaels that what Angel had said she would do on a piece of paper, and what she was prepared to do, were two separate matters; they couldn't make the paper do it for her. No, they would just have to negotiate with her to come to a reasonable compromise. In her words, "They could have half of her, or none of her."

They settled for half; she settled for half pay. That seemed fair. The Miss World publicity machine went into action. Before the Israeli papers could run their expose of Miss Israel, Miss World Inc. had dethroned her and installed Angel. The front pages of the British dailies, the next day, all featured a beautiful picture of Angel, supplied by Mood. Inside one of them, the *Daily Star*, was a magnificent spread of Angel in her lingerie, pictures for which Tony and the agency had been paid a princely sum. Jane and Dick wondered how their new Miss World's reign would work.

Meanwhile, Sally was very torn. One part of her wanted to return to South Africa with Jules. The other wanted to stay close to her daughter, who was becoming a household name in the UK. Lots of offers were coming Angel's way. Sally was nervous about Angel's ability to handle them all. On top of this, Angel had discovered the night life of London. She particularly liked Tramp, London's most exclusive disco/night club, where most evenings and early mornings were spent. Sally knew that Angel would need to be careful. Yes, she should have her fun, but not so much that it damaged her potential. Sally decided that she was needed in London. Tony, the photographer, thought so too. He had seen too many of his top models ruin their looks, and thus, careers, with too much partying. He knew that Angel was his ticket to riches, and, the fact that her photogenic mother was also in tow, might be pretty useful.

Angel trusted Tony. She also really liked him. He had not come on to her, although, she would not have said no. Instead, he somehow seemed to take care of her. He had plenty of experience, and, as co-owner of Mood, understood the fickle scene of London's fashion business. The contract she had signed with Mood was for them to act as her agent. Now, with all of the offers pouring in, she wanted more than that; she needed them to act as her Manager, as well. Tony was only too happy to agree.

"I will be your agent, your manager, and your friend," he told her. Secretly he, one day, hoped to also be her lover – but that should not now get in the way of business. Sally also trusted Tony. The pictures he had taken of them as mother and daughter on the first day she had met him soon graced the cover of *Tatler*, the London fashion magazine, two months after they had been taken. Since, by then, Angel was also Miss World, the fabulous pictures were soon appearing on the covers of practically every fashion magazine around the world. Sally and Angel were now a worldwide hit; the most beautiful mother/daughter combo in the universe.

Chapter Eleven

None of this escaped the attention of the two men in South Africa, Gerrie and Lance. As a youngster, Gerrie had been too nervous to even think of approaching the Angel of the class. Not so Lance. They had all, of course, been aware of Angel's climb up the ladder of fame, since his siter, Bibi, had been her best friend in South Africa and to this day, they still engaged in lengthy phone calls, just as they had as teenagers. Bibi had been thrilled at Angel's success in London, but also, perhaps, a little bit jealous. By contrast, even though her lover was famous in South Africa as the heavyweight champ, to a large degree life was boring. Apart from the actual fight nights and their build up, life in South Africa seemed rather dull compared to Angel's fabulous one in England.

Gerrie was not the most dynamic partner. When he was training for a fight, he spent most of his time in the gym, and, instead of coming home bounding with energy and ready for sex, he was often just plain "too tired". He had a fabulous body, but then, so did she; but he was just too tired. As a result, from time to time, Bibi played elsewhere. But, as Gerrie's de facto manager, there was plenty for her to do. She had secured all sorts of endorsements. Gerrie's handsome face appeared now on breakfast cereals, beers, sports and clothing gear, even on a motorbike. Bibi was an adept negotiator and never missed an opportunity to make hay from Gerrie's name. She knew that fame could be fleeting. One good punch might end it all.

Bibi hated going to the training gym. The place smelled of sweat. The sparring partners seemed to leer at her; she knew that they were undressing her in their heads. Sometimes, however, it was necessary for her to break into the training sessions in order to get a signature or discuss an endorsement with Gerrie. After these visits, Bibi would always go home for a shower.

In the ring, things had gone well for Gerrie. The first fight under their new arrangement with S and R and Square Ring in America, had gone according to plan. Gerrie had knocked out Bob's fighter in the fourth round. The announcement of the next fight, the rematch against Tiny Robertson, caught most sports fans and writers by surprise. Tiny was such a dangerous opponent that it puzzled many that Gerrie would risk derailing his career by allowing Tiny to get anywhere near him. Of course, Gerrie also got a lot of good press for taking this fight.

"Gerrie's a good sport," was basically the tone of their comments, but many of the pundits and fans felt that Gerrie was taking a big risk. Tiny was talking up a storm about how he was going to get revenge and take his title back. There were many that believed that he could. As a result, the estimated ticket sales were far surpassed and, on the night, the stadium was full to capacity, 60,000, a record for a live crowd at a boxing match in South Africa, indeed, probably, the world.

It turned out that Steven Shultz had done his homework. Tiny was not prepared to endure any punishment from the younger man. A glancing blow from Gerrie, after the second minute of the first round, put Tiny on his back. He didn't get up. Even Gerrie was surprised.

"Christ," he thought to himself, "I hardly hit him."

Nevertheless, hit him he had, and the path was now clear. Gerrie would meet the battling Brit, Jim London, at a place and on a date, yet to be determined. Meanwhile, in the USA, although it was the result that Bob Levin wanted, it was not achieved in the manner that he liked. Yes, he had now given Gerrie the much needed exposure as true heavyweight championship candidate, but "Those idiots down in South Africa, don't seem to understand that advertisers on TV need more than two minutes of action to get promotional value, let alone even run the ads."

Levin determined that Gerrie's next fight with the Brit must last longer. He had already done the preparatory work for the fight. He and Mickey Luff, the UK based promoter, in anticipation of Gerrie's win, had already worked out the details and how the pot would be shared. Their plan was to have Gerrie fight Jim London at the Wembley stadium. Jim was very popular in the UK. He came from a black Jamaican immigrant family in the East End of London. His father was a greengrocer with a shop in the Mile End Road. His real name was James Obunglaloosa, but Luff, quite sensibly, had insisted that he simplify it to something that Englishmen could pronounce. They settled on London; that seemed easy enough to remember. Jim was outward going, good looking, and personable, great on interviews and television talk shows. Luff realised that he could be a money well, so had carefully managed his career to date, making sure that he would look good every time he stepped into the ring. A fight against the superior ranked Gerrie Van de Merwe would be his gateway to a crack at the world title, but it could also be the end of the gravy train, so Mickey hedged his bets.

Unfortunately for Jim London, his next opponent had taken a great disliking to him. Jim had learned from his East End mates that the name "Van de Merwe" was always portrayed in South Africa as the dumb Dutchman in jokes, just as Irishmen were in the UK. During his many pre-match press interviews Jim had taken to reciting Van jokes, most of them hilarious, but all of them portraying his opponent as a boring, unintelligent, dope. Coach Brennan had put together a tape of Jim's ridiculing his opponent and made sure that his charge, Gerrie, had heard it. Gerrie, although outwardly accepting the barbs as just a piece of fun, inwardly determined that he was going to teach this black Jamaican a lesson. He was going to show the world which one of them was stupid. Nor was Gerrie paying any heed to the "instruction" from Bob Levin, to make the fight last for at least six rounds.

"He'll be lucky if it lasts six seconds," jibed Gerrie to Brennan, "I'll show him what Van de Merwes are made of!"

In fact, the fight did last six rounds. But the outcome was never in doubt. In round two, Gerrie floored the Brit. London fought on bravely but he was clearly being outboxed. In the third round Gerrie started to taunt him about what Van de Merwes can do. Brennan was worried.

"Don't get too cocky, Gerrie," he implored in the corner.

But Gerrie knew that he had things under control. In the fourth round he landed a huge uppercut, which again sent London to the canvas. In the sixth, his opponent was taking such a beating that the referee stepped in and stopped the fight. Gerrie Van de Merwe was still undefeated and when the new world rankings appeared, he was ranked number two. As Bob Levin had predicted, it would now be impossible for Louis Brown to ignore him.

The Van de Merwe/London fight had also given the two friends, Bibi and Angel the chance to re-unite. Angel took great delight in showing Bibi "her" London. Gerrie had set up a training camp in the car park at a golf course in Surrey. Brennan had insisted that for two weeks before the fight, Gerrie should do without the constant attention of Bibi, especially in bed, so Bibi had, with Gerrie's agreement, decamped to London to stay with her friend. Tony, Angel's career guide and would-be lover, was instantly taken with Bibi's sultry good looks and followed her around the flat with his camera.

"We must get you in the studio," he kept telling her, "we could really get some good shots." Although Angel was really happy to see her best friend, she was not thrilled about Tony's obvious obsession with her.

On the night of the fight, Bibi, Angel and her mother, Sally, all had seats in the front row. Jules could not be there, having to attend to business in South Africa. Sally actually hated to go to the fights. Being there, especially up so close, was a completely different thing from watching a bout on the television or cinema. For her, the sound of leather smashing into skin and bone, was awful. The squelching noise that accompanied a punch drawing blood; the sweat dripping off the fighters; the red swellings appearing on their bodies as you watched; these were all things that Sally detested, but she knew that her daughter had been a fan ever since her friendship began with a boxer's sister, years ago in South Africa. Sally, as a mother, just knew that Angel had had a girlish crush on Bibi's battling brother and that had been why she had started to go to the fights. She didn't know for sure, but she suspected that Lance had been her daughter's first lover, but she had never questioned her about it. Luckily, her infatuation with Bibi's brother had faded long ago.

"Good," thought Sally, "she is better off without him, especially now he's sitting in prison."

Despite all of this, Sally had come to the fight just to please her daughter and, to her surprise, she found the energy in the room almost exciting.

Bibi, despite a cool appearance, was all tied up in knots inside. She had every confidence that her lover could take care of himself, but each new opponent was a danger, and, sooner or later, Bibi knew that Gerrie would get hurt. Bibi wondered if this would be the night. Angel, on the other hand, was basking in the glory of being Miss World. Before the fighters appeared from their dressing rooms, to the delight of the mainly male crowd, the Master of Ceremonies, asked Angel to step into the ring – never an easy task for a young lady with a low-fronted dress. However, Angel managed the manouevre deftly and, to the delight of the crowd, had swayed her way around the four sides of the ring, waving confidently at the cheering audience. Although they were best friends, it somehow irked Bibi that Angel received all of the attention.

Tony had been accredited as an official photographer at Bibi's request, so had accompanied the three ladies to Wembley. Although he had never taken pictures at a boxing match before, he had a field day, catching all sorts of shots of the characters in the crowd, as well as several candid shots of his coterie of ladies. After the fight, once Bibi and Angel had scrambled into the ring to congratulate Gerrie, it was some of Tony's shots of the girls with Gerrie that appeared in the dailies the next morning.

When it was all over and the hubbub had died down and Coach Brennan had released Gerrie from his embargo, an almost unscathed Gerrie, Tony and the three girls, all headed back into the West End to party at Tramp. When Gerrie walked in with his ladies, the DJ reacted immediately. The thumping disco music suddenly stopped and "We are the Champions" blasted from his turntables, whilst the lights went ballistic. The whole room cheered and applauded for Gerrie, who was rather abashed by the attention, especially since he had just beaten their local man. Maybe the fact that the local man actually hailed from Jamaica had something to do with it.

Angel had thoughtfully booked a room at the Hilton for Gerrie and Bibi, thinking that they would want some privacy, which they would not get in her flat. By two in the morning, Sally had had enough to drink and enough of the thumping music. She happily detached herself from her daughter and friends and headed off, alone, in a taxi to Jules' flat in Chelsea. Meanwhile, patrons of the club kept plying the little remaining group with alcohol. Tony, had long stopped taking photos but his fascination with Bibi had been fuelled by the drink. He could feel the warmth of her body next to him on the sofa. When he started to move his hands up her leg, as surreptitiously as a partly drunk man could do, she did not react by withdrawing. Gerrie was either too tired to notice or too enraptured by Miss World, whom he had not stopped groping on the dance floor. Soon, the foursome had broken into two pairs, both on the small dance floor. But they were the wrong pairs. Bibi thought that she should be annoyed that Gerrie's hands were all over her best friend, but she found it strangely exciting.

"What was good for one, was good for the other," she thought through a haze of alcohol. Anyway, Tony had been coming on to her all evening, so why not make Gerrie envious?

The room at the Hilton did not go to waste, but it was Bibi and Tony that made sure they had good value.

Meanwhile, Gerrie found himself at Angel's flat, alone with Miss World.

All four had hangovers in the morning. They also had plenty to think about. When Sally let herself in to Angel's flat in the morning with a bag full of fresh croissants, she was amazed to find her daughter in bed with her best friend's lover. "This could take some sorting out."

Chapter Twelve

As it happened, Sally was wrong. There was not a lot of sorting out to do. Bibi had been getting more and more bored with life with Gerrie for some time now. She really enjoyed her role of managing his endorsements, and to some degree, his career, but their relationship had become quite stale. Previously she had put this down to his training ethic. His whole life centred around his desire to win the World Championship. That was his work and, like many men, he put his work before his personal life. Earlier on, she had worried that he had not proposed marriage to her, but as the years had gone on, she had got used to the idea that this would not happen. From time to time, particularly when Gerrie was in training, Bibi would take a lover. Nothing serious, of course, but enough to satisfy her needs. She did have concerns that, although she had acted as his manager, she had no formal contract with him. She had done a lot to help make him rich, but she had nothing to show for it. Not that he had been mean or ungenerous: far from it. He had always looked after her well, but if there were to be a split, she would be entirely reliant on his being fair.

Tony had the least to lose. He was not in a relationship with Angel, except through a modelling contract. He had no control over her sex life, even though, when he first met her, he would have liked to. It was her friend, Bibi, that really turned him on, so he had no regrets about the night at the Hilton. In fact, he hoped there would be many more. He realised, of course, that he had interfered with Gerrie's personal affairs, although, to be fair, Gerrie was not exactly his friend. He had met him for the first time after the fight. No, Tony did not have too much to lose as a result of one steamy night, but he would need to tread carefully. Bibi was Angel's best friend, and Angel was a hot property; so was her mum.

Angel was extremely worried that she had just slept with her best friend's lover. That is not what friends do. However, there was something about this gentle giant that really appealed to her. He might possibly be the best heavyweight boxer in the world, but, as a personality, he was gentleness itself. But, as much as she had enjoyed her night with Gerrie, no man should be worth more than the love of her best friend. If she had to choose between her friendship with Bibi and her attraction to Gerrie, Bibi would have to come first.

Gerrie had had a great time in Angel's bed. After all, not everyone gets to spend the night with Miss World. It had been a long time since he had had sexual release, not just due to Coach Brennan's embargo for the two weeks before the fight, but for several weeks of training back in South Africa. Gerrie didn't know why, or even understand it, but his relationship with Bibi seemed to have gone stale. Perhaps it was his fault, but then, what had she actually done to fire him up? The problem was that he was tied to Bibi. She had done great work for him in arranging his affairs, but, luckily, he had never signed any contracts allowing her to benefit. If he were to split with her now, he would have to be careful.

Although it was almost lunchtime, Sally prepared the breakfast. Angel appeared in her pretty dressing gown, whilst Gerrie occupied the shower. He had no fresh clothes to wear, so Sally offered to pop into nearby Kings Road to buy him a new shirt and underwear. When she returned, Angel had also showered and was looking fresh and lovely. Nobody would have known that she had spent the night partying. From the body language between the two, Sally could see that this was potentially more than a one night stand or even a mistake. Angel and Gerrie were both adults; it was their lives.

"I think you'd better call Bibi," she finally suggested to her daughter. "You and she have got some talking to do."

"Your mum's right," chipped in Gerrie, "I don't know whether I should call her first, or you. But we'd better get this sorted out." As it happened, they did not have to call. Before they had finished their croissants, the door bell rang. It was Bibi and Tony, both looking a little worse for wear and certainly a bit sheepish.

"I think I'd better leave you youngsters alone to sort things out," said Sally, almost immediately. "Tony, I think it would be a good idea for you and I to leave. Come along, I'm taking you out to lunch."

Bibi looked a little worried, but did not offer any resistance. She pulled Tony towards her, gave him a little peck on the cheek, and sent him on his way with Sally. After a long, embarrassing and pregnant silence the threesome started to talk. It was an odd triangle of friendships that had been fractured. The strange thing was that none of the three actually regretted what had happened, but would they be able to admit it?

"Well, I hope you two had a good time," began Bibi, with more than a hint of sarcasm.

"You too," shot back Angel, without admitting for a moment that she had.

"Look," carried on Bibi, "as far as I am concerned, it was just a one night stand, fuelled, I suppose, with too much alcohol. But you must admit, Angel, that you were coming on a bit strong with my boyfriend. You certainly seem to be able to rev him up more than I do. I would have thought he would have been too tired to perform after the fight and all that training. That's what he normally says." Gerrie was still quiet.

"Well, as a matter of fact, he performed rather well," countered Miss World. "I haven't had so much fun for ages."

Bibi did not like what she heard, especially from her long-standing friend.

"Well, if you like him that much, you can keep him," she screamed at Angel. "You'll soon see how fucking boring he can be."

With that she made a move towards the door. Gerrie moved to stop her.

"Look, my love," he started as he reached out to impede her exit. "Please, let's talk about this. We're all friends here. We have a long history. Let's not just throw it away." He now had hold of Bibi's arm, but she pulled away from him. He turned to Angel.

"Angel, please would you give me a moment with Bibi. We need to talk."

Angel looked a little miffed, but nodded, and slipped off into her bedroom. Through the door she could just make out what they were saying.

"Now, Bibi, you listen to me," he started. "You may be pissed off that I went with your friend last night, but what about you, shagging the photographer, just like you've been shagging guys in South Africa behind my back? Do you think I'm stupid? I don't think our relationship is the problem here, at least, what is left of our relationship. I think that that actually finished a few months ago, and you know it. No, the problem here is your relationship with Angel. She's always been your best friend. She loves you. It's not a relationship that should be broken."

"She can fuck off!," shouted Bibi, "and so can you!"

With that, she was gone, slamming the door behind her. Angel emerged from the bedroom. Without saying a thing, she moved towards Gerrie and put her arm around his waist. She pulled him towards her and kissed him gently on the lips.

"Don't worry, Gerrie. She'll get over it. I am so sorry that I have caused all of this. I can't tell you how sorry I am but hopefully time will heal."

But, time did not. The bond between Bibi and Gerrie was broken, as was her friendship with Angel. Bibi did not seek solace with her new friend, Tony, but she did, the next day, call him and ask him to go to Angel's flat to collect her clothes and personal belongings. She had not checked out of the Hilton, so she moved back and extended her stay for a few days. Tony took full advantage, not only in the bed but also in his studio. Bibi really did look good at the end of a camera lens; he would certainly be able to use these pics to his advantage one day. Bibi had fury in her eyes. It was her that was used to calling the shots with men; it was not easy for her to realise that she had been dumped by Gerrie.

What made matters worse was that, despite all the work she had done on his behalf, unless he was generous, nothing would accrue to her. However, it was way beneath her pride and dignity to ask him for anything. No, she would pack up and return to South Africa. She would go to the house that Gerrie and she shared and clear out her things before he returned, including all the contracts and paperwork that she had secured on his behalf. Then, she would go to see her brother. It was with him, that she planned to plot her revenge.

Chapter Thirteen

Lance had been allowed to watch the fight between Gerrie and Jim London on a small television in the prison. This had been a special concession to the prisoners in the boxing club. Lance's club had really blossomed. Many of the fitter prisoners were delighted to be allowed to participate in the training, and Lance had worked his way back to tip top physical condition. He was due to be released in a few weeks' time when Bibi paid him a visit. Lance was flabbergasted that Bibi had split with Gerrie after the fight. Of course, Bibi only gave her brother a sanitised version of the facts. What he discerned was that Gerrie had dumped his sister to screw her best friend.

"Well, at least I beat him to that," he thought, without mentioning it to his sister.

What was most disturbing was that Bibi was to get nothing from Gerrie after all her good work.

"Surely," he thought, "Gerrie will cough up her share when he gets back to South Africa. After all that had got nothing to do with who was screwing who," he rationalised.

"So, Sis," said Lance, "what are you going to do now?"

"I'll tell you what I'm going to do," she responded firmly, "I'm going to do for you, what I did for him. You're going to start boxing again, and I'm going to make both of us rich. You, not Gerrie, are going to become the

World Champion. Everyone thinks he has the potential to do it. I know that you were better than him, so, if he thinks he can do it, I think you can too."

"Now, hold on a minute, Sis. I'm not even a registered pro. I have no ranking. What the hell are you talking about?"

"Trust me, Lance, I know my way around the boxing block now. You do the fighting and I'll do the talking. We're going to make millions!"

Whilst Lance had been working as a policeman, he had taken a lease on a small flat in Parktown, a suburb of Johannesburg between their family home in Randburg and the City. Lance gave his sister the keys and told her to make herself at home. The next day she went to see Trevor at S and R Promotions and made her pitch. In her vision, as soon as Lance was released, he would apply for a professional boxing license. There was no way he could go back to the police. Trevor, she said, would make sure, through his influence, that the license was granted. Trevor and Steven would set up, at their expense, a training camp for Lance and provide an experienced trainer. They would organise a few bouts for Lance, which would get progressively tougher, or, at least, would appear to. Lance would quickly move up the ranks of South African heavyweights, just as Gerrie had done, until he was the champ.

Then would come the real money. Bibi would be his manager, but S and R would have a cut of 25% of everything Lance would earn, from the ring and from sponsorship *ad infinitum*. Not like it was with Gerrie, where their participation had been capped. Trevor listened with amazement. All he knew was that Lance had failed to reach the top of the amateur game, let alone have the potential to be a successful pro. Apparently, he had been too much of a playboy. On the other hand, he remembered hearing from Coach Brennan that, of the two men, Lance had the most potential. He just needed to stay fit and concentrate. What Trevor did remember about Lance, firstly as an amateur and then during the trial, was that he had the gift of the gab. Also, despite the fact that he had shot a man in the back, there was a huge amount of sympathy for him at the time from the large Afrikaans population and the white population in general. Perhaps, Bibi was right. Perhaps Lance's story could be turned into a public relations dream. Anyway, what had S and R got to lose? Only a few bucks on a training facility. They would soon see if Bibi's plan had any legs.

Trevor discussed the matter with his partner, Steven. They checked out the contract they had with Gerrie, their star client. They were just on the verge of the last fight in their contract with him and that was going to be the biggie: the world heavyweight championship. After that, they had no hold on Gerrie, although they would like to think that he would continue to use their services, by way, almost, of payback. However, they realised that such hopes may not materialise because they would have no leverage. A good run, on the other hand, with Lance, which had no financial cap nor end in the relationship, might be a smart thing to do, even though the odds on it being successful were, to say the least, extremely small. If they were to agree to take on Lance, then, they had better be quiet about it until Gerrie's world title fight was in the bag. They decided that Trevor should pay Lance a visit at the Kyalami prison, to see for himself if Lance was as fit as his big sister said.

When Trevor got to the prison and saw the set up that Lance had masterminded within the prison walls, he was astounded. Lance looked as fit and strong as any of the boxers S and R had on their books. Maybe, just maybe, Bibi's crazy plan could work.

Steven and Trevor called Bibi. "Okay, doll. You're on. But we must not go public with this until after Gerrie's world title crack, if that is going to happen. We have too much to lose, as you know, because you were the one who negotiated the deal. When Lance comes out of jail next month, we'll set him up with a gym and trainer, but nobody must know we're paying for it. The payments will need to be routed through you. Is that understood? In the meantime, we'll see that he gets a license and line up some patsies. You've got yourself a deal."

Bibi's next stop was to call on Gerrie's younger brother, Frikkie. She had noticed over the last couple of years, how Frikkie had grown up into a strong handsome young man, just like his brother. But Frikkie had been forced to live in the shadow of his famous brother. Frikkie was never just Frikkie Van de Merwe, he was always "Gerrie's younger brother". Bibi had noticed, from time to time, a little snatch of annoyance on Frikkie's face when his brother took all the limelight. Not only that, Frikkie was a strapping good looking young man and Bibi quite fancied him, even though he was a few years younger than herself.

"That would really piss Gerrie off, big time," she thought, "if I went out with his little brother. Shit, he would really be angry."

That, however, was not the reason for her visit. From time to time, Gerrie had used his little brother as a sparring partner and Bibi had seen for herself that Frikkie could give as good as he got. Her plan was simple. First, she would bed him, then she would use him – as part of Lance's team. That would really get under Gerrie's skin.

Meanwhile, back in London, Gerrie had decided to take a few weeks off, to enjoy his time with Angel. That wasn't quite as straightforward as he would have liked, since his new love was heavily involved with photo shoots and personal appearances. He also found Tony a bit infuriating because he seemed to have more time with Angel than he did. Having mother, that is, Angel's mother, living around the corner, was also a bit of an invasion of his and Angel's privacy, because mother and daughter were extremely close. On top of that Miss World Inc., kept nagging for their share on the young lady. In short, whilst Gerrie had very little to keep him occupied in London, his Angel was on a merry go round of personal appearances and other gigs.

Fortunately, after a week or so, Sally decided to return to South Africa to be with Jules, and Tony was smart enough to realise that Angel needed some time with her new lover. But Miss World Inc. wouldn't go away. Jane was insisting that Angel accompany her on a promotional tour of the Far East, which had been long scheduled and would take about three weeks to accomplish. Gerrie and Angel decided that, under the circumstances, it would be better for Gerrie to go back to South Africa, where he could commence light training, whilst he waited for his advisors to negotiate his next fight, which he insisted should be for the world title. During all of this time, Gerrie had not heard from Bibi. Of course, he was aware that she had the keys to his home in Johannesburg and he just hoped that she had not been up to any mischief.

In the moments that Gerrie and Angel did have together alone, they could not get enough of each other. Both were so happy that they had found each other. They marvelled at why it had taken so long.

Chapter Fourteen

Bob Levin had been in London at ringside to watch the Van de Merwe/London fight, even though it was not his promotion. It was clear for all to see that, somehow or other, Levin had got himself a piece of Gerrie. The beam on his bespectacled face showed that he had something to be pleased about. He was of a mind to telephone Louis Brown immediately to talk about a challenge for the heavyweight belt. However, he decided to let the mountain come to Mohamed. He knew that Brown would not be able to resist the huge revenues that would stem from an undefeated white boxer, especially one from South Africa, fighting the World Heavyweight champion, James Dubois, a loud-mouthed black man from the Bronx in New York. Dubois had now been the champ for over four years. In that time, he had fought and won on six different occasions, each time earning himself and Brown a fortune. However, Brown had been running out of worthy opponents that could add up to a big pay day, so the thought of Dubois versus Van der Merwe was eye watering. And, Brown mused, even if the South African were to win, he would have to sign for a rematch with Dubois, so, the promoter could see two big paydays looming.

A week went by without any contact between Levin and Brown. Levin had now returned to Las Vegas. He had been fending off calls from Steven Shultz in South Africa, with whom he had counselled patience.

"Steven, my boy," said Bob on the transatlantic phone, "I know how to handle Brown. Trust me."

Ten days after the fight in London, the call came.

"Bob, my man, where've you been hiding? I think it's time to talk. Is this something we can do on the phone, or shall I come to Vegas?"

"Nah, Louis, the last thing I want to see is your big black butt here in Vegas. Let's see what we can do on the phone."

The two men knew each other's game so well, it was no longer an interesting match. Within 15 minutes they had agreed a deal. They were so used to dealing with each other that a sort of gentleman's agreement existed between them when it came to promotional contracts. Except, neither of them was a gentleman. Basically, whatever revenues could be generated by the fight, other than purses for the fighters, Louis Brown would get 60% and Bob Levin, 40%. Should Dubois lose to Gerrie, there would be an automatic rematch of which the take would be reversed, i.e. 60% to Levin. For the championship fight, Gerrie would earn $1 million and Dubois $4 million. If there were to be a rematch the purses would be reversed. Both men liked to keep things simple.

They also agreed that both of them would work on finding the most lucrative sponsor and site for the fight. Bob, of course, favoured Las Vegas, his home patch, because he knew the top casinos would be begging to stage the event. He also knew that on his home turf he could rely on a kickback from a casino, before it came to splitting the proceeds with Louis. Louis, however, had other ideas. He had recently been fishing for sponsorship in a pool full of big fish with big egos: the Middle East.

Both men agreed to canvas support before comparing bids. In the end, it would come down to money, not personal preferences, although, to Bob, a Jew, doing business in the Middle East did not appeal. He knew he could not trust Louis, particularly if he was now in league with some Arabs. He started to formulate a plan. But, as he sat there working down a mental list as to how to screw his competitor, he realised that his dislike of Brown was clouding the issue. His real goal, for the first fight, was not to make a killing. His goal should be the capture of the title; then he could control the game, and this could be highway to everlasting riches. So, he would let Louis have his day in the sun.

He picked up the phone and called Louis back. "Listen, my friend," he began. "Let's not get into a pissing match here. I've been thinking. Let's keep this thing simple. You find the money from your Middle East friends for the first fight; we'll keep the 60/40 split we agreed. Then, if there is a second fight, I will find the money in Vegas. But, if you need someone to bluff up the ante, then give me a call. If you've already got some Arab in mind for this fight, I don't want to waste my time and risk annoying my sponsors. Okay?"

Louis Brown instantly agreed. He was not sure what game his competitor was playing, but it didn't really matter. He knew he already had a backer who could buy all of Vegas in one swoop.

The United Arab Emirates was awash with money, – oil money. Much of this came from the wells in Abu Dhabi, but also from over the border in oil rich Saudi Arabia. Although the source of wealth centred on Abu Dhabi, it was the neighbouring territory of Dubai which had led the way in taking the Arab world from languishing in the last century into the high-tech capital of the Middle East. Dubai was also the gateway between the Middle East and the West. Its more relaxed rules for living than its neighbours had allowed it to become a playground for Arabs, but also a commercial centre for Western companies to enter the growing Arab markets. The more publicity that Dubai could get was, at the time, welcomed by its richer neighbours in Abu Dhabi, but also by its big brother in Saudi, where very strict rules of living were the law. Dubai was the place where the Middle East met the West; a place where frustrated Saudis and other Arabs looking for a good time could find it. Dubai was the natural venue for the biggest boxing match of all time, between an undefeated upstart white man from Africa against the established black brute from New York. The Emirate of Dubai was prepared to spend big money to stage the fight. For a few weeks before the event, the word "Dubai" would be on the back page of every newspaper in the world and Dubai, with its huge hotel building programme in the works, could take all of the positive publicity that it could get.

The Dubois/Van de Merwe fight was to take place in the convention centre, since the extreme heat in the Middle East at that time of the year ruled out an outdoor event. Also, the authorities in Dubai were not too interested in attracting a huge crowd of spectators, since this was primarily to be an event made for television and the rest of the world. Nevertheless, when the eighteen thousand tickets went on sale, the computer went down, as it was swamped with "buy" orders.

The Dubois camp had decided to relocate to Dubai, several weeks before the fight. They set up a training camp in a villa on the outskirts of the city between civilisation and the desert. Gerrie and Coach Brennan decided to do their preliminary training in Johannesburg at a much higher altitude, which, in Brennan's view, would aid with peak fitness. A secondary training camp, to which Gerrie and his team transferred a couple of weeks before the bout, was created at the Hilton Beach Club in Dubai, a small members only facility with plenty of space and privacy. Despite the restrictions on access to both training camps, it seemed that there were always crowds of curious visitors who somehow knew someone to let them in. Also, a simple press card would do the trick. It was, therefore, quite hard for either boxer to train in peace, a problem that seemed to affect Gerrie more than his opponent, who, as champion, was used to, and who actually revelled in, attention.

On one occasion a wild punch from his sparring partner had landed Gerrie on the canvas. The press had a field day, with claims about a glass jaw and so on. Dubois seized upon this with gusto, predicting that Gerrie would not last more than three rounds with him, since he couldn't even avoid being clobbered in training. Gerrie responded in the press by saying that since Dubois couldn't seem to keep his mouth closed, he would have to close it for him in the fight.

By the time Gerrie stepped into the ring on the big day, he was in superb condition. His well-oiled muscular body glistened under the strong lights. The happiness that he had recently found with Angel had, somehow, helped him. The tension that had crept into his relationship with Bibi was now a thing of the past. His mind was in a good place. He was ready for the fight. After Angel's tour of the far east on Miss World duties, she had joined Gerrie in South Africa. Tony had organised a fashion shoot for her in the bush for *Vogue*, so, for once, their respective occupations seemed to gel. So did they. Gerrie did not come home from training to announce that he was "too tired".

He had not seen Bibi. She, apparently, had been into the house whilst he was still in London with Angel, and removed all of her belongings, including, much to his annoyance, all of his files and contracts. At first, he was sad that it had all ended this way, but Angel more than made up for his loss. Strom and Edna, his dad and mom, were delighted that Bibi had gone. Things had never been right in their relationship with their son since Bibi had edged them out. In their eyes, Angel was just perfect for Gerrie and could not be nicer with them. Gerrie had not exactly allowed Strom to take over the management role again, preferring to handle things himself from now on, but Strom at least felt that he was not now prevented from playing the father role.

In short, it was not only a super-fit young man who climbed into the ring at the Dubai Conference Centre, but also a man who was settled and content. All he had to do now was perform to his best ability and the world championship would be his. In training he had used a music track, "Nothing's Going to Stop me now", that Angel had given to him. As he waited patiently in his corner during the announcements, the tune floated into his head. He looked down at Angel in the front row. She looked absolutely beautiful. She smiled back and moved her lips as if in a kiss. He knew now that he loved her. He did not want to let her down. He wanted her to be proud of him.

The fight was a humdinger. At the time, world championship fights were scheduled for 15 rounds: that is 45 minutes of one on one combat. In later years the boxing authorities reduced the length to a maximum of 12 rounds. Despite all of the pundits predicting that this fight would not go the distance, with by far the biggest majority suggesting that Dubois would knock Gerrie out in an early round, both men were still standing, though exhausted, at the end of the 15th. As they collapsed into each other's arms when the final bell clanged, neither of them knew who had won. As a gesture of respect to Gerrie, Dubois, instead of raising his arm in triumph, grabbed Gerrie's arm and lifted it into the air.

The referee went to three sides of the ring, leant through the ropes, and collected the score sheets from the three judges. Most television commentators thought that Dubois had edged it, and, as is the way, if a fight is close, the verdict normally goes to the champion. Of course, judges can also be influenced by men like Louis Brown, so until the score cards were actually handed in, no one could tell who had won.

Silence fell in the arena as the referee took the microphone and unfolded the first slip of paper.

"Judge Harper scores the fight by eight rounds to seven in favour of Dubois."

A huge cheer went up from at least half of the crowd, which quickly evaporated into silence as the referee unfolded the second slip.

"Judge Maktoum scores the fight by eight rounds to seven in favour of Van der Merwe."

More thunderous noise from the crowd. Then complete silence as the man in the middle unfolded the third and final slip.

"Judge Bush scores the fight by nine rounds to six in favour of the *new* heavyweight..." The rest of the sentence was obliterated by the roar from the hall. The word *new* said all that the crowd needed to know. Gerrie was the Heavyweight Champion of the World.

The referee grabbed Gerrie's right arm and held it aloft. Dubois was the first to congratulate him. Both he and Louis Brown knew that a second, maybe even bigger, pay day would be coming. Within seconds the boxing ring was full of well-wishers. Strom helped Angel through the ropes; Edna stayed below with Sally and Jules. Gerrie's body was dripping with sweat. Angel couldn't have cared less; she was so happy for her man that she literally had to be dragged off him for the photos. Amongst the mob was Tony. He was not going to miss this photo op for anything. This had been a long road for Gerrie, but finally he had arrived. The first undefeated fighter to ever lift the heavyweight crown, and the first South African. If he did nothing else in his life, he would still go down in history.

This time, there was no drama after the fight, not like the fateful night in London after the bout at Wembley. Strom and Angel had organised a private room back at the Beach Club to which they had invited Gerrie's crew of trainers, helpers, and family, as well as the manager of the club and his wife. There was plenty to eat and drink; it was a joyous occasion, unmarred by interpersonal challenges. Strom and Edna were so proud of their boy, but also so pleased that he seemed to be in such a happy place. Likewise, Sally was pleased. Her Angel would not have to cope with defeat. She was also pleased that Jules was there to share in the glory. The joy of the occasion was not lost on two other participants; Trevor and Steven from S and R Promotions. Although the deal that they had signed with Bibi and Lance meant that they no longer had a contractual hold on Gerrie, they had just earned another $125,000. Under normal circumstances, a fighter would have kept them on to negotiate further fights, even though they now had Bob Levin involved as well. Was their clandestine deal with Lance now looking a bit foolhardy?

Two men, who were not at the victory party, were Bob Levin and Louis Brown.

They were busy sharing a coffee at another hotel, already scheming for the return match. Things appeared to have gone just as they had planned. Their bets had been well placed. Nobody could know for sure why the judges scored the fight the way they did, only perhaps one or both of the two men supping coffee. Bob was keen to get away from Arabia. He had, rather reluctantly, been in Dubai now for over a couple of weeks, helping to hype up the fight with the media. He hated it there. To him this place was a farce; a spectacular display of glass and steel in the middle of nowhere. Others, including Louis Brown, thought this criticism, coming from a man who lived in Las Vegas, was a bit rich. Basically, Brown observed, "Poor Bob's never been outnumbered by so many Arabs in his life."

The fight had done well financially. The television takings, including closed circuit takings, which was an industry in its infancy at the time, were coming in at an incredible $45 million. The sponsorship deal with Dubai had been for £10 million, offset by the gate takings, which were to accrue to a local sponsor in Dubai. Out of the $55 million income, the two men had had to pay Gerrie $1 million and $4 million to Dubois. After other expenses of around $2 million, there was about $48 million to share. Bob's take home pot would be around $19 million, not bad compared with Steven and Trevor's $125,000. And, on top of that, Bob could expect over $30 million from the return match. And that did not include a few more dollars from a few well-placed bets. Even so, Bob was not a happy camper. Some enquiries in Dubai had led him to believe that the sponsorship fee paid by the Emirate was closer to $20 million, not the publicised ten. Bob was sure that Louis had screwed him. So, at the very least, he could pay for the coffee.

Now that Bob was in the driving seat, the two men agreed that he should proceed with finding a sponsor and venue in Las Vegas, ideally to stage the return bout in about five months. Bob already had a couple of ideas in this regard. Even though there would be pressure for the rematch to be held in Dubai, that was the last thing that Bob was going to do. Nevertheless, the threat of a counter offer from the Emirates, might be quite helpful in his upcoming negotiations on his home turf.

Chapter Fifteen

Tony had been commissioned by *Tatler* to do a fashion shoot with Angel against the backdrop of the modern architecture of Dubai. So Gerrie and Angel stayed on for a few days at the beach club. Strom, Edna, Sally and Jules had all headed straight home to South Africa. The heat of Dubai was just too much for them and, in any event, they all thought that Angel and Gerrie could do with some private time. What with Gerrie's training schedule and Angel's trip to the Far East, the two lovers had only been catching brief moments of time together. None of the parent group wanted this new relationship to flounder. Tony, who was still very attracted to Angel's mother, Sally, was sorry to see her go. For a moment, in Dubai, he sensed that maybe everything was not great between Sally and Jules. He also did not want to be a spare around Gerrie and Angel, so, although they politely asked him to join them in the evenings at the beach club, he graciously found ways to decline. Gerrie and Angel made the most of their time together; they knew it would be short lived. It was so hot on the beach that most of their time was spent in the air-conditioned beach villa, either naked or almost so.

After a while Gerrie felt that he should return to South Africa, where the sponsorship contracts obtained by Bibi required him to attend several promotional events. Angel, on the other hand, was required by Miss World Inc. to go on a tour of Brazil, Ecuador and Argentina. Once again, they would be on separate continents for a couple of weeks.

When Gerrie got back to South Africa, his affairs were in a muddle. There had been several calls from sponsors, seeking Gerrie's attention. They were all reminding him of his commitments to them, should he win the title. Now he had, they all wanted a piece of him. Annoyingly he had no way of knowing what his actual commitments were, since Bibi had taken all of the paperwork. There was no way he was going to go to see Bibi, so he decided to turn to Trevor Rosenburg for help. Trevor offered to come to Gerrie's house, but Gerrie opted to go to S and R's offices. He knew that his promotional deal with the agency had now expired, but, under the circumstances, he thought that it might be worth hiring them to act as his local public relations agents, to manage all of the promotional crap that he was going to now have to endure. It would not be huge money for them, but it would also be a way of saying "thank you" for all they had done for him.

The S and R offices were not exactly "Beverly Hills". Gerrie realised that, in all the years that he had been dealing with them, he had never actually been to where they worked; they had always come to him or they had met in gyms or photoshoot locations. When he reached the rather dilapidated building in Braamfontein which corresponded to their address, he thought he must be in the wrong place, but the unpolished brass sign on the door confirmed that he was not. The interior was all brown. There was a small brown couch with two brown easy chairs and a coffee table. A brown receptionist's desk, piled high with paperwork, and a brown secretary with bright blonde hair. Gerrie, of course, did not need to introduce himself to the girl, although he did anyway.

She motioned for him to take a seat. His big frame took up the whole of the sofa. As he sat there, he could faintly hear the conversation going on behind one of the glass walls. It sounded like Steven. He was not sure, but he thought he heard the word "Bibi". Anyway, the talking stopped, the door to the office opened and out stepped a smiling Trevor, hand outstretched, who ushered him inside. There, behind the desk, was Steven, hurriedly shuffling a few papers. Greetings over, the three sat down to talk and Gerrie explained his predicament; Bibi had stolen all of his papers. A quick worried glance was exchanged between Steven and Trevor. Gerrie went on to explain that he needed someone to obtain copies of the various promotional contracts from the relevant parties, in order that they could ascertain his commitments, if any. Thereafter, Gerrie explained, he would like to hire them to handle his business affairs and local public relations. Since S and R had worked for him before, he wanted to see what sort of agreement they could come to going forward.

To his surprise, neither man jumped at the opportunity. Steven was the first to respond.

"Well, Gerrie," he began, "that's not the sort of work we normally do; so, Trevor and I would need to discuss it."

Gerrie was puzzled. He had thought they would be excited at the chance to stay involved, especially now that he was World champion. Outside the room he heard the phone ringing and then the muffled voice of the receptionist. The phone in the room buzzed. Steven apologised to Gerrie and picked up the receiver, telling the girl outside to hold his calls. The girl however was insistent and slightly raised her voice. Once again, Gerrie thought that he heard the word "Bibi". Steven excused himself for a moment and went out to the brown reception room to handle the call. Gerrie tried to eavesdrop but unfortunately Trevor did not stop talking, so it was impossible to hear what Steven was saying.

Gerrie left S and R without a new deal, but with a promise that they would get back to him within a couple of days. They would, however, as a favour, contact the sponsoring companies on Gerrie's behalf to obtain replacement copies of any agreements that he had signed.

Sure enough, a few days later, Trevor called with the good news that he had obtained a copy of all of the contracts. The bad news was that S and R did not think it was worth their while taking on Gerrie's PR work. If they could be cut into the fight deal making again, that would be a different matter. He hoped Gerrie would understand. Trevor promised to send a messenger with the contracts to Gerrie the same day, but pointed out that one of the sponsors, a cereal manufacturer, seemed to have the right for a photo shoot with Gerrie within one month of him winning the title.

When the paperwork arrived, someone had red flagged the requirement for Gerrie to go to the shoot, so Gerrie called up the cereal PR department to make the arrangements. When he spoke with the executive in charge, Gerrie took the trouble of thanking him for supplying copies of the contract. The man did not know what he was talking about. Gradually, it dawned on Gerrie that S and R were not being entirely straight with him.

"Why would they turn down my offer to let them handle my PR? How did they get the copies of the contracts so quickly?"

Gerrie looked again at the paperwork. These were not copies at all. They were Gerrie's originals! Now he knew that he had heard right. Somewhere along the line, Steven and Trevor were involved with Bibi. That could not be good news, but would explain why they would not continue working for him. He needed to find out what was going on.

Angel was in Bogota, doing her Miss World thing. Because of the time difference Gerrie waited until it was ten in the morning in Colombia before calling. When he did, he got no answer. Angel was on a photo shoot at the time, but it was taking place deep down underground in a salt mine. Salt mines and early cell phones were not compatible. Gerrie was frustrated. He wanted Angel's opinion on this matter, but he was also impatient. After two hours and no return call from South America, Gerrie picked up the phone and called Trevor.

"Thank you for sending the contracts, Trevor," he started, "but these are the originals. How did you get these from Bibi?"

"You told us that she had stolen them. I thought the quickest way to help you was to ask her to give them back," came the reply.

"So, you guys aren't dealing with her?" asked Gerrie.

"No, not at all," lied Trevor.

"Good," said Gerrie, "I would not like that."

Trevor put the phone down and uncrossed his fingers. "This could be trouble," he thought.

When Angel got out of the salt mine, she called Gerrie back. She, too, did not like what she had heard. "Sounds to me like something is going on," she agreed. "no doubt we'll find out soon. But, don't worry, Gerrie, my love. You're the champ. You hold all the cards. There's nothing that Bibi and S and R can do to hurt you; so just forget it and think of nice things, – like you and me."

Meanwhile, elsewhere near Johannesburg, in a little dorpie in the Maghaliesburg mountains, about 30 miles out of town, the ex-policeman, ex-jailbird, Lance was slugging away at a heavy bag in a makeshift gym that he had constructed in the back yard of a tiny rented bungalow, well out of the way of prying cameras. Although it was shabby, for Lance, it was 100% better than jail. The bungalow had three bedrooms, one bathroom and a grotty kitchen. It was not great, but it was better than jail. Here, Lance was holed up with two sparring partners. Trevor had persuaded the South African Boxing Board of Control, to issue his protegee with a professional licence, but asked them to keep quiet about it until they were ready for his first fight.

The sparring partners were also in the pay of S and R. One of them, Patterson, known as "Bright Boy" in the ring, had been a pro for several years, with mixed success. He was now well past his prime but was happy to cooperate with Trevor for a fee. He was also to be Lance's first opponent in a small event to be held in Port Elizabeth, a coastal city far from Johannesburg. Naturally, the outcome was entirely predictable so Bright Boy's friends would do well at the betting shop. The bout, when it took place, attracted no publicity, so went completely unnoticed in Johannesburg. Nevertheless, Lance's professional career was on its way. He was now one and o.

As it turned out, Lance did not really need to be fighting a patsy; he was now in excellent shape, not only in the body, but more importantly, in the head. Before Gerrie knew where his first title defence would be, and when, Lance had fought and won three times. After his last effort, an alert pressman, had spotted his name on a poster, and attended the fight. He smelled a story. "Ex killer cop, now a killer in the ring." Although the subsequent article only appeared in the *Port Elizabeth Herald*, it was soon picked up by the Johannesburg papers. It was Angel, now back in South Africa for a while, that first spotted it. She knew now what her ex-best friend was up to.

Back in Las Vegas, Bob Levin had been busy. His asking price of a $15 million site fee was, even by Vegas standards, on the high side. Of course, he only intended to give his "partner", Louis, 40% of the first $10 million, but, nevertheless, still wanted to get closer to $20 million. Eventually he persuaded the Starburst Hotel to agree to $20 million site fee, to be offset by 5% of the television revenue up to a max of $5 million. The Starburst would also get the live gate revenue.

Bob explained to Louis that the best he could do for a site fee was $12 million, offset by 5% of the TV money. Louis, of course, said that he could do better in the Middle East, but Bob was not having any, so Louis soon caved in. The only thing was that Louis thought his man, Dubois, should get more than $1million, even though this was the agreed deal.

"Well, give him a cut of your piece, you greedy bastard," said Bob.

"Nah, man. You know that's not a good idea," said Louis, and Bob actually knew he was right. This would be slippery slope.

Eventually, in the interests of continued business, Bob called Louis and said, "Okay, let's give him another million. It may be the last he ever gets."

"Great, man," said Louis, "I knew you was a gent."

With the deal agreed, and the Starburst signed up, Bob called Gerrie in South Africa.

"Better get your training boots on, Gerrie. The deal's done. You and Dubois are going to be fighting in Vegas on September 20," he announced.

"That's great, Bob," said Gerrie. "I'll be ready. What's my cut?"

"It's in your contract, Gerrie; you get $4 million and Dubois gets one. That's what we agreed."

"How much will you get, Bob?" said Gerrie, much to Bob's surprise.

"Well, that's difficult to say, Gerrie. I have all of my expenses, then I have to give Louis Brown half of it, and I don't know what the TV money will be......"

Gerrie interrupted. "I'll fight him, if you give me another $4 million."

Even Bob, who had seen and heard most things in his life, was taken aback.

"But Gerrie," he started, "you don't understand. You have agreed in the contract to take $4 million. That's what Dubois got to fight you. It's on that basis that I have arranged the fight and negotiated the site fee and so on. I can't give you more than the contract says."

"You know where I'm coming from, Bob. I don't see why you and that scumbag, Brown, should get rich when I do all the work. Either you see it my way, or I'm not fighting."

Bob began to get angry. "Listen, my boy. You've signed a deal. If you don't want to honour it, I'll have to sue you for damages. And, by the way, you will never get to defend your title. All the challengers are controlled by either me or Brown. If you don't defend within a year, the Board will take away your title. So, my friend, don't get too smart with me."

Gerrie listened, with half a smile on his face. Angel, who was listening in on the other line, was urging him on. After a long pause, Bob wondered if Gerrie was still on the line, but suddenly he heard a familiar phrase, "Bob, my friend, you know better than anyone, – contracts don't fight."

With that, encouraged by Angel's hand signals, Gerrie hung up. Angel fell about laughing. Back in LA, Bob Levin, smiled a wry smile. Needless to say, he had been there before.

"Let him stew for a while," Bob muttered to himself and went out for lunch.

Three days later, Louis Brown wanted to know what was happening.

"My man's the same as yours, Louis," Levin explained. "He wants a bigger piece."

"Well, there's enough skin in it for all of us," said Brown. "Offer him another million, and settle on two. Do whatever it takes."

Bob did not call Gerrie for another week. Although he had made up his mind that he would be willing to up Gerrie's purse, with a sizeable contribution from the man in New York, he thought he would let Gerrie sweat for a bit. It was not in Bob's nature to give up his share of anything lightly, and he knew that Gerrie had nowhere else to go. Gerrie, on the other hand had a different idea. By now he and Angel had figured out what was going on with S and R, Bibi and Lance. S and R had switched allegiance to Lance. Bibi must have offered them one hell of a sweetener. Maybe she had seduced Trevor.

It did not occur to him that seducing Steven, apparently a happily married man, was a better bet. Anyway, Gerrie and Angel thought it might be fun to muddy the waters. Gerrie was the champ. Gerrie held the title and it was for Gerrie to decide how to use it. He was not frightened of Bob's bluff. Yes, he had a contract with Bob, but he could always feign injury or something to get out of it. Why not let S and R think they had a crack at putting on the title fight? He could insist that it was in South Africa. Gerrie could share in the whole pot, not just fight for a fee. The whole idea was very tempting, in regard to the money, but best of all, it would screw Lance and his scheming sister.

The game of telephone Russian roulette between Bob and Gerrie needed to end. Bob was under pressure from Louis Brown to get the fight signed and the Starburst wanted to know what was happening. Reluctantly, Bob phoned Gerrie.

"Have you come to your senses yet, my boy?" asked Bob.

Gerrie quickly hooked Angel into the call. "I was going to ask you the same."

"Well," Bob carried on, "it's very difficult for me to up your purse by $4 million, that's double what our contract says, but –"

Gerrie interrupted. "Well, Bob, let's do it this way. I'll stay at the $4 mil base, but I'll sign a three fight deal with you in which I get 50% of the TV sales. How's that?"

"You can fuck off, Gerrie. You've already signed a contract. It's been lodged with the World Boxing Authority and the WBC. If you renege on it, they'll take your title away and, I'll sue you for damages for millions of dollars. Not only that, since Louis Brown is a party to the agreement, you'll probably get fucking murdered along the way. And, as for the next two fights we already have a contract, which you signed. Now, just in the interests of getting this done, I'll agree to pay you another $3million. Make up your fucking mind if you want a fight in the ring or a fight in the court."

With that he slammed the phone down. Angel giggled. "My goodness, he is upset," she said, "you've kicked him in the purse."

Just for the hell of it Gerrie called Steven at S and R. He told him that he intended to take control of his own fight arrangements in future. He didn't see why he should fight for a purse and let others cream off the television rights anymore.

"Here's the deal," he said to Steven. "Whilst I've got the title, I might as well fight at home; I know we can get a big gate here in a stadium and, as far as TV is concerned, it doesn't matter where I fight. I'll commission you to arrange the fights and I'll give you 20% of the pot. That'll be more money than you've ever earned at this game. There's one condition though, and that's that you rip up your contract with Lance. Tell Bibi she can fuck off and stop interfering in my affairs."

Steven listened. The call came as quite a surprise. He was not sure how to respond.

"I'll have to discuss it with Trevor," he rather meekly offered. "I'll get back to you tomorrow."

"No," said Gerrie, "get back to me tonight, otherwise I'll move to plan B."

Steven did not have to think long about the numbers. He knew that a first defence of the title against Dubois, could sell over 70,000 tickets in a stadium, which would be equal to at least a couple of million dollars, plus the TV rights were probably worth at least 30 million, so 20% of this would be at least $6 million. It would be a real longshot to think that the deal he had with Lance could ever be so rich. It was a no-brainer to dump Lance and go with Gerrie, but there were two problems. Firstly, Angel had almost been right. It wasn't Trevor that Bibi was having an affair with: it was Steven, and his wife did not know anything about it. Screwing Bibi when he was already screwing her could be a problem. Second, he was sure that Gerrie already had a deal with Bob Levin. The last thing Steven wanted was to be involved in a tortuous interference case from Bob in the courts.

Steven sat at his desk and thought about the whole proposition. Finally, after about an hour, he called his partner and explained. Trevor, on hearing of the deal, laughed.

"What a bastard," he said, "this is all to get at Bibi. No, Steven, we can't do this. We have a deal with Lance. He's putting everything he has into coming right. We just can't let him down now, whatever money is at stake."

"Trevor," said Steven, "that's exactly how I feel," he lied. "I'm so pleased you're willing to support my position. I'll call Gerrie back and decline."

Gerrie and Angel were, in a way, relieved that S and R had turned them down. As they mulled over the prospects of a legal battle with Bob Levin and Louis Brown, their confidence in their ability to take on the boxing world began to wane. As Angel sensibly pointed out to her lover, there was little point in being the champion if there was no one around to fight you. All Bob and Louis had to do was sit it out. Apart from Jim London in England, these two controlled all of the opponents worthy of attracting a crowd. If Gerrie pushed his luck too far, he could finish up in a year's time as the only champ in history that never defended his title. So, a couple of days later, Gerrie put in the inevitable call to Bob in Vegas. Final terms were agreed and everyone was friends again.

Bob was used to this sort of rumpus. Despite his bad temper and language during negotiation, he knew it was all just a game; a game about money. The discussion moved from the share of the earnings to the practicalities of training camps and other matters. Bob wanted Gerrie to set up camp in the Nevada desert to do his training. Ostensibly this was to get used to the climate. In practice it was so that the Starburst could maximise the publicity value, by having the world champ training in their back yard. Gerrie, after discussion with Coach Brennan, agreed. In any event, Angel had to depart the love nest for assignments in London. In some ways she was happy to do so. After all, she still rented the lovely flat in Chelsea and, no doubt, her friends at Tramp would be pleased to see her. London was just so much more cosmopolitan than Joburg.

Chapter Sixteen

Bibi now spent most of her life in blue jeans and a series of different coloured tight sweaters. Not many men passed her in the street without staring or sneaking a quick look at her magnificent body. As she reached her mid-twenties she had matured into a spectacular looking woman, not in the perfect beauty queen sense, but her sultry looks oozed sex appeal. She could easily have become a film star. No man, given the chance, could have resisted her. She was careful to whom she offered the chance. She would only use her beauty to enhance her position in the world. The affair with Steven Shultz was not a love match; it was insurance. She had always known that, once her plan for Lance had come to light, Angel might prompt Gerrie to interfere. She could not anticipate how, but thought that it would be smart to make sure that Shultz and Rosenburg were not able to renege on the deal they had struck with her and Lance. Locking Steven up, so to speak, would ensure that he stayed on side.

Since Lance lived primarily out of town in the training site bungalow, out of temptation's way, his little flat was the ideal place to carry on her affair with Steven; out of sight of Mrs. Shultz. Bibi and Lance were not flush with cash, so Bibi could not afford an expensive wardrobe. However, some of the lingerie that she had bought during her time with Gerrie now came in very useful, since that was all she needed when Steven, and sometimes others, came to call.

"Soon," she thought, thinking of a new wardrobe, "maybe a year from now, I will be rolling in dough."

Lance was training hard. He was quite determined to keep really fit. His focus was on one thing, winning the SA heavyweight title. In his view he was perhaps three fights away from it. If Gerrie did not defend the title soon, it would be taken away from him and the title would be up for grabs. There was no way, in Lance's opinion, that Gerrie would interrupt his world title defence preparations to defend the national title. According to Steven and Trevor, if Lance won three more fights against ranked South African heavyweights, it would be viable to mount a challenge for the vacant title. To do this, he would have to achieve a ranking in the country of number two or three. That meant he had to fight and beat at least two other contenders ranked in the top five in South Africa. No promoter ever wants to tell their boxer that his is a certainty to win any bout, because that often leads to a trailing off in training and fitness levels, so Trevor had been careful not to let Lance think his next fights were mere formalities. Although Lance was smart enough to realise that his success was also good for S and R, he still believed he needed to train hard. And, in any event, if he got through this phase of his career, he would have to be super fit to beat his old friend Gerrie.

The training camp was set up for a life of hardship. The old cottage was sparingly furnished and quite drab. It was not large and so, housing three big men, as it did, was quite a crush. S and R had provided an African lady to cook and clean. She lived in a secondary hut in the yard; her name was Serena. Although the food she cooked was

Peter Venison

basic, it was nourishing. Lance had given her a cookbook with recipes for athletes in training. Serena never ate any of the food that she cooked for the sparring men, preferring instead to eat her mealie meal outside in her hut. Trevor had arranged a coach/trainer to take charge of the training routines. Jake, the trainer, had been on the scene for many years in South Africa and had coached many champions at all weight levels. He was good, but also smart enough to know that Lance probably knew as much about the sport as anyone, so his role was as much as an observer than a teacher, giving feedback as he thought it was necessary or useful. Alcohol and other harmful substances were banned from the site. Instead, Jake arrived every day with a bag full of healthy drinks. None of these basic conditions bothered Lance. After all, he had just spent a year in a prison cell. From time to time, Bibi would come to visit. Lance had to smile at the way the other men ogled her. They may have been happy to exist on dietary drinks, but the sight of Lance's sister reminded them of what they were missing.

Lance's fourth fight as a pro was against the number nine ranked South African, who also happened to be a white man. Freddie Jury was tall; six feet, four inches tall. Although he was a heavyweight, his body looked quite lean. He had been on the professional circuit for three years, notching up 12 wins and two losses. None of his wins had been by knockout, but both his losses had. Lance figured that he could not have much of a punch and that he also had a glass jaw.

The fight took place in the hotel ballroom at the Castle Hotel in Pretoria, in front of a crowd of about 200 punters. It was broadcast live on South African Television. At first Lance was a bit flummoxed by his wiry opponent, who never seemed to be within reach. Each time Lance took a swing at the glass jaw, it was never there when the punch arrived. The fight was scheduled for six rounds, but after three rounds of frustration, Lance started to get a little wild. On his stool, in the corner, between round three and four, Jake earned his money.

"Slow down, Lance. Stop chasing him around. Wait for him to come to you. Then smash him on the counter. He won't last another round."

Lance listened. He was now mature enough to take advice. The fourth round started with nobody throwing a punch. Emboldened, and thinking that Lance may have shot his bolt, Freddie moved forward with a lunging right hand. It never landed. Lance countered with a ferocious left uppercut. Freddie Jury hit the deck and did not get up until, through the mugginess of his brain, he heard the referee count "ten".

Lance was now four and zero, but, more important, every boxing fan in the country had seen the cop that killed a black man fight. The fans eagerly awaited his next match. Maybe, they began to dream, South Africa might just have two champions. Over at the Starburst Hotel, Vegas, Gerrie was not able to pick up the telecast of the fight, but Strom had been relating it to him as he watched it on the television. The first thing Gerrie did was to send his old friend a telegram.

"Congratulations, my friend. When you graduate, I'll be waiting."

Las Vegas was an eye opener to Gerrie. His normal training camps had been in places of relative seclusion. Now, under the contract with Starburst, he was required to train in the grounds of the hotel. A huge tent had been erected near the ninth hole of the golf course. To keep it cool the tent had been laden with fans and air conditioning units, which clattered away incessantly. The entrance and surrounds to the training camp were heavily policed with burly security guards, but even so, there always seemed to be a crowd around the training ring. It appeared that every punter in Las Vegas wanted to see the champ up close. After a few days of this, Gerrie complained to Bob, who promised to get the Starburst to be more vigilant with their policing. Nothing changed. On the fifth day of the training schedule, Gerrie refused to leave his suite.

"If they don't clear the tent and its surrounds from anyone but my team, I'm going back to South Africa," he screamed down the phone at Bob.

"I'll do my best," said Bob, "but you must realise, Gerrie, that you're the champ now. People want to see you. They want a part of you. It goes with the territory."

"Well, I'm not going to put up with it. If this carries on, I'm going to train in Los Angeles. Fuck the Starburst Hotel."

Bob loved controversy before a fight. If there wasn't any, he would invent some. A big row about the training facility was the sort of thing that the sports writers thrived on. It all helped sell tickets and boost TV audiences. Nevertheless, Bob had been around long enough to know when a controversy was getting out of control, at which point one had to switch to a different story. In Las Vegas, this was not too hard to achieve. First time visitors to Vegas are always overwhelmed by the sheer brashness of the place. There was nowhere else on the planet like Las Vegas, and particularly the Strip on which the Starburst was located. The Strip was humming with electricity, in the form of coloured lights, flashing signs, exploding volcanoes, roaring illuminated waterfalls, blaring music, and thousands upon thousands of twinkling slot machines. There was no day and no night; one merged into the other. The whole place was designed to entertain and to seduce visitors into spending money. Temptation was everywhere, whether it came from the lure of winning money or the lure of pretty young flesh.

Angel and Gerrie had agreed that she should stay in London whilst he trained for the fight, only flying to the States a few days before, when effectively Gerrie would be winding down his preparations. Like the lovers they were, they were in constant contact with each other on the telephone. However, the time difference between London and Las Vegas was ten hours, which sometimes made communication quite difficult. It seemed that either he was in the middle of a training session or she was in the middle of a fashion shoot, so private tete a tetes were proving difficult. Nor was the press helping. Pictures kept appearing in the US papers of Angel, in skimpy disco gear, in the arms of handsome young men at Tramp and other London nightspots. Similarly, the London press kept running stories of Las Vegas showgirls draping themselves all over the champ. Angel was quick to explain to Gerrie that the pictures were just part of a fashion shoot or were old stock and, likewise, Gerrie had to explain that the pictures she had seen were fake. Both explanations were accepted, but not without a teeny speck of doubt, from both sides. These things can play on the mind. Doubt can grow bigger by the day and the constant need for denial becomes irritating.

Angel decided that she had to do something. She explained to Tony that she was dropping everything to go to Vegas; her man needed her. Tony was cross, because her departure would interfere with contracted work, but he had no choice. She did not tell Gerrie that she was coming. When she reached the Starburst, Gerrie was in the marquee, training. With a bit of sweet talk at the desk, Angel obtained the key to his suite and let herself in. She changed into the sheerest of negligees that she had bought for the occasion at La Perla in Sloane Street and, when she heard him fiddling with the door key, draped herself seductively across the super king-sized bed.

No further training took place for the rest of the day, nor the next. Brennan was very worried when Gerrie did not show up for work. The press had a field day of speculation. Bets on Dubois poured into the bookmakers. But Angel was right. She had figured that her gentle giant would be fretting about her in London, and the last thing a boxer needs as preparation for a fight is worry. Angel was the best tonic that Gerrie could have taken, and take her, he did. By the time Gerrie emerged from his suite, on the evening of the following day, rumours in the press about his condition were running like wildfire. With only a week to go before the fight, what had happened to the champ? Why was he AWOL? The fact that he emerged with Miss World was a news story itself. The Starburst management was delighted. The press had their story for the day.

The fight itself did not match up to the event in Dubai. The ring had been set up in the car park of the Starburst, and 30,000 erector set seats had been built on bleachers around it. The hotel's showroom staff had a field day with special effects. Before the big fight the whole temporary stadium erupted with a sound and light show that almost rivalled the opening of an Olympic Games. Aretha James, the world-famous blues singer, gave a mind shattering rendering of both the American and the South African anthems. It seemed from the noise that at least half of the seats had found their way into South African hands, judging from their heartfelt contribution to the singing of their anthem. Gerrie had no idea so many of his countrymen had travelled so far to support him. It brought tears to his eyes and a determination in his heart that he must not let them down. Angel, as usual, was asked to walk her walk in the ring, which, by now, she could do with aplomb: a mixture of beauty, pride and sex appeal. The fact that the South Africans could cheer for a champ and Miss World on the same occasion filled them with pride for their little country. It all added to the drama of the night. Even Bob Levin and Louis Brown had never quite experienced such enthusiasm before a fight.

It was a pity, therefore, that the fight did not live up to the expectations that had been created following the previous meeting of the two big men. A superbly fit and confident Gerrie stopped Dubois in the third round. Half way through the first round, Gerrie had sent his opponent to the floor with a flurry of hard punches ending with his famous left hook. Again, in the second round Gerrie caught his man flush on the chin, and down he went again. Since the rules state that the fight is over if one of the fighters is knocked down three times, it was now only a matter of time. Dubois was pleased that he had squeezed the extra purse out of Levin and Brown. He had quite decided that this was to be his pension and this, his retirement fight. He also had a sizeable, but untraceable, bet on Gerrie. Could it be that Louis did too? In any event his career as a boxer was now over. His face would probably appear on barbeque adverts for decades to come. That extra couple of million had just doubled.

As for Bob, he was now in control of the heavyweight division, and he meant to keep it that way. He needed to think things through carefully; he could not afford to let Louis back into the frame, even though he controlled so many of the likely challengers. This situation would need some finessing, but, for now, Bob put aside his scheming and went to the after-fight party, a very happy, and very rich, man. The Starburst certainly knew how to throw a party. The pool area had been roped off. A stage had been erected and tables for eight had been placed around the pool deck. Only the participants in the fighters' parties were allowed entry plus, of course, the hotel's special guests, including many celebrities. The beauty of an event in Vegas was its proximity to Los Angeles, and specifically Beverly Hills and Hollywood, home of many movie stars. This ensured that if you wanted a sprinkling of stardust at your party in Vegas, it was not difficult to achieve. In this case, the sprinkling had been a deluge. The pool area was dotted with famous faces, many of whom were household names throughout the world. Angel just loved it, and, since she was attached to the champ, there were many famous names on the guest list that also wanted to meet her.

There were however people in attendance who were not exactly guests: the owners of the Starburst. For many years the hotels and casinos on the Vegas strip had been operating under the shadow of the Mob. The casino business was made for organised crime and so much skimming went on that the tax man's share of huge gambling wins was severely eroded. Nothing much moved in Vegas without feeling the hand of the Mafia, whether it was the company that delivered the fruit and the milk, to the purveyors of liquor, to the very heart of the gaming control board, the Mob would be there. In some cases, they just preyed on businesses, but in others they actually owned them. The Starburst was one of those. Unbeknown to Gerrie, but of course, not to Bob Levin, the Starburst hotel was owned, through various levels of shell companies, by one of the most powerful Mafia families in the West: the Marconi brothers. Both Giancarlo Marconi and his brother Sammy loved the boxing business. Apart from the sheer joy they got, like many men, from the genuine competition involved in a good fight, the results were a mobster's dream. They were so easy to manipulate. You only needed the fighters, or the judges or the referee, to be on your team and, not necessarily all of them at the same time. Gerrie could not know that his hosts at the hotel had contributed to Mr. Dubois' retirement package. Nor could he have forecast what would happen next in his career.

The pool party was a spectacular success. The huge high-rise Starburst Hotel had been fitted out with fireworks, and an unseen wire had been rigged up to the roof of the hotel, some sixty stories up, and connected to a steel platform near the pool. A stage had been constructed poolside on which a cabaret consisting of three of the most famous vocalists in the world performed together, something they had never done before. At the climax of their show the fireworks on every one of the hotel fascia's windows were simultaneously lighted and a waterfall of flame engulfed the entire building for fully five minutes. Then, with much fanfare from the band, illuminated by the flames, the sole figure of Anita Giovanni, the slender ballet dancer, dressed as an angel, appeared, gently sliding down the wire. Even the much-partied celebrities in the crowd were impressed.

As the cabaret ended, the small dapper figure of Giancarlo Marconi was standing next to Gerrie. "We haven't met," said Marconi, as he held out his hand. "I am Giancarlo. I own this hotel. I wanted to extend my welcome to you and to congratulate you, – and of course the beautiful Miss World. We are honoured to have had you here as our guests."

Gerrie, still blown away by the firework display, managed to politely respond with his thanks for the hotel's hospitality.

"This is not the time to talk," said Marconi. "Breakfast tomorrow? I would like you to meet my brother Sammy. He is the one in charge of this business. Shall we say 11am in the Patio Room? And no word of this to Bob Levin."

Gerrie nodded. He had no problem in meeting the owners of this pile, but what was this business about Bob? Something was not right.

It did not take long for Gerrie to find out. And, it did not take long for his moment of glory in defeating Dubois again, to evaporate. Before the coffee had hit the bottom of their cups, the Marconis came to the point.

"We would like to be involved in your next fight," started Giancarlo. "That is to say, completely involved, but in a strictly confidential way."

Gerrie listened, with a growing sense of unease.

"We will select your next opponent. He will be a man that is easy to beat, so there will be nothing for you to fear. The only thing is that you will not beat him. The result will be a surprise, not just to you and your camp, but to the whole betting world. But, don't worry, Gerrie, you will not lose your title for long. There will be a rematch and you will win."

Gerrie did not know what to say. He no longer wanted the plate of fried breakfast that he had ordered.

"Come on, Gerrie, eat up your food. You need to keep fit," quipped Sammy, "We are going to be a team from now on."

With that, both men stood and made as if to leave. "You will be hearing from us soon. Bob Levin will be in touch. Enjoy your breakfast. But, don't mention this chat to anyone else, including your pretty lady. You wouldn't want anything to happen to her, would you?"

With that they swept out of the room in their immaculate suits. Various Italian waiters nodded in deference as they passed. Gerrie was no longer hungry. He just sat for a while, in silence, hardly noticing several other diners who waved and nodded in his direction as a sign of their appreciation of the events the night before. Someone else had just taken control of his life.

Chapter Seventeen

Gerrie was frightened: frightened for himself, but also for Angel. He certainly did not want to be held captive by the Mafia. He had seen too many films to know that this was not first prize. He was also angry that his moment of glory and pride should be so rudely shattered. As well as the fear of what might happen going forward, he was shaken about what might have happened in the past. Had he really outfought Dubois? Had Dubois taken a dive for money? Was Gerrie really invincible? And what role did Bob Levin have in all of this? Did Bob know that Dubois was in the pay of the Mafia? Or was this all lies? Maybe the Mob had nothing to do with the last fight, maybe they were just bluffing?

Angel, of course, noticed Gerrie's sudden change of mood. At first, she thought it might be a reaction to the build up to the fight. Then, she worried that he had cooled on her; although actually, he seemed to need her more than ever. But something was wrong. She tried asking him but this got nowhere. He just said that he was tired. Wasn't that what she had heard from Bibi about him? Was this the beginning of the end of their relationship? Suddenly, what had been a wonderful happy and exciting time had turned into a bit of a nightmare. She didn't know what to do. Her mother Sally had returned to South Africa. The only other person she really knew in Vegas was Bob Levin, but he hardly seemed like the sort of person she could share her concerns with.

So, she decided to just sit it out. She wasn't quite sure why they were still hanging around in Vegas. After a very short while the allure of the neon lights wears off. Gerrie told her that he had to stay there until the next fight had been sorted out with Bob. He said that it may be necessary to remain in America for a while, particularly if the next defence was going to be soon. But Angel had contractual obligations back in London. Tony was constantly on the phone, encouraging her to return and Jane Michaels was threatening to sue her for breach of contract. Gerrie seemed okay with her leaving, even, it seemed, encouraging it. This worried her even more. Eventually, after almost three weeks in limbo, Angel could wait no longer. Gerrie had been clinging but not loving; at least, he had not made love to her. Something was wrong, but if he wouldn't talk about it what could she do? So, it was a very worried Angel that left Vegas for London and a very depressed World Champion that stayed.

Back in South Africa, Lance had had his fifth and sixth fight in short order. In fact, he had two fights in one evening. This was strictly against all of the advice of the South African boxing authorities, but he did it anyway. Trevor Rosenburg counselled against it, citing the wrath of the boxing board of control, but actually, both he and Steven rather liked the idea of "their" man taking on two challengers in the same evening. The whole thing, of course, had been Bibi's idea and she was right on the money. The double header attracted a massive television audience as well as a full house in the stadium. Steven had also managed to sell the television feed, via Bob, to CBS in the USA. The whole thing was so unusual that it attracted huge interest, including that, of course, of a brooding Gerrie.

Needless to say, Lance won both fights, but only just. The first event was a ten rounder which only lasted for three. Lance's opponent had the misfortune to meet Lance's hammer blow of a right hook. It would have been better for Lance if the second fight had taken place immediately after, when he was all warmed up and raring to go. But S and R had decided that it might be smart to let Lance have a break between bouts, and there might have been circumstances that this would have been sensible. As it happened the cooling off period between the two bouts did not work in favour of Lance. By the time he climbed back into the ring he was feeling sluggish. In the first round he walked into a fine punch from his opponent that sent him to the floor. It had been a long time since Lance had been knocked over. The crowd was worried for him. It seemed that everyone in the arena wanted the man to win twice and here he was on his back.

The shock was what Lance needed. From here on he boxed cautiously, but finally, in the sixth round he had his moment and sent the other man flying. Lance had made boxing history. He was now a hot property and Steven and Trevor started clamouring for a crack at the South African title. The press dubbed him "the White Assassin". The back of his track suit was decorated with a gun.

In Las Vegas, Bob Levin was having a difficult time. Over many years he had learned to live with the Mob. He did not get involved in their criminal activities and, indeed, did not wish to even know what they did. But, from time to time, they moved into his patch of business and he had been sensible enough to learn how to accommodate them. Like all smart gangsters, they knew when to start and when to stop their activities. There was no point in killing off all of the operators in the businesses from which they skimmed. Boxing was the same; they would dip in and pull out as it suited them, but they never crippled the people that fed them. In the main, Bob could carry on his business with little or no interference, but from time to time, they asked him to accommodate them with a special arrangement or piece of knowledge that could enrich them. Now, after the Van der Merwe/Dubois fight they had come calling. Bob was supposed to match Gerrie up against a no hoper. The odds would then be massively in favour of Gerrie, who, up until this point in his professional career, had never been beaten. Bob's problem was that, as always, Gerrie had insisted in his contract that he should have the right of refusal in terms of opponents. Bob was sure that if he proposed that Gerrie fight the no hoper, that the Mob had suggested, Gerrie would just refuse. Bob knew that he would have to finesse the matter carefully. He would explain to Gerrie that taking on a low-ranked opponent was a good tactical move, an easy payday after two tough ones.

Bob needn't have worried. When Bob came up with the name Mickey McMurphy, currently ranked 14 in the world, Gerrie already knew why. All Gerrie wanted to know from Bob was that, should he lose to McMurphy, he must be entitled to an automatic rematch within three months. "I need to think about it," was all Gerrie could say when the situation was laid out for him by Bob. "Give me a couple of days."

Gerrie thought long and hard about taking the McMurphy fight. If he was going to throw a fight, for his own self-esteem, he would rather do so with a worthy opponent, but that, of course, would defeat the object of the fixed fight in the first place. What the Mob was looking for were good odds. The better the opponent would be, the worse the odds. Gerrie knew that much. He decided to come clean with Bob. He had been in the game for a very long time. Surely this would not be a unique situation for Bob? He also decided that if he was going to shatter his reputation of being invincible, he might as well get rich in the process. Bob could show him how. Gerrie Van der Merwe was about to turn from athlete to entrepreneur. From now on he would manage his talent, not for pride, but purely for profit. "And, one day," he promised himself, "I will get my revenge on these fucking Italians."

Once he had come to see the game as a business, rather than a sport, Gerrie's mood lightened. He called Angel in London and told her how much he loved her. He told her that he was going to take an easy fight, just for a break, until the guys could work out the next big money opportunity. He also told her that Bob had managed to secure some good sponsorship for the next fight in Ireland, because Mickey McMurphy apparently had plenty of cousins there and a good turnout could be expected. It was also far away from Las Vegas and the Italians. As soon as things were signed and settled, he told Angel, he would fly to Europe to set up a training camp; that way he could be with her, be it in Dublin or London.

Bob was coy about telling Gerrie how to bet; he had always been cautious in conniving with his boxers and he was not about to start. His reaction was to scoff at the idea that Gerrie might lose the fight. He was too long in the tooth to be making any admissions that he could predict the outcome of a fight, so Gerrie would have to make enquiries elsewhere. Gerrie was reluctant to involve Coach Brennan in anything shady. It was far better that Brennan would be taken by surprise at Gerrie's intended lacklustre performance. Brennan was so proud that his man had never been beaten. Gerrie knew that he was about to be devastated. Gerrie made a list in his head of all of the people he knew in Vegas who could place a bet on the upcoming fight, but in each case, he would be putting himself in a position where, sometime, somewhere, this information could come back to bite him. No, there was only one person that he could absolutely trust, and that was Angel.

When Gerrie reached London, he literally burst into Angel's flat in Chelsea. To her delight he was like a new man. The sullen, worried, man that she had left in Vegas had gone. Instead, he was bounding with energy, and it was not long before he proved it. Angel had missed his sexual advances in Vegas; she had also been on her own in London for a few weeks. Despite numerous opportunities in that time, she had remained constant to her Gerrie. She had thought about him each night and that had sustained her. Now, once again, her big strong, but gentle, man was in her arms. Nothing else got done that day.

The following days were busy for both of the lovers. Gerrie had to begin preparations for his training camp, which he and Brennan decided could be in Dublin, at least for the three weeks before the fight. Angel was in the middle of a lingerie shoot for the Harrods catalogue. Knowing what was ahead, Gerrie did not feel the urgency in getting back in the training ring, so, much to Angel's surprise, he seemed quite happy to spend late nights at Tramp with her and her London friends. Then, one night, when they had decided to stay in and relax Gerrie tackled the thorny issue of his next fight. Gerrie took Angel by the hand and led her to the couch.

"There is something I want to tell you," he began. Angel's heart skipped a beat.

"He's going to propose to me," she immediately thought but he carried on.

"What I am going to tell you will surprise you, my love. It might even shock you. But I want you to listen carefully and try to understand."

Disappointed, Angel, nevertheless, sat quietly and listened. Gerrie did not hold anything back. He ran through the whole scenario with the Italians and the awful position he found himself in. He told her how desperately sorry he was that she might be harmed, if he did not do their bidding. Angel listened intently, and, as he spoke, squeezed his hand in support.

"Nobody, absolutely nobody else, knows about this," he continued, "and they must not."

Suddenly, the reason for Gerrie's distant behaviour in Vegas became clear to Angel. She was not frightened; she was relieved. But Angel's first, and understandable, reaction was that Gerrie must not give way to this threat. He must not be fearful for her safety. She could look after herself, and so on. However, the more he described the menace that was the Mob, the more she could see his, and now their, predicament. Gerrie described his sleepless nights as he wrestled with the idea of her safety but also the shame of losing his unbeaten record. He then explained how he had come to believe that none of this was important. He had decided that boxing for him was no longer a sport. He had proved that he was the champion in the sport. From now on, it would be a business and, in conducting the business, there could be times when it would be smarter to lose and get rich, rather than win, and just get glory. Angel argued in vain that this was not the real Gerrie speaking.

Gerrie agreed, but added, "No, you are right, but this is the new Gerrie, and this one is the sensible one."

Finally, after an hour or so of discussion and thought, Angel, sadly, saw the sense in his conclusions. Then, for Gerrie, came the hardest part.

"Now, my love, this is how we get rich. You are going to figure out how to place a huge bet on me losing the next fight, or rather, on McMurphy winning it. When only two people are contesting something, the odds at the bookies are always close to evens. In this case, I will be such a certainty to win that we should be able to get at least four to one on McMurphy. We, or rather you, are going to place a million dollar bet on the Irishman. We just need to make sure that nobody knows the bet has come from you or, even worse, me. I am going to find out how we do that. If I am going to lose my self-respect, I need to be paid big for it."

It was a troubled Angel that wrapped her body around his in bed that night, but one that understood what a sacrifice her man was taking to protect her. She loved him for that.

Chapter Eighteen

The sporting press was quite derisory about Gerrie's choice of opponent. As much as Bob Levin tried to build up the validity of McMurphy's challenge, everybody knew that this was going to be an easy fight for the undefeated Van der Merwe. "Van the man", as he was now known in America, was taking a rest. Some accused him of taking the piss. As a result, it was quite difficult for Bob's public relations people to drum up much interest in the proceedings and the television companies who were bidding to screen the event were insisting that Gerrie made it last for at least eight rounds, so that they had time to screen their ads. Bob had been quite right to produce the show in Dublin; it was about the only place in the world where anyone had heard of McMurphy and, therefore, a good live turnout was expected.

Coach Brennan was less than pleased with Gerrie's training regime. He seemed to be putting in very little effort to prepare for the fight. This was completely unlike the Gerrie that Brennan had known for so many years. Quite rightly he admonished Gerrie for his lack of effort and enthusiasm, but his strong words of warning seemed to have little effect. On top of this, Gerrie kept packing up and flying off to London to be with his lover, something he had never done before whilst in strict training. Even the press corps noticed that the champion seemed to be taking things a little easy, and one or two hinted about this in their columns. Nevertheless, Gerrie was never far from being fit. If he had not been putting the effort into the training ring, it did not seem to be apparent from his body condition when he finally climbed into the ring on the night of the fight.

Without sharing with Brennan, Gerrie had developed a plan for losing. He would try not to hit his opponent too hard, but he would also do his best to avoid getting hit himself. He did not want any damage inflicted in the loss, because he knew that he would need to be on top form for the comeback event, and thereafter. He decided that he would wait until McMurphy actually landed a good punch and then feign that it was considerably more powerful than it actually was. He would go down, and stay down, until the count of ten. He did not care if the punch came before the six rounds that the TV company and Bob had requested; that was their problem. He just wanted the Mob to be happy and let him have his life back.

The arena was very noisy. About 20,000 Irishmen had paid big bucks to support their man. Many jugs of Guiness had been consumed. A handful of South Africans had showed up, presumably those already living or working in Dublin, but the crowd was overwhelmingly pro the Irishman. Although Angel was there, she declined to step into the ring before the fight to do her Miss World thing. Under the circumstances, and, knowing what she knew, it did not seem appropriate.

The first round was even. Nobody really landed anything of note. McMurphy was clearly somewhat intimidated by Gerrie, but, as Gerrie hardly hit him in the first round, McMurphy became a little more proactive in the second. Gerrie landed a few light scoring punches to keep up appearances, but nothing that bothered

McMurphy. In the third round, the Irishman, now full of confidence, landed a moderately hard left on Gerrie's unguarded chin. Gerrie seized the moment and slid to the canvas. The crowd went wild. The count began. Each second seemed like an eternity to Gerrie, feigning confusion as he lay on the canvas. The count reached six. Coach Brennan was yelling at his man to come around.

Suddenly, something in Gerrie's brain snapped. "What the fuck are you doing?" he asked himself.

Seven, Eight…

"I can't do this. Fuck them. Fuck them all."

At the count of nine, Gerrie stood up. He didn't stagger to his feet. He shot up like a jack in the box. The referee wiped his gloves and Gerrie started to fight. By the end of the round McMurphy was a bloody mess. He did gamely come out for the next round but, before it was over, his corner threw in the towel to prevent him taking further punishment.

Gerrie was still undefeated. Angel did not know whether to laugh or cry. All she knew was that from now on, her life was in danger. But she loved Gerrie as a winner. She knew it was just too much to expect him to lose. Now, she could admit, that despite their plan, she had not been able to place the bet against her man. She had tried, but when it came to handing over the money, she could not bring herself to do it. The thought of Gerrie throwing a fight was just inconceivable; her Gerrie would never do that, no matter what he rationalised about being a businessman. So, when Gerrie got to his feet at the count of nine, a huge weight lifted from Angel. She had been so worried about telling Gerrie that she could not bring herself to bet against him. Now, she knew that her instincts had been right.

Gerrie gamely accepted all of the normal adulation that came from a win. The crowded ring, the clamour and hubbub of reporters and cameramen, the happy faces of the punters, immediately enveloped him, but all he wanted to do was get back to his dressing room.

"What the hell have I just done?" he thought to himself. "Am I fucking mad, or what?"

He could see Angel through the crowd. She should be looking worried, but, instead, she looked the picture of happiness. She blew him a kiss and mouthed "Well done. I love you." This was not the stance of a frightened woman. This was a woman who was proud of her man, and nothing else mattered. When they reached the hotel suite that night, it was the first chance they had to talk without a crowd of well-wishers buzzing around.

"Well," said Gerrie as he sunk into the plush sofa, "I guess that's how you throw away a million dollars."

"It's also how you keep your pride, intact," countered Angel, as she slid into his arms. "Anyway, we've got two reasons to celebrate," she continued. "Your win tonight, and my terrible disobedience." Gerrie looked puzzled.

"I didn't know how to tell you, my love, but, when it came to placing the bet, I just couldn't bring myself to do it. Please never ask me to do that again. There's no way in the world, I could bet on you, my hero, to lose. I would have rather shot myself."

Gerrie looked aghast, then, as the realisation that Angel had just saved him a million dollars sunk in, a huge smile spread across his face. It was not just the money, he was thinking, but the fact that Angel's love for him was too great for her to bet against him. Also, he realised, his Angel understood him better than he did himself. Gerrie gave Angel the warmest hug, then got up from the chair, and reached for the bottle of champagne, a gift from management, which was sitting in melting ice on the bar. He popped the cork and poured two glasses, handing one to Angel.

"Angel, my love," he began, "will you marry me? I haven't got a ring to give you, but I do have a million dollars."

Angel put down her glass, pulled him towards her and whispered, "Yes, my love. I want you, not a million dollars."

Bob Levin had a hard time pretending to be pleased. He had made a little money on the promotion but lost all of it and more at the bookies. He was so thankful that he had not shared his knowledge about the Mob with Gerrie. He was sure that Gerrie had been instructed to throw the fight; so sure, that he had risked half a million on McMurphy. Naturally he had to congratulate Gerrie in front of all the fans, but inside he was seething.

"What was the matter with this moron?" he thought to himself. "Doesn't he know what the Mob will do to him now? Or worse, what they will do to his pretty Angel. Christ knows what will happen next."

Any minute now he expected a call from the Italians. But it was strangely and ominously silent.

Bob was staying at the same hotel as Gerrie and Angel. He was worried when they did not appear for breakfast; then, even more so, when there was no sight of them by 2pm. and the line to the suite was blocked. Bob was keen to get a flight back to the US, but he thought he should meet up with Gerrie before to talk about the future. He was also worried that the Mob had already reached them. As he sat in the small hotel lobby making calls, who should he see, bounding up the steps to the hotel, but Angel and Gerrie, with smiles as wide as the lobby itself. Angel let go of Gerrie and came running up to Bob.

"Look, Bob," she squealed excitedly, "Take a look at this."

She waved her hand with a huge diamond ring on it in front of him that she and Gerrie had just picked out in the jewellers nearby.

"Gerrie and I are to marry. You will come, won't you?"

What could Bob say? Gerrie had just cost him hundreds of thousands of dollars as well as put all of their lives at risk, but here, in front of him, was the picture of happiness.

"For how long?," Bob wondered. "Of course, I'll come," said Bob, giving Angel a big squeeze, "nothing would please me more."

Later, back up in Gerrie's suite, Bob got serious. "I don't want to know the details, Gerrie, and it's not really any of my business, but I suspect that by winning that fight, you have pissed off the Mob. You realise what that means."

"I don't give a fuck," replied Gerrie. "I'm not going to be told what to do by them, nor anyone. They can go fuck themselves."

"You realise, Gerrie, that you many have put Angel at risk," said Bob.

"You know what," said Gerrie, "I reckon that we're of more use to them alive, than dead. You wait and see."

Bob could not understand what, exactly, Gerrie was getting at but, for the moment, he chose to ignore it and move on.

"Let's talk about the next fight, Gerrie. Let's move on. I'll leave you to fight the Mob. Good luck with that! Now, in regards to your next fight, I was thinking that it should be against this young guy on Louis' roster, Sammy the Slammer. I think that is a fight that Vegas will…"

Gerrie did not let him finish. "I'm not fighting in Vegas again, Never, ever!"

"But," started Bob, but he didn't get very far. He could see that Gerrie meant what he said and, of course, Bob could see why. "Best to let the dust settle," thought Bob and stopped mid-sentence.

"I'll tell you what my next fight is going to be," said Gerrie, quite determined to take control of his own destiny. "If Lance Hermanus wins the South African title, my next fight will be against him – in South Africa. We'll attract the biggest crowd ever."

"But," interrupted Bob, "the television sales won't be so good, without an American or Brit in the ring."

"I don't give a fuck," said Gerrie, "I want to fight at home. I want to train at home, I want to live at home, I want to marry at home, I want to have a family at home, in fact, I want to go home!" Bob stopped arguing. He knew there was no point.

Chapter Nineteen

Lance Hermanus was now on a roll. The publicity that surrounded his "double header" had been enormous, not just in South Africa but around the world. Boxing magazines and many mainstream newspapers had carried articles about Lance. The SA boxing board of control had initially threatened to strip him of his ranking, but, in the end, it turned out that he had not contravened any laws or regulations that prohibited fighting twice in one evening. In fact, as Bibi had researched, there was no such prohibition, simply because nobody had ever thought that anyone would be so daft as to attempt it. The more fuss and debate about it, Bibi had learned, the better. Money was pouring in for endorsements. It seemed that everyone wanted a piece of Lance. Steven and Trevor were delighted; they were so happy with their 25%.

Lance, the White Assassin, remained the number one challenger for the vacant SA Heavyweight Championship. It was just a question now of S and R coming up with a suitable opponent. Lance was keen that this should be a black man; Bibi did not object. She thought there was always good mileage in having a white man beat up a black. The SA Boxing Board thought that they had the right to nominate the opponents for a vacant title and they suggested to S and R that the right opponent would be Titus Scwharz. His name would infer that he was black, but, in fact, he was a white Afrikaans miner, and a mountain of a man. When Lance refused to fight Titus, the Board members were not happy, but they knew that double header Lance was the man the public wanted to see in the ring, so they deferred to his opinion and proposed the highest ranked black man, Ironman Obangu, on the understanding that the first defence of the title would be against Scwharz. So, it was all settled and arrangements for the contest commenced.

Gerrie Van der Merwe was now back home in Johannesburg. Angel, who was getting towards the end of her contractual obligations for Miss World, had joined him, following a promotional tour of North America. Gerrie had been nervous about her safety there, given the threats from the Italians. He had insisted that Miss World Inc. beefed up their security, so that Angel was guarded at all times. Neither he nor Angel explained exactly why they were concerned for Angel's security, but Jane Michael did not want to take any risks. She just assumed that they were nervous about anti-apartheid protesters. The last thing she needed was an attack on Miss World; she had always prided herself on being so protective of her contestants, many of whom were young girls away from home for the first time. So, for much of the tour, Angel shared a hotel suite with Jane. The newly engaged Angel did not object to this set up, especially since she had no intentions of engaging in any activity that would require privacy. All had gone well. Gradually, Angel and Gerrie began to feel that the threats from the Italians were empty. It did seem strange however that Gerrie had not heard a thing from the mobsters. After all, he had cost them a bucket full of money.

Gerrie had not said a word to anyone about his intentions regarding his defence of the World Title, neither had his promoter, Bob, who was still hoping that

Gerrie would change his mind about fighting in South Africa. For Bob it was a colossal pain in the neck to have to organise a fight so far from home; he was also convinced that it would be a difficult "sell" to the TV companies.

If Lance should win the South African title, it was Gerrie's intention to announce, there and then, that he would give him a crack at the World belt, no matter what pressure he came under from the WBC or the WBA. What better place to announce that fight then in the ring after Lance's triumph?

So, the big night arrived. S and R had chosen the Rand Stadium to host the event. This was a little used rugby stadium in the southern suburbs of Johannesburg. It had a capacity of 30,000. The seats had sold like hot cakes, with very little promotional activity or advertising. Lance was now a household name in South Africa, where news travelled fast. Ironman was a potentially dangerous opponent for Lance; he carried on his back the weight of nearly 40 million South African blacks who would be happy to see the murderer, Lance, get beaten up by a fellow black. On the other hand, not too many blacks could afford a ticket to the event, meaning that 90% of the crowd would be white fans, most of whom had come to regard the White Assassin as a hero. Lance was up for the fight. Since leaving prison, he had kept himself extremely fit and his only real socialising had been to visit the television and radio studios where he was a frequent and controversial guest. Lance's cheerful personality and outspoken right wing views made him a popular guest on talk shows and in the press. Lance knew just how far he could go with, sometimes, outrageous comments, that appealed to a vast swathe of the white audience. The blacks, on the other hand, hated him, especially when he persistently called his opponent "Tinman", instead of Ironman, whenever he was interviewed. Millions of black citizens of South Africa were hopeful that their Ironman could, once and for all, put a stop to Lance's mouth, but only a handful of them could afford a ticket to watch. One such spectator was Daniel Buthelezi, the proprietor of Miss Africa South, whom he proudly displayed for all to see.

Bibi, of course, was present, wearing an exceptionally tight dress and high heels. So was Steven's wife, who thought that Bibi looked like a tart.

Gerrie and Angel were guests of honour, Gerrie in a slick Armani suit and Angel, looking radiant, in pale blue silk pants and top. Bob Levin had stayed in Vegas. He did not know that it was Gerrie's intention to announce his next fight, should Lance be victorious.

The fight, over twelve rounds, was a good one. Ironman certainly had learned how to box and move, and, with his huge bulk, he looked the part. His well-toned body rippled with muscle and, at six feet six, he towered over Lance. Both fighters started cautiously, each aware that the other packed a pretty hefty punch. If anything, however, Lance was the quicker of the two men and, in the early rounds, scored well with a constant pounding of Ironman's ribs or his protective arms. Ironman, on the other hand, was punching down on Lance and seemed to be having trouble finding his range. For the first six rounds, neither fighter landed a really killer blow, but most judges would have put Lance ahead on points. In the seventh round, Lance hit Ironman with a very hard and very low blow. Ironman winced with pain and complained to the referee, who stopped the fight momentarily, and warned Lance. Moments later, Lance did it again. This time the referee stopped the fight again and ordered the three judges to deduct a point. Lance was not phased, but his actions did have the effect of Ironman lowering his guard. That was a mistake, because seconds after the restart, almost before Ironman was set, Lance landed an almighty blow on Ironman's chin. The big black man wobbled and, like a stricken liner, slowly sank to the canvas. He did not make the count of ten. The crowd erupted with joy. The White Assassin had struck again. Lance Hermanus was the Heavyweight Champion of South Africa. The S and R camp leaped with joy. Mrs Shultz took note of her husband's squeeze of the tart.

At the press conference, after the fight, the reporters were intrigued to see that the World Champion, Gerrie Van der Merwe, was present. He was called upon to comment. Gerrie took the mic: "I would like to congratulate my good friend and fellow South African, on winning the title that I vacated a year ago. I would also like to say, that, as a special gift to the boxing fans of South Africa, I am inviting him to challenge for the world title. This is a fight that belongs in South Africa, and this is where it will be. Lance, my friend, when you have recovered from tonight, are you willing to fight again, this time for the championship of the world?"

A huge cheer went up from the assembled crowd of press and hangers on. Gerrie had just offered the biggest fight in South African history to his country, a nation that had, through boycotts, been starved of international events. Gerrie was ensuring that the world title would stay in South African hands, at least for the foreseeable future.

In the general hubbub that followed, Gerrie did not notice, a grave looking journalist come hastening into the room, carrying a piece of paper that looked like a wired message. He handed the slip of paper to the master of ceremonies, who read it and immediately turned pale. He thought for a moment and then turned to Gerrie, who was still close to the mike, having made his announcement. He pulled Gerrie towards him and whispered in his ear. "Gerrie, it looks like bad news. I've just been handed this wire. Angel's mother has been kidnapped in London."

"Christ!" said Gerrie. "I must go to her." With that he rushed off the podium without explanation and made his way as quickly as he could through the crowd to Angel, brushing off congratulatory back slaps as he passed. "Angel, my love," he started as he reached her. "Come with me. There is some bad news."

Sally had been in London with Jules. They were staying at Jules' flat. Jules had gone north in England to review a showcase of potential acts that he was auditioning to fill engagements at a chain of cabaret rooms in South Africa. Tony had taken the opportunity to shoot a series of pictures of Sally for *Cosmopolitan* magazine, which was running an article on the sex lives of older women. Tony would still have given his right arm to bed Sally, but she was clearly still with Jules, so he settled for next best, which was to photograph her in a series of suggestive poses for the magazine, and some for his private collection. For a girl in her late forties, Sally, was, for his money, the best looking gal in London. After the shoot, Sally declined Tony's invitation to dinner and went home, via the supermarket. As Sally entered the lobby area of the block of flats in Onslow Terrace, she was confronted by two men in the hallway. Before she could react, the men grabbed her and shoved something into her mouth to stop her screaming. The supermarket bags and contents spewed all over the carpeted floor. A car screeched to a halt outside the front door and before any of the neighbours came to their doors to see what the noise was about, Sally had been bundled into the car, which shot up the road and turned left into the cobbled mews. By the time the police arrived on the scene the car had disappeared into the streets of London. Nobody, it seemed, had noticed the licence plate number, not even the make of car. Sally had disappeared into thin air. When it was disclosed by one of the neighbours that Sally was the mother of the reigning Miss World, a previously disinterested London press was suddenly very interested in her disappearance. This was a story that had everything. An exceptionally pretty woman, and sometimes model, the mother of Miss World, upcoming mother-in-law of the World Heavyweight champion. This truly was a crime of public interest. Such interest, however, was the last thing that Gerrie and Angel wanted. They knew instantly why this had happened. Angel had been guarded; her mother had not. Angel felt terrible; this was all her fault.

The London police, naturally, wanted to talk to Angel to see if she could shed any light on the kidnapping. Angel knew what they were up against. She did not want to make matters worse by gabbing about the Mafia. She and Gerrie were surprised that the Marconis' reach extended to London. What they did not know was that Sally was already in a private aircraft en route for Las Vegas, still with her hands tied behind her back. The Marconis had a ranch, about 30 miles into the desert outside of Vegas. On it was a private strip, long enough for a small jet, which, although it would have been tracked by US traffic control, would be allowed to land at the private field with no questions asked, such was the control the Marconis had over the local Vegas police. Many a celebrity had been brought to Vegas via this strip, so one more plane would not attract special attention, even if it were carrying a kidnapped lady.

Gerrie knew what he had to do, and that did not include using the police, at least not at this stage of the proceedings. He and Angel assumed that Sally's kidnapping would be not just for revenge, but to regain their losses; at least, that was the best they could hope for. Whilst the London police remained baffled, Gerrie made contact with Giancarlo Marconi. That was not difficult; the man owned the Starburst Hotel and Casino. "Buona sera, Gerrie," said Giancarlo, when Gerrie got through to him on the phone, "it is nice to hear from you. It's been a long time."

"We need to talk," said Gerrie in his thick Afrikaans accent. "I am willing to talk."

"Then you must come to Las Vegas, my friend. You and Miss World."

"Can't we talk on the phone?" pleaded Gerrie.

"No phones. You must come here. We are all looking forward to seeing you." With that the line went dead.

The prison to which Sally had been taken was rather splendid. Once it was clear that Sally was not going to put up a struggle, her wrist bands had been released. She had been given a very comfortable cell/suite but was guarded night and day. The villa was surrounded by a high wall and there seemed to be guards everywhere. From the window in her cell/bedroom Sally could see expansive and well-kept gardens. Considering that beyond the wall the terrain looked like desert, the grounds looked extremely well-watered and cared for. Sally quickly concluded that escape was not an option. At first, she had no idea why she had been abducted. She did not understand why she should be of value to anyone. She could not fathom why they had gone to such lengths to take her to wherever she was. Because of the length of the flight and the temperature she assumed that she was in America, but initially she had no idea where, although her guess was that she was in the west. The man who appeared to be the owner of the mansion was also quite charming, with film star good looks. If she had not been his prisoner, she would have quite fancied him; his Mediterranean appearance was certainly charming and not at all frightening. Maybe, playing up to him could be a route to escape? But, escape to where? Giancarlo Marconi was also delighted to have such a pretty house guest. He was very accustomed to having his villa full of exotic women from the showrooms of Vegas, but this lady had a freshness and elegance which made a huge change. She was mature, yet she was still beautiful. He was, in some ways, sorry that she was his captive; he would rather have had her in his bed. To Sally, he was nothing other than pleasant; she had no idea how utterly ruthless he could actually be.

Before Sally had spent two days in her desert prison, Gerrie and Angel were on a South African Airways flight to Atlanta, with onward connections to Las Vegas. They had had no further communications from the Marconis, so had no idea when the next contact would be made. Since they had been asked to come to Vegas to talk, Gerrie and Angel simply assumed that the Marconis were involved in the kidnapping. Who else? They did not know where Sally was being held, but presumed it was somewhere in the UK, since that is where she was kidnapped. Before leaving they had spoken with Jules, who was completely distraught. They could not level with him about their suspicions that the Marconis were involved. He knew nothing of Gerrie's relationship with the Mob and Gerrie did not want him to muddy the water with the facts, which he felt would then go straight to the police. Although he had done nothing illegal, police involvement was the last thing Gerrie needed.

Jules could not understand Angel's sudden plan to go to the USA. "For God's sake," he said, "your mother has been kidnapped here in England. Why on earth would you want to go to Las Vegas?"

"Trust me," said Angel down the phone, "I know what I'm doing."

When the police asked questions in London about Sally's next of kin, they too were puzzled as to why her only daughter would see fit to go to the world's playground in America when her mother had just been kidnapped in England. It just did not add up.

When Gerrie and Angel landed in Vegas, they hurried through the airport full of jingling slot machines and took a cab straight to the Starburst. They had clearly been expected, because they were greeted at the desk by an Assistant Manager, who personally escorted them to a luxuriously gaudy suite, chatting all the way there about how good it was to have them back in the hotel. Five minutes after they had entered the suite the phone rang. It was Sammy Marconi.

"Welcome to Las Vegas. It is so nice to see you back so soon. I will be with you in an hour. May we use your suite to talk?"

"Be my guest," replied Gerrie, with a hint of sarcasm. "Come as soon as you like."

Despite their long trip, neither Angel nor Gerrie even thought about taking a shower or resting. They were far too on edge. They unpacked the few things that they had thrown into a suitcase in Johannesburg, and waited.

One hour later, Giancarlo and his brother Sammy were at the door. As they entered the suite, they were charm itself. Gerrie ushered them to a seat.

"Where is the lovely lady?" began Giancarlo, "I understand that you travelled with her."

"This is not her business to sort out," said Gerrie, "this is between you and me."

"Oh," retorted Giancarlo, "I think it is very much her business, since we know where her mother is."

Angel, who was in the next room listening, could stand it no more. She burst into the room. "Listen, you bastards," she yelled at the two men. "Tell me where my mother is. Tell me that she is okay. She has nothing to do with Gerrie's affairs. Let her go, you bastards."

"Well, well. There's a feisty lady," said Sammy to his brother, with a sarcastic smirk on his tanned face, "and very pretty, too. Just like her mother. What a pair they would make between the sheets!"

Gerrie leapt forward as if to hit Sammy.

"I wouldn't do that, if I were you," said Giancarlo, as he jumped out of his chair between his brother and Gerrie, "Sammy's only having a bit of fun. Don't pay any attention to him."

Gerrie glared at Sammy, but slowly backed away. All three men inched backwards to their seats.

"Sorry about that, Angel. Just having a bit of fun," said Giancarlo. "Your mother is in good hands – and very comfortable. The sooner young Gerrie here decides to cooperate with us, the sooner you will see her." Turning to Gerrie, Giancarlo continued, "The last time we met, I thought we had an understanding. In fact, you made a promise to us. The fact that you reneged on the deal cost us a lot of money. When we figure out how to get it back, and maybe make some more, Angel's lovely mother will be released, that is, if she wants to be."

"What the hell do they mean by that?" Angel thought, but decided to keep quiet.

The Marconis carried on, both taking it in turns to speak, as if the whole diatribe had been rehearsed. They expressed some sarcastic sympathy for the fact that Gerrie's pride had got the better of him in the ring last time. They understood that he was a proud lad, but that he ought to realise that he was not messing with the kindergarten. They would give him one last chance to make amends. What they were demanding was that Gerrie's next fight should be against another easy opponent, but that, once again, he would feign a loss. He would then be given an automatic rematch to regain the Crown, as before, but that if he failed to cooperate, Sally would be killed, only, he added with a smirk, after he and his brother had the opportunity to "enjoy her company". "And," Giancarlo added, for good measure, "maybe Angel, here, would care to join the party? You must understand, young man, that this, for you, is a reprieve. Under the terms of our previous agreement, you should, by rights, be dead. But we are practical people. Dead, would not get us our money back. Alive, will. But, if you screw up this time, there will be no third chance."

"Okay, okay," I hear you, said Gerrie. "But, if I agree to do this for you, you must release Angel's mum immediately."

"Of course," said Giancarlo, "we, unlike you, are men of our word, but if you mess up this time, the ladies will be our first port of call – and looking at Angel here, I almost hope you do."

"Okay," said Gerrie, rather meekly, "I will do as you say."

"Good," said Giancarlo, "you will be hearing from Bob Levin about your next fight."

"But," said Gerrie, "I have already announced my next fight; it will be between me and Lance Hermanus in South Africa."

"I am afraid we can't take that chance, Gerrie. He might beat you, and then where would we be? No, listen to Bob; he will tell you where and when you will be fighting."

With that the two Italians stood up and swept out of the room. As the door clicked shut, Angel ran to Gerrie's arms. "I am so sorry, my love. So sorry that you are having to lose because of me and my mum." Gerrie was sorry too, but, as he hugged the sobbing girl, he vowed to find a way to beat these bastards. First thing was to get Sally back. The Italians had left without giving him any clue as to where she was or when she would be released. He just had to trust them. He knew that, unless she was released soon, he would not be throwing any fights.

Angel and Gerrie were tired after the long journey, but they were also completely wound up. Too much had happened in the last couple of days. They called Tony in England, even though it was now late at night there. "We've got a lead, Tony. All I can tell you is that the Mafia is involved. We don't know where Sally is but we do know that she is okay and will soon be released, but only if you do not say anything to the cops. We can't tell you any more, but please relax. She is going to be okay." This was all new to Tony; the Mafia, keeping information from the police; none of this seemed right, but, what could he do? Gerrie seemed confident that Sally would be okay. He decided to keep quiet for another day and let the police scratch around as best they could. So far, they did not seem to have a clue.

Meanwhile, Sally was being looked after as if she were a superstar. Her host had reappeared that afternoon with a bag full of designer outfits for her to try. She was so grateful, since she was still in the clothes that she was wearing in London at the time of the snatch. The new clothes were stunning. "How thoughtful of my jailers," she mused, "I could get used to this."

"Pick a few things that you like," Giancarlo instructed, "and then you may join my brother and I for dinner." He left the room for her to try out the clothes.

Sally just didn't get it. Here she was, a captive who had been flown for hours across the world against her wishes, now to be gifted designer outfits and invited out to dinner. This was weird. She decided to play along. Sooner or later, she thought, a chance would come to escape, especially if she did not seem to be a flight risk.

Sally picked the most alluring of the dresses that she had been given. She walked up and down in front of the full length mirror in the bathroom. Amazingly it fitted her perfectly. Yes, she really did look good. Two days of forced rest, after the horrors of the kidnap, seemed to have been good for her. She tried the door of her room which, previously, had been locked. It now popped open and she followed the sound of the voices below. Down a magnificent flight of stairs, she found the source of the voices: Giancarlo and his brother, together with an American blonde, probably about 30 years old, who was introduced as Sammy's wife.

"Tonight, my dear Sally," said the handsome Giancarlo, "we are going to have a nice dinner. Tomorrow, you will be released."

Sally thought about requesting a change of order to the events, but, since, she did not appear to be threatened in any way, decided to roll with the punches. "Just one thing, Giancarlo," she said, as she took a seat, "does my daughter know that I am safe?"

"Yes, my beauty," said Giancarlo. "She knows you are well and she will be here tomorrow to see for herself."

Sally decided that, whatever her wishes were, she was in their hands. She would just have to play along with their plan for the evening.. Better than that, she thought, she would lure Giancarlo into her web; having some control over him might turn out to be very useful. She could see, as he eyed her in the clinging new dress, that pretty soon, she could make him the captive. That might make life interesting.

The next morning, at 9am, Gerrie and Angel got a call from the hotel manager. A car would be ready for them outside the front of the hotel at 11am, which would take them to the "family reunion". With a combination of jet lag and emotional exhaustion they had not slept well, but the news that they were to be reunited with Sally, if that is what was meant, was like a tonic. To while away the time, Gerrie put in a call to Bob Levin. Bob was astounded that Gerrie and Angel were back in town.

"That's great," he thought, "that will save me a trip to South Africa. I can have another crack at trying to talk Gerrie out of fighting Hermanus." Bob did not appear to have heard from the Italians. After a brief conversation, the two men agreed to meet the next day. A lot of things might have changed by then, thought Gerrie, as he put down the phone.

A white Cadillac with a black driver wearing a black baseball cap was waiting at 11am under the porte cochere, amongst a fleet of other stretched vehicles. The driver introduced himself as Bill and drove off at a funereal speed.

"Where are we going, Bill?" asked Gerrie, as they inched down the Strip in heavy traffic.

"To Big G's place," replied the driver. "It's about 40 miles from here, into the desert. I take it you've never been there? Lovely place, sir."

So, that was it, thought Gerrie, Big G had been hiding Sally at his home. How on earth did he get her here from London? The route took them past the airport on a road overloaded with advertising signboards. Then, once they had left the airport behind, the road was straight and boring: just dust and more dust, with the occasional weird shaped cacti. After about 20 miles the desert started to become hilly and far more colourful, until, as the 40-mile mark approached, it suddenly became beautiful. The rock formations were spectacular and the cacti were getting larger and more sculptured as the miles rolled past. Not long after the scenery changed, a few ranch houses started to appear, all with ornate gates and long driveways. Then, as they rounded one of the rare bends in the road, on the left appeared a long high sand coloured wall, only broken further on by some massive heavily worked iron gates, which, as the Cadillac approached, slowly swung open. Gerrie noticed that the guards on the gate were armed. He said nothing. At the end of the drive stood a massive ranch house, probably at least 10,000 square feet in area, with huge solid rough-carved, wooden doors. As they approached, one of the monstor sized doors was flung open and there stood Giancarlo Marconi, all smiles and welcoming. Bill slid out of the driver's seat and hastened to the passenger door, which he opened for Angel. Gerrie manovered his large frame out of the other.

"Welcome to my home," beamed Giancarlo, but Angel was not in the mood for niceties.

"Where is Sally?" she almost demanded. "I want to see my mother."

"It's all right, my darling," called a voice from inside, "I'm here – and I'm okay."

Giancarlo stepped back to let Angel pass, which she did, barely acknowledging him. Sally was in the spacious hallway behind him. Angel rushed into her arms and the two hugged as only a mother and daughter can. Gerrie, at the door, stopped to shake the Big G's outstretched hand, then moved forward to greet Sally, who had now disentangled herself from her daughter's embrace. Gerrie was shocked. Far from looking like a prisoner, Sally looked magnificent. She was decked out in a sleek suit and looked the picture of health. In fact, Gerrie had never seen his future mother-in-law look so radiant. "Being held in captivity must suit her," he thought to himself as he moved forward to hug her too.

"Thank God, you are okay," he said, as he released her, "we were so worried."

"Well, as you can see, Gerrie, I have been well looked after. I would even go as far as saying that I have had a very nice time. I know this must have come as a huge shock to you all, but actually I have been extremely well treated."

None of this, of course, could undo the angst that Angel had been through over the past few days. She and Gerrie wanted to take Sally and leave, but they were captive to the driver. "You can't leave now," said Giancarlo. "I insist that you stay for lunch and I will show you around. And, we are not far from the Grand Canyon here. I would like to take you in the chopper to see it." Gerrie looked dubious, but then Sally chimed in. "Oh no, Gerrie, you must stay for lunch and you absolutely must see the Canyon. I really do insist."

"Christ," thought Gerrie, "you would have thought that she would have been desperate to leave." He couldn't fathom it out. Far from behaving like a thug, Giancarlo Marconi acted like a complete gentleman. He was particularly attentive to the needs of Sally.

"No wonder," thought Angel, "that Mum is not in a hurry to leave."

Giancarlo ushered his guests into a magnificent courtyard in the centre of the house, where he introduced Angel to his brother and the blonde. They were all interested to hear about South Africa, in particular the bush and the wildlife. The whole atmosphere was surreal. Here was Gerrie, who was being threatened with his and others' lives, if he did not fake a performance in a fight, and here was Angel's mother, theoretically a prisoner, joining in the small talk and cosying up to her captor and enjoying a cocktail with her abusers. "America is a strange place," thought Gerrie, as he munched on the nuts.

After a beautifully prepared lunch served by an immaculate butler and a spectacular chopper ride over the Canyon, Gerrie, Angel and Sally were finally driven back to the Vegas Strip. Sally seemed almost reluctant to leave. In fact, much to her daughter's amazement she gave Giancarlo a kiss and a squeeze before climbing into the car, having first made sure that her newly acquired wardrobe was safely on board. Gerrie and Angel would have happily taken the next flight out of Vegas in the direction of Johannesburg, but for the fact that Gerrie had agreed to meet with Bob Levin the following morning. The Marconis had laid on a spectacular suite for Sally, the best penthouse in the Starburst. The three from South Africa stayed there for a while and chatted. Jules was called in London. He was so relieved to hear Sally's voice, and so thankful to Angel and Gerrie for tracking her down. He promised to advise the police in London that she had shown up. Gerrie asked him, for all their sakes, to explain that the whole thing had been a prank.

"If they think the Mob were involved," explained Gerrie, "we'll never have any peace. Please do as we ask, Jules."

Sally added her weight to the request and Jules reluctantly agreed. "I can't wait to see you, my love," he said to Sally. "When will you be coming back to London?"

"Well," replied Sally, "I thought I might go home to Joburg with Angel for a while."

Jules was clearly disappointed, just as Angel was surprised.

Gerrie and Angel offered to stay in the penthouse with Sally for the night, but Sally said she was happy to be alone. "After all this excitement, I need some quiet time. No, I'll be fine. Angel, my darling, if you like, I can see you for breakfast whilst Gerrie goes to his meeting."

With that, her rescuers were dismissed. They returned to their own suite. Neither of them had had much rest since arriving from the other side of the world. Now that they had found Angel's mother, they too were feeling exhausted, so it was not long before they hit the plush sheets of the Starburst. Meanwhile, back in the penthouse, Sally had a visitor; the owner of the hotel and casino. This was the second night that he had shared a bed with Sally. He was a greedy man and he could not get enough of her.

The next morning, it was Gerrie, the business man, not Gerrie the champ, who met with Bob Levin. By then, Bob had received the call he was expecting from Giancarlo's brother, so he was able to anticipate Gerrie's request. Bob agreed to elevate a lesser known fighter, with the help of the WBC and WBA rankings committees, into a position where he could challenge for the title. The fight would be at the Starburst. This was simply a rewind of the tape. Gerrie was concerned about his reputation back in South Africa, if he reneged on his promise to fight Lance Hermanus for the title as his next fight. Bob said that he could help out. He would ensure that the boxing authorities would not sanction an immediate fight with Lance, since there were other higher-ranked potential opponents in line. Gerrie would say that he was not being allowed to fight Lance immediately, but would certainly make sure that Lance would be the next in line.

"In other words," said Bob, "we make it the boxing board's decision, not yours. I'll make sure you get a rematch with the schmuck you're going to fight. After that, you can fight Lance. I'll arrange an easy fight for Lance with Steven Shultz in the meantime. Okay?"

Gerrie was not okay, but this seemed to be the best way to move forward with his business. This time, he thought, he will not let pride come before the dollar.

That evening Angel and Gerrie caught the plane back to Joburg. Sally did not join them. "Since I'm here, I think I'll stay for a few days and catch some shows; after all, you don't get the chance to do this in South Africa or London, I got a free ride here, so why not take advantage of it?"

Angel offered to stay on with her mother, but Sally was insistent.

"No, my darling. I will be perfectly alright on my own – and I might never get the penthouse again."

The service in the suite was impeccable. Word had quickly spread that the mature beauty staying there was the owner's latest grind. Nothing would be too good for her, until the wind changed. Back in London, Jules was worried. But his business there was done, so he, too, was soon on his way to Joburg.

Chapter Twenty

In Johannesburg the winter had arrived. Winters on the Highveld are spectacular. It rarely rains and the bright clear sun arrives every day, making it possible to plan outside events with a high degree of certainty that they will not be interrupted by inclement conditions. So, the marriage of Angel and Gerrie was planned and executed. The actual ceremony took place in the garden of Gerrie's home in Atholl, with the reception inside the spacious house, as the cool of the evening approached. Sally had returned to assist her daughter with the wedding plans, but not as soon as Angel had expected. It was also a surprise to Angel and Gerrie, as well as Jules, that she was delivered to South Africa in a private jet, organised by none other than her former captor.

Jules was furious with Sally and, whilst the loving relationship between Angel and Gerrie was blossoming, the one with Jules was running out of steam. Sally was fond of Jules and he had been very good to and for her over the past few years, but their relationship had not seemed to blossom after their coming together in London. Jules was a man of limited intellect and Sally found herself wanting something more. Maybe she needed more excitement in her life. Maybe she needed more of an intellectual challenge. Jules had made no moves to marry Sally and now, in retrospect, she was glad about that. However, she was confused. It was an overwhelming physical attraction that she had felt for Giancarlo Marconi, when he first showed up as her captor in the desert house in Nevada. There was something almost dangerous about him, certainly, something mysterious. Whatever it was made him strongly attractive to her. So, she had formulated a plan that being nice to him might lead to her release. What she did not anticipate, at the time, was that her instant physical attraction to Giancarlo, would quickly mature into something more serious, almost an addiction. She was, of course, aware of the potential dangers of a relationship with a mobster. At first, she had decided to lure him into a relationship from which she and her daughter could benefit. What she was not expecting was to actually fall for his charms. She was beginning to feel that Giancarlo, despite his hard-nosed reputation, was actually looking for love. Clearly, he did not get it at home. The Big G was a charming, but dangerous, man. For the moment, at least, he had been caught in Sally's web. This is just where she wanted him to be, when she had first conceived the idea of seducing him. She now found herself not only wanting to control him, but, alas, also wanting him.

If nothing else, the budding relationship with Giancarlo did have the effect of clarifying her feelings about Jules. The excitement that she felt in Giancarlo's presence did not exist with Jules. It was time to end the relationship. Jules knew that he could not compete with a man who owned a casino and several jets. He just feared for the happiness and safety of Sally, whom he still adored. However, Sally made it quite clear that their romance was over; she just wanted to remain friends. Devastated as he was, he decided to accept it for the moment. He was hopeful that things would change.

Gerrie and Angel could not figure out what was going on with Sally. Here she was, cozying up to the very man who had first kidnapped her and then threatened her daughter and her fiancée. They hoped that Sally had just been taking advantage of Giancarlo, so that she could have a good time in Vegas. They had no idea that she had been sleeping with him.

When Gerrie announced that he was being obliged to fight Rocky Jones before he could do battle with Lance, he was, for a while, the most unpopular man in South Africa. "Coward! Reneger! Liar!" were the headlines on the sporting pages. The White Assassin took full advantage of holding the higher ground and insisted that Gerrie was a coward and ducking the fight. It was Bob Levin that came to Gerrie's rescue. He flew to Johannesburg, at Gerrie's request, and held a press conference. Bob was held in high esteem in South Africa. He was seen as the World's tsar of boxing, and a good friend of South Africa. He quietly explained that the switch of Gerrie's next opponent and venue was beyond Gerrie's control, and that he was bound by the rules of the World Boxing Association and the World Boxing Council, to fight someone higher ranked than Lance. This was his obligation. If he did not honour this he would be stripped of his title. Of course, this was all bullshit, but it seemed to be accepted by most of the public, so the outcry against Gerrie died down, particularly since Bob explained that the fight after the mandatory defence would definitely be against Lance Hermanus and definitely in South Africa.

And so, the world moved on. Angel and Gerrie, now married, flew back to Las Vegas, so that Gerrie could prepare for his fight against his designated opponent, Rocky Jones. Mother-in-law went too. In the weeks before the upcoming fight, Angel brought her mother, with whom she was now spending a lot of time, into the secret of the upcoming fight. Who was better placed than Sally, at that moment, to organise a bet against Gerrie? Sally was the one that seemed to have the ear (and other parts) of the Marconis. If anyone in the world could place a large bet against Gerrie for Sally, it would be the Mob.

Sally had enhanced her position with the mobsters considerably. When she arrived back in Vegas to accompany her daughter whilst Gerrie trained for the fight, Giancarlo installed her, once again, in the penthouse at the Starburst. Nothing was too much to ask for, including, bizarrely, a bet on the fight that they were controlling. Giancarlo would have been in a difficult position if she had asked him to put her money on her son-in-law. That would have been a huge test of the value of their relationship. But, Sally did not. Instead, by trusting him to place a bet against Gerrie, she quietly acknowledged that she was prepared to be one of them, part of the family.

Unfortunately, that was not quite the case. Giancarlo already had a family, which included his wife, Guilietta, whom he had married shortly after she was out of school. Guilietta had long learned that she was not the only bed partner of her husband. She had seen many beautiful young ladies come and go. But, Guilietta was still there. Sally was too new on the scene to be regarded as a threat and, from what she had heard through her informants at the Starburst, too old for her G. "Why would he want to trade in one old wife for another one?" she rationalised. "Sally is just Gerrie Van Der Merwe's mother-in-law. That's why Giancarlo is looking after her."

Gerrie approached the fight with a clear head. He was no longer confused or driven with concerns about his wounded pride or reputation. This was just business. He would make a fortune on the upcoming fight, partly because of the deal he had wrenched out of Bob Levin in which he shared in the television and closed circuit revenues, and partly because Angel had confirmed to him that the huge bet he had placed on his opponent had been safely lodged. Furthermore, he relished the opportunity to score heavily again in the rematch. The only person he felt sorry for was Coach Brennan, his loyal trainer over so many years. Brennan was fiercely proud of Gerrie's unbeaten record. To lose it would be devastating. However, that aside, Gerrie was at peace with himself as he stepped into the ring. He had met his opponent at the weigh in. He could see that Rocky was frightened of him. He just hoped he was not too frightened to get the job done.

So, it was a completely cool-headed Gerrie that stepped into the ring with the full intention of losing his title, until he looked at the faces in the crowd below. Suddenly, as he glanced into the second row, he got a shock. Sitting there, as bold as brass, were Bibi and Lance.

"Shit," thought Gerrie as the bell went for the start of the round, "there's no fucking way I can lose a fight in front of Lance. Why didn't someone tell me they were coming?"

Gerrie's mind was no longer in the fight. His head was all over the place. He had been completely flummoxed by the appearance of his ex-girlfriend and her brother. Such was his lack of concentration that in the 45th second of the first round, Gerrie did not see a right hook coming from the fresh and fired up Rocky. It landed fair and square on Gerrie's chin. It knocked him clean out. Gerrie did not get up from the canvas; he was out cold. The crowd, many of whom had paid mega bucks to be there, booed and yelled, imploring Gerrie to get up. The only people who were not surprised were Angel, Sally, and her gangster friends. They did not realise that Gerrie was not acting.

It took several minutes for Gerrie to come completely around. By then, Angel and Sally were getting worried. Could it be that Gerrie had really walked into a big punch? Had this been his way of getting the thing over quickly? Slowly it dawned on them that Gerrie was not acting. He had been seriously hurt. It is a requirement of the boxing authorities that a doctor is always in attendance at a fight. Whilst Angel and Sally looked on, the doctor nursed Gerrie's head in his hands, as he carried out the normal cognisance checks. Then, some full five minutes after the knockdown, he finally pronounced that Gerrie would be okay to make his way to the centre of the ring for the announcemts. As Gerrie heard the words "for the new heavyweight champion of the world", he cringed a little inside, but his now-alert brain started counting the money. Gerrie had survived the ordeal without knowing too much about it, and without too much pain, hopeful that his sore head would soon mend.

There were two celebrations in Vegas that night. The new champ still had plenty of energy to paint the town. The dethroned champ celebrated his new found wealth in the penthouse. His happy clan included Bob Levin, now even richer, Angel and her mother, and the Marconis, ostensibly there as the owners of the Stardust and the hosts.

The Marconi's party included, for the first time, Guilietta Marconi, who had clearly showed up to protect her assets. Sally had dressed to impress, with a chic Versace outfit that clung to her body like clingwrap.

Guilietta realised, for the first time, what competition she actually had. Sally looked stunning. This was something Guilietta would have to deal with, but, not tonight. Two other invitees did not show up: Bibi and Lance. Sally, who, of course, knew Bibi from her childhood friendship with Angel, had sought her out at ringside. Naturally she had invited them to the after-fight party in her suite. She knew they were no longer best friends, but, hell, they had come a long way to see the fight, and, as they both knew, their two men would be soon fighting each other for the title. When Gerrie went down, Lance had been devastated. Lance had been in touching distance of holding the world title belt; now, it seemed his chance might have gone. What the hell was Gerrie playing at? Now he had ruined everything. There was no way, in his mood, that he was going to a party. It's a pity that he didn't, because had he done so, he would have found Gerrie and Angel in a jubilant place. Then he would have realised that something was up.

Chapter Twenty One

Rocky Jones thought that he might have got lucky. As Rocky saw it, landing a knockout blow on Gerrie Van der Merwe's jaw so early in the fight had, perhaps, been a bit of a fluke. Although he had signed a contract which obliged him to give Gerrie a rematch as his first defence, he had absolutely no intention of doing so. The last thing he wanted was to immediately lose the title that he had won so quickly, which he was convinced would happen if he fought Gerrie again. Louis Brown, his "manager" also knew that was a good possibility, so when Rocky told him that he wanted to get out of his contractual obligation, or, at least, postpone it for a few fights, Brown could see the sense in that. After all, during Gerrie's short reign as heavyweight champ, Louis had been out of the picture. Now, on the back of Rocky Jones, he was in the driving seat, not Bob Levin. He called Bob in Vegas.

"Bob, my friend," started Louis, "my man says that he doesn't want to fight Gerrie again. Ain't nothing I can do to talk him out of it. Do you think we can come to some arrangement? Maybe, I give him a couple of easy defences first. You know? Build up the interest before the big return."

Bob Levin did not buy it. He wanted Gerrie to regain his title as soon as possible. He knew that there was big money to be made in the fight between Gerrie and the

White Assassin and to do that, Gerrie had to get his title back. "Forget it, Louis," he began, "there is no way we are going to let you or your fighter off the hook. It's down in black and white; he must give Gerrie a rematch. If he doesn't, I shall move to get the WBC and the WBA to take his title away from him. Do you understand?"

The conversation went nowhere. Louis Brown insisted that he could not force his fighter to honour his contract and Bob Levin insisted that, if that was the case, he would go to the boxing authorities and, if necessary, the courts. Louis stuck to his guns, but was far from certain how this would all end. He knew that Bob's relationship with the world boxing councils was probably better than his. Bob had been funding them for many years and they were really in his pocket, particularly the WBA. Nevertheless, he also knew from experience that muddying the waters often produced surprising results. The argument between the two men continued for weeks, with neither side giving way. Bob took his case to the press, arguing that Rocky Jones was in breach of contract. Nobody seemed to dispute that, but Rocky insisted that he had not read the contract when he signed it and that he had been manipulated by Levin to sign something he did not understand. Eventually, Bob took his case to the boxing authorities. Almost immediately, the WBA ruled that Rocky must make his first defence of the title against Gerrie, or lose it. However, the WBC took a different view, probably coached by Mr. Brown. It pronounced that Rocky must, at some time, defend his title against Gerrie, but, not necessarily as a first defence. Levin was furious, but apparently powerless to change their view. He knew what had happened and, after blowing off steam in the press, quietly accepted the decision.

He explained to Gerrie that all was not lost. The WBA title was still a "world" title. This was not the first time that the boxing authorities had split. Also, as far as a South African crowd was concerned, the WBA title would be good enough to draw a big crowd.

"Nobody is going to be interested in Rocky Jones fighting a nobody for the other title," explained Bob. "The WBA is where the money is." So, with Gerrie's agreement, plans were made for Gerrie to fight Lance four months later. Meanwhile, the WBA removed the title from Rocky and endorsed the all white, all South African, title fight. This time there was no interference or pressure from the Mafia. Everybody, it seemed, in the Marconi family wanted Gerrie to win. After all, he was the son in law of the boss' latest squeeze.

The relationship between Sally and Giancarlo had been flourishing. Sally, having shed herself of Jules, now moved back to Las Vegas, where Giancarlo installed her in a luxurious apartment in a classy new residential development on the fringe of the city. It was difficult for her at first, because, outside of the Marconis, she had no friends in Nevada, and because Giancarlo was married, it would be impossible for her to be accepted by the Italian diaspora. Italian families in the USA are incredibly tight knit and supportive of each other, so, whilst Giancarlo was married to Guilietta, Sally would not be welcomed in their community. She understood that, and accepted it – at least for the time being. Luckily, Bob Levin was not subject to any Italian family loyalties, so he was able to introduce her to many well-connected people in the city, as indeed were the Mood model agency, which had tentacles across the world. Mood was also able to organise several photo shoots for Sally in nearby Los Angeles, so, gradually, Sally was able to develop a social life beyond the trysts with Giancarlo.

Giancarlo was also exceptionally generous and showered Sally with gifts, many of which were extremely expensive. The shopping mall at the Starburst was also the source of Giancarlo's generosity to his lover. Sally, of course, had no idea that Giancarlo never actually paid for anything he bought there. Despite all of these good things, the situation with Giancarlo was not entirely satisfactory for Sally; she did not like this sharing arrangement. Although Giancarlo made no secret of his affair and the whole arrangement seemed perfectly normal to most of his friends, Sally wanted more. She was convinced that Giancarlo actually loved her, but she needed to put it to the test. She could see no future in the current arrangement, cosy as it was.

Giancarlo also had many friends outside of the family. For many years he had led three lives. One, with Guilietta and their children, second with friends and associates outside of the family, mainly people involved in his legitimate businesses, and third, his life as the head of a criminal syndicate. He had been careful not to confuse the three. However, he had never really been in love before. Love, to him, had seemed a soft option and one that could only lead to weakness. Weakness can be dangerous. True, he had had a litany of glamourous female companions outside of his marriage, but none that had been so serious as to threaten the foundations of his marriage to Guilietta. Sally was different. Certainly she was sexually attractive and experienced, but she was so much more. Giancarlo did not want to lose her and every day that he spent with her reinforced his desire to be with her. He was infatuated by Sally; some would call it love.

She was so far out of his normal range that every day with her was fresh and surprising.

Guilietta knew that Sally was trouble. From the minute that she had met her at the after-fight party some months before, Guilietta had been on the alert. But, she did not really know what to do about it. Giancarlo was his own man. Long ago in their marriage she had accepted that he could screw around, as long as he continued to keep her in the luxury that she had grown used to and as long as he kept up appearances at the traditional times of family celebration. Italian men were allowed to have mistresses; that was just the way it was.

This, however, was different. It had become apparent to Guilietta that Sally was a rival, not a sideshow. She decided to confront her husband. That did not go down well. In fact, it ended with a screaming match in the desert villa, with Giancarlo stomping out. He did not return for over a week and, this time, it was with a lawyer. Sammy and others in the extended Italian family did their best to counsel Giancarlo against divorce, especially after over 25 years of marriage and three children. But he was not interested. Sally had opened his eyes to what personal happiness could mean. What Giancarlo wanted, Giancarlo got. However, let no one tell him that he was not fair with the mother of his children, at least, in terms of money. The lawyer had already drawn up the terms, which were not ungenerous. However, in true Giancarlo fashion, Guilietta was given no choice.

"Sign here, or forget it," said the lawyer in a tone that was trying to be forceful, yet kind. "In my experience this is exceptionally generous, especially for a woman that has a history," said the lawyer, rather ominously. Guilietta understood. Several years before she had engaged in an affair with one of the security men at the ranch. She always suspected that Giancarlo had been informed of this, but assumed that it suited him to keep silent, knowing that he also engaged in extra marital dalliances. Now she knew that this had been a big mistake. She signed.

Sally was taken by surprise when Giancarlo told her that evening that he was going for a divorce. She was happy that she would now be able to come out of the shadows in regard to her social life with Giancarlo, but she was nervous at the thought of marrying for the second time. Not that Giancarlo had actually asked for her hand. Marriage into the Italian family would be a big step; hopefully she would not have to face that decision for a while. What did please her, however, was the thought that it would now be very difficult for the Mob to lean on her son-in-law again, and, the longer she could maintain that state of affairs, the better it would be for her lovely daughter, Angel. Now, what she needed Giancarlo to do was to buy her, or them, a house in Los Angeles. Sally found Las Vegas quite weird. She did not think she could live there.

Chapter Twenty Two

The fight for the vacant WBA world heavyweight belt
was scheduled to take place in the largest rugby stadium
in Johannesburg, which normally accommodated
70,000 spectators. Given that this was a boxing match,
the capacity could be boosted even further by placing
thousands of seats on the turf, surrounding the boxing
ring. Although Gerrie's reputation had been somewhat
tarnished with his first minute knockout at the hands of
Rocky Jones, he still boasted a fantastic record of 14 wins,
one draw, and one loss. Nobody else in the heavyweight
division had such a good record, except, of course, his
challenger, the White Assassin. Lance, of course, had had
far fewer professional bouts, but he was still undefeated.

Never before, in the history of the professional game,
had two South Africans been ranked so high. The local
interest in the fight was at fever pitch. Gerrie had been
quite right. Johannesburg was the natural venue for this
event. In America or Europe, the interest would have
been negligible.

The nation was torn. Most sporting fans in the country,
at least the white ones, were proud of Gerrie Van der
Merwe, the first Afrikaans man to have held the world title.
But Gerrie, as a public figure, was quite difficult to relate
to. He certainly was not a PR man's dream. In interviews
he came across as a nice young man, but not a terribly

interesting one. On the other hand, his opponent, Lance, was the darling of the Afrikaans community, particularly, the women. His frequent appearances on the radio and television had boosted his popularity enormously. His comments were always controversial and direct. Sometimes he could be very funny. He was the PR man's dream. Needless to say, in the weeks before the fight, Lance absolutely milked his popularity. He was ruthless in his scorn for his opponent; he exuded confidence.

Many pundits, of course, commented that pride comes before a fall, so, popular as he was, most of the money at the bookies had been placed upon Gerrie to win. It appeared that the public were not fooled by all of Lance's boastful talk; they just enjoyed it. His sister, Bibi, was, of course, a great help. Everyone knew that Gerrie was married to Miss World, even though they were puzzled by this relationship. Everyone also knew that Lance, despite all of his big talk, was actually managed by his sister, and most people thought that Bibi was the sexiest thing on two legs. Many wondered why she had not been snapped up by a wealthy suitor. Lance always had a different girl on his arm, but none came close to the sex appeal of his glamourous sister. The team of Bibi and Lance in the television studios was just electric.

The whole of South Africa held their breath in anticipation as the two large white men climbed through the ropes to be introduced. There was a carnival atmosphere in the stadium. A South African crowd at a rugby match can be awesome; this was a level beyond. There were Mexican waves galore, raucous renderings of all the favourite Afrikaans songs, fireworks (even though they had been banned) and multiple wisecracks. As the sun set, the lights in the stadium focused on the little square of canvas in the centre of the huge arena, like a tiny tropical island in a vast dark sea. Those with seats at the back of the stands almost needed binoculars to make out the two fighters. Gerrie wore black shorts that were quite long. Lance was kitted out in red and white. Coach Brennan, Gerrie's loyal trainer, was present, as ever, but everyone noticed the gesture he made to Lance, by walking over to his corner before the fight commenced and giving him a friendly hug. Gerrie, good sport that he was, did not seem to mind.

Bob Levin, of course, was in attendance. Before he had been introduced to Gerrie Van der Merwe by Steven Shultz a few years before, Bob had never thought of visiting South Africa. Now, it was like a second home. It had also become the source of huge revenue. Sally and Giancarlo had also flown from Las Vegas for the event. They looked a really handsome pair and attracted much interest from the photographers. Even Tony from London had made the trip. There were many pretty girls in the audience, but, as usual, two of them stood out: the old friends, Bibi and Angel. Neither spoke or acknowledged each other. Both had dressed to impress.

The fight was unbelievably tough. Both men were spurred on, not by the need to be the heavyweight champion of the world, but by the need to determine who actually was the best boxer. They had a long history. The thought that they had thrown their first punches in the same ring on the same night as two schoolboys was actually amazing. Nothing like this had ever happened in the world of professional boxing. Both recognised that they owed so much to Coach Brennan. The last time they had fought each other, Brennan had been the referee; now he was in Gerrie's corner.

On that evening, many years before, Brennan had scored the fight a draw. Many people in the stadium would have said the same for this latest fight, it was so close. However, when the judge's slips were called in, referee Roufus, still going strong, announced the winner as Gerrie Van der Merwe. For the first time in months, Lance was speechless. He could not believe the verdict. Nor could his sister. The crowd, by and large, was happy with the result. Lance and Bibi thought they had been robbed, but Bibi's good public relations mode kicked in and she forced herself to be gracious. Inside, she was seething.

At least, she could fall back on the thought that they had all made a huge pile from the event and maybe, since the fight had been so close, there would be many more paydays to come. Steven Shultz and Trevor Rosenburg were very pleased with their percentage; it had been the best payday in the history of their little company. They were all, however, sorry that this might be the end of the gravy train. "Who knows when Gerrie will ever let Lance have another crack at it?" said Steven. "If I were him, I would keep Lance well away."

As it happened their concerns were short lived. At the after-fight press conference, Gerrie surprised everyone by suddenly announcing his retirement from professional boxing. Against all the advice he had received from all of those who relied on him winning, including Bob Levin, Gerrie had decided that he had had enough. He had made a fortune on the last couple of fights. The only person with whom he had discussed his intentions was Angel, and she was delighted with his decision. He would use his money to buy trucks, just like his dad. However, Gerrie's company would be the biggest haulage firm in

South Africa. "Van the Man", had decided to go into the real van business. He knew that his dad would be pleased.

This, of course, meant that the WBA world heavyweight title would be up for grabs, yet again, and Lance was obviously going to be the number one contender. It was like a low fruit hanging before Lance that he could not quite grasp. He was obviously pleased at this turn of events, but was still smarting from his defeat. Should he gain the belt at the next attempt, it would not be the same as defeating Gerrie. Somehow, he felt that he had been robbed, that Gerrie had deliberately retired so that Lance would never have the satisfaction of actually beating him.

It did not take Bob Levin, Steven and Trevor long to be in deep conversation with Bibi. It was agreed that Bob was in the best position to guide the WBA in the direction that suited Lance and themselves. But, once again, Louis Brown controlled the most likely challengers to be approved by the boxing boards of control. The big money fight, however, they all knew, was the one to re-unify the two titles, WBA and WBC. Rocky Jones was already set to defend his new WBC title against one of Brown's convenient stable; hopefully he would clear that obstacle. If so, it looked as if the stars were aligned for a Rocky versus Lance match in a few months' time. Bob agreed that he would set about negotiating the terms of this with Brown when he got back to the USA. Bibi announced that she should be there when he did so. Bob did not object because any real meeting of minds between Brown and Levin would not take place in Bibi's presence anyway. So, Bob Levin returned to the USA, followed a few days later by Bibi. Before she showed up, Bob had already alerted his arch rival, Louis Brown, that when he called to negotiate the merging back of the two heavyweight titles, that Bibi, Lance's "manager" would be on the line with him. In other words, whatever deal they agreed upon, could be reworked between them later.

At this stage, Rocky had yet to defend his newly won title, but this event was imminent. Rocky would be fighting another American heavyweight, managed by Louis' son, so the result was entirely predictable and did not seem to pose a threat to a future White Assassin versus Rocky event. Bibi found her way to Bob's office and they called Louis.

"How's that big white brother of yours doing?" said Louis, in an attempt to be as charming as possible to Bibi.

"He can't wait to take out your big black journeyman," shot back Bibi.

Louis laughed, a sort of loud derisory laugh.

The actual negotiation didn't take long. Louis said that, subject to his man winning his next fight, he would be willing for Rocky to take on Lance, in America, for a purse of $2 million. Bibi immediately countered by stating that Lance would not get in the ring for less than $4 million.

"Jesus, Miss Bibi," yelled Louis through the speaker on Bob's desk, "your goddam brother didn't even win his last fight. My man is already a champ. Rocky has every right to earn more than your brother. Lance is just a challenger. We could always fight someone else, so get real, lady."

"But Lance has more crowd appeal" interjected Bob, in support of Bibi's case, "although we do accept that he has yet to actually win a title."

It did not take Bob long to convince both parties to settle for $2 million each.

"Will you agree to an automatic rematch?" asked Louis, clearly nervous that his somewhat untested champion might not be successful.

As Bob said "no", Bibi said "yes". Louis laughed, a big even noisier laugh.

"Looks like you two are not on the same page," he chirped. "Well, what is it, yes or no?"

Bob put the phone on hold and the two at his end had a little chat, in which he convinced Bibi that more money could be made without having Rocky in the picture.

"We'd rather kick for touch on that one," he told Louis as soon as he had pressed the unmute button. "We'll agree to give Rocky another crack within eighteen months, provided that you still think it's worthwhile at the time."

Louis sort of growled. "Agreed, or not?" prompted Bob.

"Okay," said Louis, "but only on the basis that I select the venue for the first match."

"No fucking way!" replied Bob.

"Well then. Looks like we don't have a deal," said Louis.

"Looks like it," said Bob. And with that, to Bibi's astonishment, he rung off.

Bibi was taken by surprise. "What are you doing, Bob? Lance won't mind where he fights in America. Why don't we let him pick the venue?"

"Because, my dear Bibi, if he picks the venue, he will be sure to get a kickback and we will have no way of knowing how much or from whom. No, my dear, we must be in control of the site. Let him stew for a few days. He needs the fight, because nobody is interested in his Rocky. Trust me."

The words, "trust me" coming from a boxing promoter seemed like an oxymoron to Bibi, but, in a strange way she did trust Bob. He seemed to have been in their camp for quite a while now. And who else could she trust in America?

A few days later, a deal was agreed between Bob and Louis. The deal was struck whilst Bibi was busy shopping in Beverly Hills. As in any deal the two made, it was all quite simple. Each fighter would get $2 million, no immediate rematch clause, but words of good intention for a further fight within 18 months, Bob and Louis to share 50/50 in the venue and broadcast rights, both promoters to pursue site deals, with an agreement that they would go to the highest bidder. Bob called Bibi to say that he had heard from Louis and that this was the deal on the table. She was a bit annoyed that she had not been there, but decided not to kick up a fuss. In her mind, the real deal for Lance would be just how much he and she could muscle in to the profits of the fight. It was not about how much Lance would get paid. That would have to be a discussion between her and Bob alone and it could not wait until she got back to Vegas. Right now, she was busy in Beverly Hills.

Whilst Bibi was in the Prada store on Rodeo, she noticed a short middle-aged man, wearing a sharp grey suit, looking at her intently. She half thought that she recognised him, but then this occurs quite frequently in the golden triangle of Beverly Hills. One tends to think that many of the people you see there resemble someone you know, or you think you know, or you think you may have seen in the media. As she waited at the cash desk to secure her purchase, she quietly asked the server if she knew who the short man was.

"It's Ron Fleming," the girl whispered, "Supreme Pictures."

"Thanks," said Bibi as she collected her beautifully wrapped package.

Bibi stuck out her chest and paraded past Fleming en route to the exit. As she went by, he addressed her. "Excuse me, young lady," started Fleming, "I must compliment you on how elegant you look. It's such a pleasure to see a well-dressed young lady here, after all the casual gear that young people seem to wear nowadays. If I had to guess you are from overseas?"

"Well thank you, sir," responded Bibi, her South African accent immediately giving confirmation to his suggestion. "That is very sweet of you. I am glad that somebody appreciates it." Bibi had moved into full flirtation mode. A little fluttering of the eyelids, and a slight pout as she finished her sentence. Bibi was now pleased that she had decided to dress up nicely for her trip to the shops.

Ron Fleming was glad that he had approached the young lady. She had a sultry sort of beauty that reminded him of Gina Lollobrigida; slightly Mediterranean. He wondered if she was an actress. If so, he thought it was odd that he had never seen her before; Fleming prided himself on knowing who was who in Los Angeles but, in this case, he had not set eyes on Bibi before.

"Forgive me for asking, young lady, but are you from Cape Town?"

"No," Bibi replied with a broad smile. "Close. You are very close. Johannesburg, actually."

"Oh, what a lovely part of the world," said Fleming. "I do love it there. Say, we must have some mutual friends. I know lots of people from Joburg. May I take the liberty of buying you a coffee? There is a nice place immediately next door."

Bibi did not need to be asked twice. When the boss of Supreme Pictures asks you for a drink, you don't say no. With a little wave to the shop assistant, Ron Fleming escorted Bibi out of the door and into the cute street café adjacent. He was as smooth as silk; Bibi wondered how many times before he had carried out this manouevre.

Over coffee Bibi made sure that she captivated the man. She shared with him the reason for her mission to the USA and he was fascinated. He knew a few folk in the boxing game, but they were all men. Never before had he heard of the manager of a heavyweight champ being a woman. And, in all his years in the movie business, rarely had he seen such a beautiful woman as the one now sitting in front of him. He wondered how good she could be as an actress. He wondered how good she would be in bed. He intended to find out the answer to both questions. Although Bibi knew who he was, she did not let on. Rather, she waited for him to tell her, which, of course, he did almost as soon as the coffees were served. She did her best to be unimpressed. She needed him to want her more than she appeared to want him. The chance to get a foot in the door of a Hollywood studio was irresistible, but he must not know that.

The Beverly Hills Hotel is slightly removed from the Golden Triangle, about half a mile away. Too far to walk in stiletto heels, but an embarrassingly short ride for a cab. With coffee over, Fleming offered to give her a ride. Two minutes after a phone call from the café, a white Rolls Royce appeared outside. At first Bibi did not recognise it as a Roller, because, in comparison with some of the cars in Beverly Hills, a Rolls Royce seems quite small. Nevertheless, it is still *the* car to have, so Bibi felt quite important as the doorman at the hotel rushed forward to open the door. He certainly knew who Ron Fleming was.

When Bibi got back to her room, she saw that Bob Levin had called. She called back. Bob gave her the good news about his deal with Louis Brown and arranged for her to visit his office upon her return from Los Angeles. Bibi did not take issue with Bob on the phone, but she had no intention of signing a contract on behalf of her brother on the terms that Bob had agreed. If Bob thought that she would allow Lance to fight for $2 million dollars without any share of the gate, the sponsorship, or the broadcast rights, he was mistaken. But, for now, the matter in hand was how to seduce Ron Fleming. Lance's contract would have to wait a few days. Bibi picked up the phone, called the front desk, and extended her stay for three nights. "Three ought to do it," she said out loud to herself.

If one were to listen to the squealing from some actresses about the way they had to undergo the ordeal of the audition couch, you would think that they were all seduced whilst they screamed and shouted for their freedom. It became Bibi's goal to be "seduced". What was wrong with that if the seducer owned a Hollywood film studio? What was wrong with the fact that Ron Fleming was already married to an ageing actress?

The process did not take long, and was, in fact, quite enjoyable. Ron showed her places in town that she would otherwise not have been to. More importantly he arranged a screen test, which Bibi just nailed. She could lose the South African accent in a flash. The studio, and Ron, were very happy with the results of the test; the studio executives knew just how to please their boss. Incredibly, three days after the encounter in Prada, Bibi had been offered a small part on the silver screen, to be filmed in a month's time. Naturally, she accepted, then headed back to Las Vegas, mission accomplished.

When Bibi walked into Bob Levin's office, he was all smiles. When she walked out, he was seriously livid. Bibi had done her homework. She had called Gerrie Van der Merwe in South Africa. At first, he was nervous to take her call. He did not want to upset his darling Angel. It was not long however before he returned her call, having first obtained cautious approval from his wife. Bibi wanted to know what, in Gerrie's estimation, the site fee and broadcast fees could be for a Lance versus Rocky title fight. Gerrie thought about it, and then gave a number. Bibi halved the number and demanded that this would be the amount that Bob should share with her brother, if she were to sign the contract on his behalf. Bob was apoplectic. He thought about walking away from the whole thing but his instincts to have half an apple, rather than none, prevailed upon him. He eventually settled for a number that actually equated to three quarters of an apple, so he would need to make sure that the real numbers remained a secret. Even so, giving away a quarter of his profits was not something that Bob Levin liked to do. "What is it with these South African boxers?" he asked himself. "Why are these people so smart?"

Bibi decided not to return to South Africa for a while. After all, her brother would soon be coming to America to fight Rocky and she had one foot in the door of a Hollywood studio. She also decided that she could not live in Las Vegas. No, Los Angeles was the place for her; so, she set about finding a nice apartment. It was not long before she had moved into a high-rise building on the southern cusp of Beverly Hills, just off Sunset Boulevard. Her small apartment had a magnificent view of Beverly Hills and Santa Monica, with its wide beach, in the hazy distance. Bibi had arrived in Hollywood.

The affair with Ron Fleming was hot. Ron was in the process of divorcing his third wife, so he was free to escort his new protege about town. And Ron knew the town, and the town knew Ron. Bibi was having a wonderful time. Bibi looked stunning. The warm weather of Los

Angeles suited her. It was not long before the whole of Bel Air knew who Bibi was. The studio enrolled Bibi in acting lessons, but, in truth, Bibi needed very little instruction. In her small part in her first film, according to those on the set, she stole the scene. There would clearly be more to come. But it was on the television that Bibi made her biggest impact. The film studio had secured her a spot on one of the late-night talk shows as a guest. With her great looks and quick wit, she was an instant success. Other television stations wanted to book her, and soon her name and picture were all over Los Angeles. She was the perfect foil for an interviewer. She made a point of always wearing a lowcut dress. She always had a new joke or story to relate and her quick brain was a nice challenge to the hosts. In a short time, from the fortuitous meeting with Ron Fleming, Bibi had become a celebrity. Her picture and name started to appear in magazines and adverts. Tony, at Mood in England, had a field day. The LA press were hungry for photos of the gorgeous newcomer to Hollywood. Tony had some marvellous photos of Bibi in lingerie, just what the media needed. It was not long before Supreme studios had plastered a fifty foot high billboard on Sunset Boulevard of Bibi in one of Tony's pictures. Ostensibly it was to advertise the film in which she had a bit part, but clearly, Ron was positioning his new girlfriend for stardom. Bibi had arrived.

Chapter Twenty Three

Back in South Africa, Gerrie and Angel were enjoying a much quieter and calmer existence. Gerrie, with welcome advice from his dad, had acquired a fleet of spanking new diesel trucks as well as a huge depot just south of the railway yards in Johannesburg, which spread across several acres on the edge of the city, close to the emerging network of motorways. Gerrie installed his dad as President of "Van the Man" enterprises, although Gerrie was a quick study, and pretty soon had a good handle on how trucking worked.

He and Angel still lived in the big house in Atholl, in the northern suburbs. In the year following Gerrie's retirement Angel had produced one beautiful little daughter. Now, sixteen months on, another baby arrived, this time a robust boy. Gerrie wanted to call him Strom, after his dad, but Angel quietly objected; it was far too Afrikaans for her. Eventually they settled on Luke.

When Angel's mother, Sally, now installed as the new queen of the extended Marconi family in Nevada, discovered that she was about to be a grandmother, she was torn. She had been enjoying a renaissance; firstly, in regard to her sex life, which had flourished with her mature and experienced Italian man, but also with the explosion of possibilities in her life. However, the accessibility of Giancarlo's personal long-haul jet and the complete absence of concern about money, made visits to South Africa to see Angel and the babies relatively easy. Gradually Sally eased into the role of grandmother and, to her surprise, such a role did nothing to detract from her sensuality or beauty. From time to time, Giancarlo accompanied Sally to Johannesburg. His relationship with Gerrie had come a long way since he and his brother forced him to lose. Now, he was most helpful to Gerrie in teaching him some of the tricks of the trade in the trucking business. Things that Gerrie's dad would never have known about.

Giancarlo, with his extensive interests in the casino business in Nevada, had also spotted an opportunity in South Africa, where casino gambling had been banned. He very quickly realised that it was less than three hours' drive from Johannesburg and Pretoria to Swaziland, an independent nation and neighbour to South Africa. In Giancarlo's view, a casino and adult entertainment centre in Swaziland would be very attractive to South Africans, who were being deprived of their right to gamble and have fun. He shared his thoughts with Gerrie. He knew that Gerrie was a national hero and an Afrikaner, as were all of the influential politicians. Gerrie could be his key to getting a project approved. The government in Pretoria exercised a huge influence on its tiny neighbour, Swaziland, which was still ruled by the local tribal chief, or, in this case, king. If the king wanted to build a casino resort in Swaziland, it would be pointless without the support of the South African government. Giancarlo knew exactly what to do, but he would need Gerrie's support. His relationship with Gerrie's mother-in-law would be a big help. A project outside of Nevada might also be of great assistance in laundering money from the Starburst.

Sally was delighted that her man was so interested in her adopted homeland; it made things so much easier for her and Angel. It was not too long before the Swazi Starburst project started to get real legs.

Meanwhile things had moved on in the USA. Rocky Jones had successfully defended his heavyweight crown and cleared the way for a reunification of the title fight with Bibi's brother, Lance. Once again, this fight had taken place at the Starburst in Vegas, which had now firmly established itself as *the* boxing venue for the west coast, as opposed to Madison Square Garden in the east.

The fight was pretty much a walkover for Lance, who disposed of Rocky in the fourth round. The after-fight party was much more of an event than the bout, itself. Bibi's first film had been released and Bibi received good notices for her cameo role, not so much for her acting, but for her sizzling personality on the screen. This had been followed by another film in which she had a much bigger part as the mistress of a criminal. Again, she impressed. She had managed her affair with Fleming to perfection. He did not excite her sexually except through his power. She made sure that he had a good time and was careful not to let any sideshows she engaged in get in the way. So, everybody who was anybody wanted to be seen at the party, and Sammy Marconi excelled himself by organising the party to end all parties, including a rare appearance of the King himself, Elvis Presley.

But, despite the fire power of the celebrity guests and performers at the Starburst, the real star of the show had been Lance, himself. Lance was the consummate entertainer. He had lost none of the ability he had displayed as a teenager in being able to captivate an audience. He was articulate, entertaining and funny during the pre-fight and after-fight press conferences. During the training sessions before the fight he had been readily available for the press, and, during his frequent appearances on late-night TV shows he was often hilarious and always controversial. The public loved him. And the fact that he was the brother of Hollywood's up and coming superstar was just icing on the cake for the tabloids and talk shows.

In the two years following the Rocky fight, Lance went on to defend his title successfully five more times and, with the smart management of Bibi, amassed a fortune. He too had moved to Los Angeles, and the days on the Highveld of South Africa and jail in Kyalami, seemed long ago. Bibi had secured, under Fleming's patronage, a couple more film parts, but it was becoming clear that, as sizzling as her presence was on the screen, her ability as a serious actress was limited. So, Fleming had another ace up his sleeve for his lover. A television show with her charismatic brother. Fleming had frequently seen how relaxed both Bibi and Lance were in front of a television camera. They didn't need to act; they just needed to be themselves. They were both characters in their own right. They did not need to impersonate anyone else.

With that in mind, Ron decided to move into TV production and converted one of the Supreme Pictures film studios into a TV production unit. From there he conceived and produced the Bibi and Lance show, a late-night talk show, hosted jointly by the brother and sister team. The B and L show quickly became the number one TV talk show in America, with the combination of wit and beauty it offered. The fact it was hosted by two non-Americans also made it stand out from the rest, because both host and hostess found ways to politely make fun of their new country without being offensive. They made

America look at itself and that, combined with the beauty
and the wit, was an unusual and winning combination.
It was not long before the B and L show attracted the
most interesting, talented, handsome and beautiful guests
in the country and from overseas. And, Lance was still the
reigning heavyweight champion of the world.

Two years after the launch of the talk show, and
three defences later, Lance retired from boxing, still
the undefeated world champion. Bibi and Ron's sexual
relationship had cooled, but their business relationship
and friendship had grown exponentially. Ron had accepted
that Bibi was a free spirit but had also recognised she was
a superb and ruthless businesswoman. He saw how she
had taken on the male dominated business of professional
boxing and manipulated and milked it. He saw the ease
with which she had conquered the male dominated space
of the late-night talk show business and he saw what an
influence she had on the nation and, indeed, the politics
of the nation. He could not expect to have exclusivity in
her personal life. He was better off being her friend, ally,
and mentor in a broader sense. He was comfortable with
that, and so was she.

Bibi and Sally had not maintained a close relationship,
despite coming from the same suburb of Johannesburg
and both now having homes in Los Angeles. Perhaps
the memory of that fateful day in London, when Sally's
daughter had stolen her boyfriend, Gerrie, was too much
of a bridge to cross? Perhaps the difference in their ages
was a factor? Whatever the barrier was, the paths of Bibi
and Sally rarely crossed, even though they lived so close
in a town so foreign to both of them. Bibi was, therefore,
quite surprised to get a call one day from Sally, to tell her
that Gerrie and Angel were coming to visit her with the

grandchildren. "Perhaps," said Sally, "you'd like to come around one day to see your old friend and the kids. It would be nice if you two could make up. You used to be such good friends and so much time has now passed."

Bibi was tempted by the idea of seeing Angel and Gerrie again. Sally was right. Angel had been Bibi's best friend as a teenager and they had both behaved badly to each other when they split. On the other hand, Bibi wondered what it would have been like to have stayed with Gerrie. In truth, she had never met anyone else that she wanted to marry and now, Angel had a happy marriage with two children, whilst, she, Bibi, had nothing, except of course, fame and money. Maybe she should have stuck with Gerrie, boring as he might have been.

"Okay, Sally," she finally responded, "yes, it would be nice to see Angel again – and her little ones. Please let me know when you want me to come, but remember I work late, so, if possible, from lunchtime on. Thank you."

A couple of weeks later Bibi broke out of her busy schedule to visit Sally and her family at Giancarlo Marconi's villa in Bel Air, carrying several little parcels of gifts that she had bought at the cute little toy shop on Canon Avenue. Gerrie was not there. Angel greeted Bibi warmly enough and proudly introduced her little girl and boy. The little girl, Samantha, was the prettiest and cutest little thing Bibi had ever seen. Bibi instantly fell in love with her. Luke was still little more than a baby, so interaction was more limited, but Bibi and Samantha clicked from the minute they met. Angel was pleased. Sally produced some coffee and cold drinks and the three ladies caught up on the state of each other's lives. Although Angel spoke glowingly of her husband, Gerrie, she did not explain why he was not present. When the opportunity came Bibi raised the subject. "And how's Gerrie? How's the business going?"

"Thank you for asking," replied Angel, "he's very well. Hopefully you'll see him whilst we are here. This morning he had to attend some meeting or other; something to do with haulage. I don't exactly know what."

"No real information there," thought Bibi. "He's probably just avoiding me."

Then Bibi had an idea. "You know that Lance and I host this TV talk show five nights a week?" she started, "well, do you think you and Gerrie would be prepared to come on the show as our guests? It might be fun, what with you having been Miss World and Gerrie the champ, and the fact that we all come from the same place and so on."

"Oh, I don't know, Bibi," said Angel, "you know what Gerrie's like. He was never a great one for publicity. I'd love to come on the show, but I doubt Gerrie would agree."

Sally, who had been listening without comment, now piped up. "Then I'll try to persuade him," she said, "I think it would be terrific. It would make a great show and loads of people would be interested."

Bibi's mind was whirring. If she could get Gerrie and Lance together on the TV set, she had an even bigger idea. Both men had stopped fighting professionally and both retired whilst still the champ. The last time they fought each other was in Johannesburg in the never to be forgotten bout which Gerrie shaved on points. Her brother had never had the chance to show the world that, given an even playing field, he could beat his compatriot fairly and squarely. If Bibi could get the two men together, maybe, just maybe, she could engineer a final showdown between them. She could hype the thing up to the heavens. Both men had plenty of money, so it must not be for money; it must be for honour. Such an old-fashioned thought could appeal to the show's audience – big time! The idea began to formulate in her head that, through such a fight, the show could raise millions of dollars for good causes. If that were so, it would do Bibi no harm at all.

The first step was to get Angel and Gerrie on to the show. She decided to keep quiet about her scheme. The request for the couple to come on the show would be for an innocent chit chat about old times. There was enough meat in the backgrounds of Angel and Gerrie to interest viewers and, between Lance and her, she was sure that they could make the conversation interesting enough. That's what she had to convince her brother and the show's producers. She would spring her "charity" bout idea on air, and surprise them all.

After a couple of hours in Sally's Bel Air back yard, with its splendid view over Los Angeles, Bibi made her farewells, with big hugs for the kiddies and lesser ones for Angel and Sally as she, once again, urged them to prevail upon Gerrie to be guests on the show. Angel was quite excited about the idea. She had not been in the public eye for a couple of years now. This would be a nice adventure. She had regained her perfect figure after childbirth; she had nothing to fear in a TV appearance. All she had to do was convince her husband.

When Bibi got to the TV studio and discussed her invitation to Angel that she and Gerrie come on to the show, at first Lance was cool on the idea. He had never had a childhood friend on the show and was not sure that it would be of interest to the audience. Bibi convinced him otherwise. "You have so much to talk to them about; as do I. We all go back such a long way. It would be different if they weren't achievers in their own right, but, look, he's been world champion and she's been Miss World. That's not a shabby record. We've had plenty of guests on the show with less talent and fewer achievements. No, Lance, this will make a great show. Believe me."

And so it did. As predicted, Gerrie was extremely reluctant to participate. In fact, he had been extremely reluctant to even meet Bibi, which is why he had gone out when she came to coffee. Now he was being asked, not only to meet his ex-live-in lover and her brother, but also to meet them in front of millions of other people.

"That's what makes the meeting so easy," Angel explained, "because so many other people will be there, nothing unpleasant can happen."

So, after an evening of not only Angel, but also Sally, going on at him, he reluctantly agreed and Sally called Bibi to make the arrangements.

The Bibi and Lance show was taped live. It was screened 15 minutes later in New York and three hours later in Los Angeles. To keep it fresh, most of it was unrehearsed, especially the actual interview sequences with the studio guests. The 15 minute time lag was purely to edit out any profanities or other slip ups that might occur and would need to be deleted. Gerrie and Angel were asked to show up at the studio one hour prior to the taping session, just to check on dress, make up and the general procedure that would be followed. They were ushered into a dressing room with five golden stars on the door. The room was large and plush. The walls were covered in photographs of previous guests on the show, a wonderful gallery of some of the world's most interesting people. There was a deep pile carpet, a comfortable sofa and easy chair, and a dressing table with a mirror surrounded by light bulbs, just like you see in the movies. For a couple of South Africans from Randburg, it was awe-inspiring to think of whose footsteps they were following in this room. Angel checked herself out in the mirror. She was wearing a light summer dress, with a fairly short skirt that really showed off her legs nicely. She was nervous about that because, now she thought about it, the easy chairs on the set were quite low. "It might be a bit difficult for me in such a short skirt," she thought to herself, "but too late now." Actually, Angel looked absolutely stunning; as Gerrie looked at her he was so proud of her and pleased with himself. The most beautiful wife who had produced two gorgeous children. What more could a man want?

Whilst Gerrie and Angel examined the wall of celebrity photos, a knock at the door signalled the arrival of their hosts. Bibi and Lance burst through the door. Lance gave the warmest of hugs to his old adversary, Gerrie, and then moved on to Angel, who did her best to avoid the bear hug approach. Angel had a long memory in regard to the ebullient Lance. The greeting between Gerrie and Bibi was more awkward, and Bibi began to wonder whether she had done the right thing in inviting him on the show.

"Now, let me explain how this all works," began Lance, after he had welcomed them and thanked them for coming. "Bibi and I will be asking you questions that we think might be of interest to the viewers. We'll try to keep it away from our personal entanglements. I can ask you about boxing things. I can tell them how you helped me in Kyalami. It's not a secret here that I once went to jail. We can discuss how we felt about winning and losing fights and so on. Okay? We can talk about our common ground. What it was like going to school in Apartheid South Africa etc." He stopped for breath. Angel and Gerrie had not commented.

Bibi picked it up. "I think the viewers will be interested in your Miss World experiences. I'll ask you about that – and what it's like to give it all up to be a wife and mother, that sort of thing. Okay?" Most of this seemed harmless to Angel and Gerrie and they both said so. Bibi and Lance swept out of the room just as they had swept in. "See you on the set in ten minutes," said Bibi, "and remember, if anything happens you're are not happy with, this is a tape. We can always cut it out." With that, brother and sister were gone.

Both Gerrie and Angel had been used to performing under bright lights; Gerrie in the ring and Angel on the beauty pageant stage, but the brightness of the set in the studio took them both aback as they were introduced to the audience with the cameras rolling. They did look a handsome couple as they walked in, hand in hand. Angel looked stunning in her short white dress and high heels which displayed her beautiful legs; Gerrie, tall and handsome in a dark blue suit without a tie, could have been a male model. He was unmarked from his boxing career. No cauliflower ears, scars, or other marks to spoil his good looks. The studio audience clapped and cheered, urged on by a stage hand with a huge plastic sign. Both Bibi and Lance got up to greet them and seat them on the comfortable guest sofa. Angel tried to pull her skirt over her knees, but to no avail. Bibi had changed from the outfit she had been wearing in the dressing room. Now she had a skirt even shorter than Angel's; there was no way she was going to be outshone by her old friend. Gerrie, of course, could not help but notice.

"We four go back a long, long way," Lance explained to the audience. "We've all been friends since around our tenth birthdays. We were born in the same suburb in Johannesburg. We spoke the same language, Afrikaans, and went to the same schools. We're all here today, in Hollywood, because the Gods have been kind to us, and we've all made our mark on the world. But none more so than Angel and Gerrie. Both have conquered the world, which is some feat coming from where we all started."

With that, the discussion began. Everything went according to plan. The two guests began to relax. There was much laughter and some fond mutual reminiscing. The studio audience was enraptured. Then, Bibi suddenly broke from script.

"Gerrie," she began, "a lot of people think the judges should have scored your fight against Lance for the World title differently, – and I agree with them. It was clear to me that my dear brother actually beat you that night. What do you say?"

Gerrie thought she was joking, then realised that she wasn't. He refused to take the bait. "Well, my dear Bibi, there were three judges and only one of them appears to have agreed with you. Luckily for me, the referee didn't have to ask your opinion on the night."

"But Gerrie," Bibi carried on, "wouldn't you admit that Lance is the better fighter? Just look at his record after he, so-called, lost to you. He never lost another fight. Before you took on Lance, you got knocked out by a nobody."

Gerrie began to get a little irritated with Bibi's aggressive stance. He had not agreed to come on their show to be belittled.

"I've never fought a 'nobody' said Gerrie, "even your brother's not a nobody."

"He certainly isn't – and most people think that he was a better boxer than you."

"Well, if that's what you think, maybe I should prove you wrong." As the words came out of his mouth Gerrie leaped off the plush sofa in the direction of Lance, his fist clenched, as if to start a fight. He was, of course, only pretending to be annoyed, but, for a moment, the audience thought they were about to see an actual fight, since Lance too jumped up with his fists at the ready.

This is just what Bibi had hoped for.

"Now boys," she started. "Calm down. We're all friends here. But I've got an idea. Why don't we put on a real fight? I know you've retired Gerrie, but it wasn't that long ago so that shouldn't stop you from having a showdown to see who really is the best."

"But, Bibi," chimed in Angel, "Gerrie stopped fighting over three years ago. He's not going to start again now. I don't want him to fight anymore. That's all finished now."

"Wait a minute, my love," came back Gerrie. "I think it would be a very good idea to show Bibi, once and for all, who is the king of the ring. Of course, I'll fight Lance, but not for money. This time it will be for charity."

Bibi squealed with delight. This was just the result that she had wanted. In her mind a fight between two retired champions, one of which was a household name through their talk show, could raise millions of dollars for good causes. This could only help the cause of Bibi Hermanus.

"Okay," said Lance, "let's do it, Gerrie. We'll fight. Twelve rounds. Big Arena. Six months from now. Give you time to get into shape. All proceeds to charity. You name yours and I'll name mine. 50 50 split." He got up and extended his right hand. Gerrie grinned, and shook it. The deal had been struck. No details, but a very public commitment had been made. There was no turning back for either man.

Bibi was very pleased at the result of her manipulation. Angel was not. She was cross with Gerrie for reacting to the goading. They had a good life back in South Africa. The trucking company was going well and Angel was enjoying being a young mother of two. This whole thing could only bring chaos to their lives. As they left the studio to return to Sally's Bel Air house, Angel was not in a good mood. She could only see trouble ahead.

Chapter Twenty Four

The prospect that two ex-champions were going to have a grudge match immediately fired the imagination of the public, not just in North America but also in South Africa, Europe and South America. There were plenty of clips from the B and L talk show for other news agencies to use and thousands of pictures of Gerrie, Lance, Bibi and Angel to decorate the press stories. Gradually details about the fight and how it would raise money were released, mainly by the glamourous Bibi, who took it upon herself to be the promoter in chief. Bibi wanted the fight to be in a big venue. She envisaged raising millions through ticket sales as well as from worldwide television. The TV companies from every continent were clamouring to broadcast the fight, so the timing of the event would be crucial in maximising international viewership across time zones. Gerrie had agreed to hold the event in the USA, so that Bibi and Lance could continue with their TV show, even though that would be more disruptive to him and his family and business. In fact, he wanted it to be there. He was determined to beat Lance, even in his own backyard. Also, Gerrie knew just how popular the White Assassin was in South Africa. He did not really want to fight in front of a hostile crowd, even though he was a South African himself. Angel, of course, was not keen on this, because it would mean her husband having to spend at least a month away from home, if not more.

Bibi investigated suitable venues and eventually settled on the Staples arena, an indoor stadium in downtown Los Angeles with a capacity of 24,000. All of the necessary broadcast facilities were built into this venue and it would mitigate any worries about weather disruption. Bibi also left no stone unturned in regard to potential money raising. First, of course, there would be the revenue from the sale of TV broadcasting rights, then from the ticket sales and ancillary income from the venue, and then the documentary movie rights surrounding the fight and its back story.

But the big money, in Bibi's head, would come from opportunities for the worldwide public to bet on the fight. To do this, Bibi enlisted the assistance of one of the world's leading betting sites and together they dreamed up all sorts of phone-in competitions, designed to suck money from the public before and as the fight proceeded. You could bet on almost anything regarding the fight from simple things to how long it would last, to how many right hooks would be thrown, to how many knock downs there would be and so on. All proceeds from anything to do with the fight would go to the chosen charities and Bibi wanted this promotion to become the biggest world fund raising effort ever made. Neither Bibi nor Lance would have their fingers in the pot, but the kudos they would gain as fund raisers and benefactors would be of huge commercial and political value – especially to Bibi, whose sights were now firmly set on bigger things.

Winning this fight was now the most important thing in Gerrie's life, save for his wife and kiddies. Most people in the world had thought that Gerrie had been smart to quit when he was at the top. Many boxers in history had failed to do that and come to regret it. Now, it seemed, Gerrie was no different from those that went before him. He was determined to get fit and be sharp on the night. He sought out his old mentor, Sean Brennan, who was delighted to be asked to help. Since Gerrie's retirement life had become quite mundane for Sean. Now he had the chance, once again, to be on the big stage. Sean and Gerrie's plan was for Gerrie to reach maximum fitness over a three month period of strenuous training in Johannesburg. Sean tapped into a couple of current heavyweights as sparring partners and rented a small private gym in Sandton, not far from Gerrie and Angel's home. Then the plan was to move to a training camp in the USA a month before the fight. Giancarlo Marconi kindly offered his ranch house in Nevada as a headquarters for Gerrie, Sean and his sparring partners, where there would also be room for Angel and the children, should she decide to come over before the fight. A marquee was set up in the walled garden of the villa. Since the house was mob proof, and surrounded by a high wall and dozens of security cameras, the press would have a hard time getting to Gerrie in training.

Lance, as was his way, was far more cavalier about training for the fight than Gerrie. After all, it was not that long ago that he had retired as the World Champion. He still believed that he could outpunch his old friend. He hoped that he would not have to outlast him. Not to say that he didn't work out at all. Far from it. It was just that, in comparison to Gerrie, Lance took things relatively easy. On top of this, he still ran the nightly show, which of course, was a relentless vehicle for Bibi to keep plugging the fight, and to raise more and more money.

When Gerrie and his team arrived in Nevada, four weeks before the fight, Bibi really wanted him to make another appearance on the show to increase the hype, but Gerrie declined. Nothing was going to take his attention away from being fit, not even Bibi at her most alluring. And Bibi really tried. To her, Gerrie was still a very attractive man. Now that he was here in Los Angeles, without Angel, Bibi thought she might just have a chance to rekindle her relationship, whilst, at the same time, weaken her brother's opponent. Gerrie wasn't having any of it. Bibi could have walked stark naked through the doors of his training villa and Gerrie would have looked the other way. That is how badly he wanted to win. And that his how badly he wanted to honour the promises he had made to his darling Angel.

Tickets for the fight were like gold dust. Bibi, of course, had held the best ones back for careful and well considered distribution to the Hollywood "A" list. This was a glorious opportunity for Bibi to thank old friends in high places as well as to gain new ones. The front five or six rows of the floor seats at Staples Arena would have more celebrities than the Oscars show. Bibi suddenly found out how difficult the task of sorting out the pecking order of famous people is. There were, after all, only a limited number of seats in the front row. Fortunately, the tickets were so "hot" that just having one was a status symbol. Nevertheless, having a ticket for the front three rows had become the ultimate sign of super stardom – and Bibi found herself in the role of kingmaker.

Despite the fact that Gerrie had promised Angel he would not allow Bibi near him in her absence, she was not convinced he would be able to fend her off. She really did trust her Gerrie, but she knew how clever and devious Bibi could be. As a result, Angel could not stay for too long in South Africa when Gerrie was training in the danger zone. The thought of travelling to Las Vegas with the two little ones did not appeal. Once in the US, she knew that she could stay with her mum, so help with the children would be on hand, but the thought of the journey terrified her. Nevertheless, the thought of Bibi getting her hands on her husband terrified her even more, so Angel decided to make the journey.

To mitigate the trauma of the trip Angel booked the front four seats in the first class section of the South African Airways jet. At the time, the positions of air steward were reserved for gay whites by the national airline. Angel placed the crib for the baby boy across the two front left seats and strapped little Samantha into the seat next to herself. The gay steward arrived with the menu, beautifully printed on a gold card. "And what would madame like for dinner?" he enquired of little Samantha.

The young lady thought for a moment as she glanced over the menu, which, of course, she could not read. "I think I will have a peanut butter jelly sandwich," she finally piped up.

This threw the steward into complete disarray. "I'm afraid we don't have any peanut butter jelly on board, madame," he managed, "but I can give you a caviar sandwich." Angel smiled and in perfect Afrikaans, told him not to worry.

Giancarlo had arranged for chauffeur Bill, with the baseball cap, to pick up Angel and the children at Las Vegas airport. When Gerrie was not there, Angel was disappointed that he had not taken time off training to come the short distance from the villa to the airport. After such a long journey with the kiddies her heart sank when she did not see him with Bill. He was, however, pulling her leg, having been hiding behind a pillar, out of sight in the crowd. He watched his gorgeous wife and children greet Bill, then, whilst Angel was attending to the task of folding up the push chair, he crept up behind the little group. Samantha saw him first. "Daddy," she cried out, as the broadest possible beam spread across her little face, "Mummy, Daddy is here." Angel looked up. Her heart jumped. She was thrilled to see her handsome man. Bill took charge of the children whilst Angel and Gerrie hugged and kissed.

Although Gerrie continued to train hard, his family, at least, was around him. Any worries he might have had about the trucking business in South Africa were soon put behind him as Angel reported how well his dad was coping. Being President of Van the Man Trucking had breathed new life into Strom. So, Gerrie was free to concentrate on being as fit as he could possibly be and, somehow, that cause was helped considerably by having his family around him.

As Angel and Gerrie reflected in the evenings in the desert, they thought about how life had treated them well, as, indeed it had their fellow life travellers, Lance and Bibi. All four of them had led a blessed childhood in Apartheid South Africa; they had all been born on the right side of the tracks. All four of them had profited from the sound education that was available to white citizens of South Africa and all four from the economic opportunities that had been available to them. Yes, it is true that they were all exceptionally adept at taking advantage of the chances they had been offered, but all four of them had found a way to carve out and profit from these opportunities, when so many others failed to do so. In some ways, however, their lives had been selfish. One did not have far to look in their homeland for extreme poverty and hardship. Whilst our four compatriots enjoyed a life of comfort, privilege and luxury, most of their fellow citizens simply did not have the same opportunities. South Africa was a very uneven playing field and none of our four favoured citizens had done anything really meaningful to help raise the standard of living, health or happiness of their fellow black citizens. This was fine, as long as it lasted, but change in their homeland was well overdue. As Angel and Gerrie were served their dinner each evening by Giancarlo's attentive staff, the plight of 40 million blacks at home did not cross their minds. Gerrie was focused on one thing: beating his old friend, Lance, in the ring. Angel was focused on looking after her handsome man and their offspring.

Bibi's fundraising efforts, with only a few days to go before the fight, had raised an incredible 125 million dollars for charity; none of it was earmarked to help their underprivileged black citizens in their homeland.

PART
TWO

Chapter Twenty Five

It is January again in 1970. Two little boys are starting school for the first time. They both live in Alexandra, a sprawling black township nestling up against the richest suburb in the north of Johannesburg and possibly the richest suburb in the country, if one were to measure these things by the number of swimming pools and tennis courts per square mile. Nobody in Alexandra is rich, and nobody has a white skin. Nobody has a swimming pool. There is not even a public one. The wealthy suburb of Sandton is separated from Alexandra by a newly constructed motorway which joins the administrative capital of South Africa, Pretoria, to the commercial capital, Johannesburg. The sprawling scar on the landscape of Alexandra is in stark contrast to the glistening suburb of Sandton. Alexandra township is not supposed to be there at all. It is, what is known as, an informal township. It has sprung out of a cluster of hostels, which were built to house black male workers, who were needed for service in the rich white suburbs or in the factories to the east of the city. The official black township, Soweto, is situated some twenty miles away from white Johannesburg, out of sight and mostly out of mind. Alexandra has emerged and grown without any urban planning or commensurate services slap bang next to the white wealth of suburban Johannesburg. Despite the fact that it officially does not exist, it grows bigger by the day, inching northwards to the other new motorway which connects the wealthiest white suburbs to the airport. There are very few brick-built houses in the township and only a small scattering of anything higher than one storey, and those are soulless hostels for single black men, overcrowded and filthy and a breeding ground for homosexuality. Most of the homes are literally shacks, mainly made of corrugated metal. They are freezing in the winter and like little ovens in the summer. Most have no running water, this has to be fetched in pails from communal taps. A few shacks have been formally wired up with electricity. Most residents have tapped into the mains supply and are in one way or another stealing it. Nobody knows how many people live in Alexandra because non-persons do not fill in census forms. There is no pressure from the wealthy white citizens of Sandton to eliminate the township; this would wipe out the source of their cheap workforce.

The two little boys are both starting their first day at the Emfundisweni Elementary School in the middle of the informal township, so it is not too far for them to walk. That is a good thing because there is no form of public transport available, only unlicensed taxis. There are no school buses. The school is rudimentary. The one-storey block is riddled with asbestos. There are no playing fields nor tennis courts. There is not even a proper gymnasium. The school "hall" has to double for all activity that does not take place in a classroom. There are 50 children in each class, but not 50 little desks. The truancy level is so high that overcrowding is not actually a problem. The children are taught in Afrikaans, which is not one of their native languages nor one that is spoken in their humble homes. The most common language of communication across the ethnic groups is English. Despite such poor standards of education most black children speak English and at least two African languages which is considerably more than their white counterparts.

Although our two first timers at school both live in the township with their parents, they come from completely different backgrounds. Daniel Buthelezi was born in Alexandra township. His father, Sam, runs a shabeen, which is an informal (illegal) bar and meeting place, operating from a tin-roofed extension to the Buthelezis' little tin-roofed house. Sam's wife is Surprise – such a lovely name! Surprise is always smiling, no matter what difficulties she may be enduring. Everybody who knows her in the township loves Surprise and many who have not met her have certainly heard of her. Both Sam and Surprise were born in Zululand, although they did not know each other there. Sam had come to "Goldies" (Johannesburg) many years ago in search of work, where he had found employment at South African Breweries, first as a labourer and eventually as a driver. Surprise had arrived in the township initially as the girlfriend of another Zulu man, long gone. She had found employment at the Clinic in the township, a charitable local hospital set up by a group of white doctors from Johannesburg. There, she had started as a cleaning lady but, due to her friendly outward going nature, had risen to receptionist and general factotum. From this desk she got to know a huge amount about the struggles and joys of the people of Alexandra. She was there when babies were born and there when the elderly passed on. There are few surprises in Surprise's life. Most of Sam and Surprise's relatives still live 600 miles away in Zululand. In all the years that the Buthelezis have lived in Alexandra, they have only been able to afford to go to their homeland once. Their little boy Daniel has never been; in fact, he has never been anywhere out of the sprawling township.

Daniel has two brothers and two sisters. His elder brother, Shaka, was born out of wedlock. It is quite common in many African tribes that a woman must prove that she can bear children before a man will take her as his wife. Shaka, in fact, is the son of the "long gone" boyfriend of Surprise. Sam Buthelezi married Surprise, not just because he loved her, but also because she had proved herself to be fertile. And fertile she was, producing three more babies for Sam before the clinic, unbeknown to Sam, secretly supplied her with some "pillies". Daniel's younger brother is called Solomon, and his two sisters, Sindiswe ("saved") and Mthunze ("shade").

Mthabisi (pronounced "umtarbisi") Skosane, the other little boy in our story, is a newcomer to Alexandra. His parents are from the Ndebele tribe. They had recently moved to Alexandra from miles away, because Menzi, Mthabisi's father had secured a job in a factory to the east of Alexandra. He had been living in a hostel, away from his wife and children, but this had been extremely disruptive to family life, so he had found a shack in Alexandra which could accommodate himself, his wife, Londiwe, and their two children. Menzi's new job is in the administration at the factory. He is very quick with numbers and is highly regarded by his white bosses. He is paid a wage considerably higher than most of his black peers. The move has meant that Londiwe has had to give up her job in Witbank, so, at the time of Mthabisi starting school, she is on the lookout for paid employment somewhere near to Alexandra.

Mthabisi takes after his dad, in terms of his numeracy. It does not take him long at school to grasp the fundamentals of reading, writing and particularly arithmetic. He is a very quick learner and a delight for his teachers. Daniel Buthelezi is less interested in learning, but he is extremely sociable. He is large for his age and seems to the other boys to be quite worldly. Clearly, the effect of having the men of Alexandra township descending on his home night after night to sup at his dad's illegal hooch den, has made him much more aware of what goes on in the world than Mthabisi would have been in the black township on the outskirts of the Afrikaans coal mining town of Witbank. Witbank is not known as the seat of learning, even in the Afrikaans community.

Mthabisi and Daniel find that they have been assigned to the same classroom. Daniel already knows several of the new recruits to the school, having played with them in the mud or dust of the streets of Alex. Daniel can see that Mthabisi is a bit bewildered by his new environment, so kindly takes him under his wing and attempts to bring him into his ever-growing group of little followers. Mthabisi is grateful and, for many years to come, will never forgot this act of friendship. It is not long before the newcomer's name has been shortened to Thabi, but strangely, Daniel never becomes Dan, but will remain Daniel throughout his life.

The two young lads become friends. Daniel has many other friends, but Mthabisi is quite a loner. Menzi and Londiwe, his dad and mum, are concerned about him. Back in Witbank, he was not exactly a gregarious boy, but he did have a cadre of pals that he kicked around with in the dirt. Now, after the move to Alex, he has not made friends easily. Luckily however, that boy Daniel seems to have taken him under his wing. Londiwe, although glad for her son, is also cautious. She has heard the rumours about what goes on in the tin shed next to Daniel's home.

She does not want her little man to get caught up in anything like that.

Also starting school for the first time is a pretty little girl named Gloria Lukhele. Like Daniel, Gloria is a Zulu. Her mother, Lulana, has taken the name "Lukhele" after the father of her daughter, even though she never married him. In fact, Gloria and her little brother, Brightboy, have no idea who their father is and have never met him. Lulana runs what is effectively a brothel in Alex. She has built up quite a thriving business and has gradually expanded her modest little hut into a rambling cacophony of little tin houses, which she has decorated in garish, mostly red, colours. Gloria and Brightboy live with Lulana in a tiny bungalow behind the brothel premises. Although Lulana, from time to time, frequents Daniel's father's shabeen, Gloria and Daniel have never actually met, prior to enrolment at Emfundisweni, where they have been assigned to different classrooms. It is possible that they have met in the playground but neither has shown any interest in the other.

Fast forward five or six years. The two lads are now progressing to High School, also known as Emfundisweni. It is really more of the same. There is one difference, however, the High School facilities and structure have been much abused by the students over the years. The classrooms are littered with broken furniture, and most windows have been smashed and not replaced. There are very few books available and most of these are in Afrikaans, the language which most residents of Alexandra hate. There is an acute shortage of trained teachers.

Gloria too has progressed to the High School. She is now developing into a very striking and beautiful teenager. The word is out that her mother runs an illegal whore house and the older boys at the school are particularly interested in getting to know her, partly because she is so pretty, but also because of her intriguing background. It is not long before Gloria is being dated by a much older boy. Then, for some unknown reason, Gloria just disappears from school altogether. Her absence does not go unnoticed by Daniel, whose interest in girls has suddenly escalated.

The older students at the High School resent the use of Afrikaans. This is the language of their oppressors, the language of the ruling class who have beaten their tribes into subservience. Whereas, most of the adult residents of Alexandra township keep their heads down and are grateful to have a roof, however flimsy, over their heads and a job to bring in some money, the teenagers do not see it that way. Their prospects of bettering themselves and of exceeding the achievements of their parents seem to be ethereal. Unless the circle can be broken, they see themselves as perpetually subservient to their white overlords. This is not something which sits easy with teenagers, particularly the boys. As a result, gangs of black teenagers regularly cause trouble, not just in the township itself but in the areas nearby. Frequently, the youth of Alexandra find themselves in confrontation with the armed white police and from time to time the army is sent into the township to frighten the gangs of dissidents. This intervention normally takes the form of armoured vehicles, known by the residents as "hippos", from which trained soldiers are able to fire into the crowds without risk of being hurt themselves.

Very little teaching takes place at the High School. White teachers are fearful of working there and there are insufficient trained black ones to do the job. As a result, youngsters like Thabi and Daniel get out of the habit of learning. Idle teenagers can only get into trouble, one way or another, and our two boys are no exceptions. By the time they are 14 years old, both Thabi and Daniel have both been arrested several times for being involved in rioting. The jails are not large enough to hold so many youngsters so they are often convicted, then freed shortly after. But, the more the Afrikaans police maltreat them, the more resentful they become.

During this period a black political party has been making considerable progress, particularly by alerting the rest of the world to the injustices that are occurring in South Africa. The Africa for Africans party (AFA), although painted by the white South African leadership as a violent and criminal organisation, is, in fact, led by a man of peace, Nkosi Mabendla, who is serving a long sentence in jail for terrorism. Despite being depicted differently by his captors, Mabendla is a fervent believer in non-violent revolution and, even from jail, has been able to mastermind an international public relations offensive to discredit the political system in South Africa, which denies his fellow blacks a vote. As a result, most countries in the world have banned trade with South Africa and almost no international sporting events are allowed to take place which include a team from South Africa. Overseas sports teams are banned from visiting the country. More and more pressure is being exerted on the ruling white government to release Mabendla and allow black citizens the vote. The teenagers of Alexandra, however, are not interested in waiting for things to change; nor are they interested in obtaining change through discussions. Violence is in the air.

Luckily for Mthabisi and Daniel there are a few good teachers at the school, and one of these, Moses Mwahli, has made a point of identifying a small number of pupils who, in his view, seem to have potential. One of these boys is Mthabisi, who Moses believes has outstanding ability and understanding of anything to do with numbers, and another is Daniel, who has demonstrated significant leadership and social skills. Moses is determined that he is going to steer his little group of special students, at the very least, to university. Moses is an active member of the AFA. He is convinced that sooner or later, the ruling Nationalist party will feel the stranglehold of the world's boycotts and will need to adjust its electoral arrangements to appease the rest of the world in order to restore its normal trading links. If this does not happen Moses believes that the country will face civil war and armed uprisings. This is not what anyone really wants. Moses is far sighted enough to know that his beloved political party will need trained personnel and seriously minded people to participate in the future operation of the country. It is his job, as he sees it, to help discover and develop such talent.

Both Daniel and Thabi respond well to Moses. He has the gift of making learning interesting. He also is inspirational about his vision of a future black run country. Gradually the teacher convinces most of his little hand-picked group that there is a future for them and that it is senseless trying to destroy such structures of governance that already exist. It makes much more sense to follow the leadership of Mabendla and work towards a peaceful change. Thabi and Daniel are encouraged to join the AFA Youth Wing and start to attend clandestine meetings in the township.

Daniel's dad, Sam, is nervous about this. He certainly wants his boy to succeed in life and is pleased that he appears to be working hard now at his schoolwork, but he is concerned about his boy's sudden interest in politics.

Sam has learned to live with Apartheid. He has learned to weave his way around it and, where possible, use it to his advantage. His whole livelihood depends on the good relations he has built up with white commerce. South African Breweries, for whom he still works as a driver, unbeknown to the management, is the major supplier of the booze he sells in his little shabeen. He doesn't get it for nothing, but he certainly is supplied at a cost far below market value through a network of SAB employees who sell "surplus" beverages to small traders like Sam. Since SAB manufacture and sell 90% of all beer in the South African market, there is plenty of room for the odd barrel or bottle to go astray. Some of this reaches Sam and ultimately his shabeen customers. Any major shake up in how the country operates might be bad news for Sam, so he is not in favour of disturbing the status quo, even if his heart tells him that it needs to be changed. Basically, Sam is looking for a quiet life. He does not want his son to attract the attention of the ruling Nats. On the other hand, he is proud that his son is not out on the streets causing mischief like so many of his customer's kin. He is nervous and decides to keep an eye on Daniel's activity, just in case! Surprise, however, is quietly proud of her son.

Thabi's parents are more supportive. They are pleased that their boy seems to be taking his education seriously and is no longer following a gang of hoodlums. There is only one university in the country which allows black and other non-white students to attend. Fort Hare is located 100 miles away from Johannesburg, but it really is the only option in the country for further education for non-whites. Both Menzi and Londiwe continue to encourage their boy to work hard and follow the example of Moses. If Moses suggests that Thabi join the AFA, then it must be a good idea.

Menzi is also in a position to discuss the future of the country with his colleagues at work, most of whom are white. To his face they readily accept that the system of governance in their country is unfair and unsustainable. The company that Menzi works for is also forward thinking. Under the laws governing workplaces, the company is supposed to provide separate facilities for whites and non-whites on its premises. In theory this means that Menzi should take his lunch in a separate seating area from the white employees. This rule and many others are not adhered to by the company. Like so many rules and laws, if they are widely ignored, eventually they get changed. Laws tend to follow practice and this is the theory of Menzi's employer, hence his policy of allowing his staff to mix freely and encouraging them to discuss everything from sport to politics. As a result, Menzi is convinced that change will take place in his country; it is only a matter of time. He admires the passive leadership of Mabendla and is pleased that his son wants to play an active role by joining the AFA.

In the rest of the country feelings are running high, particularly in the African townships. Young blacks are refusing to go to school whilst the teaching language is Afrikaans and all tests and examinations are carried out in that detested medium. Rioting and civil disobedience are becoming rife and, when they occur, are being put down with a heavy hand from armed police. Meanwhile, the economy is being crippled. Exports have slowed to a trickle and it is extremely difficult to import anything, except on the thriving black market. As the economy worsens, so, ironically, does the number of jobs available for black workers. The country is in a vicious downward spiral and yet the politicians remain as stubborn and resistant to change as ever. The wheels of the country are not yet coming off the rails, but they are certainly creaking and groaning badly.

Chapter Twenty Six

A few years have passed. Thabi has successfully attained a place at Fort Hare, and his studies are going well. He is the brightest student in his group and displays an exceptional aptitude for mathematics. The leadership of the AFA is acutely interested in keeping close ties with Fort Hare. The leadership, both those in jail and those operating from overseas, realise that the bright young men at Fort Hare could play an important role in the future of the country. Mabendla and his colleagues believe it is only a matter of time before the Nationalist party will have to concede to universal suffrage in order to restart the economy. The trade boycott stranglehold is getting tighter and tighter. Furthermore, much of the white-led business community has been lobbying for change and this feeling is seeping through the white population, particularly the English speakers. There is a strong feeling in the air that change is not only inevitable, but also imminent.

At the same time, the diehard Afrikaners are not giving up. As part of their clandestine operations, they have infiltrated the University in an attempt to marginalise any rising stars in the AFA. Thabi has been indentified as a risk. Some of his friends and colleagues have mysteriously met with accidents. Thabi is worried. He is two years into his degree programme. He wonders whether he will ever finish it. When one of his fellow students fails to return after the summer break and he can find no trace of him, Thabi begins to seriously fear for his own safety. He decides to discuss the situation with his dad, Menzi, as well as with his old mentor from school, Moses, who seems to have the ear of the top leadership of the AFA. A plan is hatched. Thabi will be sent to England. Menzi has enough money saved for an air ticket and Moses has the strings to pull to get Thabi connected to the clandestine office of the AFA in London. Londiwe, his mother, is devastated but realises that it is for the best.

With most of the leadership of the AFA incarcerated on Robben Island, near Cape Town, one would have thought that the fangs had been removed from the banned political party. Far from it. Many of the brighter revolutionaries have fled overseas and organised themselves into an effective lobbying force in the UK, Scandinavia and the USA. From here they have applied pressure on their host governments to ramp up trade, political and sporting boycotts of their homeland. Such activity requires a good measure of organisation and, of course, funding. As a base to carry out this work in the UK, the AFA has rented an old terraced house in the back streets near Kings Cross station in London. From there they plan their activities and fund raising. It is to Kings Cross, therefore, that Thabi heads for from Heathrow. The bureau chief, Oswald Dhalame, has been alerted of his impending arrival by Moses, who has requested that assistance should be given to his protege in getting the right papers, finding a place to live, and getting a job. In return, Moses has suggested, Thabi would be quite capable of handling the accounting function for the local AFA, which Moses, quite rightly guessed, is currently shambolic.

When Thabi eventually finds the little terraced house, it is not what he had been expecting. He thinks he has come to the wrong address. The grubby looking terraced house has a few steps up to the front door, and further steps down to a basement flat. The net curtains in the windows are dirty, stained and ragged. The lower space outside the flat is piled high with rubbish. The paint is peeling off the front door. "Hardly a great advertisement for a political party which was angling to take over a country of over 40 million people," Thabi thinks as he prepares to ring on the doorbell.

As he stands outside, waiting for a response, he notices, across the road, the net curtains move in the window of a house opposite. Behind the curtains is a slight dark shape. It looks like a man. Somebody is watching him. He rings the doorbell again. When nobody appears, he gives the door a slight push. It opens to reveal a small hallway, with stairs ahead and an old bicycle leaning on the wall. The carpet is filthy and the wallpaper in the cramped entryway is peeling. At the end of the hallway he can hear voices, somewhat animated, and laughter: the sort of hearty African laughter that you might hear in a shabeen. A game of poker is in full swing. He knows he is in the right place.

Oswald Dhalame and his pals give Thabi the warmest of welcomes. Oswald is a big fat man whose belly overflows between his shirt and his trousers. His big generous smile, however, is a tonic for a young man in a strange country. For the first couple of weeks Thabi bunks down in an attic room in the house, but soon finds his feet and manages to rent a room in a tidy little house about two blocks away. Whilst looking for a job, in the informal sector, Thabi begins the process of applying to colleges, armed with glowing testimonials from Fort Hare. He also piles into the mess that is the "bookkeeping" for the London division of the AFA. This is going to take some sorting out and, clearly, new disciplines will need to be applied. Thabi knows that this will not make him popular.

Little by little Thabi's life in London comes together. He takes an entry exam into college and passes with flying colours. He manages to get a job as a bookkeeper for London Transport, aided by a network of black English union workers who support the revolution in Africa, and everywhere else it seems. And he acquires a girlfriend. The surprising thing is that the girlfriend is white. He is not sure how this will go down at the AFA headquarters, but he does not really care.

Thabi's girl is Gillian. She comes from quite a wealthy middle class family in the north of England. Her dad has a business making screws. She is currently enrolled at the Royal School of Music in Kensington, London. She is very pretty, but in a Bohemian sort of way, little make up, red hair tied back with an elastic band. Although the School of Music is located south of Kensington Gardens, she lives in a flat in Holland Park, with a couple of other university students. Thabi and Gillian met in a coffee shop in Bayswater, which was home to a skiffle group and other visiting jazz artists. In this environment it is not unusual to witness a black man with a white girl. Out of London, this would be a very rare sight indeed. Gillian's mother and father have no idea that their daughter is sleeping with a black man.

Thabi finds London really liberating. Here, he does not need to worry about passbooks or curfews. He feels free, released from the continual dance that he had to engage in in South Africa around the rules of Apartheid. Here, in London, he is treated like anyone else. If he went to look for racism he would find it, but, so far, it has not found him. He has had no trouble finding accommodation. He does notice the sideways glance that some people give him when they see him with Gillian, but these instances are few and far between. "This," he thinks to himself, "is how

South Africa will be one day." The weather however is not to Thabi's liking. The skies are so often leaden. He longs for the bright sunshine of his homeland. But, given all of the advantages, he is happy to have landed where he has. He also knows, that with a white girlfriend, even wife, he could not live in South Africa. According to the infamous Immorality Act, if caught co-habitating, he would go to jail and Gillian would be deported.

It is not long before Thabi has sorted out the bookkeeping at the untidy headquarters and installed some discipline into expenditure and record keeping. Not only has he tidied up the books, but he has somehow managed to instill a sense of pride in the premises. He has supervised a redecoration of the ground floor and no longer do bicycles litter the hallway. He has turned the untidy lounge area into a reception/waiting room, and the other rooms into reasonably tidy offices. He has strongly made the point to Oswald, that, if the AFA is to be taken seriously as the government of the future, it had better, at least, look more organised. At first Oswald Dalwhene is a little put out that Thabi has come in like a new broom, but soon realises that the improvements reflect well on him. Thabi has also engaged with the South African secret service people who are spying on them from the other side of the street. He has accused them of harassment and told them that, unless they desist, he will report their activity to the British police. For a while the curtains in the front room of the house opposite are still. All in all, Thabi is happy with his lot, and his contribution does not go unnoticed by the leadership of the AFA.

Back in Johannesburg Thabi's old friend, Daniel, is also doing well. Upon leaving school, Daniel's dad, the long-time employee and "fixer" at South African Breweries has managed to find him a job at the firm. SAB, aware of the fact that change will almost certainly come in the fabric of the nation, have decided to put in place a trainee management scheme for non-white applicants. Needless to say, Sam, has enough pull in the firm to make sure that one of the trainees would be his son. Daniel has been the star recruit, demonstrating, right from the get go, his ability to learn quickly and to lead. His natural temperament to get on with people has propelled him into the marketing department. Since the Breweries has huge sales in the non-white market, Daniel's presence is instantly useful to SAB.

So, as Thabi is making his mark with the hierachy of the overseas division of the AFA, Daniel is laying the foundations for a business empire in the black economy of South Africa. Daniel has seen how his dad has made a living from the supply of liquor in the township. He sees no reason why his dad's success cannot be duplicated on every corner of every black township in the country. "You just need to control the supply chain."

Daniel also has a girlfriend, who is none other than the long lost Gloria from High School. Daniel had always been curious about the disappearance of Gloria from school. Her pretty face had been etched on his mind, but gradually his interest had faded. Until one day, whilst visiting his parent's house, he stepped into the shabeen. It was rare that women frequented the place, at least as customers, so it struck him as odd to find the men gathered round a young lady with a skirt so short she had difficulty concealing her underwear. Suddenly, he recognised her.

"Good Lord," said Daniel, "it's not Gloria, is it? You don't remember me, do you?"

"I'm afraid not," said Gloria, "but I'd sure like to know a handsome young man like you, instead of all these old farts." She motioned to the other men, but with a wickedly teasing smile.

"Oh, this is Daniel," offered one of the men. "He's far too young and inexperienced for you." The rest of the men laughed.

Despite the put downs, Gloria found herself instantly attracted to the young man, and was even more interested to learn that he was Sam Buthelezi's son and a budding executive at South African Breweries. So, a romance was started, although one driven purely by sex as opposed to love.

Gloria's teenage life had probably conditioned her against love. She had, it turns out, dropped out of school because her mother Lulana had become very ill, and unable to continue her role as the Madam of the establishment. So Gloria was not only placed at a very early age in the position of being carer for her mum, but also as the Madam of the illicit brothel. As such, Gloria had grown up in an atmosphere of sex, not love. Her only love had been for her sick mother and her little brother. Everything else in her life revolved around sex and money. But young Gloria had been a quick learner, not only from her mother, but also from the other girls who offered their services to lonely men. From them she learned how to make the best of her already outstanding looks, with make up and clothes, as well as how to please the customers. Gloria, at her mum's behest, had decided to learn the tricks of the trade. After all, her mother explained, you will not get any respect from the staff unless you can do the job as well as they can. It did not take Gloria long to master the art of pleasing men, as well as collecting "rent" from the girls working for her mum.

After a few years, Lulana sadly passed away, but by then, Gloria was the real Madam. She had made substantial improvements to the premises, had learned how to keep the police at bay, and was earning some serious money.

The meeting with Daniel is indeed fortuitous, for both of them. In fact, Daniel has many girlfriends, but the new one, Gloria, does not know about the others, or so Daniel believes. Just like his mother, Surprise, Gloria has the right name. She is absolutely drop dead gorgeous to look at, one could say, glorious. She is very happy to be seen on the arm of Daniel, especially as Daniel becomes more and more the man about town, or rather, the man about the townships. Gloria would like nothing more than to be able to move out of the seedy atmosphere of the brothel, and, as she sees Daniel's career progressing, she begins to believe that he may just be the key to her future.

Daniel works hard to impress his bosses at SAB. After a couple of years on the road, Daniel has cemented his position as the best sales person in the country, in regard to beer and alcohol outlets in black townships and villages. What SAB does not realise is that Daniel has worked out how to play things at both ends. The shabeen owners across the country are, in the main, selling alcohol without the necessary licence, so they need to be low profile as regards the Afrikaans police. They also only have one source of supply and that, now, is through Daniel. Dozens of the most successful shabeen owners now find themselves extremely reliant on Daniel, who can increase, decrease or stop altogether, their supplies at the stroke of a pen. He also has all the information he needs to shop them. Although Daniel had never heard of, nor read about, the protection rackets in the USA, he quickly developed his own version. If you wanted to get supplied by the Breweries, especially at the lowest tariffs, you had better make a contribution to Daniel's "fund", or in some cases, cede some of the ownership of your business to him. Bit by bit, Daniel was becoming rich. Gloria, of course, loved it.

Riches and power also give Daniel a good standing in the AFA, to which he remains affiliated. Daniel is now the President of the Small Business Association for Africa. As such he controls the votes for a huge swathe of blacks. This, in due course, could be tremendously important when the AFA comes to decide upon its leadership, particularly since that leadership might one day run the country.

Daniel's siblings have not been quite so entrepreneurial. His elder brother Shaka has not been particularly enterprising. As the first born he has been quite mollycoddled by Sam and Surprise, who have never really pushed him into a career. He is not particularly lazy but his motivation to do well is negligible. And why wouldn't it be? He has always had a roof over his head at the Buthelezi home and, compared to the rest of Alex, a comfortable way of life. From an early age he has been required to help out in the shabeen and has got quite used to this fairly easy and sociable life. Both Sam and Surprise have showered him with first born love. Why would he need to do anything else? Ultimately, he assumes, when Sam gets too tired to work, Shaka will take over the business. He is a very sociable young man, with lots of friends, both male and female. As the son of the owner of one of the few "pubs" in the township he is the right person to know.

Solomon, Daniel's younger brother, is more adventurous. At the age of 15 he started driving a taxi when one of his dad's customers, a taxi driver, had an accident and could not drive for a while. Solomon had taken over the old man's rusty taxi and kept the flag flying, sharing half of his take with the cab owner. When the man recovered and wanted his taxi back, Solomon had saved enough money to put down on his own vehicle. Now, after a couple of years of driving morning noon and night, Solomon had put enough money aside to buy a second vehicle, this time a mini bus. Neither his car nor his little bus were licensed, of course, so the business was always a bit precarious. But, as long as he had enough cash on hand to pay off the police that occasionally stopped him, things were okay. Solomon no longer lived at home with Sam and Surprise. He had his own tin shack about a mile away from the shabeen, just far enough for him to enjoy a healthy and active social life, and one, of which he knew his mother would not approve.

The two girls were completely different. Sindiswe took after her mother. She was a very caring young lady. Surprise had introduced her to the doctors at the clinic and through their influence she had undergone training as a midwife. The women of Alexandra were very suspicious of the nurses at the clinic, especially when it came to their advice on childbirth. It was the tradition of African families to have many children; this was a route to having many helping hands, especially in old age. It was also a route to outnumbering the white overlords. When Sindiswe tried to give advice on birth control she found herself fighting an uphill battle. The "pilly" was a way for the white man to cut down on black births. Sindiswe's customers would take the pill that she prescribed, but would discard them. In some cases, when they really wanted to stop having more babies they would take the pill but were fearful of telling their menfolk, for fear of a beating. Sindiswe was always saddened by the women to whom she was prescribing the birth control pills turning up nine months later with a baby waiting to drop. Sindiswe was dedicated to her job. She had not married and lived in the staff hostel of the clinic, with her own little room and television set.

Mthunze, the daughter whose name meant "shade", was most inappropriately named. She had started teacher training but was kicked out having seduced one of the teachers. She then joined a fledgling girl band, which plied its trade around the shabeens of the townships with knock off Africanised versions of Spice Girl numbers. The girls, including Mthunze, were all very vivacious and attractive and soon came to the attention of an alert entertainment agent, who started to book them at white events out of the township. This had led to much broader exposure and eventually to a film part for Mthunze, who was encouraged to change her name to Blossom. By the time her brother had become an important member of the AFA, Blossom was a big enough name to be regularly booked as a cabaret act across the country. As far as the public were concerned, at the time, Blossom was a bigger name than her brother.

Chapter Twenty Seven

Several more years have passed. Thabi is still in London. He has gained his degree from university and has a fulltime job as Deputy Financial Controller of London Transport. His rise in the company has been astounding, but it is solely based upon his talent. He is now married to Gillian and they have a little boy, Thomas, and the prettiest little girl, aptly named Belle. Although Gillian and he are living happily in a terraced house in Afghan Road, Wandsworth, Thabi still pines for his homeland, not so much for Alexandra, but for the sights and smells of Africa in a broader sense. However, if they decided to live there he would be arrested under the Immorality Act and Gillian would be deported. He knows that returning to South Africa with a white wife is impossible. But he is still active in the AFA, and now sits on their highest offshore committee. He knows that progress is being made. If things go well, he is determined to lobby immediately for the abolition of the Immorality Act. He is deeply disturbed that he cannot take his family to his homeland. It just seems wrong.

The talks being held between the leadership of the AFA and the white government of South Africa are quietly making substantial headway. The government has offered Mabendla his freedom, but he, craftily, has decided that he has more clout as a prisoner than as a free man. His stance has been, "I will walk from jail, when the government has agreed to 'one man, one vote'." Thabi's offshore committee has been told by their counterparts in South Africa, that the government is on the verge of capitulating. His committee has also had this confirmed through diplomatic channels in London.

Thabi has quite made up his mind that, should Mabendla be released, he will return to his homeland to do whatever he can to assist the cause and help establish a new government. Gillian is not at all sure that this will be the best thing for her and her little family, but she loves and admires her husband, so has quietly prepared herself for this fateful day, even if it means breaking the law in her husband's homeland. Gillian too, is a rebel at heart.

Daniel, meanwhile, has been coining it. As the President of the South African Small Traders Association, he now represents almost all of the small black businesses in South Africa. This is a hugely influential position because he has the ability to influence thousands of potential voters. He is now sure that universal suffrage in some form will soon come to his country. He knows that he will be able to exercise considerable power. His personal wealth has also grown exponentially. Through forcing "protection" payments out of a host of small shabeen owners he has been able to amass a fortune. With this he has bought many legitimate businesses and expanded them. He now controls a huge slice of the cement business throughout the country and has a major stake in the steel industry. If South Africa is freed from the stranglehold of trade sanctions, he anticipates a construction boom. Daniel is well positioned to become very rich indeed.

Daniel has been smart enough not to move from Alexandra, which is his power base and where he is extremely popular. He has not built a mansion, but has continued to live in a rather modest brick building in the centre of the township, not far from his dad's shabeen. Despite his humble surroundings, he does own a white Rolls Royce, which sits incongruously on the dirt driveway of his house. He has bought Gloria a pink one (her choice). Strangely, this is not frowned upon by the less affluent residents of the township. In fact, they regard it as cocking a snook at the white government and wave and cheer every time Daniel or Gloria drive along the dirt roads of their township in their special vehicles, which are regarded as a symbol of success in the face of the white authorities.

The great day has arrived. The Afrikaans government has finally understood that it has no option but to agree to work towards electoral freedom for all citizens, black, brown, or white. A new constitution will be devised and written by a committee led, on the one hand, by Nkosi Mabendla and, on the other, Piet Mostert, the sitting President. The goal has been set for the new constitution to be devised, written and presented to the voters within two years. It is envisaged that, within the framework of this constitution, anyone will have the right to form a political party and all citizens over the age of 18 will have a vote. On this basis Mabendla has agreed to be released.

After 27 years in incarceration, Nkosi Mabendla, leaves jail on April 2nd, 1990. He is greeted by his long-suffering wife, Aretha, and his children, as well as Piet Mostert, the President of South Africa. He insists on walking for the full length of the prison driveway, maximising his chance to meet the crowd who have been waiting all night in anticipation of this never to be forgotten moment. His stride is weak and yet determined. This long walk to freedom is witnessed on television by countless millions of people from around the world. One in the audience, overcome with tears, is Thabi, who sits mesmerised, surrounded by not only his family, but many of the overseas members of the AFA. This is the best day of their lives. None of those watching have ever experienced such emotion. Everything they have been working towards is now, on this historic day, beginning to fall into place. Even the general public in the rest of the world who have no connection with South Africa are mesmerised by the drama and emotion of the occasion. Gillian is, of course, amongst those celebrating, but with an enormous sense of foreboding. She knows that her life is about to change; she is nervous that it will not be for the better.

Daniel and Gloria are, of course, in the crowd outside the jail. Or, more correctly, they are at the forefront of the crowd. Mabendla has not actually met Daniel, but it is almost certain that he soon will. Daniel has not come to the ceremony of the walk for any other reason than he just wants to be there. He too knows that this day will probably be the most important day of his life; something to tell the grandchildren. "I was there!"

Before the negotiations for agreeing a new constitution begin, Mabendla asks for a month's delay. He realises that the Afrikaans government will have their sharpest brains at the negotiating table. He wants to make sure that he shows up with the cleverest people in the AFA. So it is not long before the call comes to London for Thabi, who has now returned to London. The leadership in South Africa is well aware of the impact Thabi has had in cleaning up the act of the AFA overseas. He is probably the best accounting and economic brain in the organisation and is recognised as such. Mabendla would like to have Thabi on his team.

Thabi is honoured. He discusses the situation with Gillian. She pretends that she is thrilled for her husband; she is certainly very proud of him, but is still nervous about how all of this will affect their lives and the lives of their little ones. Thabi is determined to be part of the history of his country and Gillian understands. London Transport however is not so understanding. Thabi asks for a sabbatical; he is refused. There is no option but to resign. However, the AFA in South Africa has limited funds and cannot pay Thabi even half of what he earns in England. Gillian is becoming even more dubious about the wisdom of a move. She now insists that she is given a guarantee that she will not be arrested, nor will Thabi. She half hopes that this will not be forthcoming but, on Thabi's request, Mabendla makes this a condition of the upcoming negotiation. Piet Mostert is happy to oblige. He is well aware that one of the first things to go under a new constitution will be the Immorality Act, so what if it starts to self-destruct? Gillian receives this news with mixed feelings. But she knows that her husband has given up a fantastic job in London to fight the cause of his people in Africa. As a mother, she thinks this is a bad idea, but as a dormant rebel, it also stirs her heart. What else can she do but give him her full support?

Thabi decides to ask his childhood friend for help. He knows that Daniel has been very successful and that he still has his connections to the AFA. Maybe Daniel will be able to help fund the move. After all, it is solely in the interests of their country. Daniel has not heard from Thabi for some time, although he had got in touch when each of the babies were born, and Daniel had sent through some very nice Christening gifts at the time.

"How are you, my old friend?" asks Thabi, when Daniel answers the phone, "It's great news, isn't it?"

"Yes," said Daniel, "it's fantastic news. Everything that we could have dreamed for."

The two men chat for a bit about old times and the future. Daniel is impressed that Mabendla has called for Thabi. This is only good news. If his old friend Thabi is going to be something important in the new government, it could be very helpful for his future business enterprises. Favours given now could pay excellent dividends later.

Thabi explains that he would be severely out of pocket if he returned to South Africa to help. "If I didn't have a family to consider, I would be there in a flash," he explained, "but I do have responsibilities."

"Stop right there, my friend," interjects Daniel. "Tell me what the shortfall is and I will fund it with a donation to the AFA. Consider it done. No favours asked."

"That's fantastic," said Thabi. "I don't know how I can ever repay your kindness."

"I do," thinks Daniel, but does not say it.

So, within a few weeks of the conversation, Thabi is back in his homeland and ensconced in a hotel room near to the Johannesburg airport convention centre, where the constitutional talks are scheduled to take place. The plan is that Gillian and the children will travel to South Africa in more leisurely fashion – by ship. This will give Thabi time to get organised.

The goal of the constitutional talks is straightforward enough; to give every citizen, over the age of 18, a vote as to who should represent them in parliament as well as to clear the decks of all laws which support racism and segregation. As in anything regarding the law, the devil is in the detail, and what seems like a fairly cut and dried issue, is actually wrapped in many layers of thorny issues, each one needing individual attention and solutions. The amount of detail that is needed to be worked through is mountainous. A very special sort of brain will be required to do this. It soon becomes clear to Nkosi Mabendla that Thabi is blessed with such a brain and he thanks God for providing such a talented man at such an important time.

The constitutional talks drag on for almost two years. The business world does not need to wait for the outcome. As usual the stockmarkets of the world deal with the future and businessmen need to think ahead. The South African economy starts to boom in anticipation of the good times ahead. Orders for steel and cement come pouring in and the shabeens are doing record business. Daniel is now probably the richest black man in South Africa, yet he persists in living in his tin-roofed house. Gloria, on the other hand, has branched out. Her pink Roller is seen less and less in Alexandra. Rumours persist that Gloria has a second, more luxurious, existence than that of a housewife in the township.

President Piet Mostert is insistent that the white voting citizens should have some protection in regard to their future representation in the governance of the country. He is working hard to ensure that there will be a framework wherein the whites will be able to block or veto new laws. Mabendla is adamant that whilst there shall be proportional representation in parliament, matters will still be decided by a majority vote, with no special safeguards for minorities. The talks have reached a point where Mostert is threatening to walk away, stating that he will not countenance any changes and that South Africa will remain governed as it has been for decades, under the control of the whites. Riots start to break out in the townships. There is a sudden increase in the murder of white farmers, the easy targets.

Gillian starts to fear for her safety and that of her children. She and Thabi have rented a nice little house in Parktown, Johannesburg. Parktown is one of the more progressive suburbs, where there is much support for political change. She and her black husband are, in the main, welcomed by her new neighbours. However, when the constitutional talks start to run into difficulty, the mood in the street begins to change, particularly when unruly mobs of black youths start to vandalise the neighbourhood. One night a small firebomb is posted through Thabi and Gillian's front door. Nkosi Mabendla is furious when he learns of this and makes an appeal on television to his followers to desist from violent behaviour.

"Violence will not get us what we want," he solemnly states, "persistence, logic, tenacity, and the fact that right is on our side, will. You must stop this violence. It is harming our cause. Have patience. We will succeed."

Gillian has come to love the old man. He has been so kind and thankful to her husband. He is a font of gentleness and wisdom. And yet, he is strong. She is grateful for his intervention. The people listen. The violence tails off. Mabendla has pleaded with Mostert not to send in the troops. An uneasy truce takes hold and the constitutional talks resume. Mabendla uses the violence to demonstrate what will happen in the country unless the Nationalists of Piet Mostert agree to the AFA's terms and finally, after about 18 months of negotiation, a new constitution is unveiled. Thabi is proud to have been a co-author of the most important document ever written in his country. Gillian is proud of her man.

Chapter Twenty Eight

Daniel Buthelezi finally moves out of Alexandra. He buys a mansion in Atholl, the richest suburb in Johannesburg, but only three miles as the crow flies from his old home. He now rationalises that a new house is a badge of his success, rather than an embarrassment. Whereas his support base was once primarily in Alexandra, it is now across the country. He wishes to demonstrate just how successful and powerful he has become. He offers to buy a new home for his mum and dad, but Sam and Surprise do not want to move. Sam no longer drives for SAB but he still runs the shabeen in his back yard. All his lifelong friends are in Alex; why would he want to move? Surprise is also happy to stay. She loves her job at the clinic and her life, too, is full of friendship. And life is not too uncomfortable; their son has had their shack completely refitted, with a new tile roof, a large screen television, and all the kitchen mod-cons that anyone could want. Sam and Surprise are both enormously proud of their son, and have no problem with him moving on, but they are not going anywhere. The rest of Daniel's siblings, however, are not too proud to turn down his offer to rehouse them and, although his generosity does not extend to Atholl, they all manage to find nice comfortable homes in Kempton Park, a white middle class suburb abutting Alexandra.

Daniel's new house is spectacular. It sits within a high-walled site of about three acres, complete with swimming pool and tennis court. The architecture is very modern. White concrete walls, high ceilings and a sea of glass. Daniel has become interested in art and the walls are a splash of bright colours which reflect the new bright hope for his country. And South Africa surely is a country of hope. It is gearing up for the first elections in which all of its multi-race and multi-tribe citizens will be allowed to vote. Even the initially nervous white population seems to be buying into the concept of universal franchise, greatly encouraged by the sudden economic boom that is benefiting the nation. The "haves" seem to be getting more; the "have nots" are hoping that their turn is coming. The country seems full of hope and, even, goodwill.

Nkosi Mabendla is preparing to become the first black President of South Africa. Although he is already President of the AFA, he has not yet been elected President of the country but, when the time comes, his appointment is a certainty. He is busy encouraging suitable members of the AFA to stand for election and, together with his closest advisors is allocating safe constituencies for them to represent. He is also choosing which members he will appoint to cabinet positions. On the advice of his trusted Thabi, he decides to approach Daniel. Mabendla's experience of business and commerce is negligible but one of his strengths is that he understands his weaknesses. He knows that his cabinet will need to include a Minister of Commerce. He also knows that almost all of the suitable candidates will be white, but he would much prefer to appoint a black businessman, hence the suggestion from Thabi that Daniel might be the right man.

Daniel gets a call from Nkosi. He invites the future President to his Atholl mansion for tea and a chat. When Mabendla steps into the world of Daniel he is a little taken aback by the stark opulence. Daniel is clearly not a humble man. For Daniel it is a huge privilege to have this famous man come to his home. As Mabendla walks through the front door, it is, to Daniel, as if Jesus Christ has just walked in. The aura of saintliness is eerie.

"It is an honour to have you in my home," says Daniel as Nkosi holds out his hand in greeting, "May I offer you a tea or coffee?"

"You may," replies Mabendla, "but will there be one for my driver too?"

"Of course," said the host, a bit surprised at the request.

Daniel ushers his guest to a sofa, set amongst the objets d'art, and calls the order for refreshments through to the kitchen.

"You obviously have mastered the art of making money," Mabendla observes, as his eyes sweep around the large room and beyond. "I shall be needing someone who knows how to do that for the country," he continues. "Your good friend, Thabi, believes that you are the man to help us."

"Ah, Thabi. Such a clever man. And such a good citizen. That was nice of him to recommend me. We go back a long way – right to primary school in Alexandra. You know, Mr President, that until a few months ago, I still lived there. Despite all of this (he says, waving his arm around the room), my roots are still there in the township."

"Well, Daniel, it looks to me as if you've well and truly left them behind," says Mabendla, with a slight gesture towards the room. "But that's what I need. Someone to help me lift our people out of their poverty and hardship; just like you have done for yourself. As you know, Daniel, my training is not in economics or business. Before I went to prison, I was a lawyer – not a terrorist as they tried to say. As a lawyer I've played my part in helping to write a new constitution; I now need a businessman on my team to get the country moving again..."

As Mabendla is speaking, the maid walks in with a tray of coffee and biscuits. To Mabendla's astonishment, he sees the maid is white. For once in his life, the great man is speechless.

Back in the AFA's offices Nkosi Mabendla fills Thabi in on his visit to Daniel. He does not mention the white maid in the black uniform, but does comment on the sumptuousness of Daniel's home. It turns out that Daniel has turned down this invitation to join the prospective government. He has too many conflicting responsibilities. Privately, Nkosi is pleased. He is sure that Daniel would be extremely competent, but would he be extremely honest? Mabendla just wonders how Daniel has been able to amass such a fortune in such a short time. Whatever other qualities his hand-picked government will have, complete honesty must be one of them. Nkosi is quietly glad that Daniel has turned down his approach; he will need to fill the vacancy from elsewhere.

When Thabi gets home that evening there is a message from Daniel, thanking him for the introduction and inviting him and Gillian to dinner in Atholl. Thabi, without even asking his wife, accepts, and a week later, he and Gillian find themselves sitting on the same sofa that Mabendla had occupied a few days before. Gillian is astounded by the house and the vivid artwork. She is also astounded by Gloria, or rather the dress that Gloria is wearing – or almost wearing. It is the skimpiest piece of blue silk that clings to her body. Her long black legs seem to stretch forever between the shortest of skirts and the highest of heels. Gillian has to admit that Gloria looks spectacular. It is as if she is challenging the artwork.

Daniel, of course, is absolutely charming to Gillian and spends much of the evening reciting tales of the boys' shared youth. She is touched by the story of Thabi's first days at school and how Daniel took him under his wing. Daniel seems to be genuinely very fond of Thabi; she can see now why Thabi admires his friend so much.

The sight of Gloria telling the white maid what to do and what not to do, at first seems quite embarrassing to Gillian, until she realises that the young girl did not seem to mind in the least. "How strange," thinks Gillian, "if the girl had been black, I would not have given the situation a second thought. But, because she is white, I feel sort of sorry for or embarrassed for her. When you think about it, that's just stupid, isn't it?" What Gillian does notice however, is that Daniel seems quite taken with the white maid. She wonders what Gloria thinks about that. "Maybe Daniel and Thabi have something else in common; they both like white girls," muses Gillian, as the two men knock back brandy and reminisce.

The evening is a great success. Thabi has really enjoyed seeing his old school friend and Gillian has been completely charmed by him. Even Gloria seems to have enjoyed herself.

"I do like your friend," says Gillian, as they drive back to their more modest home, "and he is very fond of you. He has been amazingly successful, hasn't he?"

Thabi can't help feeling that somewhere, hidden in his wife's thought, is a touch of longing. It is true that he has not been such a good provider as his old school friend, but he was shortly going to be a Minister of State in the new South Africa. Surely, that would be something for Gillian to be proud of?

Over the next few days, Gillian thinks about Daniel a lot. His charismatic charm has captivated her but his incredible rise from poverty to extreme wealth also intrigues her. She wonders how he has done it. On the other hand, she must admit the potential progress of her beloved and clever husband from street urchin in Alexandra township to the Minister of Finance in his country is also astounding. Together the two friends are a living advertisement for what can be achieved from humble beginnings. Gillian is also enraptured by the fantastic feeling of hope that is flowing through the country. Many of her new white friends in the neighbourhood had been convinced that the country was heading for civil unrest, if not civil war. They had all been fearful for the future of their children. Many had made plans to leave the country and emigrate to whoever might have them, even if they had to leave their life savings behind. Now, there is new hope. A civil war seems to have been avoided and the future, although not clear, is certainly full of hope for a less fearful life.

Gillian is caught up in this euphoria and the atmosphere rubs off onto Thomas and Belle, who seem to be loving their new life, their school and their newfound friends, albeit if they all speak with a funny accent. Their schoolfriends are clearly impressed that their dad is such an important man.

For a number of years, Gillian has put her music on hold. Now, with a new sense of purpose, she begins to play again, both on a little upright piano that Thabi has bought for her, and the violin that she brought from England. She also volunteers to teach music, not just in the school in her neighborhood but also in Emfundisweni, Alexandra, the alma mater of Thabi and Daniel. There, as the wife of Thabi, she is welcomed as if she is Father Christmas. It gives her such a kick.

Election Day in South Africa is one of pure joy for everyone except the very hard right wingers who have resisted this change with every sinew in their bodies. They have threatened huge disruption at the polling stations, but, in truth, their numbers are too small to have any impact and the security forces are out in numbers. As it happens massive lines of voters turn up at polling stations across the country. Some would-be voters have to wait for many hours to cast their vote, but, in most cases, it is the first vote they have ever been allowed to cast, so a long wait is a small price to pay. The lines in Sandton are not so long, but, for the first time, the owners of the houses find themselves in line with their servants. Everybody is in a good mood. Gillian and Thabi join the line holding hands as if this is a symbol of times to come. Many residents can't wait to tell Thabi how proud they are of him; everybody in the suburb knows just what a good influence Thabi has been in the negotiations; they feel privileged to know him.

That night, Thabi and Gillian make love. It will be some time before Thabi will have time for such things for several weeks; the next day Nkosi Mabendla announces his cabinet. As expected, Thabi is his new Minister of Finance. There is a sharp learning curve ahead for him.

Daniel, on the other hand, is not too busy to keep in touch. He is delighted that his old friend is now in such an influential position and is determined not to let their rekindled friendship falter. On the other hand, he has been quite taken by Thabi's lovely wife. Keeping both balls in the air might be tricky, but Daniel is used to juggling.

Chapter Twenty Nine

A year after the election Daniel embarks on a new project, ostensibly for the glory of the nation, but privately for his own enrichment. He, and other leading businessmen, ironically including the Managing Director of his first employer, SAB, have formed a committee with the goal of attracting the Olympic Games to South Africa. The Olympics, to this point, has never been held in Africa, so it seems to Daniel to be a no-brainer, now the country has rejoined the world community, that the Olympic bosses would jump at the idea of holding the games in South Africa. Daniel's interest, of course, is in constructing an Olympic Stadium, which would need a lot of concrete and plenty of steel. It is important in this new age that the government backs the Olympic bid, so Daniel's group invite Nkosi Mabendla to nominate a couple of government employees to be on the committee. Nkosi, asks Thabi and his Minister of Sport to participate.

Things go wrong, however, when it is discovered by the committee, that, in order to get the votes of the African delegates of the global Olympic movement for the games to be held in South Africa, most of them will need to be bribed. There is in existence a shopping list, so to speak, of how much each African delegate would need to be paid to cooperate. This list has kindly been provided by previous national hosts of the Games. Naturally, Daniel's committee is shocked by this news and the two Ministers refuse to cooperate. The commercial members of the committee are less bothered by this discovery but realise that, should the games take part in South Africa, they would need the full cooperation of the government. In these early days, Nkosi's virgin government would not be likely to countenance bribes, so, reluctantly, Daniel and his gang of entrepreneurs decide not to press the issue.

Daniel, however, has a better idea: the WIFA World Soccer Cup. To host this event would require the construction of at least two 60,000 seat stadia, as well as another four 40,000 seaters around the country. This was far more concrete and steel than for the Olympics and he knows that WIFA is "bent".

"What a wonderful opportunity," Daniel exclaims to himself one day. "If I can keep the politicians out of the negotiations, I might just have a chance."

Daniel applies himself to the task with his usual enthusiasm. Not just because he is salivating at the prospect of making so much money on the construction materials, but also because he loves soccer. In South Africa soccer is the black man's sport, as opposed to rugby which is entirely dominated by whites. If Daniel can bring the famous World Cup to South Africa, he will be a hero. So, of course, will be the new President of the country and anything Daniel can do to ingratiate himself with the President should be useful.

For window dressing, Daniel pulls together a multi-racial group of South Africans from the world of sport, broadcasting, tourism and potential commercial sponsorship. There is no question, however, that Daniel is the driving force and public face of the bid. The buoyant mood of the country gets behind Daniel. The politicians take note.

As part of the process, WIFA, the world body controlling soccer, insists on sending delegates to each country planning to participate to inspect the plans and proposed facilities as well as the capability of transporting and housing thousands of overseas visitors around the country. The newly emergent and previously forbidden country of South Africa is high on WIFA officials "must see" list, so streams of low and high level officials need to be entertained and escorted around the country. Daniel is the ideal host. Naturally a networker, his worldwide network is now growing exponentially.

After an elimination process of about a year, WFIFA finally announces its short list of host countries. The four finalists are the USA, Brazil, Sweden and South Africa. All 120 competing nations will be given a vote and, in a straightforward process, the country receiving the most votes will become the host for the World Cup seven years hence. The voting is to take place in Switzerland in a hall near the WIFA headquarters. The four finalist countries are invited to send a delegation of six people. Daniel understands from others who have had this experience that lobbying for votes will go on right up until the time of the ballot.

Daniel decides that it would be smart to ask Nkosi Mabendla to become part of his delegation. Mabendla is undoubtedly the most loved black man in the world, not only by black people but by others of all shades. He is the man who miraculously brought an end to segregation in South Africa and did so peacefully. According to Time magazine, Mabendla is the "Man of the Century". Who wouldn't want to have such an icon on their delegation?

Needless to say, Daniel has done plenty to grease the palms of many of the 120 delegates, but his is not so foolish as to believe that the competing nations have not done the same. For him, this relatively modest down payment could reap millions in return. He is, however, shocked when he is pulled aside on the morning of the vote, by a high ranking WIFA executive. The man has a simple message; "The voting is quite tight, but there are a still a few 'undecided', who can tip the balance. A payment of ten million dollars into this WIFA nominated bank account will ensure victory."

Even Daniel is shocked. He has already paid out God knows what, so to be tapped up for such a huge amount at the last moment is mind blowing. Much as Daniel loves his country and soccer, there is no way he is personally going to subsidise the event to such a degree. This is something for the government to decide – and they must do quickly and, obviously, quietly. Daniel decides to reach out to Mabendla.

Only Daniel, Mabendla, and his Minister of Finance, know exactly what went on that day, but, somehow or other, the sum of ten million dollars finds its way from South Africa to WIFA a mere hour before the final voting commences.

When the results are clear and South Africa is announced "winner and host", South Africans around the world rejoice and Chief amongst them is Mabendla himself, although his stomach is churning with anger and disgust. Subterfuge is not in Mabendla's being but, for the sake of the country he has made a judgement. He is using the people's money to give the people what they want, but it will leave a stain on his heart forever.

Daniel and his victorious group return to Africa and the planning begins. Needless to say, Daniel will be chief planner and chief beneficiary. As Minister of Finance,

Thabi is troubled. Clearly, he has no alternative to follow his boss' instructions, but he is determined to make sure from now on any government funds for the project will be closely controlled. He is, of course, concerned that this is putting him on a collision course with his oldest friend, but he has no reason to believe that Daniel's interest in the project is anything but altruistic.

When Thabi reads the conditions that Daniel's committee have agreed to he is curious. From Thabi's perspective the World Cup Soccer finals are more of a global television event than anything else. WIFA has insisted that the host country must have the infrastructure to stage the semi-finals in separate stadia, no smaller than 60,000 seats each, and all other matches in stadia with a capacity of not less than 40,000. South Africa has agreed to build six new stadia, some of them in rural parts of the country where they would never get used again. This seems like complete madness to Thabi and a complete waste of tax payers' funds, when Africa is crying out for more hospitals and schools. Thabi rightly points out to his friends on the organising committee that this represents a massive misuse of taxpayers' money. The committee and Daniel, of course, maintain that the die is cast and that, unless the country is prepared to renege on its commitment, there is no alternative to the construction programme.

Although Thabi has signed various confidentiality and non-disclosure documents before taking up his role as a Minister, it is not unusual for him to discuss matters that trouble him with Gillian. He calls it "pillow talk".

He explains the problem, or, in this case, the three problems. The first being the fact that a legally binding commitment has been made to WIFA, the second, the huge proposed waste of taxpayers' money and the third that an obvious beneficiary will be his best friend, Daniel. Both he and Gillian have not forgotten that a few years ago it was Daniel who had effectively financed their family's return to South Africa. They do not relish the thought of antagonising their benefactor.

Gillian sleeps on the issue, but, over the next day, she thinks it through. That evening she is ready to offer a suggestion to her troubled husband, not one that will save money, but one that will ensure that the money is put to good use.

"What you do is this, my love," she starts, as she hands her weary husband a cup of coffee that evening.

"You explain to WIFA that, despite your agreement to build these stadia, as designated, it is your intention to cut down on their size and number, on the basis that this is primarily a television event and the TV audience will never know whether there are 40,000 spectators in a stadium or 25,000. They will also not care whether the match is being played in Bloemfontein or Kimberly. Furthermore, you will explain that instead of building two 60,000 seaters, you will be converting and renovating two existing rugby stadia. And here is the selling point. The World Cup finals have never been played in Africa before. Everybody knows that Africa needs more hospitals and schools. You will explain to WIFA that all of the billions of Rand in savings will be channelled into 'good causes' new projects, not just in SA, but across the continent. WIFA will be able to say that it is their idea and, in order to help Africa, they have agreed to a reduction in their normal demands of live spectator seats, for one time only, to commemorate the African, not just South African, World Cup. This can come as a joint announcement from the WIFA president and Mabendla. They will both be proclaimed heroes."

Thabi listens intently. Gillian is right. This is a wonderful approach. Everybody should be able to get on board with this, even Daniel. There will still be plenty of work to spread around, because hospitals and schools still need steel and concrete.

"Thank you, my love," says Thabi. "That is so helpful. I do love you so much."

Unfortunately, for whatever reason, Thabi's colleagues in government are not so easily impressed with Gillian's idea. Some argue that it would be embarrassing to go back to WIFA and ask for a change in the conditions. Others argued that this approach would cut down the number of tourists that would come, even though Thabi points out that there are not enough hotels in the country anyway to house the larger numbers. Others, who at first find the idea intriguing, strangely and slowly change their minds. Daniel, of course, is not a member of government, so he has little to say – at least in public. He is, however, greatly relieved when Mabendla finally vetoes Thabi's proposal. It is easier for him to help build the stadia on his home turf than countless little schools and clinics across the continent.

Thabi is dejected. He promises himself that, as Minister of Finance, he will now follow every penny that is spent on these stupid stadia, even if it does mean upsetting his benefactor in the process.

Elsewhere in his portfolio as Minister of Finance, Thabi has more important battles to fight. For obvious reasons most of the jobs in the massive civil service are held by white citizens, particularly at the senior level. It is AFA policy to phase out the whites and replace them with trained blacks. Thabi, of course, keeps reminding his colleagues that the important word in that sentence is not white or black, but "trained". He realises that offices and services, such as the Post Office, have been operating more or less efficiently for decades. The removal of the strata of white management and their replacement with blacks can only work if the incoming managers are thoroughly trained. Alas, many of Thabi's cabinet colleagues are too impatient for change. White supervisors are being let go, paid off at great cost, and replaced with inexperienced and untrained black personnel across the board. Efficiency is beginning to suffer. Thabi is worried. However, the short term effect is positive on the economy. The departing whites have large redundancy payments to spend and the incoming black supervisors, with their increased salaries, are also splashing out. To most people, everything looks rosy. The only trouble is that the letters are not getting delivered.

The same phenomenon is occurring in non-state and quasi-state enterprises, such as rail and air transport, electrical generation and supply, the telephone services and so on. Thabi's ministerial colleagues are quick to push these companies into changing their internal racial structure of management. There are jobs for the boys everywhere and the boys find plenty of previously hard earned funds in the coffers of the companies they now find themselves managing. On the back of this windfall a new black middle class is rising. Things are good for all concerned, but Thabi is sure that these gains are a one time windfall and that, sooner or later, the reality will be that badly managed companies will crash and burn. His is a lone voice of sanity in the cabinet.

Chapter Thirty

The seven years that pass between the securing of the football World Cup and it actually taking place, have been good times for South Africans, whatever the colour of their skin. There is plenty of money flushing through the economy and great hope for the future. Staging one of the most prestigious world events is a far cry from the days of sanctions and boycotts. White South Africans, who had fled abroad, fearful of civil war and economic ruin, are flocking back to their homeland, confident that things will continue to improve. Life for white South Africans has not suffered a massive deterioration as predicted and people are not being mugged or killed by unruly mobs. The so-called Rainbow Nation is doing very well.

Nkosi Mabendla, partly due to his advancing years and partly to his own recognition that he is not a "manager", has decided to step down as President. His legacy is intact. The AFA has appointed another long-term member as its new President, who has in turn been appointed President of the Country.

Julius Indiki is a bureaucrat and intellectual by nature; he is not a revolutionary nor a great public speaker. According to his predecessor he is "safe hands".

Thabi Skosane has been retained as Minister of Finance. Despite the booming economy, his worries are growing by the day. In his view efficiency is being massacred by inexperience, greed and, maybe even, robbery. His warnings have been falling on deaf ears. He is regarded by most of his colleagues in the AFA as a massive pain in the neck.

His old friend Daniel Buthelezi has continued to prosper. He, like many other black entrepreneurs is known as a Black Diamond. Black Diamonds have, in their private enterprises, been able to secure all sorts of work at all levels from the new inefficient managers that dole out the jobs. Daniel still lives in his Art Deco mansion, where he frequently throws rumbustious parties. He is still not married and the pink Rolls Royce still graces his driveway, or, at least, a newer version of the original. Gloria is still the official girlfriend. The loose arrangement suits them both – and loose it is. Daniel, like his old friend Thabi, is also partial to white girls. The white girl that served the coffee seven years ago has been replaced with a younger model. Sometimes her services are required in the bedroom, rather than the dining room. The one white girl that Daniel really fancies is off limits; that is until she indicates to him otherwise.

Daniel has set Gloria up as an impresario. He has bought the Colosseum Theatre, the largest downtown entertainment venue in Johannesburg, which Gloria uses as her base. As the previously banned television service has taken hold in the country, so have the names of international performers become widely recognised. There is a hunger, Gloria has recognised, for South Africans to see their favourite entertainers in the flesh, so Gloria had, one by one, brought them to perform in South Africa. Even though her enterprises were often not financially viable, Daniel is happy to soak up the losses, for the sake of the kudos that it brings him. The arrival of a famous stage or TV star in the country normally coincides with one of Daniel's famous house parties to which, naturally, Gloria brings her international stars.

Thabi and Gillian are usually invited to these bashes. Gillian always wants to go, particularly because of her love of music and the arts. Thabi is less enthusiastic but does not want to disappoint his wife. In truth, he now finds it difficult to deal with his old friend Daniel. As Minister of Finance he is effectively in charge of auditing the government's books. He just knows that one day something will come up that could embarrass Daniel; it is only a question of time. Thabi is concerned that a too friendly association with his colourful friend will come back to bite him. Nevertheless, he goes to the parties. He likes to see Gillian happy. Also, it gives him a kick to see his wife getting so much pleasure from talking with some of the world's most famous entertainers, most of them of course, in one way or other, musicians, like her. In some instances, Gillian has been able to persuade a superstar to come with her to Emfundisweni, to meet the kids in her music class. These occasions are like magic to Gillian and she is so grateful to Daniel for affording her the opportunity.

There are occasions when Gillian and Thabi are not able to go to Daniel and Gloria's soirees. This is normally because Thabi can't, due to work. From time to time he is required to attend conferences overseas, particularly in New York. There are other times when the pressure of work is just too great for him to take time out. Up until now Gillian has not suggested that she go to the parties alone, but, since Thabi's work seems to clash more and more with the party nights, Gillian is becoming a little resentful. She even suspects that Thabi, who is never that keen on a party, is deliberately finding reasons not to go. However, her loyalty to her husband is so great that she never complains.

It is, therefore, quite a surprise when Thabi suggests that, if work prevents him from going to Daniel's house, this need not stop her. Gillian initially baulks at the idea. "Of course I won't go on my own. That is not right when you are having to work," she says, but with little conviction.

"I don't mind, my love," says Thabi, "I know how much you love meeting people from the performing arts. It is only fair that you go alone, if I can't." With that, Gillian's protests evaporate.

A few evenings later Gloria calls. She is having a soiree at the house for a famous American jazz pianist, Dizzie Jones; she knows that Thabi is away, but would Gillian like to come anyway? It is almost as if Gillian was writing the script. "Of course, I'd like to come," she instantly replies, "it would be fantastic to meet Dizzie."

"That's great," says Gloria, "it's not a huge party, just dinner, probably no more than eight. Okay?"

"Of course," says Gillian, "It will be a thrill."

The dinner amongst the artwork is a lot of fun and the eight participants get through a lot of wine. Dizzie is all that Gillian had expected, loquacious and witty, with many stories from around the world. Gloria is particularly attentive to him; in fact, after several glasses of wine, she is flirting with him unashameably. Dizzie is lapping it up. His wife is in Los Angeles, but clearly he does not care too much. The other four guests are Dizzie's manager and a young pretty South African girl who has very little to say, as well as two gay men from the advertising agency used by Gloria to promote Dizzie's tour.

Daniel, as always, is the perfect host. Amiable, charismatic, charming and full of stories and jokes, some of dubious nature. The fact that Gloria is practically making out with their famous guest does not seem to bother him at all. When dinner is done, Daniel reaches for one of the many control pads lying around the place and activates some music.

"Would you care to dance, Mrs Skosane?" says Daniel with a huge, cheeky, but assured grin. Gillian, by now, has had far too much to drink.

"Of course, I would," says Gillian, with the faintest slur.

Whilst Dizzie explores Gloria's body on the couch, Daniel and Gillian smooch and sway to the music. Daniel pulls her close. His hands slide down to her bottom which he begins to caress. Suddenly, Gillian, through the fog of the wine, realises what is happening. She pulls away abruptly.

"Daniel," she says, as firmly as she can muster, "we must stop. We can't do this. I must go. Thank you for a wonderful evening." It all pops out like a machine gun.

Daniel smiles. He is not angry. Disappointed, but not angry. In fact he has been surprised that he even got so far as a dance and a touch. "Better not push it," he thinks to himself, "her husband will be too much use to me. Don't spoil everything, you randy bastard."

Gillian makes a rather hasty exit. Gloria and Dizzie hardly notice. As she drives back home, she is excessively cautious. She knows she has had too much to drink. She is also shaken up. She really enjoyed the forbidden feel of her host. She really wished she could have stayed.

She is ashamed.

Chapter Thirty One

The soccer World Cup is a huge success. South Africa is now really on the world map. The television companies have made sure that the beautiful scenery of the country has been displayed for the world to see. The economy is booming, the streets are peaceful, and the weather is the best in the world. Who would not want to live in or visit such a wonderful country? There is no question that the perpetual display on the world's televisions for over a month is a tremendous advertisement for South Africa. Some would say that this is publicity that "money can't buy", yet it is money that did just that.

Thabi is the first to admit that staging the World Cup has been good for South Africa's economy, particularly in the construction and tourism industries. But he just abhors the waste. He has the strong suspicion that several of his co-workers, even at the highest level, have enriched themselves during the handing out of contracts related to the Cup events. He cannot help but notice the dramatic improvement in lifestyle that has appeared amongst many of his cabinet colleagues. He knows it is not possible to buy a Ferrari on a minister's salary, nor a Bentley, but the parking lot at the parliament buildings is beginning to look like a luxury car showroom. It is true, and Thabi recognises this, that the trickle down effect has raised the employment opportunities for many citizens, both black and white, but he is fearful of the short term nature of this boom. Most of all, however, Thabi is concerned about the principle of building a sound economy in a corrupt society. History has shown that this does not work. However, in the short term, South Africa has never had it so good, unless, of course, you are stuck at the bottom of the pile. Some black citizens have seen no improvement in their standard of living. Having been induced to move to the white mans' cities to cast their votes, they have found themselves jobless, penniless, and hungry. The only thing they succeed at is producing offspring and sometimes tapping into the electrical supply system.

However, whilst Thabi ponders, unhappily, about the future of his country, Daniel and his cronies are thoroughly enjoying the present. He has retained his power base as the President of the Small Traders Association as well as his membership of the AFA. In fact, having secured his wealth, Daniel has decided that the time has come to move into politics, not for any altruistic purpose, but purely to protect his status quo, his power base, and his personal future. Daniel lets it be known that he is willing to stand as a candidate for the Presidency of the AFA, a position which almost automatically leads to President of the nation, if the voters continue to give support to the AFA.

At this moment, the President of both the AFA and South Africa is still Julius Indiki. He is widely regarded by the membership as a caretaker President, who is easily manipulated by the top men in the AFA. These loyal supporters however are pressing on in years. It is in the nature of Africans to respect their elders, but as these old men have now enriched themselves and not necessarily their younger voters, there is a growing resentment within the party. Many members of the AFA believe that it needs fresh blood and fresh leadership if it is to retain its power base. Daniel has emerged as a candidate at just the right time. He is regarded as a natural successor to the old guard, a black man who has proved himself in business to be successful, a gregarious, warm and outward going man of the people.

The AFA annual conference is held in a huge marquee in the bush. There are well over a thousand delegates present, representing the party from all corners of the country and from all the nation's tribes. Daniel's Zulu roots stand him in good stead, since the Zulus are one of the most powerful tribal groups in the country. The other large group is Tswana, but it is represented by the unimpressive current President. To the outsider, the conference appears to be a complete shambles. The speeches drag on and on, each one getting more verbose than the last. The sound system is shambolic, with constant crackling and screeching. The busiest place on site is the food tent, where an unappetising buffet is constantly being restocked. The bar tent is packed.

Daniel's speech is an outstanding piece of rhetoric. He really gets the crowd going. He achieves what none of the other speakers have done so far; he empties the bar and food tents. His every sentence is followed by whoops and cheers from the noisy crowd. It is as if his audience has been gripped by a frenzy. He is loving every minute; his smile is getting wider and wider, and his voice stronger and louder. The perspiration is pouring down his face; there is no air conditioning in the marquee. Finally, he thunders to a stop. The noise is as if two Concorde jets had screeched through the tent. There can be no doubt who the people are going to vote for. Daniel Buthelezi, the most famous son of Alexandra, will be the next President of South Africa. Thabi, his childhood friend, watches like a deer caught in the headlights. Gloria jumps up and down with glee.

Three months after the AFA congress, South Africa, once again goes to the polls. Indiki's term had run. Despite all of the corruption that has clearly been going on, for many South Africans, this has been a good time. On Julius' watch a black middle class, which previously did not exist, has grown exponentially. This group will all be voting for Daniel and the AFA, recognising that he will be pro-business. The masses of poor people in the country will also be voting for him in the hope that some of the magic will rub off onto them. The old guard of the AFA, having secured votes for all, is now out of touch; Daniel represents a new, younger and savvy era, so even the poor will vote for him in anticipation of change. To most observers, Daniel has got it made.

The election is a landslide victory for the AFA. Daniel gives a surprisingly lowkey acceptance speech; he seems to be taking his appointment with gravitas. When he appoints his first cabinet, Thabi is surprised and deeply hurt that he has not been included in Daniel's cabinet. He is no longer the Minister of Finance, the position he has held through the last two governments. Daniel has not given Thabi any prior warning; this also seems strange to Thabi. After all, the two men have known each other since early childhood. What, wonders Thabi, is Daniel up to?

It is not long before Thabi finds out. The day after Daniel has made the names of his new cabinet ministers known he calls Thabi and requests that he attend a meeting with him at his home in Atholl.

"I'm sorry I didn't speak with you before my cabinet announcements," starts Daniel, even before the two men have sat down in Daniel's office in his house. "I should have done. I apologise."

Thabi can see that his old friend has not lost any of his charm. "That's okay, my friend. It would have been nice to have had a heads up, but I accept your apology. Let's move on. I can assure you I'll do my utmost to give a smooth transition to my successor as Minister."

"Thank you, Thabi; I am sure you will. However, I have a much more important role for you to play, for me and for the country. As I'm sure you're aware, this last government was mired in bribery and corruption. Both you and I know corruption leads to inefficiency and that will lead us to ruin. The politicians have let us down. I could have bought any one of them, and you may think I did. However, we need to stop this culture, and fast. I'm sure you can already see the inefficiency starting to erode our big state enterprises." Daniel stops for breath. Thabi tries to not look surprised at what he is hearing. Here is the arch briber, telling his friend that bribery needs to be stopped. Thabi is tempted to say something but decides to let Daniel finish, wherever he is headed.

"I've decided to set up an anti-corruption bureau. I need it to be run by somebody I can completely trust. I only know one such man, and that's you. I'll give you all the powers you need to bring down even the highest officer in the land. Will you do this for me?"

Thabi, of course, agrees that it is essential to wipe out corruption, but there is something incongruous about this proposal coming from one of the most corrupt men in the country. Nevertheless, Daniel is right. Something must be done about this culture or the citadel will fall. Maybe Daniel is for real.

"Give me a day to think about it," says Thabi. He knows that this work needs to be done, but, the complex relationship between Daniel and himself needs to be factored in somehow. He is highly suspicious of Daniel's motives. He knows that Daniel had built his fortune sailing close to the law. He suspects that Daniel would really like to steal his wife from him. He owes Daniel for supporting him financially when he first returned to Africa. There are so many things to think about which might be at conflict with the appointment. He needs time to think it through.

"Okay, Thabi. But one day only. I need to know."

Thabi leaves Daniel's house with plenty of food for thought. He really wants to discuss things with Gillian. This subject really is a candidate for pillow talk.

In some ways Thabi is relieved to no longer have the responsibility of the Finance Ministry. He, and he alone, it seems, is extremely nervous about the state of the economy and its sustainability. Under his watch he has seen the country's major industries effectively nationalised, except that this is a form of nationalisation which has only benefitted a few; those few that have found themselves in positions of authority without even a soupcon of the required training, experience, or knowledge required to perform their new duties. Thabi has watched hopelessly on whilst his colleagues have plundered the resources within the national electicity, water, and transport companies, whose once full coffers have been drained and where planning for the future has stopped. Most competent white managers have left, clutching their redundancy payouts, or been pushed aside under the new rules that mandate certain percentages of formerly disadvantaged citizens must be adhered to on company payrolls. Futhermore, all listed companies have been obliged, under the new rules, to "sell" large percentages of their shares to black groups, thereby relinquishing control of South Africa's premier companies. Thabi is aware that Daniel has taken full advantage of new share ownership, being one of the few competent and experienced black entrepreneurs available.

Thabi is also concerned about the new "management" of national services, such as the police, the country's infrastructure, the postal and health services. He has started to witness gross inefficiencies as the experienced managers and workers have been dismissed, retired, or just left. As Minister of Finance, Thabi feels that he has been singularly unsuccessful in stopping the rot. Part of the problem has been that his colleagues in cabinet do not recognise the malaise. In fact, many of them have been its biggest cause. Whilst the economy has been buzzing along and these new "free" shareholders have been receiving bumper dividends, none of his colleagues have shared his foreboding. Most of them think that Thabi is a colossal pain in the neck and there is much rejoicing in the cabinet that he is going. Thabi knows that the buck, eventually, will stop with the Ministry of Finance. In many ways he is glad that he will no longer be the Minister.

On the other hand, if Daniel is being truthful, he has pinpointed the most pressing issue of the day: corruption. "And," thinks Thabi, as he mulls on the conversation he has just had with Daniel, "Daniel should know!" To be successful in the role of curbing the rampant corruption that is now endemic, Thabi knows that he must be given the teeth to do the job. If that was to happen, perhaps this task would be the best possible way he could serve his country.

Gillian's view is quite straightforward and, indeed, encouraging. She is, of course, a big fan of Daniel. She really believes that he cares for Thabi. She knows that

Daniel would like to have a closer relationship with her and only assumes that he does not press the issue out of consideration for Thabi. She believes, therefore, that Daniel's offer to Thabi is genuine, born out of necessity as well as friendship. On her pillow that night she gives her husband encouragement but her thoughts are with Daniel.

The next morning Thabi calls Daniel. He is too busy to meet during the day but asks Thabi to come to his house that evening. Thabi spends much of the day thinking through what he would need to set up an effective anti-corruption unit. On one matter, he is sure. He must report, not to any member of government, but to the Chief Justice. Nobody, including the President, shall be able to interfere with his enquiries.

That evening, over a convivial dinner, as usual served by a white maid, Thabi talks through his plans and requirements for his anti-corruption unit. He is calling it "Ferret". Daniel nods his head in agreement with his friend's early plans until it comes to the tricky issue of to whom Thabi shall report.

"No, my friend, you have to report to me. I must know what is going on at all times. It is not feasible for you to report to a judge."

Thabi begs to differ.

"Think about it Daniel," he says, "by removing my enquiry from the supervision of a politician, especially one who has sprung from private enterprise, you are legitimising the function. No other single act can signal how seriously you regard this matter."

Daniel, however, continues to insist that Thabi should report to him. He makes the point that they will need to work as a team, not against each other. But Thabi is equally insistent and Daniel can see the political points he will score if he relinquishes control of Ferret. Finally, he agrees. Round one to Thabi.

The announcement that Thabi has been appointed the chief of an independent anti-corruption agency is met with huge approval from the press and much superficial praise from the newly elected members of parliament. Those that have been guilty of misdeeds in the past join in the praise, but are certainly surprised that Daniel has opted out of control. The good life, however, goes on. It will be months before Ferret has the ability to pursue any cases, so the "live for the moment" attitude prevails. Luxury goods are flying off the shelves. New shopping malls are opened in Johannesburg and Cape Town and tourists are amazed to find that every brand name in Bond Street has a shopfront in South Africa. After all they have heard about the poverty in Africa, tourists are flabbergasted to witness the customers in the high end shops, amazed that they are almost all black citizens of Africa. The same tourists are also amazed, as they drive out of or into the major cities and even the smaller towns of the country, at the sight of millions and millions of black Africans living in abject poverty in plain sight. These are the people that the Black Diamonds have left behind: their own.

Chapter Thirty Two

Gloria is, of course, delighted that her long-term lover, protector, investor and housemate, has been elected Premier of the country. She is really enjoying the publicity and attention that it has brought to her. Some people in the land, however, are not happy that Gloria is not actually married to Daniel, especially in the many strong religious communities. In all the years that Daniel and Gloria have been together there has never been any question of marriage; both are too free spirited and the lack of commitment and loose arrangement has suited them equally, particularly since both of them frequently have dalliances on the side. However, now that Daniel is a public servant, he and she are far more in the spotlight than before. Every move they make is subject to scrutiny. Furthermore, because Gloria is not officially the "first lady", she is excluded from many of the state ceremonies and events which Daniel must now attend.

Gloria is not happy about this and, on several occasions, attempts to discuss marriage with Daniel. He is not interested. He is very happy with the status quo. He does not want to give up his freedom. The office of the Premier is shackling enough. Gloria will just have to put up with things the way that they are. Besides, Gloria is becoming something of an embarrassment to Daniel, now that he is the Premier. Her background as a Madam in a brothel was not a problem to him in business, but in the lofty atmosphere of parliament and the international diplomatic world, it is a different matter. Daniel does not feel that he can take Gloria with him on high level diplomatic missions to New York or the UK. Their relationship turns ugly when the British government invite the Premier of South Africa to the UK on an official State Visit. This will entail Daniel staying at Buckingham Palace with the Queen and her consort. Such invitations are normally extended to the wife of the visiting Premier, but, on this occasion, the British ambassador has quietly suggested to his counterpart in the South African embassy in London that it would be diplomatic to leave Gloria at home, on the basis that she is not married to the Premier. Actually, the thought of Gloria staying with the Queen is just untenable to the stiff men in the upper reaches of the British civil services. Daniel is not at all bothered, but, when he tells Gloria that she will not be joining him in London, she is furious.

"So, I'm not good enough for your fancy friends, am I?" she shouts at Daniel in their ritzy lounge. "I'm good enough to meet the Zulu King; so why shouldn't I meet the Queen of England?" she rants, shrieking at the top of her voice.

"Because we're not married," says Daniel, as quietly as he can, in an effort to stop the screaming.

"And who's fucking fault is that?" she screams even louder.

Daniel tries to calm her, but he is reaching a point with her when he really doesn't care if she leaves.

"I'll tell you whose fault it is…" she carries on at the top of her voice. "It's your fucking fault. All you want to do is to fuck me just when you feel like it. That's all I am to you. Just a fucking fuck machine."

With that she stomps out of the room. Ten minutes later Daniel hears the doors slam on the pink Rolls Royce and she is gone. Daniel does not know where to and he does not care. The State Security police assigned to protect the Premier and his family are quick to tail Gloria. Her whereabouts will not be unknown to Daniel for long.

These rows between Daniel and Gloria have become more frequent of late. Gloria preferred life with Daniel before he acquired the trappings of greatness. She is sick of being followed around by secret policemen. Her previously adventurous life is now being seriously impaired. Recently she had booked a top black American crooner, Johnny Spade to perform at her Colosseum Theatre. Spade had taken a shine to Gloria and, as she had done with so many of her celebrity bookings, she enjoyed accommodating him on frequent visits to his hotel suite. Unfortunately, these clandestine meetings were no longer private affairs, since she was aware that she was being tailed. She did not know whether her activities were reported back to Daniel or were just sniggering fodder for the local cops. Whichever, she was not happy about it.

Johnny Spade was really taken by Gloria's charms. Physically, she was everything a man could desire, but her assured personality was unusual for a black African woman and really appealed to him. When his short string of stage appearances was over he had asked Gloria to return to Los Angeles with him but this would have been too complicated for Gloria, with her relationship with Daniel and her private business concerns in South Africa. Now, however, as she drives away from Daniel's Atholl mansion, she starts to have second thoughts.

"Screw Daniel," she shouts out loud, as she drives around to nowhere. "Screw him. I've had it with him.

I shall go to fucking Los Angeles!" With no one to shout at and nowhere to go, Gloria begins to calm down. A plan begins to formulate in her pretty head. She pulls into the Intercontinental Towers, tosses the keys of the pink beast to the doorman and checks herself into a suite, with a request to the assistant manager that her presence in the hotel remain confidential. From here she begins to plan her retreat and the next phase of her life. The South African secret police, of course, know exactly where she is.

Meanwhile, back in Atholl, Daniel is pleased that Gloria has gone. They have had a good ride together. Coming from the same neighbourhood they were soul mates. Gloria had also been magnificent in bed. She had been a good student at the brothel and knew how to please a man. She had also been a lively and interesting partner, at times, even an exciting one. Yet, despite her physical attractiveness, she was not intellectually challenging. She was also becoming something of an embarrassment.

Preparations for the State Visit to Great Britain had been moving ahead. Her Majesty the Queen had been very fond of President Mabendla. Like everyone else in the world she admired the way he had engineered massive change in South Africa from a prison cell. During the years of sanctions against the Nationalists, South Africa had been banished from the British Commonwealth. When Mabendla was finally elected President, the Queen, through the British government, had invited South Africa to rejoin the Commonwealth and Nkosi had accepted with alacrity. Shortly after his election Mabendla had been invited to stay at Buckingham Palace and he and Her Majesty had struck up a warm friendship. Now, with this new State Visit, both the palace officials and the Queen herself are nervous about the new incumbent. The

Queen's advisors have been desperately trying to ascertain with whom Daniel will be travelling. The word has gone out that Gloria may not be an ideal guest to have in the Palace and it looks as if this advice has been heeded. It is with a certain relief that the Palace is finally informed that Daniel will not be bringing Gloria to London. The Palace is, however, surprised with Daniel's request that he should be accompanied by his mother, Surprise. The first instinct of the courtiers is to refuse but, just to be on the safe side, the Queen's personal secretary decides to run the request past Her Majesty. To everybody's surprise the Queen is enchanted by the idea, even more so when she learns that Daniel's mother is called Surprise. Without hesitation Her Majesty sees to it that Surprise is included in the invitation and even instructs her staff to make sure that Surprise is actually sent a personal invitation. The shriek of delight that emanated from the shabeen in Alexandra as Surprise opened her hand-delivered gold-embossed invitation from Buckingham Palace, could be heard as far as Pretoria. One elderly lady had made another very happy indeed.

Daniel is his normal affable and approachable self and Her Majesty is relieved to find him an easy house guest. Naturally she does not regard him with the same esteem as Mabendla, but he is easy company, although extremely respectful of Her Majesty and treats her with the reverence he holds for his own mother. Surprise is the hit of the visit. Everybody just loves her. The wonderful mixture of awe and exuberance, charm everybody that she meets, none less so than Her Majesty herself. Daniel has done the right thing in bringing his mother. The State Visit is a huge diplomatic success and the newfound popularity of the mother and son duo in Great Britain reverberates back to South Africa, where things auger well for the newly elected Premier.

Those that doubted the wisdom of allowing a black majority to rule the nation are beginning to have second thoughts. Fresh capital is pouring into the country and business is booming on all fronts. New skyscrapers are emerging from the African soil in all of the major cities. Massive new conference centres have been built in the three largest cities in the country and the price of real estate is rocketing. The fresh new shopping malls are teeming with the new black middle class and there are few signs of overt racism. The hopes for a rainbow nation seem to be justified.

Thabi, however, continues not to be fooled by this apparent economic miracle. He is alarmed by the flamboyant spending patterns of the newly enriched black investors. As part of the drive to enhance the wealth of previously disadvantaged citizens, all publicly listed companies have been forced to sell shares to non-white citizens. These shares are to be paid out of future dividends from these companies, which, until such time are still managed by the mainly white management teams. As a few years pass the dividends from the well-managed companies have paid off the loans and the non-white "investors" are now taking control of many of these companies. As a result of white managers being paid off and replaced by untrained black men, standards of performance are falling and financial controls are sometimes being ignored. Thabi has witnessed a deterioration in the efficiency of many of the largest companies listed on the Stock Exchange.

Similarly, any companies that are providing essential services to the nation, have been nationalised by successive AFA controlled governments. Existing management have been paid off and replaced by untrained black executives. The effectiveness of public service businesses is beginning to suffer. Mail is not being delivered, capital investment is not being made in infrastructure projects, sporadic power black outs are beginning to occur, water is in short supply and so on. Whereas most citizens view these matters as teething troubles, Thabi is not convinced and a cursory examination of the accounts of many listed and nationalised companies demonstrates to him that he is right to be concerned. Assets are being frittered away and nothing is being put aside for a rainy day. Thabi is convinced that these assets are actually being stolen and he is determined to find a way to stop the rot before it is too late. This new job that he has been assigned is going to be an uphill battle. It is also going to be him against the power of the AFA. He needs Gillian by his side now more than ever before. For many years the whites have had their noses in the trough but they, at least, managed to keep it well stocked. The new trough is hastily being sucked dry. Meanwhile, nobody seems to notice, and those that do are getting so rich that they do not need to care. Unfortunately, the ones that will suffer are the ones that have not yet even reached the trough.

Chapter Thirty Three

Gloria is now living in Los Angeles with Johnny Spade. Johnny has not divorced his wife who he has more or less abandoned in their penthouse in New York. By substantially overpaying Johnny on successive performances at the Colosseum in Johannesburg, Gloria has managed to launder a substantial amount of cash out of South Africa so she is not entirely dependent upon her host and new lover. As usual, Gloria has no intention of losing her independence. As soon as she is able, through Johnny's well-connected lawyers, to obtain a Green Card, she will establish herself in her new homeland, where her connections to the entertainment business will stand her in good stead. In addition to that her lawyers in Johannesburg have managed to extract a multi-million dollar "alimony" payout from Daniel, the Premier, in exchange for her silence in regard to much of Daniel's pre-public service life.

Johnny Spade is unabashed at having the beautiful Gloria on his arm in Los Angeles. Much to the chagrin of his abandoned wife in New York, Johnny and Gloria are frequently photographed for the tabloids at various very public venues. It does not take long for Bibi and Lance to invite them as guests on the talk show, especially since Gloria and the brother and sister show business team have roots in South Africa, albeit from astoundingly different backgrounds. In fact, Gloria is such a hit on the show that

Lance and Bibi are keen to invite her several times. Bit by bit, Gloria is beginning to be more famous than Johnny.

Bibi's one time lover, but now established friend, Ron Sterling, has become aware of Gloria's presence in Los Angeles. He asks Bibi for an introduction. He is fascinated, not only by her outstanding beauty but also her history. Always on the lookout for a good story line for the studio, he senses that Gloria might be an interesting subject. Bibi organises a dinner party, to which Gloria and Johnny are invited. She makes sure that Ron is invited. Gloria does not disappoint. The other dinner guests are enthralled by her tales of Alexandra and her rise to fame and success on the coat tails of the now Premier of the country. Gloria's narrative sparks a hundred film scripts in Sterling's head. Her beauty and obvious sensuousness do not go unnoticed.

Lance has not been invited to the dinner party. Believe it or not, although Bibi and Lance are practically joined at the hip as brother and sister, they make a point, outside the TV studio, of living separate lives. Gloria is disappointed. Although she is pleased to have had the opportunity to meet Fleming, who will no doubt be extremely useful in furthering her career, it was really Lance that she wanted to meet in a social setting away from the television cameras. Of all the men she has met since arriving in America, Lance is the one that interests her most. Naturally the subject of the upcoming fight between Lance and Gerrie comes up in the dinner talk and Bibi explains that Lance is now in strict training. Dinner parties are off the menu. So, according to his sister, are girls: just the sort of challenge that Gloria needs!

Back in South Africa, the country is experiencing the biggest economic boom since the gold rush. Most of the world is amazed that the revolution has occurred peacefully and since Mabendla walked from jail. Investment has poured into the land. With Daniel at the helm there is even more confidence in the future of the country and new commercial enterprises are proliferating. The amount of cash slushing around is stupendous. The opportunities for Daniel to make hay whilst facilitating development and business projects are numerous, but he has been elected as the candidate to stamp out corruption. He also has his friend Thabi looking over his shoulder.

Thabi has decided on two concurrent strategies in his quest to uncover corruption. He will go for low hanging fruit, so as to score some quick victories, but he will also quietly pursue the biggest cases, which he knows will take time to unearth and secure convictions. Daniel gives him every encouragement. The more cases that can be proven against his former AFA colleagues, the less attention will be directed at him. There have never been any accusations against the first black Premier nor his regime. Thabi is convinced that Mabendla was as honest as the day is long and that for the first couple of years of his tenure, he was so revered that nobody would have been tempted to rob the State. However, by his own admittance, Mabendla was a leader, not a manager, and his grip on the detail of fiscal management was not solid. Furthermore, Mabendla was an old man when he came to power and, quite sensibly, he passed over the reigns of power to younger colleagues, once his work of establishing a new constitution was complete. Thabi's investigations therefore began with Mabendla's successors.

Two cases particularly interested him. One included the purchase of armaments and military equipment and the other the purchase of railway rolling stock. Both purchases were for billions of Rand and rumours were rife that the backhanders from the overseas suppliers ran into multimillions of Rand. Gradually, Thabi and his team were piecing together substantial evidence linking payments to politicians who were stupid enough to purchase with state funds, railway stock that would not pass through the bridges and unwanted submarines for the navy. Daniel, of course, was delighted that Thabi and his men were gathering evidence against his predecessors; that way he wouldn't have time to look closer to home – or so he thought.

Daniel's private life had changed. The house in Atholl seemed dead since the departure of Gloria. Although, at the time, Daniel had been pleased to see Gloria leave, her departure had left a gaping hole in the atmosphere at the house. Also, as Premier, Daniel was able to live in the rather grand houses which were the formal residences of the State Premier. There were two of these because the seat of parliament in South Africa alternated between Cape Town and Pretoria. These state-owned houses were a far cry from Daniel's garish town house in Atholl. They were both relics of the colonial era of the country – all pillars and marble – no place for the white maid. On the one hand Daniel hated these state homes, but, on the other, he felt rather satisfied that he, Daniel, ex-resident of Alexandra township, should now be living in the grandeur of the country's colonial past. Daniel only visited his home in Atholl when engaged in sexual conquests, which, although still under the watchful eye of the security services, at least seemed a little more discreet than amongst the marble pillars of his official homes. Everything in Daniel's life was good, with one exception. The woman that he really desired was married to Thabi.

Daniel was frequently required to attend official functions. As President of the AFA his presence was also needed at party meetings and gatherings. His officials were often embarrassed by not knowing who would be accompanying their boss on these occasions. Often Daniel did not know himself until the last moment. This gave those that were protecting him an unenviable task. However, from time to time, Daniel would throw a private dinner party at the Atholl house, with minimum interference from the security officers. Now bereft of the services of Gloria in securing guests from the show, with Thabi's permission, he turned to Gillian to gather interesting guests, mainly from the arts. Gillian, from her early work in introducing music to the children in the primary school, had developed her involvement in the music and arts scene in the nation. She had started a national society for the development of the arts, which had attracted a large membership from all walks of life in the country – the National Association for the Promotion of the Arts (NAPA). As such, Gillian was the perfect person to arrange the most interesting soirees.

Thabi, in regard to his role as an investigator, was never keen to attend Daniel's soirees. As far as possible he had decided to keep his distance from Daniel, at least in so far as social events. The fact that his wife was attending in her role as an arts coordinator seemed appropriate. If there was anything going on that he should usefully know about, he felt sure that Gillian would tell him. Gillian enjoyed her new found role as arts and social agent for Daniel. No budget was too high in regard to her activity. She was given a free rein and the freedom and scope to put together the most interesting dinner or lecture guests. She was also given the freedom of Daniel's Atholl house and quite frequently found herself alone with him without the incumbrance of security personnel. Bit by bit Gillian found herself falling for Daniel's charm offensive. To his credit Daniel did not force the issue but he gradually wore down her resistance to his charms. It was not long before she found herself deliberately checking on what she looked like before meetings with Daniel, making sure that she was appealing. She dreamed of Daniel. Thabi was so busy with his work that she felt neglected. Daniel was far from disinterested. His goal in life, as far as relationships were concerned, was to bed the English woman who, for so long, had intrigued him.

One night, whilst Thabi was out of town on investigative business, Gillian finally succumbed to her desire. The Atholl house guests had departed and the pull of the magnetism that existed between her and Daniel finally overcame her. Daniel was, of course, receptive and they made love. Although it was a physically powerful moment for Gillian, she instantly felt ashamed. She hastily gathered her things and left. As she drove home she cried the whole way. From that night on she never organised another event for Daniel. Others wondered why she was no longer involved. There was plenty of speculation, but Daniel took it in his stride and never uttered a word. Gillian had penetrated his thick skin unlike any other woman. He still desperately wanted her. He had never thought this way about any of the women he had bedded in his life, but, maybe, because of that, he decided to give her time and respect her. He could wait.

He also had plenty to do. He had inherited a booming economy and his pro-business leadership had only strengthened and prolonged the progress. But he was smart enough to know that this new found wealth had not trickled down to the black masses. Daniel understood only too well that unless life improved for all South Africans, the trickle of unrest could turn into a torrent. South Africa was on the brink. Daniel had to decide if he really cared.

PART THREE

Chapter Thirty Four

So many chapters in this story begin with a fight. Both Gerrie Van der Merwe's and Lance Hermanus' lives were determined by what happened for short periods inside a square ring. This fight, however, was to be different. This would be the last boxing match that either of the two protagonists would take part in. So, in so many ways, this would be the most important fight in each of their lives; neither was willing to lose.

The Staples arena was packed to the rafters. The celebrity residents of Hollywood, Beverly Hills, Bel Air and Malibu Beach had turned out in force, grateful, this time, that they did not have to schlep to Nevada to see the action. Thousands more donations came pouring in as the arena filled. Somehow, in a way that was hard to define, the atmosphere was different to a regular title fight. Nothing was at stake here except honour. Hence, it was more of a carnival fever that filled the hall, more of a joyous than a serious occasion. To the boxers, however, nothing could have been more serious. This was the final opportunity for each man to prove to the other, and the world, who was the greatest champion of them all: the outward going and outspoken television star or the modest family man from Joburg. All the big money was on Lance. All of the local enthusiasm was for Lance. In Hollywood, Lance was THE man of the moment, and Lance's glamourous sister was his greatest accessory. The crowd in Los Angeles had come to see Lance win. Notwithstanding that, Gerrie did have his fans; the crowd would not be 100% for the White Assassin.

The Staples centre was exceptionally noisy that evening. Bibi, with the help of the professionals from Ron Fleming's film studio, had decorated the arena as if it were a Roman colosseum, heavily draped with South African and American flags. There was a real buzz of excitement in the air. The hospitality suites were crammed full and, as more and more alcohol was consumed, the noise got louder and louder. It took the sound system at full volume to announce the arrival of the fighters with a blast of bugles, followed by the playing of the South African and US national anthems. Gerrie was the first of the two men to be announced. As he made his way to the ring through a cordon of well-wishers, he was entirely focused on the battle ahead, and barely acknowledged the applause. Lance, on the other hand, swaggered to the ring amidst a bevy of scantily clad Las Vegas showgirls. He was dressed like a Roman gladiator. He looked super confident and stopped en route to exchange greetings with many famous faces, just as if he were the President of the USA arriving for the State of the Union address.

In the ring, Gerrie was ready to fight. Lance, ever the gamesman, took his time in removing the toga outfit. Gerrie ignored him. The referee, American Jo Stoppa, called the men to the centre of the ring and recited the ritual instructions. Then, the fight began. As predicted, the first few rounds were very evenly matched. Coach Brennan, who had been invited by Bibi, afterwards showed his private scorecard. After Round Five, he had it dead even, everything to fight for going forward. But there was no going forward.

As Gerrie went to his stool at the end of the fifth he suddenly, without warning, collapsed, clutching his chest. He had suffered a massive heart attack. At first, nobody knew what had happened. Some thought that his collapse was due to a punch in the last round from Lance, but in fact, for the last minute of the round, Lance had not managed to land one solid punch. Others thought that he was throwing in the towel, but, up until that point, he had shown no signs of fatigue or being hurt. The ringside doctor was in the ring within seconds, but he could do nothing for the stricken man. Gerrie was dead before he could be lifted out of the ring. Never before, in the history of the Staples Center, had an event ended so abruptly. Jo Stoppa did not know what to do. He didn't need to stop the fight because everybody knew it was over. Out of an abundance of good sense he refrained from raising a confused Lance's hand and for once in his life, Lance was not celebrating. His concern was for his friend and not himself. Like everyone else he was in a state of shock. The change from joyous partying to complete surprise was instantaneous. The packed house went silent, save for the screams of anguish coming from Angel, as, realising what had happened, she had clambered into the ring to comfort her dying husband. There was no need for any announcements, although the Master of Ceremonies gamely tried; it was clear to all in the arena that life had left Gerrie – cruelly and suddenly. What had started as a gala, now finished as a horrendous nightmare. Nobody had beaten Gerrie, except his own heartbeat. Angel was completely crushed. No matter what Sally did to console her it was no use; nobody could stem her cries of agony. She had had a bad feeling about this fight from day one; now she knew why. She blamed herself for allowing it and nothing anyone could say would change her mind – ever!

The appalling news of Gerrie's death went viral. The crawl bars on millions of television sets carried the news. It was of universal interest and a sense of sadness spread quickly across the world. At Lance's request, the talk show was taken off the air for the next week and replaced with recorded material. Lance and Bibi turned down all requests for interviews and comments. Although everybody assured Lance that Gerrie's death could not be attributed to him, for a while, he wondered if it really was caused by one of his punches. Not until the post mortem exam concluded that the death seemed to be unrelated to the boxing match, did Lance rest easy.

There was, however, no consoling Angel. Despite being pronounced dead by the ringside doctor and the paramedics, Gerrie's body was taken to Mount Sinai hospital for further examination. Angel, Sally and Giancarlo travelled in the ambulance, but, soon after the physicians at the hospital confirmed that there was nothing that could be done. Giancarlo called for a car to take himself and the two ladies back to his LA house, where the children were being cared for. By now, Angel was in a daze. The doctors had given her something to calm herself and she fell into a fitful sleep. When she woke, her first thought was for the children. She decided that she needed to be strong. Her two little ones would never see their daddy again. It was now all down to her. She decided that Gerrie's body must be flown back to his beloved South Africa; that was where the funeral must be, not in the tinsel town of Beverly Hills. Arranging to fly a deceased body from the USA to South Africa is a daunting task riddled with beaurocracy. Thankfully, Giancarlo knew just how to deal with bureaucrats. Without him Angel would have struggled, but a few days after she had decided on this course of action, the whole family and the coffin were in the air, heading for their homeland.

The funeral, a few days later in Randburg, was one of the largest ever attended in the history of the Republic. The streets en route to the cemetery were lined several people deep, all silently bowing in respect, with, here and there, some polite clapping. And, for once, the crowd was not all white. Gerrie's courage and ability in the boxing ring had gained the respect of many black South Africans and more than a few turned out to pay their respects. Gerrie had brought a pride to South Africa which had been denied the country for many years. When all was done, Angel and the little ones went home to what now seemed like a cavernous empty house. Angel could not stop crying. A few weeks ago, her little family had been jumping for joy as Gerrie surprised them at Las Vegas airport. Now, he was gone – forever. For many weeks Angel mourned. She hardly went out and for the first time in her adult life she did not apply make up. It was her old friend and admirer, Tony from the Mood Agency, that brought her out of her depression. Tony, having spoken with Angel a few times on the phone, realised the state she was in. One day, some six months after Gerrie's heart attack, he paid Angel a surprise visit from England. "Come on, my baby," he declared, as deliberately upbeat as he could be, "put on your glad rags. I'm going to take you out to lunch." Angel, at first, declined. But Tony was insistent. "Come on, my love. I've flown all the way here from London to take you out to lunch. You can't disappoint me." Angel decided she had no choice. She asked him to wait a few minutes and then, half an hour later, she emerged looking radiant. Tony was stunned, but decided not to comment. He wanted her to believe that this was the new normal.

Strom, too, was completely devastated at losing his son, as was Edna, his mom. Luckily, Frikkie had been learning the ropes of the trucking business and Frikkie was a fast learner, as Bibi had once discovered. This meant that Gerrie's business was in competent hands, so Angel need not be worried about an income to bring up the little ones. Frikkie had loved his brother. He would make sure that his children wanted for nothing.

Sally and Giancarlo, of course, stayed for the funeral. This suited Giancarlo well because his casino project in Swaziland was moving forward apace. All of the necessary permissions had been granted and building of a new super resort for the South African market was proceeding. Giancarlo had hired the top architects and interior designers from Vegas, and, whilst Sally stayed home to help Angel's adjustment, Giancarlo busied himself with the Swazi Starburst. Giancarlo, the mobster, was used to death. But the sudden demise of Gerrie had also been a shock to him. Since the days when he first tried to bribe the young man, Gerrie had become almost a second son, and, as an Italian, family was the most important thing in life. Giancarlo felt this loss to his family, but strangely, there was no one to avenge, no one to blame. Only God.

Back in America, with Bibi's encouragement, after a week, Lance agreed to return to the TV studio, to restart the talk show taping, but it was clear to the producers that some of his spark had gone – at least, they hoped, only for a while. Bibi and Lance had not flown back to South Africa to attend the funeral. Before Angel had left America with her husband's coffin, she left the brother and sister with the strong feeling that they were to blame for her husband's death. "If it hadn't been for Bibi proposing the fight on the TV show, this would never have happened," Angel thought and what was in her mind seemed quite apparent to Bibi and Lance. Despite all medical opinion that Gerrie's heart attack had been unrelated to the fight, Angel was not buying it. In her view, if Gerrie had remained in South Africa running Van the Man, this disaster would not have occurred. She was quite happy that the couple did not come to SA for the funeral; they would only have attracted media attention and robbed the occasion of its dignity.

Bibi carried on with the talk show as if nothing had happened. She was clearly the least affected person by the tragedy. She had been hoping that Gerrie's spell in Los Angeles without Angel might have been an opportunity to re-ignite the spark between them, but Gerrie's refusal to even meet her, had put a quick end to that thought. As such, Bibi had been feeling a little spurned. Nevertheless, Gerrie's untimely death had been an awful shock to her, but not one that was going to derail her career. Now she had to make sure that it did not derail her brother's.

The ill-fated boxing match had raised almost 100 million dollars for charity and Bibi set about distributing this in a way that brought her the maximum personal positive publicity. Several of the talk show guests in the past had suggested to Bibi that she should enter politics. She would not have been the first from show business that had successfully carved out a political career in California. Being the benefactor to several popular charities would do no harm to her political aspirations. But first, she had to fulfil her contract with the television company in regard to the talk show. For this she needed an upbeat contribution from her brother, at least for a couple more years.

Lance, however, could not get out of his head Gerrie's untimely death. He too had been assured that it was an accident waiting to happen, but he still wondered why it had when it did. For several months the normally ebullient talk show host was depressed and it seriously affected his performance on the show. His spark had gone and despite Bibi's valiant attempts to overcome this on air, the audience noticed and the show's ratings began to fall. Lance had sunk into a total depression. Bibi encouraged him to seek professional help, which he did, but the counselling did not seem to work.

Lance seemed to be in a deep trough, with no apparent desire to clamber out. It would have helped if he had had a partner to turn to with his grief, but his soul mate of a sister was no help, having apparently shrugged off Gerrie's death, as if she had been swatting a fly. Lance was returning to an empty apartment night after night; he could not escape from thinking about Gerrie's death. This was not helped by a so-called guest on the show who, without any prior warning, laid into Lance, blaming him for the murder of his old friend.

Then, one day, something wonderful happened to Lance. The producers of the talk show had invited a young French film star, Brigitte Sandos, to be a guest on the show. Brigitte was an unusual beauty. She was not the full-busted glamour puss that one would normally have associated with French films, but, in her pixie-like way, was extremely attractive, with a sparkling personality to match. Lance had, as usual, made his pre-interview visit with his sister to the guest dressing room at the studio. He had instantly been entranced by their guest and the attraction stayed and grew during the live show. Brigitte was very quick witted and, with her cute French accent, was very provocative. She was physically very attractive to Lance, who for the last few months had shown no interest at all in women, but it was her lively and sometimes quite cheeky mind that sucked him in. When the show was over, Lance asked Brigitte to join him for supper. She declined, but left him with hope. "Some other time?" she teased.

"How about lunch tomorrow?" persisted Lance. She demurred. And so started the recovery of Lance Hermanus.

Four years later, Bibi was on top of the world. Her political career had flourished. She was now the mayor of Los Angeles and had launched a campaign to be elected Governor of California. She knew that she could never become the President because she had not been born in the USA, but Governorship of California was an excellent platform to propel her to further fame and riches. Although still unmarried, in the run up to the State elections, Bibi had formed a close friendship with one of Hollywood's leading heartthrobs, George Bentley, also known, of course, as Gorgeous George. The popularity of George had done nothing to dent Bibi's chances in the elections and the glamourous couple were continuously featured in the supermarket check out rags. What Bibi had not done to or with George was indescribable, even though the rags attempted to do just that, and what George had done to Bibi was mind blowing.

However, whilst Bibi's life in California had flourished, having shrugged off the death of Gerrie, her old friend, the now-widowed Angel was having a very difficult time in South Africa, whilst Bibi had hardly given her a second thought.

Chapter Thirty Five

In the four years following Gerrie's death, Daniel Buthelezi had ruled South Africa. During that time he had also strengthened his grip on the AFA, but he had needed to continuously fend off strong opposition from the Youth Wing, led by "Fighting" Felix Mobumbo, a firebrand and rebel rouser who had captured the imagination of the poor black youth, most of whom were unable or unwilling to secure and hold down jobs.

For the first two years of Daniel's presidency things had gone really well. The economy had boomed and the black middle classes had mushroomed. Despite that, the wealthier sections of the white population had held their ground economically. Indeed, in most cases the white rich had got even richer and, although there had been a massive handover of shares to handpicked black "investors", the rich whites had managed to keep control of most private enterprises.

In the public sectors, however, the wheels were really falling off, especially in regard to the county's infrastructure. The once pristine road system was crumbling. Major highways were full of potholes and no new transport initiatives were planned. There were constant water shortages in most provinces, despite often heavy rains. Millions of residents in the shanty towns were stealing electricity and there had been no new investment in the nation's electric grid. Blackouts were becoming more and more frequent, even in the mainly white and affluent suburbs. Those that could afford it insulated themselves from these hardships by drilling wells or installing electrical generators, but the majority of citizens, particularly the poor blacks, could not afford to do so. Unrest, due to these poor conditions, was growing. Hospitals were also severely understaffed and undersupplied with the necessary drugs. Private hospitals flourished, but, naturally, only the rich could benefit. Bribery at all levels of society was endemic. Traffic police stopped cars just for the purpose of eliciting cash and airline check in staff took cash for "overweight" luggage without the slightest hint of guilt. Everything was rotten.

Many older blacks were beginning to think that they had been better off under the previous system of Apartheid. At least then, they had jobs, water and heat when required. Many young blacks in the poorer districts had never known white rule or Apartheid. Despite the fact that the black politicians blamed the problems on the legacy of Apartheid, after many years of black rule this argument was wearing a bit thin, especially amongst the younger population.

The Christian Church which had once been so powerful had also lost its appeal to the younger electorate and its sense of order was being replaced with a growing sense of unrest.

Daniel was, of course, worried about this underlying mood, but the power still stayed with the older members of the AFA, on which he had a firm grip. Africans respect their elders, so, in Daniel's view, the youngsters, despite being unhappy, would continue this tradition. After all, they would be the elders themselves one day.

What Daniel was most worried about was the work of his appointee, Thabi. Thabi, as predicted, had been extremely thorough in bringing many prosecutions for corruption against leading AFA figures who had bled the public services through bribery and theft. Ferret had proved to be one of the few departments set up under Daniel's government that had real teeth. These prosecutions were good for Daniel's overall image amongst the population but were creating enemies for him in the old guard of the AFA. Furthermore, Daniel knew that Thabi had been systematically gathering evidence about the biggest heists of all, many of which had been at the hand of Daniel himself. Daniel had thrown every obstacle in the way of Thabi's investigators but, little by little, Thabi was building a case against his old friend that would be devastating. It would not be feasible for Daniel to fire Thabi because his record of success in bringing many crooks to justice had made him a popular figure amongst the electorate. On the other hand, he needed to impede Thabi's progress in regard to uncovering his own corruption.

Daniel sensed that things were coming to a head. He half hoped, since he had been so good to Thabi and his family in earlier times, that Thabi would repay him by not aggressively pursuing evidence against his benefactor. After all, not only had he aided his friend at a time of need but he had also resisted, at least to some extent in his view, the advances of Gillian. "I have been a good friend to Thabi over the years," thought Daniel, "why would he want to shaft me now?" Unfortunately, Daniel knew the answer to this question. Thabi was the most diligent and honest man he had ever met. There was no way Thabi would rate friendship over duty. So, Daniel had to consider drastic action. He needed to eliminate Thabi as a threat, and to do it soon.

Contact between Daniel and Gillian had almost ceased, except on formal state occasions when it was necessary for them to be in the same room. That is not to say that there was not a huge sexual attraction between the pair, but both realised that acting on this would be a dangerous path to follow. Thabi had obviously questioned Gillian about her sudden withdrawel from Daniel's soirees, which she seemed to have enjoyed so much, but, when Gillian explained that it was in order not to embarrass or impede Thabi with his enquiries, he accepted that and was most grateful. The less Thabi and his family had to do with Daniel, the better.

Frikkie Van der Merwe had proven himself as a worthy successor to his late brother, Gerrie. He had done a splendid job in operating Van the Man, much to the pride of his dad. He had also been a staunch support to Angel, ensuring that she and the children had everything that they needed, or almost everything. Frikkie was tremendously attracted to Angel, who was still a gorgeous young woman. Angel too was often tempted to take up with her late husband's brother, who reminded her so much of Gerrie, but she resisted temptation, as indeed did Frikkie. This mutual but forbidden attraction, which was obvious to many of their friends, made their relationship difficult to conduct so Angel did her best to keep out of Frikkie's way and just accept the financial benefits that flowed from his management of the company.

Notwithstanding that, Angel was still a young woman with all of the normal sexual urges of a young lady of her age. Tony from Mood was the most obliging in this regard and had made frequent visits to South Africa, whilst Angel, children's needs permitting, made frequent trips to England. Tony had successfully relaunched Angel as a photographic model and this enterprise provided perfect cover for their ongoing relationship. However, Angel was not in love with Tony and, after a couple of years, had had to accept this and just be happy with the relationship as it stood.

Frikkie's job of running a trucking company was becoming more and more difficult. As the mood of the country and the normal standards of living deteriorated, even for the poorest folk, unruly behaviour grew, particularly amongst the worst affected. Small but frequent riots and political protests were breaking out all over the land, and often in places where Van the Man trucks were plying their routes. A laden truck, no matter what the load consisted of, was very attractive to a hungry mob. As a result, Frikkie's fleet of trucks was frequently hijacked or raided, costing the company many thousands of Rand, since insurance was now impossible to get. Soon, Frikkie found it necessary to employ armed guards to travel in each truck, but this too was expensive and quite frequently the guards could not bring themselves to fire on their own folk, the hungry crowds. At the same time, the economy was grinding to a halt. Civil unrest and government mismanagement were not a recipe for investment. Within a couple of years, the world's view about the prospects of South Africa had turned quite sour. Nobody had much faith in the future of the country.

Van the Man started to haemorrhage cash. Since the company was, in effect, owned by Gerrie's widow, Angel, the pile of money that Gerrie had earned as a fighter started to diminish. As far as Angel could see, if things did not improve, her resources would, within a few years, be drained entirely. Although she was able to earn a good living from her renewed modelling career, she did not wish to see Gerrie's inheritance entirely squandered by chasing the lost cause of trucking in South Africa. After all, she had the future of Gerrie's children to consider. Frikkie, of course, saw things differently. Van the Man was his livelihood. He needed it to continue, however difficult the circumstances might become. Strom and Edna too needed the support of the company. For the first time in her marriage into the Van de Merwe family, Angel felt isolated. Yet she was determined to do what she knew she must and, in fact, what she felt Gerrie would have done. She announced that she would close down the company, sell all the trucks, and in future rely on her modelling earnings and the interest on what remained of Gerrie's stockpile of cash. Her responsibility, she announced to her in-laws, was to her children, Gerrie's children, and not to the rest of his family. She proposed to take a quarter of the proceeds as well as a quarter of her remaining capital and give it to Frikkie and his parents in compensation. In her view, she had no need to be so generous. In their view, she was being exceptionally mean. The disruptive effect of the unruly state of the country had found its way into the lives of the Van der Merwes

The situation at large in the nation was becoming more and more toxic. The AFA youth movement had all but broken away from the AFA and was continuing to urge unrest. White communities were attacked by mobs armed with sticks and stones, but, increasingly, with AK 47s. AFA Youth encouraged this behaviour and sooner or later the mobs were starting to occupy abandoned properties in white areas. This activity then escalated into young black gangs simply invading occupied white homes and turfing out the owners. The predominately black police force did very little to stop them. Needless to say, white communities formed their own militia to defend their homes but they might as well have been King Canute. The tide was coming in and nothing was going to stop it.

The last straw for the white communities was the day that AFA Youth proposed that all black domestic staff should turn on their employers and poison the food that they prepared for the "madams". This resulted, almost immediately, in the most loyal of home employees being dismissed, even if their intentions were as pure as fresh snow. Fear spread amongst the white community with a devastating effect on the economy. Black unemployment soared and with it came more and more violence and crime.

Daniel Buthelezi, the incumbent President, needed to act.

Chapter Thirty Six

Daniel Buthelezi's first term as President was drawing to a close. If he wished to serve a second term he would need to get re-elected as the President of the AFA first. The President of the AFA would be the party's candidate for the general election and, given the strength of the party within the electorate, it was certain that an AFA nomination would carry the national vote. So far, Daniel had proven himself adept at fending off challenges from the young Turks in the party, but since there was so much unrest and unruliness in the community as well as failing public services and declining law and order, it was far from certain that Daniel would be able to carry the day. He needed to win because without the protection of the position of head of state, he might find it more difficult to keep the upcoming accusations of corruption at bay.

Thabi, of course, was aware of the approaching deadline and was doing everything in his power to complete his investigation into the cases of alleged corruption involving the President. Finally, he was ready to take his evidence to the Chief Justice, evidence that Daniel would have great difficulty in explaining away. It would appear that prior to becoming President, Daniel had been involved as a middle man in purchases authorised by his predecessor. These purchases, which were for train rolling stock and armaments, were for massive amounts and Thabi had evidence that a substantial and illegal commission had been paid by the German suppliers. A complicated paper trail proved that half of this had finished up in Daniel's account in Switzerland and the other half in his predecessor's account in St Kitts and Nevis. Thabi had absolute proof that this was the case. When the kickback was taken into consideration the public of South Africa had paid almost 50% more than they needed to for the arms and the trains. To add insult to injury, the rolling stock was useless because it could not pass through the tunnels of much of the country's network and the country had no use for two nuclear submarines. This news could be devastating, not only to Daniel but also to the AFA itself. As far as Daniel was concerned this evidence must not come to light.

Daniel knew that it would be useless trying to persuade his old friend not to file the evidence. Also, he assumed that, even if Thabi were to meet an unfortunate and sudden death, he would have left a trail of damning evidence with his investigatory team. Daniel had to be sure to take a different route.

Three days before the AFA national convention, chaos broke out in the country. As a show of strength ahead of the convention, masses of young blacks staged a simultaneous protest in the three largest cities in the country. Hordes of young men and some women, armed with spears, sticks, bats and a sprinkling of automatic guns rampaged through the streets of the cities, destroying property, cars, taxis and buses before them. The police were powerless to stop them and, in most cases, were sympathetic to their cause. Pictures of the riots flashed around the world. This was a massive blow to South Africa's teetering economy. The value of the Rand fell by 60% in one day and the normally steady Johannesburg stock market fell off a cliff.

Daniel seized his moment. He called in the army. Armed troops and tanks flooded into the affected cities. Appearing on television, alongside the leaders of the three South African armed forces, Daniel announced a national emergency. He suspended parliament, cancelled the AFA convention, shelved the constitution, and declared a State of Emergency in which he devolved all power in the land from parliament to himself. Within two days the army had taken control of the cities, and armed troops were patrolling the streets. For a while the cities and towns were quiet. As it happened the heads of two of the armed services, the army and the air force, were both white men with many years of military training and experience behind them. The third, in charge of the navy, was black, but he too had been a long time serving officer of great repute. These three men did not speak during Daniel's announcement of martial law, but the resolute look on their faces spoke volumes. They were not about to brook any trouble.

Meanwhile, the move for blacks to take over white property continued unabated. Whilst the soldiers were able to prevent further damage to public property, they were not able to cope with the ongoing takeover of much white private property. Black servants were rebelling against their employers in huge numbers, street by street. It was not uncommon for the servants, assisted by relatives with guns, to simply take over the households, either evicting their rightful owners or, worse still, condemning them to the servants' quarters. Many white housewives were abused or raped, whilst the man of the house was held at gunpoint, unable to prevent his loved ones' humiliation. The rule of law had simply been tossed out of the window together with the property owners and their possessions. White families were lining up at the airport clutching what little belongings they could carry. The prices of international air tickets soared, whilst the value of the Rand plummeted even further. The country was in complete chaos.

Daniel, whose ill-gotten gains had been long ago converted into Swiss Francs, was not personally bothered. He now cared less about impending prosecution but, nevertheless, in anticipation of a return to normality at some point in the future, decided that now was the opportunity to rid himself of any threat. Under military law, he disbanded the Ferrets and other government agencies and, in so doing, dismissed Thabi. Not that Thabi had waited for this. Seeing the danger coming, he, Gillian and the family, had fled to the UK, where he promptly set about organising a government in exile, gathering around him other early escapees. Back in South Africa, elections, or any thought of them, had been cancelled. Thabi would have plenty of time to regroup.

During this mayhem, Angel and the children were still living in the house in Atholl which Gerrie had purchased when he was living with Bibi. Since Atholl was also the suburb where Daniel lived, Angel felt fairly secure. The whole area was crawling with armed soldiers so any risk of danger, either personal or to the property, seemed unlikely. She also still employed the gardening "boy" that had been there when Gerrie first moved in and "Blossom" her trusted maid, whom she had decided to keep despite the threats and warnings.

Things were not so rosy at Van der Merwe senior's home in Randburg. Strom and Edna still lived in the little house where Strom used to keep the trucks. Frikkie lived in the same street but in a larger homestead. He had arranged security guards to protect his home and that of his parents, but was quite concerned because many of the "so-called" security firms were discovering that their employees were complicit with black squatters. The Van der Merwes were living in constant threat of invasion. On top of that the trucking business had become a disaster. Angel had not found a buyer for the company nor indeed for many of the individual trucks, so the promised share of the proceeds had not materialised. Like many white families their livelihood had gone up in the smoke of the civil disobedience rampage.

Angel, from a financial point of view, was, however, more fortunate than most. Despite not being able to sell the trucks she had, well prior to the riots and the plummeting of the Rand, wired Gerrie's remaining fortune to her mother Sally in the USA, where Giancarlo had made sure that it was earning well. From a security standpoint, although reasonably happy that she was safe for the moment, she knew that she must now plan to leave South Africa. Sally would have had Angel's family come immediately, but Angel wanted to leave in an orderly fashion. Alas, she had waited too long. One evening there was a kerfuffle at the front door. The garden boy and Blossom appeared to be having an argument with some of the soldiers, who were demanding entry. It was well known that an ex Miss World lived at this address. The soldiers had been drinking and decided that a visit to Miss World would be fun. There were four of them. Angel would never forget the crazy look in their eyes as they gang-raped her on the sofa in her lounge in front of the screaming Blossom. As, one by one, they had their brutal way with her, she tried to think of something else, something nice, but the screaming of Blossom would not let her do so. Even as she was being ravished, she just wished Blossom would stop screaming. Their business done, the soldiers left, just as suddenly as they had arrived. Angel, in a daze, went to shower. She was strangely and perfectly calm. The whole episode had been extremely unpleasant, but what stunned Angel was that, despite the resistance that she had put up against the soldiers, and notwithstanding the horror of what was happening to her, she had actually experienced multiple orgasms during the rapes. Not only did she feel defiled but she also felt ashamed. She knew that she now had to leave her beloved country.

Two days later Giancarlo sent a plane to rescue Angel and the children. She contacted Frikkie and offered him and his folks a ride to safety. They declined. Despite all of the turmoil, they could not bring themselves to leave their beloved homeland. Three days later they were hacked to death as they resisted a takeover of Strom's home. Angel and the children were in Los Angeles. Angel was strangely flat. When she heard the news about Gerrie's family she seemed devoid of feeling. It was going to take a long time for feelings of any sort to come back to Angel, such was the depth of her trauma.

Even for Daniel, things seemed to be spiralling out of control. He went on television, accompanied by the heads of the three military services, and appealed to the masses to calm down. "In the name of Jesus Mabendla," he began, "I implore you to desist from breaking the law; I implore you to return to your homes; I implore you to behave as good citizens. This is OUR country; we must not destroy it. Please don't steal what is not yours. We are all citizens of this beloved country, whether we be black, white or brown, whether we be men or women.

This looting and rampaging must stop now. It is not what Jesus would have wanted. Together we should be building this country, not destroying it."

His words were effective. Gradually the wave of violence subsided as the rioters grew weary, but those that had gained during the riots were not going to give back what they had taken. Society had been turned upside down.

Chapter Thirty Seven

A year after Daniel's suspension of the Constitution nobody was happy. Many white citizens had lost their homes and many of those that hadn't found themselves with black squatting neighbours. Therefore, a typical street in a Johannesburg suburb might have four or five white families in a row of houses that now included three "stolen" properties. In many cases the lost neighbours had fled abroad or moved elsewhere. Everyone in the street knew that their new black neighbours were thieves so there was little dialogue between the residents and the interlopers. Within months the gardens of the stolen properties were overgrown and the actual houses were overfull. The new occupants had no money for maintenance and no will to refuse their extended families a place to live. There were not many attempts to expand into other homes by the squatters because the streets were regularly patrolled by armed soldiers who had become vigilant to this sort of thing. In many instances court proceedings had been initiated by the evicted white owners against the squatters but there were so many cases pending and so few working judges that it would take many years before any case would come to court, if ever.

The downtown business districts of the large cities also suffered badly. Offices and shops had been ransacked and were providing temporary accommodation for hungry blacks who had streamed in from the country or the surrounding shack townships. Whole high-rise buildings were occupied as living quarters for the homeless, and ad hoc committees were set up to control the activities of the "tenants" in each block. The office blocks were crawling with young children and old people huddled together in little groups. Soon the power supplies were cut off. The elevators stopped working and the toilets became clogged. With no electricity there was no way to pump water so buckets of water had to be carried up multiple storeys. Soon the buildings were filthy and stinking. The men could not get work to sustain their oversized families and, obviously, there was nowhere to grow crops or keep chickens or livestock. Eventually, when the conditions in the high-rise buildings became too putrid, the inhabitants started fanning out into the suburbs, where the patrolling soldiers and police had little chance of stopping them.

The situation in the black townships was not much better. Food and water were in short supply. Black acrid smoke hovered above Alexandra and the other townships for days. The schools, which had clung to teaching in the hated Afrikaans language had been burned down and ransacked, even Emfundisweni, where Daniel and Thabi had met, was burned to the ground. The clinic where Surprise had worked for so many years, had been closed shortly after the white staff, who had gamely and bravely continued to work, had been brutally murdered. Sadly, the three white doctors who had spent their lives helping the blacks of Alex, were the first to be killed in the riots and the clinic was badly damaged. Sam and Surprise could make no sense of anything. They were ashamed at the mess that their son Daniel had led the country into.

Daniel's siblings suffered mixed fortunes. Shaka, still living with his mum and dad at the shabeen, had no customers and, even if he did, he had nothing to sell them. Surprise had tried growing a few vegetables in the little plot. What savings they had were rapidly being used up and, in any event, their value had melted away with the decline of the Rand. If their son had not been the President of the country, they too would be dependent on the food parcels that from time to time were tossed out of patrolling army vehicles.

Solomon, who before the riots had amassed a fleet of seven minibuses and now lived in a house in Randburg, acquired with the help of Daniel, had no gasoline to operate the fleet. He too, was now eking out his savings. Luckily, he had not married any of his lady friends, so he only had his own mouth to feed. After a while he offered a safe haven to his nurse sister, Sindiswe, and together they made do. From time to time, they visited their brother, Daniel, who still had access to his overseas funds which he drew on to help them.

Mthunze, the actress, was, of course, well provided for. She had made herself available to the army, so rations were never a problem.

Most social services stopped or slowed to a crawl. Uncollected garbage started to pile up in the streets or in the front yards of the stolen houses. The towns started to smell. Previously well-kept public gardens soon became overgrown and replete with rough sleeping families, many of whom had lost their homes in the riots. Vandalised shops were left unrepaired and not replenished, their smashed windows a grim reminder of the unrest. The contents of the shops had long been emptied by angry and rapacious looters. The streets were littered with broken glass and unwanted packaging materials. Traffic lights had stopped working, but this did not matter, since there were almost no vehicles on the streets. Petrol stations, in the main, were closed. Black market (mainly operated by whites) petrol was available, but at a huge cost.

In the country side things were worse. Most white farmers had been ejected from their land and any useful or productive farming had ceased. Tractors and farm machinery were rusting in the fields or were now unworkable due to a lack of spare parts. The traditional harvests had not taken place and no new crops had been planted. Shops and supermarkets that used to be overflowing with local produce now looked desolate, with row upon row of empty shelves. The once proud nation which could feed itself with some to spare was now becoming reliant on foreign aid. Gasoline was almost impossible to obtain so a car was becoming an expensive but unusable asset. Car payments naturally had fallen behind but banks and lenders had no way of recuperating; taking back cars that could not be used seemed futile. In short, South Africa, once Africa's shining example of a fully functioning economy, was now the basket case of Africa. Nobody was investing. Anyone who had somewhere to go to had left and those that could not leave were living a life of misery, a life that they never conceived as possible.

Daniel, now seen as a Dictator, not a President, continued to go on television with promises of a better future, but not many people had the luxury of a working television set, and, if they did, they did not believe him. Since he had suspended government, there was no one to come up with a rescue plan for the country, no economists to advise on and direct a route to new prosperity. The white leaders of industry had either fled with their earlier gains to overseas territories or were hunkered down in fortified homes. Nobody, it seemed, had the will or ability to help Daniel plan his way out of this economic and social disaster. Those that did, were busy making plans in London with Thabi.

The military chiefs had proven themselves competent at stopping most of the violence and restoring order, though falling short of law and order. Bit by bit the servicemen started to clear up the streets. The navy took over the garbage companies and commenced the huge task of cleaning them. Some good citizens of all colours came out to help. But the military commanders realised that this could only be a holding exercise unless something could be done to restart the economy and restore the Constitution in order to re-establish the rule of law. They quickly came to the conclusion that Daniel and his old AFA cronies were not capable of doing this. In fact, these were the men who had ransacked the economy in the first place. Continuing to prop up Daniel seemed to them to be futile.

The most important of the military triumvirate was General Patrick Wilkins, the commander in chief of the army. The two leaders of the other forces, air and sea, although fully supportive of Wilkins, had little to offer by way of assistance due to the nature of their forces. However, they were not blind and could see with Wilkins that continuing to take direction from Daniel was futile. Daniel had nobody around him with the competence, desire, or experience to get the country back on its feet. The army was able to protect the Courts and support the police but, in terms of restarting the economy, the armed forces were helpless. They soon concluded, however, that they were no less helpless than Daniel himself. What was needed was new leadership, a leader who could attract the talent back to South Africa that had once made it great, and which could provide a platform for law, order and prosperity. To do this Wilkins and his colleagues decided that they must take control. So, one day, shortly before Daniel's first year of effective dictatorship, Wilkins and a small force of soldiers, walked into his office and informed him that the military was taking over the running of the country and that he was to be imprisoned in his house in Atholl, pending a trial for corruption. It was futile for Daniel to resist. He had nobody to turn to for help. The rats that had supported him had fled the sinking ship.

The day that found General Wilkins announcing on television, radio, and to the press that the military had staged a peaceful coup d'etat was met with relief amongst most foreign diplomats but with a good deal of shame in the population. Whites were deeply upset that their glorious country, once the showcase of Africa, had now sunk so low as to require military governance. These were the sort of things that happened in the rest of Africa, not here at home in South Africa. The Blacks were mainly ashamed that their opportunity to run their own country, as conceived by their hero, Jesus Mabendla, had been so badly squandered. Nobody had any confidence that things were about to get better.

Meanwhile, back in the UK, Thabi Skosane, with much assistance and cooperation from the British government, had been gathering around him, a cadre of younger black professionals and a powerful group of expatriate South African entrepreneurs, who were mainly white millionaires. Their common goal was the re-establishment of their homeland as a prosperous democracy. Thabi was the one black leader in whom they had confidence and the one that had demonstrated his political skills in gathering around him this government in exile. It did not take long, through diplomatic assistance from Great Britain, for Thabi and his advisors to connect with General Wilkins. Plans were hatched for a return to constitutional rule.

The traditional powerhouse in South African politics had been the AFA, the party of their late leader Jesus Mabendla. It was the AFA and the AFA in exile that had brought about change in South Africa, it was the AFA that had secured all black citizens the vote. But it was the AFA that had mismanaged the country once given the chance to run it. The AFA was also the political party which almost all of the black citizens had faithfully supported and, like night follows day, AFA Presidents had become President of the nation through the popular vote. Thabi, however, had taken the bold decision that, if he could form a new national government, it would not be as a member of the AFA. He had decided to resign from the AFA and start a new political party, which he nominally called AIP (African Indaba Party). This was a huge risk because, even though the AFA had clearly demonstrated its incompetence, people's voting habits were hard to shift. Some of Thabi's advisors thought he was taking an unnecessary risk. Gillian thought differently; she absolutely supported her husband's position, although she was not at all thrilled at the prospect of returning with her husband to the chaos of South Africa, especially as her children had settled down at school in the UK.

And so it came to pass, some five months after General Wilkins had staged the peaceful coup d'etat, that he once again turned to the media to announce plans for the military to organise a new general election one year hence, with a declaration that there would be a return to the Constitution within the next six months in order that normal electoral procedures could function. Within days Thabi Skosane also took to the airwaves and announced the formation of the AIP together with an impressive list of founding members, many of whom would make up his first cabinet should he be elected. He also announced that he had negotiated a huge financial aid package from the World Bank, more or less stating that this would be at risk if he were not elected. At the same time he made it crystal clear that the rule of law would be reintroduced and upheld. People who were occupying property illegally would be given fair warning to vacate, but he wanted to be clear – "I will only govern, if elected, by the rule of law, not by the rule of chaos. Those of you who do not agree with this principle should look elsewhere for leadership."

With new hope for a corruption-free and orderly government in the country, the economy began a cautious rally. With the value of the Rand so low, there were plenty of bargains to be had and money started to flow, albeit slowly, back into the system. Thabi and Gillian returned to South Africa and moved back into their home in Randburg, the military having first removed several families of squatters. Gillian was horrified that her home had been trashed, but nevertheless set about cleaning it up. For the moment the children were left with Gillian's mother in England, at least until the end of the school year and till after the elections. The fact that the prospective candidate for the Premiership of South Africa had a white wife seemed appropriate for a country that was so divided. Membership of the AIP grew astoundingly. Correspondingly membership of the AFA plummeted. All the signs were pointing to the fact that Thabi Skosane would be the next Premier of the country.

Chapter Thirty Eight

In America, the diaspora of relocated South Africans looked on in horror at the events that had transpired in their homeland. They were thankful that they had escaped this predicted mayhem but deeply saddened by the ruination of their beloved country. Sally thanked God every day that her daughter Angel had narrowly escaped, even though she was clearly deeply wounded. It was as if her daughter had become a zombie. She wore no make up and paid little attention to, nor interest in, her clothing. Whilst she attended in a perfunctory way to her children's needs, she did so in an extremely unemotional manner. There were very few hugs and cuddles, just at a time when they were most required, since the children had suddenly had their old familiar world taken away to be replaced by the strange new world of Beverly Hills. They had also lost their dad.

Giancarlo's hospitality was, as usual, unsurpassed. However, he did not spend a great deal of time in Los Angeles, since there were pressing needs for his leadership in Las Vegas. He was extremely annoyed that his plans in Swaziland had come to nothing, but at an extreme cost. Work had stopped on the almost complete Swazi Starburst Casino and Hotel, because the market for the product, South Africa, had just imploded. Naturally, Giancarlo was hopeful that one day things would return to normal in South Africa, but he was not confident.

When he did come to the house in Beverly Hills he now found that he had lodgers and that Sally's attention was taken up with her grandchildren, rather than with him. The worry of this upheaval for her family had impacted greatly on Sally, who was no longer the blooming and beautiful 50 year old that had attracted him some years before. Attending to business in Las Vegas was not the only reason that Giancarlo spent so much time there. The penthouse at the Starburst was being put to good use. However, the other reason that he stayed away was fear: fear of the sudden attraction he had for Sally's daughter. Despite the fact that Angel was so dejected and, to some degree, unkempt, Giancarlo found himself almost lusting after her. Beneath the sadness, there was still a beautiful woman. Beneath the dull and lifeless attire there was a woman who could rightly claim to be the most beautiful woman in the world. Giancarlo wanted to jump start her back to life, but he knew this was forbidden fruit. Best to keep out of the way – at least for the moment.

Lance Hermanus was relieved that Angel and the children had escaped the mayhem of Johannesburg. He immediately reached out to her, offering whatever help he could, including financial. She politely declined and also avoided seeing him. She just wanted to be left alone with her guilt. Lance realised that he had a "history" with Angel. He knew that she must still blame him for Gerrie's death. Nevertheless, he had known her since she was a teenager. They had shared the same upbringing; they had shared the same classroom. Despite everything, he still wanted to be her friend. He did not, of course, know that she was still suffering the devastating effects of being raped.

Lance had finished with the television talk show. His sister had abandoned him for politics. He had enough money in the bank to see him through the rest of his life in comfort. He had girlfriends galore, but no life partner. The affair that he had had with the French film star, Brigitte, had lifted him out of his own depression. She had succeeded in getting Lance to shed his feelings of guilt regarding Gerrie's death. She had been terrific but, ultimately she was French and wanted to live in Paris, not Los Angeles. "The Americans are all mad," she would say, "they have no culture!" For several months their affair was torrid. After all Lance was strong, supremely fit, and handsome. He had much appeal to the young French woman. When the talk show had finished its run Lance did, for a while, move off to Paris to be with his lover, but he found the language and the life style too foreign. Also, in Paris, Brigitte was the star and Lance, although never a "nobody", was not a household word.

The affair ran its course and Lance reverted to living in a big house in Los Angeles on his own. In many ways, despite his gregarious nature, he cut a lonely figure. He played around with property investments, had the odd fling with interior designers and real estate brokers, but was never able to develop a serious and loving relationship. In a strange way, even though he had been living in America now for many years, he missed his homeland. All South Africans miss their homeland. Angel, therefore, was a connection to his past. He decided that he must persist. However, as it turned out, Lance's persistence was not required.

For a few months Sally put up with Angel's despondent mood. She knew, of course, that her daughter had been raped, she knew that her daughter had been uprooted from her homeland, and she knew, above all, that her daughter had suddenly lost her much loved husband. What she did not know was that Angel was desperately ashamed of the fact that she had "enjoyed" the gang rape. Angel thought that she must be the only shameful person in the world who could have had any "pleasure" from being raped. If she would only have gone to counselling, she would have learned that she was far from being unique. But Angel was not about to share these dark thoughts with anyone, especially a Los Angeles shrink. Angel felt unworthy.

These feelings of shame and guilt would not be improved by what happened next. Sally had taken the children to the Aquarium at Long Beach for the day, just to get them away from the depressing atmosphere in the house. Angel was taking a shower when Giancarlo showed up unexpectedly. What followed was almost predictable. Giancarlo, having suppressed his sexual attraction to Sally's daughter for so long, could not deny himself any longer, particularly because she was taking a shower in his and Sally's bedroom. Angel did not resist. Nor did she really join in. For all the pleasure it gave him, Giancarlo might as well have been making love to a Barbie Doll. It was not exactly rape, because Angel made no attempt to fight him off. Instead, she just accommodated him. On top of this, once again, she was roused to orgasm, emotionless orgasm.

When it was over, Angel was immersed in shame, even deeper than before. She did not cry. She was just flat. She asked Giancarlo to leave, which he did. She sat, naked, on Sally's bed for hours, enveloped in a cloud of self-pity, self-hate, and despair. Finally, she decided that she must act. She could not stay in this house any longer. She had betrayed her own mother and, at the moment of truth, physically enjoyed it. Maybe it was time to die?

It was Lance who found her. Having decided to act on his thoughts about reconnecting with Angel, he got in his car and drove to Sally's house. Nobody answered the door, but it was slightly ajar. It was not long before he found Angel, lying on a bed wrapped in a white sheet. She was unconscious. Ten minutes later, in the emergency room at the hospital, Angel's life was saved by an alert ER team.

Sally never knew that Angel's desperate action had been triggered by Giancarlo. She was, therefore, puzzled and hurt that once Angel had recovered, at least physically, she had moved out of Sally's house with the children and moved in with Lance. Sally might have felt that her daughter was ungrateful for the refuge she had provided, but she realised that her poor daughter was still suffering mentally from the trauma of leaving South Africa and all that was happening there, as well as from losing her husband so suddenly. Sally forgave her daughter for her apparent unkindness. Giancarlo kept quiet. He also kept his distance from Angel's mother.

It took a long time for Angel to recover. A more energised or interested Angel would never, in a month of Sundays, have moved in with Lance, given their history of animosity. However, she blankly accepted that Lance had saved her life and given her refuge. Not at first, of course, because she had actually wanted to die. But as she saw Lance, with his ebullient personality, playing with her children, as if they were his own, and as the fair weather of Los Angeles shone down on her, she began to be thankful that she was still alive. Lance shared with her his feelings of despondency after Gerrie's untimely death. He told her how he had recovered and how good life now was. He treated her more like a sister than an ex-lover, even though he did love her still. Gradually, bit by bit, day by day, Angel recovered, and, one day, she finally decided, all on her own, to go for counselling. In less than half a dozen sessions she discovered that she was not alone in feeling guilty about being raped. According to the statistics proffered by the doctor, at least a third of women raped report feelings of pleasure, even during the horrific act. Angel began to see that she was not actually at fault; she was the victim, not only of the rapes, but also of the thoughts that had paralysed her for so long. Slowly, the real Angel emerged. The Angel who was capable of giving and receiving love. But not, she decided, with Lance. She was pleased to have him as a renewed friend, but not, as he had hoped, as a lover.

It was now Sally's turn to be upset. She had loved having her grandchildren in her home. Now, they, and Angel, were gone. Suddenly! Her daughter had tried to commit suicide and steadfastly refused to share her feelings with her mother, and, on top of this, her own lover, Giancarlo had suddenly become almost invisible. He continued to pay the bills for the house in Los Angeles, but rarely visited, citing extreme "work" pressure. Sally did not believe him. She sensed the relationship with Giancarlo had run its course. She was now in her late fifties, menopausal, and lonely. Now it was Sally's turn to be depressed. Just then, another refugee from South Africa showed up, her ex-employer and sometime lover, Jules. The circle of life was turning.

Chapter Thirty Nine

The election in South Africa returned Thabi's new AIP party into power with a sweeping majority. The percentage of people who actually voted was, predictably, very small since so many citizens had been displaced or moved from their traditional voting communities or where they were registered to vote. Furthermore, a large swathe of the population saw no point in voting. To them, all politicians had proven themselves to be either inept or crooked. In the countryside there was a strong hankering to return to the old tribal chiefs for leadership. Nevertheless, the organising committee of the military declared it to be a legal election and this was supported by a large team of foreign observers.

Part of Thabi's election platform was based upon the fact that his victory would secure the massive package of financial support he had wrestled out of the World Bank and a few wealthy nations. Subject to South Africa's return to a democratic state, billions of aid money would be made available for investment in infrastructure, schools and hospitals. The injection of this money was designed to trigger new faith in the country which would then encourage private investment to return. Everyone knew that underpinning this generosity was the fact that beneath the soil of the country lay a wealth of unmined minerals that the world needed.

With Thabi in the driving seat, most of the electorate understood that their new leader was an accountant and an economist: just the person needed to attract new investors and to encourage previous ones to return. Thabi's new Cabinet of Ministers was soon in place: handpicked and experienced business men and managers, who understood the size and complexity of the task ahead, but with the previously displayed ability of knowing how to think big and plan accordingly. Many of them had joined forces with Thabi whilst in exile in England. The problem was, that with the exception of the ministers of sport and the arts, the rest of those appointed were white.

This did not sit well with AFA Youth and Felix Mobumbo continued to stir up trouble across the country, but especially in the partly destroyed townships. Part of Thabi's foreign aid was slated for housebuilding in the African townships, not tin shacks, but proper homes built with bricks and slate roofs. But getting a programme of this size started takes time. Sites have to be cleared and infrastructure put in place. This does not happen overnight. In addition to this, Mobumbo commenced upon a plan of disruption to the programme, insisting that the new homes should not be replacements for those destroyed in the black townships, but built in previously predominantly white neighbourhoods. Mobumbo described the proposed houses as "foot out the door" homes, mocking their size and scope. Most white suburbs were punctuated with parks and green areas. The AFA Youth wing was now demanding that these green areas be made over as new home sites, homes for black families.

Another slug of aid money was slated to upgrade the electrical generation industry and water supplies. Unfortunately, those that knew how these things work had all retired, left or been paid off. Competent executives had been replaced with incompetent ones, who were now entrenched. They were all black, so for Thabi's government to be replacing them would not be popular with the electorate. Although Thabi's AIP had won the election handily, the AFA had not exactly gone away. With the imminent dismissal of thousands of useless black executives, the AFA swung into action. The head offices of various state owned companies were picketed across the country and always the racial card was played. All of the promises from Thabi would take time to implement. He may have negotiated billions in aid, but the results would not be obvious for quite a while. Thabi was in a race against time.

One of Thabi's problems was what to do with Daniel. The revival of the Ferrets did not now seem to be a pressing issue. Nevertheless, he knew that his old friend had been guilty of robbing the nation and that he had the necessary proof to convict him. Daniel was, however, still the President of the AFA, even though he was under house arrest. Stirring the pot between the AIP and the AFA by pursuing Daniel did not seem to be a very sensible policy for the moment. Thabi's nature however was not to leave work unfinished. He sincerely believed that Daniel should be punished and he resisted all attempts and counsel from others to have him released. Eventually, as he often did, he turned to Gillian for advice. Pillow talk.

It was hard, of course, for Gillian to be objective, particularly on the subject of Daniel. She was also nervous that, under pressure, Daniel might reveal that they had, on one occasion, been intimate. Thabi could not know it but Gillian was the worst person he could possibly have asked for impartial advice on the subject of the ex-Premier.

Gillian, of course, opted for leniency. "What's done is done," she told her husband. "If you pursue him through the courts, it will be a long messy and damaging process. In fact, you run the risk of kicking off a civil war. It's just not worth it. He's lost his position of influence now, but it will spring back if you pursue him. Why don't you do a deal with him? Persuade him to leave the country. Persuade him to quit politics and go back to what he does best... making money." So that is what Thabi decided to do.

"Daniel, my old friend," started Thabi, as they sat together in Daniel's art deco mansion, "let's see if we can't sort things out...for the good of our country." Daniel ushered his visitor to one of the many comfortable couches that Gloria had so often graced in years gone by. Daniel, under house arrest, had put on a lot of weight, his belly was overflowing his trousers and he waddled slightly as he walked. He offered his visitor a drink.

"I'll just take water, if I may" replied Thabi, who was anxious not to let this meeting turn into a social event. A few security men hung about the room. Thabi asked that they all step out into the garden. He wanted no record of the conversation he was about to have.

Water in hand, Thabi laid out the possibilities to Daniel, making it quite clear all of the time that he, and he alone, would be the one to decide what to do. He understood that it would be better for everyone if Daniel would go quietly, but he knew that Daniel was not the quiet type. Daniel listened patiently to Thabi's recital of the possibilities for his future. All of the time he was thinking of Thabi's wife. Somehow, Daniel had the feeling that, in Gillian, he held the ultimate trump card. On the other hand, he had a genuine fondness, almost an infatuation with Gillian, that held him back from using her as a pawn in the game. Nevertheless, even if he would not play that card, the fact that he had it gave him a feeling of superiority over his jailer.

After a lengthy discussion, Daniel could see the sense in withdrawing from politics on the basis that he could keep all of his ill-gotten gains and stay out of jail. As far as he was concerned South Africa was a lost cause. He had never wanted to be in politics, as such. His only motivation was to use politics as a route to enriching and protecting himself. The solution that was being proposed to him allowed him to achieve everything that he desired, except access to his jailer's wife. Still, that was an issue that could be dealt with later. If he were to be released and, at the same time, keep all of his wealth intact, this was a no-brainer. He would, of course, complain that he was being robbed of his right to lead the nation, but, in truth, he did not care. In exchange for his freedom and his estate he would happily leave South Africa, never to return. He would either go to the USA or the UK and Thabi, through his diplomatic connections, would have to ensure that these were real possibilities. Deal done!

A few weeks later, Daniel slipped out of the country on a South African military jet. His destination was London. Part of the conditions was that he should not address the AFA membership but should submit a written resignation. Addressing their convention would, in Thabi's view, have given him a dangerous platform. With Daniel out of the country, Thabi addressed the nation. "I today bring you the news that your previous Premier, Mr Daniel Buthelezi, has been released from house arrest and has decided to leave politics and, indeed, South Africa. In the spirit of reconciliation in our beloved country, your government has decided to drop all pending charges of corruption and treason against Mr Buthelezi. The case against him is closed and will not be re-opened. We wish him well for the rest of his life and thank him for his services to his country. Thank you."

The press, of course, had a field day. "Stitch up" screamed the headlines. "Traitor flees with all the Gold" and so on and so forth. Thabi was blamed for being soft on crime and even suspected of being paid off by his predecessor, but, generally speaking, there was an air of relief that a potentially difficult and explosive episode had been successfully sidestepped. Daniel next appeared in the gossip columns in England, waving the keys to his new mansion in Chelsea. The house in Atholl was given to Sam and Surprise, but they declined to move in. Instead, Surprise insisted on selling it and donating the proceeds to a fund to rebuild the clinic in Alexandra. This did not please the actress in the family.

Within the first two years of Thabi's presidency much was achieved. Two million new "foot out the door" houses were built, as were 200 new schools. Crumbling roads were repaired across the country and electrical power supply was renewed. Tourism had begun to flourish and several international companies invested in new hotels. The management of the national air carrier was replaced and, once again, the airplanes proudly carried the flag. The Rand recovered to slightly less than before the riots and the stock market edged even higher than before. However, this progress came at a cost. Not only the amount of money borrowed from the World Bank and other sources but also in the structure of the country. The whites were back. Back as leaders of industry, back as owners of the press, back as managers, and back as land and home owners; in other words, back in charge. Not that blacks were prohibited from taking part. After all, the Premier was black. But somehow or other, the revolution that had taken place some years ago, when basically blacks took over the country, had now been reversed, but with a black man at the wheel. This did not sit well with the AFA Youth movement, many of whom were no longer youths. Their leader Felix Lebombo began galvanising his forces, continuously raising the imbalance regarding the wealth and governance of the country. Rallies were held all over the country, at which Lebombo made impassioned speeches, urging his fellow blacks to "stand up and demand justice". His slogan "one bullet, one white man" was chanted across the country at rally after rally. With the upcoming annual convention of the AFA, things were not looking good.

Gillian was particularly perturbed by this re-emergence of civil unrest. She had refused to bring her children back to South Africa to carry on with their schooling. Instead, she insisted that they stay on at school in England and that her parents should continue to look after them. Gillian made frequent trips to England, and her stays became longer and longer. She could not bear to be parted from her young ones. But she also had another motive...Daniel.

Not only had he acquired a large house in Chelsea but also a magnificent country estate in the Cotswolds. Gillian became a frequent guest. At first, she hid her new liason from her parents, the children, and, of course, her husband in South Africa. But as Thabi paid less and less attention to her and his young family, due to the enormous pressure of his job, Gillian became more brazen in regard to her friendship with Daniel. Nobody knew for sure if she actually slept with Daniel, but there were plenty of rumours buzzing around the British press. In fact, Gillian had stopped short of actually making love to Daniel, despite his continuous entreaties, but it was a dam that sooner or later had to burst.

When the shooting took place, Gillian was actually with Thabi. The children were at school in England. It was convention time in South Africa. The AFA had just held their annual convention in the newly built Durban convention centre. This was the first time that this convention had not been held under canvas. Somehow the tribal chants of the different factions of the membership seemed strange in the steel and concrete building. It just did not seem right. No longer were the impassioned and lengthy speeches echoing across the veld. Maybe, or maybe not, this contributed to the aggressive atmosphere in the hall, but things just did not seem right or normal. The AFA needed to choose a new leader following the defection of Daniel Buthelezi. A few of the old guard put themselves up for election but this new, and younger, membership, were now solidly behind Lebombo, who was elected by a landslide. His policy was clearly racist. Blacks must be re-installed in all positions of authority. Whites must surrender their land and their shares in public companies. Nothing less would do.

Thabi Skosane had listened to the reports coming from the AFA convention with alarm as he prepared for his own African Indaba Party rally, which he had decided to hold in the same hall. His was now the party of law and order, the party of prosperity and efficiency. His party, according to the latest polls, still enjoyed a healthy majority in the overall electorate but the AFA seemed to be making large gains. Thabi was worried. He would need to make a good showing in front of his faithful.

He never got the chance. As he arrived at the door of the convention centre to open the conference, a shot rang out. The bullet went straight through his heart. He died minutes later in the arms of Gillian, who had been travelling in the car with him, surrounded by a ring of security men shielding her in case of any more shots. The assassin was instantly jumped upon and detained by further security forces. He appeared to have acted alone. The screams of shock and horror from the crowd who had gathered to watch Thabi and Gillian's arrival at the hall, reverberated into the packed convention centre. Word travelled through the crowded room like a massive and vile wave until the room was a seething cauldron of wailing humanity. Their leader was dead. How could that be? Their leader was dead. Nobody seemed to know what to do. The organisers of the planned meeting were stunned. The mood of the crowd turned from shock to anger. Anti-AFA chants started to ring out across the hall. Realising that things could get really unpleasant, even dangerous, Gillian, who could hear the chanting from the assembly hall, decided to act. She released herself from the body of her dead husband, into the hands of an arriving medic, and hurried into the auditorium. A minute later she was standing on the platform, microphone in hand. The unruly crowd was startled to see her and, as she started to speak, suddenly, almost abruptly, fell silent.

"In the name of my dear husband, Thabi Skosane, I would ask you to remain calm. This is a tragic day for you all, but also, for me and our children. I do not know the motive of the deranged man who did this to my husband, and your leader, but we must not jump to arms. My beloved husband was not a violent man; he would not want any violence or retribution now. I therefore ask you, in the name of Thabi, please leave this hall now, in a quiet and reverent manner. Do not seek revenge. Pray instead for the well being of our country, Thabi's country. That is what he would want." With that, Gillian burst into tears and was quietly led away by an unknown lady from the crowd.

Once again, Jesus Mabendla's hopes and dreams for the country had been smashed. The country at large immediately saw this latest atrocity as a tribal matter. Thabi, an Ndebele, had been gunned down by a Zulu from the AFA. This was not true but the truth did not seem to matter. The Xhosas, historically enemies of the Zulus, would come to the aid of their Ndebele friends. The Zulus must not be allowed to ride roughshod across the land. Never mind the fact that the actual gunman had turned out to be an illegal immigrant from Swaziland, the Zulus had it coming from a coalition of other tribes. Gillian's words had landed on deaf ears. Law and order, once again, in South Africa was beginning to break down. All of the good things that Thabi had injected into the nation were at risk. The newfound investor confidence in the country was about to crumble. The new found harmony in the country was smashed. Things could get bad in a hurry.

The Constitution of the land did not envisage the role of Deputy Premier. The Premier, in fact, was voted into power as the representative of the winning political party in national elections. In the event of a Premier dying or resigning the Constitution called for the ruling party to elect a new leader within ten days, who would then assume the role of Premier. On the evening of Thabi's assassination, the ruling cabinet came together to discuss the urgent situation. Wisely, they decided to act unilaterally and immediately. They were concerned that any hiatus in leadership could be very dangerous with the imminent risk of tribal warfare. Within one hour of meeting, the cabinet unanimously chose Harry Richemont, the incumbent Minister of Finance, to be their new leader. Harry, in turn, immediately mobilised the army. Once again, General Wilkins would be a key player. Troops were deployed in all of the major cities and the opportunistic looters who followed unrest like flies over a corpse were soon sent packing. But feelings were running high. The new Premier realised that the country was split, not just along tribal lines, but also in regard to policy. Opinion polls were indicating that, despite the strong economic progress that had been made under the late Premier's leadership, there was a growing concern amongst the general population, particularly the young men, that their country had once again been hijacked by white men. Indeed, there was so much unrest and civil disobedience that Richemont decided that the country was becoming ungovernable. He decided to call for a general election, with the hope that he could command a new mandate to govern. Many thought that he was putting his head into a noose. The roller coaster that was South African politics was about to take a new turn.

Chapter Forty

Bibi and Gorgeous George were still together in America. They had been an item now for over four years. This was a record for both of them. Due to the nature of their work they spent a lot of time apart, which maybe was what kept them together. George's career as an actor had flourished in the time he was with Bibi and he had been a massive aid to her campaign to run as State Governor. For a while they were probably the most famous couple in the USA, if inches in the press is the yardstick. Bibi had narrowly won the election, but she was now, a year into the work, bitterly regretting it. Life in Sacramento, the capital of California, was not the same as life in Los Angeles. Sacramento was boring. Sacramento was stiflingly hot in the summer. To Bibi, it was like living in Bloemfontein as opposed to Cape Town. True, as Governor she did have to travel throughout the State and beyond, but the day to day grind work was in boring boring Sacramento. Two years into her four year stint, Bibi had had enough. She was also tired of reading the headlines in the supermarket rags that Gorgeous George was having flings with just about every starlet in Hollywood. George, of course, vehemently denied any wrongdoing. This did not exactly worry Bibi, but it certainly annoyed her.

When Bibi read about the renewed troubles in South Africa her interest in her birthplace was stirred. Her parents,

Rudy and Becky, had, long ago, at Lance's insistence moved to the USA, and Bibi had not kept up with any cousins or other relatives. Her only real contact in her homeland was Steven Shultz, the boxing promoting lawyer with whom she had briefly had an affair in the interests of promoting her brother's career. Steven would warily make the odd call to Bibi, and, although their small talk was not often about the state of politics in South Africa, through this pipeline she did get the occasional on the ground assessment.

Bibi called Steven. "What the hell is going on there?" she asked.

"Since Skosane was shot, things are shit," replied Steven. "There is unrest all over the country. Lebombo is stirring it up big time. This new guy, Richemont, is not strong enough to lead the AIP. I don't know what to do."

It was as if a light bulb had suddenly switched on in Bibi's brain. "When is the next AIP convention? Is that when they will choose their leader to fight the election?" asked Bibi. Steven explained the process. There would be an indaba for the AIP in three months' time, at which Richemont, or another, would be elected to lead their party into a general election. As far as the AFA were concerned, they had already chosen their leader, Felix Lebombo.

"In a straight contest between Richemont and Lebombo, I am sure Lebombo will win," said Steven, "it will be a race issue."

"Steven," interjected Bibi, "do me a favour. Find out what I have to do to get elected as leader of the AIP. Find out if that is feasible. If it is, I am going to stand for election and you, my friend, will be my campaign manager."

"What the fuck are you talking about?" replied Steven, who was totally taken by surprise. "Nobody is going to elect you as leader of the AIP."

"How do you know? You're a boxing promotor. I'm the politician!"

"But you're the fucking Governor of Los Angeles. And you don't even live here."

"But, Stephen, I am a South African and I'm almost halfway through my term here, and, by the way, in case you didn't know it, the economy of California is three times larger than that of South Africa. Of course, I can get elected."

"Christ," thought Steven, "she may just be right."

Two weeks after that call, Bibi had announced her intention of standing down as Governor. She would be the first Governor in California's history who had opted out before the end of her term. But, in true Bibi style, she had turned what could have been a public relations disaster into yet another triumph. She was going to do the patriotic thing. She was going to "rescue" the country of her birth. Their need was greater than that of California, which would be left in good hands. This move would not be self-serving; it would be self-sacrificing. Bibi would save South Africa!

Some of the California press bought it. Most were much more sceptical, accusing her of hypocrisy. California had been good for Bibi when she had "fled" from her own country. She had "used" California. One very telling article in the *LA Times* quite accurately described Bibi as the "Queen of Self-Preservation." The public, it seemed, saw things differently. Bibi had nobly given up her privileged and safe position in America for the dangerous and difficult task of "saving" the country of her birth. How gallant and how romantic!

Gorgeous George was not happy. Firstly, he had not been consulted and second, he had no intention of spending the next phase of his life in darkest Africa. The break up between the film star and the Governor did not take long. It was just another chalk mark on Bibi's scorecard of failed relationships.

Bibi, as usual, shrugged it off.

Meanwhile, elsewhere in California, Bibi's brother, Lance, still had house guests. Luckily Lance had a very big house, so the fact that Angel and her two youngsters were still guests was not a huge inconvenience. Little by little Angel's mental health had improved; her frequent visits to the shrink had been invaluable. By the time Bibi announced her resignation as Governor, Angel had all but ceased her psychotherapy sessions. She had regained most of her enthusiasm for life and was enjoying her little family, who were now at school in Beverly Hills. Lance took trouble not to interfere in her upbringing of the children, but since they were all living under the same roof, albeit a sizeable one, he in many ways had become a substitute Dad. Angel was thankful for this, but she still managed to avoid any sexual involvement with her host. She was helped, in this, by Tony. Angel's modelling career had resumed and Tony was a constant companion. Since the rapes, Angel could not bring herself to have sex with any man, no matter how much her desire. It had been Tony, who, having patiently waited for the right moment, cured her of her fears. Although she did not love him, she found that she did love him making love to her. When they went on the road for a photo shoot they invariably slept together. But when he visited the house in Los Angeles this never happened; Angel would just not allow it. Her gratitude to Lance was too great. As Angel slowly recovered from her trauma, with a steady income from her modelling activity, she thought hard about her future and that of her children. She should really move out and establish her own home, but the two little ones seemed content and so, it seemed, was Lance. Maybe she would stay just a little bit longer.

When Lance's sister, Bibi, announced that she was returning to South Africa to enter politics, both Lance and Angel thought that she had gone completely mad. However, that did not stop Lance from inviting Bibi to stay at his house whilst she made preparations to leave for Africa. Although the atmosphere between Angel and Bibi was cool, the visit was not a disaster. Lance did his best to dissuade Bibi from her mission, but that was clearly a waste of breath. Bibi would have loved Lance to come with her to help win the election, but she was mindful of the fact that he had once shot a black man in the back. Felix Lebombo would certainly have a field day with that!

For a couple of weeks, Lance's house was turned into a political contender's office. Back in South Africa Steven Shultz was preparing all of the paperwork that needed to be done to establish Bibi as a candidate. There were forms to be filled in and tax returns to be submitted and so on. The most important election as far as Bibi was concerned would be the one for the AIP Presidency. If she could win that, she would automatically become the Premier of the Nation. Her opposition, Richemont, had the advantage of being in situ, but Bibi was banking on the fact that he came across as an elderly accountant, completely charisma free. In any normal race, Bibi could have won at a stroll, but she had not been in the country for many years now and that would surely play against her. On top of this, once one scratched the glamourous surface Bibi had no background nor track record in economics, other than the economics of enriching herself. None of this bothered

Bibi, when, after a couple of weeks in Los Angeles, she set off for her homeland.

When Bibi walked into Steven Shultz's office in Johannesburg his jaw dropped. Bibi, who had been the sexiest young lady he had ever met, had now matured into a stunning and sophisticated woman. She had film star magnetism. She was still sexy, of course, but now she oozed glamour. The years had not been so kind to Steven. When he had his brief affair with Bibi, he had not been a young man, but, since then, the difficulties of doing business in Johannesburg and the monotony of his marriage had worn him down. Bibi was shocked. How could she have made love to this wreck of a man? She wickedly thought of Georgeous George, what a difference! Nevertheless, actress that she was, she gave Steven a warm and close embrace, thrusting her bosom into his chest as she did so. "My God," thought Steven, "where did all those wasted years go?"

Bibi was now all business. Never mind that she had just stepped off a plane from the other side of the world. She disentangled herself from Steven and pulled up a chair opposite his desk. She noticed that the office was still brown. "We will need a campaign headquarters," she announced, "but it must not be brown!" Steven looked a bit perplexed. He had never really noticed that his office was all brown. Bibi continued to rattle off a long list of all of the things that they needed to do. Steven took notes, but it was hard for him to concentrate; his mind kept going back to Lance's little flat. Bibi galloped on for at least an hour, outlining her plan of attack, and listing all of the things that Steven would need to do for her. Then, her instructions finished, she stood up to leave. Steven came around his desk, and as he did so, Bibi suddenly pulled him towards her. She looked straight into his eyes. "Steven, this time things are different. This will be strictly business. Do you understand?"

Steven backed away and nodded. "Yes, Bibi. Understood – but it will be difficult."

Bibi smiled and released her captive. "Let's see what happens after we've won," she said as she left with a nod to Miss Brown at the desk outside the door.

It had been some time since Bibi had last been in the town of her birth. She opted to stay at a new hotel set in the Hyde Park shopping centre, less than a mile from the house she had been brought up in. The area was almost unrecognisable. During the economic good times of the first few years of AFA rule much had changed on the ground. New roads had been built and the city of Johannesburg had spread like treacle northwards towards Pretoria, enveloping the old suburbs of Sandton and Randburg where she had been raised. Nevertheless, nature had not changed. The winter air was still fresh, sharp and crisp. Such a difference from the traffic-polluted air of Los Angeles. The sun shone all day, every day. The land was brown, but where humans had intervened with sprinklers and hoses it was full of vibrant colour. From the balcony of her hotel suite Bibi could see as far as the Maghiesburg mountains, almost blue in the distance. Yes, Bibi was glad to be home. Maybe this was where she was meant to be.

It was not difficult for Bibi to charm the pants off the members of Richemont's cabinet. Mostly they were white captains of industry or commerce who had rallied around Thabi at the country's time of need. They had agreed to elect Richemont as their leader, but under extraordinary stressful circumstances. He was the least contentious member of Thabi's cabinet and, as a result, the least threatening to each of them. That of course, did not make him a great leader; in fact, he was probably the least appealing candidate to both his colleagues and the electorate. His fellow Ministers understood that but none of them was prepared to back any alternatives amongst their number. Another black leader would have been ideal for the AIP, but there was no such candidate in their midst. So, when Bibi first appeared upon the scene, announcing herself as a candidate to lead their party and the country, she had arrived at an interesting time. The party did not actually have an outstanding candidate for its leader; it actually needed one, but nobody had thought of a woman, nor a white one to boot.

Bibi had seen the gap. She knew exactly how she could fit in. The question was how would she be perceived by the majority of AIP members, who were black? As far as the black delegates were concerned there were two strikes against Bibi before she even started. She was a woman and she was white. The other party, the AFA, had a leader who was a black man and a confident and accomplished orator. What Bibi understood was that half of the voters, both for the party and the country were women. It would be the women who could put Bibi in power.

When it came to the AIP congress, at which a new leader would be elected, the contest was already over. Bibi had campaigned almost entirely on the basis that it was now the women's turn to run the country. The argument that successive men had made such a mess of things played very well across the membership of the AIP. Whereas rural women may have been more conservative and traditional in their views, Bibi understood that she did not need the nation behind her to become President, she needed the votes of the AIP members. Bibi understood that any women who had actually joined the AIP would probably be, by definition, less traditional than the broad spectrum. In examining the membership rolls Bibi discovered that women members were just over half of all membership. From straw polls she felt that she could count on about three quarters of these women to vote for her as well as a sprinkling of men. It could be a close race, so much would depend on the speeches at the actual convention. Also, according to the rules, if you wanted to vote, you had to be in attendance at the convention. This played into the hands of Bibi, the arch organiser. She badgered Steven and his team to lay on buses from all over the country to bring women to the convention: women only buses. Richemont and his followers were far less active in this regard; to them, such action was almost foul play.

On the day of the membership election, both candidates for the top job were allocated one hour to speak. They drew lots as to who should go first and Bibi was delighted that it was not her. Going second on this platform should be a definite advantage. Richemont made a predictably measured but dull speech. Everything he said made a lot of sense. He was clearly a diligent and organised man. However, as a number cruncher, he had never learned to speak with passion and much of what he said went over the heads of the largely female crowd. As he droned on for his full hour his audience became more and more bored. There was no fire in his belly, just old-fashioned good sense. He did his best to raise the tone in his concluding remarks but by now he had lost his audience.

Bibi had struggled with what to wear. She was known for her chic and fashionable outfits and for what she had worn on the television talk show. However, she was well aware that the bulk of her audience would never have been able to afford her wardrobe, and may not even aspire to. For once in her life, Bibi could not answer her own question. She decided to ask Steven for his opinion. He did not answer quickly. He was a lawyer; this was not the sort of question he was used to. Finally, he spoke, "You've already got the women's vote, unless you do something to turn them off. You haven't yet got the men's vote, so you need to do something to turn them on."

"That's a great help, Steven" jumped in Bibi. "You've just described the problem, not given me the answer."

"Well, what that tells us," continued Steven, unperturbed by the interruption, "is that you have got to go down the middle. The fact is, Bibi, you look good in anything. So, keep it plain, keep it chic, but keep it almost affordable. You know, the sort of thing you could buy off the peg in Woolworths."

After a ten minute break following Richemont's lifeless speech, it was Bibi's turn. She had bought a simple, but striking, dress in Woolworths, but, just to please the men, she had unbuttoned it at the top, just enough to show her form. She spoke of her roots in South Africa. She spoke of her fight to succeed in a man's world. She spoke of the experience she had gained in politics in California. She spoke of her experience of the world outside of her homeland, but also of her great love for where she had been born. She spoke of her heartbreak about the state of South Africa, but also about her hope for the future, since, beneath all of the turmoil, South Africa was potentially rich. She spoke of her love and esteem for Jesus Mabendla and her determination to carry out his wishes for a successful, peaceful, and prosperous nation. She spoke of the dangers of the AFA youth movement. She spoke of the dangers of violence. She spoke of her commitment to peace. But finally, as her speech reached a crescendo, she spoke about the role of women. "The men have failed us," she almost shouted from the lectern. "It is now the turn of the women!"

The audience rose and burst into spontaneous applause, even many of the men. It was a powerful speech and despite the fact it did not contain one iota of detail about how Bibi was going to govern, or what her policies would be, or who would be involved in government, she had pressed all the right emotional buttons. When the vote took place for the new leader of the AIP the result was a landslide victory for Ms Hermanus. Bibi was back and Bibi was in business.

Chapter Forty One

Bibi's victory at the AIP convention took everyone by surprise, not least the older men of the party. They could not believe that their hopes of continuing to rule the nation were in the hands of a woman. This was not how things were supposed to be. But, under the charter of the AIP, there was little they could do about it, at least publicly. Whether they would extend their cooperation to Bibi when it came to their constituents' support would remain to be seen. The AIP was a new organisation, created by the late Thabi. It would not take much for some of its members to revert to their roots in the AFA, even if it was now being run by the hothead Lebombo. Bibi understood that her tactic of blindsiding the convention with women may not be enough to win the Premiership. She would need to come up with Plan B.

Bibi was quite surprised when she received a call of congratulations from Felix Lebombo. She had listened to tapes of his inflammatory speeches several times. As far as she could ascertain he had one policy and that was to rid South Africa of white domination and to return the nation to his people. There never seemed to be any plan beyond that. He was all about destruction, not construction, and, as such, on a level playing field, provided that she could offer comprehensive and sensible policies to re-establish a viable South Africa, she should have no difficulty in defeating him in an election. However, the playing field was not level. The bulk of the population had never been treated properly, and this hurt would take years and years to dissipate. Common sense alone would not prevail in a general election and Bibi knew it. The deprivations of the past affecting Blacks would need to be addressed, as would the unfair treatment of women, be they black or white.

Yet, here was Felix, on the phone to her, talking like one reasonable person to another, with not a hint of rancour or racism. Felix was challenging her to a televised debate. She could not refuse. For a moment they discussed arranging a meeting of their representatives to iron out the rules of a debate, but suddenly Felix interjected. "Hell, no, Bibi. Why do we need others to tell us the rules? Let's you and me meet for a drink and agree together how we should do it. What do you say, Bibi?" What could Bibi say? Within seconds they had agreed to meet the next day. Felix proposed that he would find a nice, secure and private place which the press would not know about and that he would get her a message that afternoon with the details. Bibi, intrigued, agreed.

There was only one suite at the Holiday Inn at Johannesburg airport. Bibi had received a text from Felix. "Suite 600, 6th floor, Holiday Inn. Airport. 3pm. Go straight to suite. Do not stop at front desk. See you tomorrow." He did not sign the message. Bibi was suspicious that she might be walking into some sort of trap but intrigued to come face to face with her opposition. At least this would give her some feeling as to what she was really up against in an election.

Bibi slipped into the Holiday Inn unnoticed and joined the bevy of tourists gathered on the ground floor outside the elevator doors. She stepped into the cabin and pressed six. The scratched button illuminated. The rest of the passengers all disembarked at the fourth floor. They were Americans; none of them recognised Bibi, even though she was clearly not a tourist, having donned an ultra-smart business suit with a fashionably short skirt and high heels. You couldn't miss suite 600; clearly it was the pride and joy of the Holiday Inn. The double door onto the hallway was surrounded by a gaudy golden frame. She rang on the bell and Felix himself opened it and welcomed her with a broad, white tooth smile. Felix was more handsome in the flesh than in the papers or the newsreel. He was over six feet tall and dressed in an immaculate dark blue suit. He looked nothing like the African rabble rouser that Bibi had seen on the newsreels. This man could have worked on Wall Street.

Felix welcomed Bibi into the gaudy suite lounge and gestured towards the leather couch. Bibi sat. The couch was so low that Bibi had some difficulty keeping her skirt down over her legs. There was something mesmerising about the black man. He was certainly handsome, but there was something unusually penetrating about his dark brown eyes. The snarl that accompanied his "one bullet one white man" screeching had now turned into an alluring smile. Bibi could not take her eyes off him; he was so striking, even attractive. Bibi knew that she should proceed with the utmost care.

Felix was, in turn, not unattracted to Bibi. Felix knew just how much he appealed to the opposite sex and his many encounters had not been exclusively with black girls. Although he was married, now with three children, this had never stopped him from playing away and his amorous adventures had from time to time crossed the colour line. He noticed Bibi's struggle to cover her legs on the low sofa and smiled to himself. Finding a way to smother the opposition, in this case, might be quite enjoyable.

It did not take the two political opponents long to agree upon the rules for a televised debate. That done, Felix broke out the whisky. Bibi declined, but Felix insisted. Just being in the room with her rival for the position of Premier, seemed oddly inappropriate. On the other hand, she rationalised, the more she could find out about her opponent, the more ammunition she would have to crush him. Presumably, she thought to herself, he must be feeling the same about her. Becoming friendly with Lebombo could only end in tears. And yet Bibi found herself fascinated and attracted to her rival and actually did not want to leave. She imagined him in bed. His body, through the suit, looked rock hard; his handshake was firm, and his manners, so far, were top drawer. That firebrand act that she had seen so often must have been, just that, an act. Maybe Felix was smarter than she thought?

As Felix poured the second whisky, Bibi came to her senses. She had accomplished what she had come for; she had no need for further accomplishments that afternoon. Refusing the second drink, Bibi suddenly got to her feet and announced that she had to leave. Some gentle persuasion by her host failed to make her change her mind, and soon she was back in the elevator, speeding away to safety. "He sure is a handsome brute," she thought to herself as she stepped out of the hotel, "there will be a lot of 'my' women voters who will not be able to resist him."

Two days later Bibi witnessed on the news a completely different Felix Lebombo berating a black crowd to vote for their liberty and their rights. His speech was full of unbending criticism of white leadership, criticism that bordered on hate. The smart suit had gone. Now dressed in jeans and a Mabendla shirt, Felix Lebombo screeched for the overthrow of the white racist settlers, demanding that they should be stripped of their land and removed from all positions of power. "Let them see how they like living in a foot out of the door," let them see what it is like to have no electricity or water, let them know what it is like to be on the end of a rubber bullet! Take their bullets. One bullet, one white man!!!!" Felix's delivery was perfect, working from calm and reasonable to screaming and dangerous. The all-black crowd, with the exception of a few white policemen, became more and more worked up, with countless ululating and anti-white chants. As Felix finished his tirade he was met with a roar of support, followed by a tidal wave of black bodies swarming down the street, smashing shop windows, street lights, and overturning parked cars. For a long while the police just watched until a water cannon appeared and dissipated the mob.

"How could Felix possibly defend these actions?" thought Bibi from the safety of her couch. "Let him explain that, if he can."

This frightening scene was carried out, over a few weeks, time and time again, much to the consternation of the business world and South African watchers. Bibi did her best to condemn this behaviour, in and on the media, but riots were more newsworthy than lectures or speeches. Radio achieved a broader reach than television, but being calm and reasonable on the wireless commands far less attention than a riot. Once again, the slowly recovering economy of South Africa started to take a further hit. White South Africans, of course, stood firmly behind Bibi and many black women, sick of the lawlessness and the wanton destruction, also supported her. But would that be enough to prevent Felix from winning the election? Bibi, could see, after her brief encounter with Felix, that he was smarter than his public image would suggest. He could not really want the nation to disintegrate on his watch. Surely, this was just a tactic to get him into power. After that, things might be different. She wrestled with whether it was good for her to point this out in her campaign, or just keep quiet. Bibi, on the face of it, was representing the party that was pro-law and order, but also pro economic recovery. The latter was needed so that the inequalities between the races could be redressed from a position of economic strength, not weakness. This would be the stance that she would adopt in the upcoming and important debate.

Bibi also thought about seducing Felix. This approach had worked well for her in the past, when she had needed to get something done. Physically, this would not exactly be an unpleasant task. She had never screwed a black man, but this one was such a hunk, that it might even be enjoyable. She also thought she could achieve it. Something told her, during that brief meeting in the Airport Holiday Inn, that Felix was taken with her. If she had stayed that afternoon, he might even have fancied his chances of bedding her. Maybe the way to defeat Felix was through his trousers? Bibi began to hatch a plan.

Steven Shultz was turning out to be a first-class campaign organiser. He had never done the job before, so possibly a fresh approach was useful. He was, however, good at organising events and knew intimately many venues across the country, so when Bibi embarked on a nationwide campaign of speeches, everything went smoothly. No riots, just questions and answers. Again, particularly in the townships, Bibi aimed her remarks at the women, especially the mothers, on whom she was relying so heavily. Children, albeit of a voting age, can still be influenced by the mama of the house, so, in Bibi's view, this was one route to the younger generation as well, presenting them with an alternative to the rioting of some of their chums.

It was Steven who negotiated a series of three one hour televised debates between Felix and Bibi. The participants were not allowed to know the questions they were to be asked before the live programmes, but Steven, as canny as ever, had arranged to have them leaked to him a few days prior to the debates, but not, of course, to Felix. The result was that Bibi, in the first debate, had her answers down pat, whereas, from time to time, Felix appeared to struggle with framing an orderly reply. Street soap boxes were clearly the better venue for Felix. However, given the fact that he was starting at a disadvantage in the first debate, Bibi was still impressed with the way Felix managed to marshal his thoughts. She was also even more impressed with how he looked, dressed in black slacks and black shirt, undone at the neck, revealing a forest of dark hairs on his chest. She wanted him, but she didn't know how. She also thought that by having him she might, in some way, neutralise his political threat. The question was, how to proceed?

This was a question soon to be answered. After the first TV debate, the two participants and their teams were invited for cocktails in the TV studio. Naturally the two contenders found themselves together, light heartedly awarding themselves points from the debate. Felix was as charming as he had been in the Airport Holiday Inn. How could this be the same man that led riots from a street soapbox? The more Bibi spoke with Felix, the more she fancied him, not to win the election, but as a man. She had so often wondered what it would be like to make love to a black man; she hoped that she would soon find out. For Felix, having Bibi would be a real feather in his cap, never mind what harm or help it might be to his election cause and never mind that he was a married man. In both candidates' cases, nature was taking over from logic and good sense.

Felix, sensing some reciprocation, slipped Bibi a little note. She excused herself to go to the ladies' room. "11pm. Suite 600"; that's all that was written. Not much, but enough for the message to be understood. The platform was ready for Bibi to put her plan in motion. She would seduce Felix and see where that would take her. Either she would get him under her spell or she might be able to compromise him in some way. Either way, she would have some fun. It had been a while since she had been with a man and she was ready for Felix. Wearing a short skirt and a provocatively low cut and sheer blouse, under an outdoor coat, she slipped, once again, unnoticed into the Holiday Inn and pressed the button for the sixth floor. At the stroke of 11 she tapped on the ugly framed door. From inside, she thought she heard laughter: female laughter. "Must be the television," she thought as she waited for the door to be opened. When it was, by Felix in a dressing gown, Bibi was shocked. There, dressed as provocatively as herself, was none other than Gloria. There was no sign of Johnny Spade. Bibi remembered Gloria from the Hollywood talk show, where she had been a lively guest on more than one occasion. "What the fuck are you doing here?" she blurted out, "I thought you were still in Los Angeles."

"Well, my dear, I'm not. I'm here to help. Johnny is otherwise engaged."

As Felix removed Bibi's topcoat, she felt a little foolish. It was obvious to all that she was dressed to seduce. But then, she thought, so was Gloria, and why was Felix in his dressing gown? Questions whirred around in Bibi's pretty head. Her strategy seemed to have disappeared. Gloria was a curve ball that she had not been expecting and Gloria still had some curves. Whatever reason Felix had had for inviting Bibi to his suite so late in the evening, no longer seemed obvious. Maybe, thought Bibi, she should, for once, just go with the flow and forget about politics for one night.

Chapter Forty Two

Since raping his partner's daughter in Beverly Hills, Giancarlo had hardly been home. Sally knew that their affair had run its course. Her infatuation with the man had worn thin, and her efforts to please him were half hearted. It was time to call it a day. Everything in Sally's world seemed to be falling apart. Her daughter Angel was distant and the grandchildren were clearly affected. Sally was lonely. What was the point of a beautiful house in Bel Air if there was no one to share it with? When Giancarlo did come home, he barely tried to hide the evidence that he had been with other women. The final straw came when Sally discovered, almost by accident, that Giancarlo had been, from time to time, staying with his ex-wife. This really hurt her. She felt as if she had been used. However, she realised that she had also been the user. After all, it was her that broke up the marriage in the first place. She had had some good times with Giancarlo, but she knew that it was over. She wondered why every one's lives were falling apart.

At first, when her old employer, Jules, showed up, she was curious to find out how his life had evolved, but only that. She had met him quite by chance. Jules was in Los Angeles on business. He still had the talent agency in South Africa and was on the search for some American acts for one of his clients. He was pushing a trolley around Whole Foods on Canon, when he caught a glimpse of a middle-aged woman at the other end of the dry goods aisle. She was examining the small print on a package of rice. He was sure it was Sally. He hadn't seen her for at least ten years but there was no mistaking her. She still radiated loveliness. He cautiously steered his trolley down the aisle. She still had not seen him. When he got within four feet of her he softly called her name. She looked up with a start. "Oh, my goodness. It's Jules. How wonderful to see you! What on earth are you doing here?" The initial awkwardness evaporated in ten seconds. The thought that she must look like the wreck of the Hesperus flashed through Sally's mind; she so wished that she had put her make up on before venturing out to the shops. The trolleys were pushed aside and the two ex-lovers hugged each over in sheer joy. Over a cup of coffee in the neighbouring deli the two swapped life stories, and pretty soon Sally was giving Jules a ride back to her house. He was staying, he explained, in the Beverly Wilshire at the end of the road. "Screw that," said Sally, "you must come and stay with me."

Jules was tempted. The Beverly Wilshire was not cheap and Jule's business in South Africa of late had been precarious. With all of the rioting and civil disobedience at home it had been difficult to tempt people out of their homes after dark. This had had a massively damaging effect on the entertainment and night club business, and for over a year now Jules' business and his cash flow had been suffering. He still had some clients in countries in East Africa but collecting his fees from these was often tricky. He still owned the little flat in Oakley Street, Chelsea, and was endeavouring to pick up more clients in England and the rest of Europe, but he was not getting any younger, and everything in his life seemed a bit precarious. Saving money on the room at the Wilshire would be welcome, but at what cost emotionally? Sally had loved him and left him before.

"That's very kind of you, Sally, but let's give that a rain check for a few days. I love you dearly and I am so so pleased to see you, but let's take one day at a time." Sally was disappointed, but tried not to let it show.

"Well, in any event, come back to my place for some lunch so that we can carry on catching up. I have so much to tell you." Jules agreed.

Meanwhile, not far from Sally's house, her daughter Angel was making her own plans. She had decided to leave America and resettle in London. Her revitalised modelling career seemed to be going well with the Mood Agency and she was spending more and more time with Tony. But most of the work seemed to be in the UK and she had found herself more often away than at home, that is, at Lance's home. Lance had been terrific with her two children and they doted on him, almost as if he were Gerrie, their dad. Angel was seriously torn between what was right for her and what was better for the children. Lance, of course, wanted her to stay in America; he had given up on any romantic link with Angel but had grown to love the children. They now were his family. Nevertheless, Angel had taken her decision. She would go to England, and the children would go with her. Tony was keen to marry her, but Angel was not ready and, anyway, the children did not accept Tony as a surrogate father. To them, that was Lance.

When Sally learned of Angel's decision, she was horrified. Although her relationship with her daughter had cooled when Angel suddenly left, she had still stayed close with her grandchildren. To lose all of her family to the UK would be a huge blow. The idea of spending her old age, alone, in Beverly Hills did not appeal to her. She would rather be back in South Africa with all its perils, or back in her birthplace, England. Maybe this chance meeting with Jules was fortuitous? Maybe, this was a second chance?

Over a few days Sally and Jules swapped stories and, as they did so, Sally became more and more comfortable with him. He did not move in and he was careful not to be too hasty in initiating any physical contact. It had, however, been a long time since Sally had received a hug from anyone, including Giancarlo, so the presence of an ex lover was tantalising. Sally longed for Jules to make a move. She realised just how much she had missed having the strong arms of a man wrapped around her body.

Despite the fact that Sally was living in Giancarlo's luxurious home, it was obvious to Jules that he never came there anymore. It was also obvious that Sally was no longer infatuated by him nor his jet set style of life. Jules had always been in love with Sally. He had been heartbroken when she broke away from him so many years ago. Now, just maybe, he could have a second chance.

After four days of reminiscing, and much laughter, Jules took the plunge. "Sally, my love, – come back to England with me. Forget all this nonsense here in Los Angeles. With all the crap in South Africa, I am going to relocate to London. Nothing in the world would make me happier if you would consider joining me. I have loved you from the day you stepped into my office. I still love you – so please, jack all of this in and come home with me. I want to make you happy."

As he spoke, he wrapped his arms around Sally and held her tight. When he had finished speaking, he gave her a big kiss on the lips. She found herself responding eagerly. For a long time they held each other, tightly. Sally was sobbing, but they were tears of joy. "Of course, I'll come with you. Nothing could stop me. I should never have left you all those years ago."

For a moment they just sat there, hugging and kissing each other. Sally's phone buzzed; she decided to ignore it. Nothing was going to spoil the moment. It buzzed again and this time it persisted. Reluctantly she freed herself from Jules to answer. There was an Italian voice on the other end of the line, high pitched and excited. "Giancarlo's been shot. Outside Smith and Wollensky in Vegas. He's in bad shape. He's calling for you. I'm sending a plane!" It was Giancarlo's brother, Sammy.

"Shit," said Sally, not to the phone but into the room. "Giancarlo's been shot. He wants me to go there. Christ! What shall I do? They're sending a plane. Oh, fuck, what a mess!"

"Oh Christ!," said Jules, "how awful. Will you go?"

"What else can I do? I'm living in the man's house."

Jules was distraught, but now was not the time for him to consider himself. He would do whatever it took to keep Sally, even if that meant helping her through this awkward time. "Its sod's law," he thought to himself, "just as you think you have got something, it slips away from you."

"I'll come with you," he announced. "At least as far as the airport – and beyond if you want me to."

"Thank you, Jules. I do want you to."

Giancarlo died later that night. Sally had reached his bedside before he became unconscious. His wife was already there. When Sally arrived, Giancarlo indicated that he wanted to be left alone with Sally and so the sobbing wife moved out of the room, from where her wailing could still be heard. "Thank you for coming, Sally," he croaked, "I have not been fair to you; you truly were the love of my life and I have treated you badly. I am sorry. I do really love you" The words were getting more and more difficult for him to say. The attending nurses were showing signs of worry. "Just one more thing," whispered the dying man, "I have left you the house in Los Angeles and five million dollars. They are my loving gift to you. Now, I must see my family." With that, he closed his eyes and died. When the nurse realised what was happening, she summoned the wife and family from the corridor. When Guilietta realised what had just happened she became hysterical, screaming Italian obscenities at Sally. Sally left. Jules, who had flown on the plane with her from LA was waiting outside.

When Sally saw him, she burst into tears. "Thank God you are here, Jules. I love you."

Chapter Forty Three

The combination of Felix and Gloria was too much for Bibi. Not in the bed, but at the ballot box. Bibi's gambit that she could capture the women's vote in the general election was dashed by Felix's recruitment of Gloria. Not only was Gloria a woman, but she was a woman who had made a big success of her life. From orphaned little girl to successful businesswoman in a man's world in South Africa, to film star in Hollywood USA. The combination of firebrand Felix and glorious Gloria, was just too much for even Bibi to overcome. Most importantly, both Felix and Gloria were black, from considerably underprivileged backgrounds. Bibi, although successful was white middle class. When nine tenths of the electorate are of the same ethnic background as the candidates, the result is fairly predictable. On top of that, both Felix and Gloria were Zulu, as were the biggest block of voters and the grass roots of the AFA. Bibi managed to rouse many Xhosa and other smaller tribes and, naturally, most of the white vote, but it was not enough and a few hours after the polls closed, she graciously accepted that Felix had won.

Several hours later, the glamourous Bibi found herself in jail. Felix had trumped up some charges about electoral fraud. Bibi was arrested and tossed into the Kyalami prison, ironically the same place that had held her brother, Lance, so many years ago. Her one telephone call, before her phone was confiscated was, in fact, to Lance in LA. Clearly, she would need all the help she could get, because, a fair hearing did not seem likely under the principles which guided Felix. Bibi was not alone. Members of her AIP party were being rounded up all over the country and also imprisoned on the same sort of trumped-up charges. Any opposition to Felix in power was being extinguished before it could even spark. Yes, there had been an election, but it might just as well have been a coup d'etat.

When Lance had been in Kyalami prison almost the entire staff were white Afrikaners. Now from the prison governor to the cleaners the place was staffed entirely with black personnel. The glamourous Bibi was in all sorts of physical danger. Lance, through his old television connections, made sure that the story of Bibi's imprisonment was headline news throughout the world and, as a result, considerable diplomatic pressure was brought to bear on Felix and his new government. This was brushed aside with disdain. In Felix's view the rest of the world needed the minerals from South Africa more than it needed Bibi out of jail. After a few weeks the clamour to have Bibi released from overseas died down and, despite Lance's efforts to keep the story alive, it soon moved from the front pages and the crawl bars. In the meantime, Bibi was denied any privileges in jail. She had been placed in solitary confinement in a tiny, filthy cell, with one small iron-barred window, which was too high for her to see out of, an iron bed with a dirty stained mattress. On numerous occasions she was raped, not only by other inmates, but by the guards, both male and female. The conditions in the jail were appalling and, for the first time in her life, Bibi did not know what to do. For a person who had always been in charge, she now felt wretched and helpless. Physically, she was deteriorating rapidly. Ironically she thought that this might be a blessing. "At least if I look like an old hag, maybe no one will want my body."

Lance was still remembered by most people in South Africa as a gallant heavyweight champion, but, alas, he was also renowned for shooting a black man in the back. He flew to South Africa to see what he could do to get his sister released, but the broadcasting company was now well and truly controlled by the AFA and Felix. Lance was given short shrift and there were even rumours that he might be re-arrested and re-tried for his earlier offence.

Even Daniel Buthelezi, the popular ex-Premier, was unable to help, following a plea from Gillian Van der Merwe in the UK. Although he was still a towering figure in the AFA, Felix had painted him as a man who had turned his back on his country of birth and escaped to England. Daniel could not be denied air time on the South African media, but his voice no longer carried any weight. There seemed no way that anyone could relieve poor Bibi of her misery.

Under Felix's racially fuelled administration, the wheels, once again, started to fall off the country's economic train. White flight from the country continued at even a faster pace than before. The white management class disappeared and thousands of businesses closed. Public services, once again, started to crumble and crimes, at all levels, seemed to go unpunished. The remaining white farmers gave up or were murdered in their beds. The shelves in the supermarkets were empty. Fearful of the military, Felix moved swiftly to remove the white generals and officers from their positions and promoted black men from the ranks. Worst of all, the rural Zulus, sensing that they had the support of the primarily Zulu AFA, started to muscle in on the property of the minority tribes, and, if resisted, had no qualms in murdering their victims.

The biggest opposition to the Zulu gangs of marauders were the Xhosas and frequent mini wars broke out between the two tribes. When these occurred no prisoners were taken and the streets of the villages were stained with African blood.

On the other side of the world, the Chinese sensed an opportunity. For some years Chinese workers had started to populate some of the mineral rich countries surrounding South Africa, as the Chinese government offered "help" to the failing local powers in exchange for the mineral wealth in the land. It was now the turn of South Africa to benefit from the "generosity" of China. Felix welcomed the arrival of Chinese "entrepreneurs" and, in exchange for all sorts of personal favours, offered state-controlled Chinese companies easy access to the gold, diamond, platinum and other industries in South Africa. Soon, most of the major industrial companies in the land were either controlled by China or the benefactors of heavy Chinese investment. The period of the second colonialization of Southern Africa had begun. This time the masters were not European but came from the East, and the colonial architecture which graced many small African towns, was overshadowed by ugly tower blocks housing Chinese workers. It was clear that they were there to stay.

Chapter Forty Four

40 years have passed. Fighting Felix is now an old man, clinging on to his Presidency and battling ill health. Any pretence of democracy in South Africa is a distant memory. From the day that Felix defeated Bibi and subsequently incarcerated her, he has clung on to power with a steely grasp. Elections have been held periodically but they have always been rigged in Felix's favour. Several years ago, most citizens stopped even bothering to vote, such was their disenchantment with the system. That glorious day when Jesus Mabendla secured the vote for all is a distant memory in the minds of many South Africans. The young and middle aged have never known what it is to not be allowed to vote; now they just think it is a waste of time and effort. More and more black South Africans are turning to their traditional tribal chiefs for guidance and leadership. The country, once briefly united, is now splitting into tribal groupings. It is a question of time before the different tribes break away from their democratic homeland and maybe a question of time before they start squabbling over land, water and mineral rights.

When Felix took over the reins of power the country was already at the top of a slippery slope. Some citizens, like Thabi, recognised this and battled to correct it. Others knew it too, but continued to milk the system for personal gain, thereby committing the country to the inevitable descent into mediocrity. The white citizens who had either stayed in South Africa through the transition to black rule and those that had returned in the early days of hope and success had long gone and their diaspora spread mainly throughout the United States, the UK, and other English-speaking countries.

The coffers of the country were quickly emptied. First through massive corruption, starting with the politicians and civil servants, but spreading throughout every aspect of daily life. In the first ten years of Felix's Premiership, it is estimated that over 160 billion dollars were stolen from the exchequer and deposited overseas. AFA members who had fought so hard for their right to govern their country had, in a few short years, squandered everything they had fought for.

The Chinese have been and gone, although they too have left their ugly mark on the nation. Whether it be for gold, copper, platinum or any other valuable mineral, they raped the country, taking more and more to satisfy the avaricious needs of their homeland and their billion-person population. They have left the country scarred, not only through their mining, but also through their infectious greed. Their remaining hostel block homes are now an eyesore on the once pretty landscape and their sperm has left a legacy of "Chinese" Africans who are now misplaced adults, hated and despised by their fellow countrymen and belonging to no tribe at all.

Out of the five million whites who lived in South Africa before the release of Jesus Mabendla, only roughly a quarter of a million remain. The familiar twang of South Africans can be heard in everyday life in many suburbs of the developed world. South African doctors and dentists are sought after in Manhattan, Los Angeles and London. Those that are old enough to remember the good old days in South Africa still pine for it. Their offspring have moved on.

Of those that remain in their homeland, almost all of them are in Cape Town. None are farmers, not even grape farmers, in the Cape. The isolation of farms was just too dangerous. Farmers were being murdered faster than they could plant a seed. Not that life in the cities has been easy. Electricity power outages occur on a daily basis. There is even a schedule for these outages, just like a railway timetable, although, like the trains of 20 years ago, somewhat unreliable. Now there are no trains, with the exception of the short ride from the airport in Johannesburg to the filthy city. A nation, once proud of its luxury Blue Train and its protege, Rovos Rail, cannot now operate a single train service between its cities. The tracks have long been stolen, valuable steel and sleeper wood for the ramshackle townships. Where tracks still exist, they are completely overgrown. Nature has taken control where man once trod.

Even the roads are virtually unpassable once you venture 20 miles from the major cities. What roads do still exist are full of dangerous potholes, which grow larger and larger each rainy season. Very few new cars grace these roads. The once thriving motor car factories established by European marques in the Apartheid era have all been closed down. Vandalism and absenteeism made it impossible to carry on and, even if they had done, the market for selling new cars evaporated long ago. The few remaining passable roads in the country are reminiscent of Cuba 30 years after the Castro revolution; the only vehicles are decades old and patched together with sticky tape.

Tourism, which had been thriving prior to Felix's first electoral victory, has now dried up completely. The broken infrastructure could not support visitors from overseas and the few that did arrive were in constant danger of being mugged. Besides that, one of the chief drivers of tourism had been the wildlife, but this was decimated by the Chinese, who had overseen the slaughter of wild animals, mainly for the sale of their tusks and horns back in their homeland. The once well-organised system of wild life sanctuaries had disappeared. Now life was wild on both sides of the broken fences.

Of the participants in our story only a few remain alive. Many would consider Gerhadus Van der Merwe lucky to have died of a heart attack before he could witness the decline of his beloved country. Angel, his wife, has survived and is now just turned 70. She is still remembered fondly by older Afrikaners as "their" Miss World. Her two children are also now middle aged and they, in turn, have each had two children. All of the Van der Merwe clan now live in the UK, where Angel long ago accepted the love of Tony and allowed him to marry her. Under the guidance of Angel and Tony, the Mood agency has grown into one of the largest fashion model and photographic agencies in the World.

Her childhood friend, Bibi, did not fare so well. After several months in jail, despite enormous efforts from her brother Lance, to have her freed, she finally took her own life. By then, it was not a life worth enduring any longer. She had been repeatedly raped and abused, not only by the other prisoners, but by the staff, including the Administrator of the jail. Lance had spent months in South Africa, desperately trying to get a reprieve for his sister against whom no charges had actually been brought.

In fact, no proceedings had ever been brought against her in Court. She was merely a political prisoner of Felix who saw her as an ongoing danger to his Premiership. Lance had used all of his political and show business connections in Los Angeles to put pressure on Felix's government to offer clemency to Bibi, but it was useless. Finally, one sad day, at the repeated pleading of Bibi, Lance had smuggled enough pain killers into the prison, for Bibi to end her own life. After her huge success as a television star and politician in the USA, Bibi just could not cope with her catastrophic fall from grace. She was a broken woman when she died and the brother that she left behind could never come to terms with her appalling treatment and her death. Lance and Bibi had been as close as a brother and sister could be. When Bibi died, although he was still alive, Lance might just as well have been dead too. Unmarried, lonely, and totally distraught about the collapse of his homeland, he too, some five years after Bibi's death, had been found dead from an overdose in his Beverly Hills mansion. Without his sister, he was a dead man.

Daniel Buthelezi, on the other hand, was not too perturbed about the downfall of his homeland. Now, also, just turned 70 years old, he is quite content with the success he has made of his life. As he sees it, he has been smart. He got out of South Africa at the right time. Of course, he had stolen from his country of birth but he saw that as a victory, not a crime. Although he had briefly been a politician, for him it was simply a means to an end: a way to personally enrich himself that he had achieved. He had overcome almost every hurdle in his life on the way to his enrichment; he had achieved every goal that he had set himself, but one had eluded him: Gillian Skosane. After Thabi had been shot outside the political convention hall, Daniel had been sad. After all, he had known Thabi since they were schoolboys. However, he had also seen this as an opportunity. Gillian was now a widow and Daniel still lusted after her. He had had a brief taste, now he wanted the whole meal.

His advances to Gillian were tempting. Thabi had not left her a rich widow. Daniel offered to look after her and her family should she move in with him. It would certainly solve a few problems for her, but at what price? Fortunately, Gillian's parents in England were good to her. Her dad's business had continued to prosper and, like most parents, he loved his daughter and her offspring. She would not need to go hungry and she could, if she wished, take over his business in due course. Daniel was thwarted, but his feeling of emotional emptiness had not lasted long. Gloria, tired of her life in America, had re-emerged and finally got her way with super rich Daniel. The wedding between Gloria and Daniel had taken up almost half of the pages of *Hello* magazine. Finally, Gloria had nailed her long-time companion. The pair of them had several white servants. Gloria lusted after the handsome gardener at their country home, but, even she, at 70 years old, had lost her sexual magnetism, if not her appetite, so she just had to dream of what could have been.

Angel had not been home to South Africa for many years and, due to the chaotic situation there, had not encouraged her growing family to visit. She had read how difficult life had become in the country of her birth, but, nonetheless, like most people, missed the sights and sounds of Africa. To compensate, on a couple of occasions she had taken some of her offspring to other parts of Africa for mini safaris, and from time to time had arranged photographic shoots for various magazines on the African continent, but never in her homeland. It had been on one of these trips, on which she had been joined by her mother Sally, that Sally contracted malaria and, sadly, never recovered. Sally had moved to England to be with Jules as well as near to her grandchildren. A devastated Jules was still alive but struggling with dementia in a care home in Sussex.

Tony understood how much Angel missed her homeland. After all she was one of South Africa's icons, still referred to in the local press as Miss South Africa and Africa's only ever Miss World. For her 70th birthday, Tony had decided that it would be a nice idea for the family to take Angel back to South Africa for a nostalgic trip. He thought it would be great to let the children and their children see where Grandma Angel had been born and raised.

Arranging the trip had been difficult. First, almost all of the decent hotels in Johannesburg and the other cities had been closed, and he had had less than encouraging reports about the standards of those that remained. Secondly, although he wanted to cross the country by road, so that the family could really experience the place, he had been warned that this might be dangerous. Everybody encouraged him to arrange to travel by air, or not at all.

Determined to press on, Tony managed to locate three ancient Volkswagen "people carriers": front wheel drive mini-buses that had been popular as "Kaffir" taxis. After some protracted negotiations with the VW owner about the terms of the rental, Tony had arranged that the vehicles would be available in the car park at the Felix Lebombo airport in Johannesburg. Angel was excited about the trip. She was so keen to show her children where she had been born, where she had been to school, where she had met their late Granddad and so on. She was aware that things would have changed dramatically, and had prepared herself for that. No amount of preparation, however, could have prevented the shock that she experienced upon arrival. The jetways from the buildings to the aircraft were, apparently, inoperable. There were no buses available to transport the passengers to the terminal buildings, which were in a ghastly state of dereliction. The steel rebar was showing through all of the concrete buildings, manifesting itself as huge rust coloured stains on the cracked and pitted infrastructure. Nothing mechanical moved. Her little party had to climb dirty and stationary escalators, some with missing steps. Obviously, these had not been operational for many years. There was a long line at the passport control booth with no special provision for returning South African passport holders. Notwithstanding that, Angel and her party all noted that some black passengers seemed to have a fast track. None of the luggage rotundas worked. In fact, they were piled high with unclaimed bags and suitcases from a multitude of previous flights. After a half an hour wait some trolleys of luggage from their flight were wheeled into the hall and just left there, piled high with bags. Passengers were left to "fight" for their personal belongings and there was no control as to who took what. The whole procedure was disorganised, shoddy and disgraceful.

Things did not improve. As Tony and his little group headed for the exit, an official stepped forward and demanded that certain suitcases be opened. As he painstakingly rummaged through the first case which they had opened, it became obvious to Tony what he was doing. The flourish of a 20 dollar bill from Tony hastened the end of the search. The case, now totally untidied, was closed, the 20 dollars pocketed, and Tony and Angel's group were on their way.

The next shock was the vehicles. The smart, brightly painted minivans ordered by Tony were not as advertised. Instead, Tony was led by the "representative" of the hirer to the end of the parking lot, where stood three rusty, dirty and ancient VW vans, covered in dents and scratches. The bright patterns on the paintwork displayed in the sales pictures were hard to make out through the filth. Inside, the seats were torn and, here and there, a spring protruded. Tony cast his eyes around for an alternative, such as one of the international car rental agencies, but none were in evidence. Having tried to search online for alternatives to no avail, he decided to make the best of what was on offer. The grandchildren were becoming restless after the long flight. Although excited to be in Africa, they were now getting tired and irritable. After a brief debate about who should drive, the little party headed off in the direction of Sandton, the once upmarket suburb of Johannesburg, and a stone's throw from Angel's birthplace. Their destination was the hotel from which Gloria had fled upon her separation from Daniel, so many years ago.

The road from the airport to Sandton was an obstacle course of pot holes and man-made barriers. There was some evidence that pot-hole filling crews had, at one time, been working on the road because various barriers had been abandoned there. The journey from the airport to the hotel covers about 15 miles, which, in years gone by, could be completed in about half an hour. This time it took over an hour. Twice, on the short journey, the little procession was pulled over by police. On each occasion the flourish of another 20 dollar bill seemed to satisfy the cops and they were allowed to proceed. Various road signs urged drivers not to stop. "Thieves operate in this area." It seemed the thieves were none other than the police.

The hotel was a shock. Although still designated "The Intercontinental", it no longer lived up to this billing and had long ago been abandoned by the chain of that name. The doorways were crowded with down and outs, who clearly camped there, waiting for the occasional tourist, diplomat or businessman to leave a coin or two. The uniforms on the staff inside the lobby were threadbare, as indeed were the lobby furnishings. Although there was still a whiff of the original grandeur of the place, this was now overcome by the stench of dirty human beings. The air conditioning obviously no longer worked and only one of the four elevators was still operational. Angel and Tony shuddered to think what the rooms would be like.

They were, therefore, not surprised to find that the rooms were equally squalid. The stained carpets and threadbare soft furnishings screamed out that nothing had been replaced nor properly cleaned in the room for many years. This was not an auspicious start to the holiday. In fact, things could not be worse. But they could. No sooner had the little party arrived in their allotted rooms than the lights went off. Their luggage, of course, was still downstairs in the lobby and the lack of power meant that the last workable elevator had no possibility of moving. They were on the 14th floor and their luggage was at ground level. On top of this, the hotel was now almost dark. There was apparently no fuel available for the emergency generator.

One of the grandchildren, exhausted from the journey, began to cry. This set off another. Parents began to bicker. In-laws began to wonder why they were there. Things were not going well. Angel and Tony had taken a suite, so that there could be a communal meeting area for the family. The whole dishevelled group were there. Suddenly the phone rang. Angel picked up.

"Angel Van der Merwe speaking,"

"Ms Van der Merwe," started an African voice, "please forgive my forwardness. I am Jacob Ntweni. I am the General Manager of the hotel. Forgive my intrusion but I could not help but notice you when you checked in. I seemed to know your face. Are you not the one who was called Angela from Bryanston, the daughter of Miss Sally and the one who became Miss World? The one who was married to the boxing man?"

Angel did not know what to say. She was amazed that someone in South Africa would still recognise her, but was that a good thing or not? Her vanity got the better of her.

"Yes, Mr Ntweni. I am the one. I am amazed that you recognised me."

"Well, Miss Angela, I shall never forget you. I am the son of Supreme. The lady that worked in your house for Miss Sally. I was the little boy that sometimes stayed in Supreme's room. When we were little, we played together."

"Good God! You are that Jacob. How amazing. How is your mother?"

"Long gone," replied the Manager. "Long gone," he repeated with melancholy.

After a few more small talk exchanges it was agreed that Jacob should meet the rest of the family. They were all tired now from the journey so a time was set for late afternoon. Despite all of the chaos and dilapidation, Angel was beginning to feel at home.

And so it transpired that Angel and her family met Fighting Felix, the ailing Premier and Dictator. Jacob had, apparently been one of Felix's right hand men during the days of the anti-white rallies. He was still in touch with the old man, even though he professed to have distanced himself from him as a result of disillusionment.

"You know, Madame Angela," Jacob told Angel, "you are still famous here. You are the only South African who has been Miss World. Nobody before you and nobody after. Many people here still remember you."

"Would Felix remember her?" asked Tony.

"I am sure he would. One way to find out. I will phone him and ask him."

Of course, Felix remembered Angel. Naturally, he wanted to meet her. She was part of the history of the country. So, it was not a surprise on day two of Tony's little tour, that Angel received another call from Jacob. "The Premier would like to invite you and your husband to the Premier's palace in Pretoria tomorrow for afternoon tea." To Tony and Angel this invitation sounded all too colonial for a black dictator but nevertheless, out of sheer inquisitiveness, they accepted. A car would be sent from Pretoria to fetch them.

Chapter Forty Five

Tea at the Presidential Palace was such a contrast to the mediocrity of the Intercontinental Hotel that it was quite shocking and the Intercontinental itself was a palace compared with the living accommodation of most of the citizens in South Africa. Whilst intrigued, both Tony and Angel were also disgusted. How was it possible for someone to live in such opulence when surrounded on all sides by abject poverty? The absolute arrogance of the man was unbelievable. If ever Felix had been an idealist it was no longer apparent.

Felix was, of course, absolutely charming to Angel. He had always fancied himself as a lady's man and the opportunity to meet an ex-Miss World had been too much for him to resist. Just as Sally before her, Angel had aged very well indeed. Although now over 70, she could have passed for 50. Sometimes people had difficulty in delineating her from her daughter, or, at least, that is what they said. Angel, knowing that she was to have an audience, had also made the effort to apply her make up carefully, as if she were going on a photographic shoot. Felix was clearly impressed.

"My goodness," he exclaimed on greeting Angel at the door of the reception room, "how stunning you still are, my dear. If your husband were not here today, you would not be safe in my presence."

"That's what you think," thought Angel. "You wouldn't get near me, old man."

As the meeting went on it became clearer and clearer that Felix seemed oblivious to how the rest of his fellow citizens lived. How he could be immune from it Angel just could not fathom, but to hear him chunter on, one would have thought that he was ruling over Utopia. The more he boasted about his achievements and about himself, the more Angel's dislike of him grew. His arrogance was so total that he did not seem to notice. Nor did he seem to notice Tony, or even attempt to bring him into the conversation. As far as he was concerned, Tony could have been the chauffeur, not the husband.

Felix seemed in no hurry to say goodbye to his visitors. It was as if he did not often have the opportunity to meet real people from his past, surrounded as he was with sycophants and yes men. "Tea" and small talk trundled on for well over an hour. Angel was anxious to get away from this unpleasant old man but he showed no signs of wanting her and Tony to leave. In fact, at about 4.30 he announced that it was "now time for a proper drink" and moved towards a small table on which sat several bottles. "Time for a gin and tonic," he exclaimed, playing the friendly host. "What will you have?" Despite the early hour Angel accepted a gin and tonic and Tony a whisky. Felix poured three very strong drinks. No ice was offered, nor seemed available. Within minutes he had downed his and poured himself a second.

"Signs of an unhappy man," thought Angel. "He certainly likes his gin."

Two things came out of the meeting. First, both Tony and Angel solidified their preconception of Felix; in fact, he was far worse than they had thought. Maybe they could have forgiven his ineffectiveness as a ruler, but not his arrogance. Second, such was his infatuation with Angel, that he offered to loan Angel and her party the presidential jet to ferry them around the country. This, of course, was not what Tony had planned. He had wanted to show his little group the country from the ground, but given the state of the vehicles he had hired, the odd ride in the Presidential plane might turn out to be very helpful. Both Tony and Angel accepted with alacrity but also a slight sense of guilt.

And so it was that Tony's little birthday trip for Angel and the gang turned out to be quite luxurious, at least the travel part. Tony quickly revised his plans to go on side trips from the major cities. The jet would be on standby at all times for the group in Durban (now "Elangeni"), Port Elizabeth (now "Port Mabendla) and CapeTown (now, "Felixtown"). There was no point in using it to visit the game parks because they quickly learned that the game parks no longer existed, nor did most of the game.

What they found on their little tour was that everything dear to them in their homeland had been ruined. Whilst still in Johannesburg, Angel took them, in their battered vans, to see her old school in Randburg, where she had first laid eyes on Gerrie. She was devastated – so was the school. Where once there had been neat little gardens and well-kept playing fields, there was nothing but a weed filled wasteland. The school buildings were derelict and no attempt had been made to clean them up or refurbish them. Like so many other things in the city, the school was a wreck. Angel did her best to paint a bright picture of her youth to her family but it was simply no use. The devastation of her childhood memories hung over her like a heavy dark cloud. She wished that she had not come back. All happy memories were obliterated by the sheer vastness of the desolation that she witnessed. As each day of the trip went by her anger against Felix grew and grew. She had to do something to avenge her lost generation.

Cape Town and Durban were in no better state than Johannesburg. What were once pristine and pretty streets were now littered with temporary homes made of corrugated metal and cardboard. All the neat little suburban gardens had disappeared, garbage was piled high on every street corner, drains were blocked, and many roads were impassable. Angel and her party became more and more depressed. Since they had arrived by plane, they needed to rent vehicles to travel around the cities and to make side trips out of town. The international car hire companies had long ceased trading in the country, due to high levels of car theft and impassable and unsafe roads. It was not difficult, however, as Tony soon found out, to rent vehicles, at rip-off prices, from hotel staff, so on a couple of occasions some of his party ventured beyond the suburbs. There, the scenes of desolation were even worse. Nature had regained control and all man-made infrastructure was slowly becoming eradicated. Everything that the white residents had built up over half a century had almost disappeared in half that time. The motorbike had become the favourite means of motorised transport for many, its flexibility in bypassing potholes and undergrowth trumping four wheeled vehicles.

When Angel's family group boarded Felix's plane back to their starting point in Pretoria, they were all looking forward to leaving the country as soon as they could. "We have one last thing that Tony and I must do," announced Angel. "We must go to see the President to thank him for the use of his plane." Nobody in the party thought that this was a good idea or even necessary, but Angel insisted. Unbeknown to the rest of her family she had a present for the President as a "thank you" for the loan of the plane, a present that she knew he would enjoy.

Tony very rarely put his foot down in a discussion with his beautiful wife, but on this occasion, he did just that. "Whatever it is that you want to give him, my love, you can give to the captain to pass on. I am sure that he will be willing to do that."

And so it was that the bottle of special gin that Angel had acquired for the hated President was wrapped with a thank you note and given in safekeeping to the captain of the jet for safe delivery, to his employer. Angel had taken great pains to select a fairly sweet tasting gin which she had made even tastier with a large slug of ethylene glycol. Felix died of kidney failure whilst Angel and her family were still winging it back to Heathrow. Since ethylene glycol is virtually untraceable in the body, it was assumed that the old man had died from natural causes, even if they had been accelerated by his habit of knocking back several slugs of gin each day. Angel did not feel an iota of guilt. As far as she was concerned the world was now rid of the man who had ruined her birthplace and the lives of so many of her fellow citizens.

And so, our story concludes. The rise and fall of a nation does not take long. Some say that history has shown that each period of dominance by a nation on Earth lasts for 240 years. To paraphrase Sheik Rashid, the founder of Dubai, "As a boy I rode a camel, my son has ridden a Mercedes, my grandson rides in a Land Rover, his sons and grandsons will ride on a camel again." The world has seen dynasties come and go. The world has seen superpowers rise, dominate, and then fall. South Africa was never a dominating world power, but it was, for an all too brief period, the powerhouse of Africa, richly endowed as it was, with minerals and raw materials coveted by the rest of the world. Its rise to power was driven by white men, using the labour of blacks. These white men chose the route of trying to dominate the majority of their citizens. For a while they were successful and the rise of South Africa in the world was impressive. But it was built on an illusion and it did not last 50 years, let alone 240. The fall from the peak of success was, as always, due to greed. Greed is the foundation of corruption. Corruption is the enemy of efficiency, and so South Africa, a country that had the potential to give so much to all of its citizens, fell short. So short that it joined the rest of Africa in the abyss of poverty and chaos.

Some of its citizens, like Angel, managed to escape. So too did some of the creators of the chaos, like Daniel, each one ferreting dirty money to be washed in a compliant tax haven. They were the lucky ones. Of our original cast, most have been caught up in the fall of their, once beautiful, homeland. In many ways Gerrie Van der Merwe, South Africa's world heavyweight champion, was lucky to die on the crest of South Africa's wave. In many ways, he departed at the pinnacle. His parents, Strom and Edna, as well as his little brother Frikkie, all died soon after him in the violence kicked off by Felix. His one-time lover, Bibi, having sparkled so brightly, only to be extinguished brutally by corruption and his one-time arch opponent, but sometimes friend, Lance, mentally checked out when Bibi died. Only Angel survived, as Angels do. Nobody connected her to Felix's death, that's how inefficient South Africa had become. Or perhaps nobody cared anymore. This beautiful country, raped by the Chinese and robbed

by the politicians, had been consigned to the garbage heap of Africa. The once abundant mines no longer operated, the police were corrupt, the wild life had been decimated, the power and water supplies had dried up, violent crime was endemic, the once beautiful jacaranda trees had been cut down and chopped up and, in the main, the white men had left. Central political power had petered out and the Africans returned to their tribes. The candle of South Africa had, for a short period, burned brightly; now it had been snuffed out. The final bell of the last round had rung. The colourful rainbow that had become the symbol of the new multi-racial culture of the country had turned black. The black rainbow cast a shadow across the land.